M.C.

MW00718739

The Ultimate Paradigm

Literary Lights Publishing
TALLAHASSEE

ISBN: 0-9727127-0-4
Library of Congress Control Number: 2002096321

Author's First Edition

www.ultimateparadigm.com

Printed in the United States of America

To my wife Susann, and to our Creator: the Author of life, breath, and hope when hope is lost. May the words in this book, which would not exist without you, bring forth something tangible and true.

To LaVonne —
Enjoy!

End and Beginning

Johnny is dead, but she is alive. She has fled like a dove before the cruel wind, but Johnny could not flee.

He didn't even see it coming.

She saw trouble brewing when it was barely a blemish on the horizon, before it unleashed the smoking bolt that hissed and crackled as it snaked to earth and struck them suddenly out of an indigo sky.

She saw trouble coming a mile away, but Johnny didn't have a clue.

His childhood was spent in insular safety, wrapped tightly in the arms of the American dream: two loving parents, a big sister, a cat, and happiness unmarred by life's harsher realities. And yet, as far as she could see, his sheltered upbringing had given him a skewed take on human nature.

Johnny didn't - no, he couldn't - hear the hungry cruelty in the man's voice or feel the pressure building as the deadly static stirred around them, whispering hypnotically in the thick summer air, slowly coiling its lambent strength and spoiling for a chance to strike. He didn't sense danger for one simple reason: Johnny trusted people. If he had experienced an intuition of evil, he would have dismissed it out of hand.

She had tried to warn him. She really tried. And now, despite her efforts, the memory of the past few minutes returns to her as if a film of the events were scrolling, uninvited, through her mind.

THEY WERE RIDING in his car, cruising the lonely byways of their rural Florida county as they talked and laughed and enjoyed their time together. By the early hours of the morning they had driven into the distant reaches of Homeland Estates, an elaborate maze of deserted roads in an unfinished housing development that long ago had been abandoned, unfinished and unwanted, in the wake of a notorious local bankruptcy.

It was hard to pinpoint the moment when they first noticed the lights.

The distant cluster of lights was an anomaly in the darkness, a luminous island in an expansive sea of night, an unfolding mystery that danced and swirled in the roadway until their car drew closer and they could see two dark shapes standing on the desolate blacktop, signaling with flashlights for them to pull over.

"I don't like it," she said, tensing and moving away from him. "Johnny, don't stop. Turn around. Let's get out of here." There were bigger, brighter lights in the road behind the two men. A bitter, unfamiliar scent filled the humid air, pressing hotly into their car through Johnny's open window. Something was happening here: something bad: something dangerous. She could taste it.

"Come on, Jamie, relax," he pleaded, reaching out to push her shoulder playfully. She pulled abruptly away. Her muscles were taut, her senses so acute that his touch was almost painful. "You're so paranoid," he observed, shaking his head. "There's nothing to be afraid of." She seized his arm and squeezed it fiercely.

"Turn around, Johnny! Listen to me! Get out of here! Get out, now!" she begged fervently, aching deep in her chest. But he shrugged her off, frowning in annoyance as he pulled over to the side of the road, stopped the car, and rolled down his window. In the ditch to their right, tall cattails slowly nodded in the car's headlights, and a chorus of crickets whirred abrasively in the late night heat.

Stepping up close to the car, two men wielding long chrome flashlights shined their stainless spots into the vehicle. They gazed without expression at the fresh-faced youths revealed by the light: just two local kids, cruising in an outsized, 1968 Plymouth, raising their hands to protect their eyes, blinking in the garish blast of harsh, blinding light.

The boy looked about 20, the girl about the same. They had unsullied, innocent faces: Barbie and Ken out for an evening drive. The boy was sunburned, with short blonde hair; the girl's face was framed by cascading burgundy locks. She had flawless, milky white skin, naturally crimson lips and bright blue eyes open wide with dismay. They were both ripe for the picking, two fair-haired peas in a shiny Plymouth pod.

With a swift glance, no more than a flick of her eyes, Jamie confirmed that her door was unlocked. Nervous and uncertain, squinting into the bright light, she slowly slid her hand to her right and gripped the cool steel handle. *Johnny was right; everything's okay. You're being paranoid,* she told herself. *When will you get over it?*

Then one of the men spoke, and his voice sliced through time, connecting her to another city, another life. The voice was not familiar, but the tone was one that she knew too well.

In the man's voice, she heard the probing, greedy rasp of predation.

She recognized the chilling undertone as surely as she knew her own face in a mirror, and the undeniable realization stunned and almost paralyzed her. She stared fervently at the two men, straining to make out their faces.

"What are you kids doing out this late? Don't you know that the woods are full of monsters?" The man spoke conversationally, his voice a pleasant purr as he leaned over towards the driver, his left hand carelessly lingering on the smooth, polished hood. She saw his face now, and it was seared into her memory: darkly tanned and delicately featured, perversely handsome and supremely insolent, with an aquiline nose and long, dimpled chin.

"We're just driving around, sir," Johnny replied. "What's going on?"

"Nothing that you'd want to see."

"What do you mean?" he asked, surprised.

"This is what I mean," the man hissed, spitting the words out as his hand snaked behind his back.

Somehow, Jamie knew what would happen next.

The action slowed to a tantalizing crawl as the man began to pull out the gun, and Jamie's ears rang loudly as time, the arbiter of intensity, ground to a virtual halt. Then her heart leaped into her throat, and the pace of events accelerated exponentially.

"JOHHNYYY!" she heard someone scream, recognizing the sound of her voice as the man's hand flashed up and blew fire through the exploding windshield, promiscuously spraying them with luminous diamonds of glittering glass. Her door banged open of its own accord and she dove, crashing down onto the cracked asphalt, ignoring the jagged stab of pain in her shoulder as her weight slammed hard against the ground, using the car for cover to roll into the watery ditch.

She began to run, foot-sure and fast, making the most of her wonderful speed, slicing through the weed-choked gully as bullets blistered the air about her. She leaped over the embankment, cutting through spiny bushes and mud and cattails and lily pads, plowing deeper and deeper into water that appeared miraculously before her until, without thinking twice, she plunged into the depths of a warm Florida lake.

The recumbent lake murmured contentedly as she slid through its smooth waters. The lake invited her into itself, yielding to her presence without complaint: its glistening arms dripping snakes, its warm bed filled with alligators that huffed in indignation, unsettled by the girl's intrusion. The surprising, comforting warmth of the water engulfed her, soporific in its effect, as she tried to steady her breathing.

JOHNNY IS DEAD, *but I am alive,* she thinks as she swims quietly toward the center of the coffee-dark lake.

But for once, for just this once, she is wrong.

Johnny is not dead.

Unfortunately, but quite definitely, he is painfully - and frighteningly - alive.

Black Water Slough

Numb with fear, too shocked to feel her cuts and abrasions, Jamie slowly slips through the root-stained waters. Buoyed by the viscous, blood-warm slough, she is as she always has been.

She is the sole survivor.

She is the last one standing.

Or at least, that is what she thinks.

Holy Mary . . . full of grace . . . blessed art thou among women, and blessed is the fruit of thy womb, Jesus.

As the young woman prays, she is awash in a profound, mysterious peace. The staccato gunshots and the brittle percussion of splintering glass, like the terror of that moment, are perceived from a distance, filtered through fragmented chambers of memory. Yet a deep, unknowable peace rolls through her like a river, momentarily taking away the pain.

Johnny's wretched shrieks, accompanied by the shooter's cruel laughter, are refracted in the chambers of her memory. But even in the midst of such wrenching remembrance, she feels, somehow, secure.

She would remain in these thick, musty waters if she could. She feels safe with the alligators for company, hidden here among the hyacinths. But her mind is clearing, and she knows what she must do.

She must keep moving.

The broad lake is preternaturally calm. It lays flat and still, clean and black beneath the thick strands of fog and the trembling sheets of delicate mist: a pristine oasis of silence in the middle of a chaotic nightmare.

The lake is a jewel in the heart of the Florida scrubland, a slinky, steamy sheet of warm black liquid that ripples softly, glinting dully beneath the dazzling, unfathomably profound clouds of shimmering stars. The lights tremble above her, far beyond her reach.

The stars are alive tonight, revealing themselves with unsullied clarity: breathing pale, sweet light like the dust of living diamonds set in an ocean of night. They are beyond the touch of cruelty, buried safe in the bottomless vault of the deep: breathtakingly beautiful, pulsating pinpoints of cold white fire extravagantly strewn across the darkened face of the heavens.

The shadowy shoreline framing the wild lake sings with jubilant life. The quiet of this place and the purity of the moment are not touched by the evil that has just sprayed death into her young life. But the dim glow of lights beyond the shoreline - and the distant, angry shouts - remind her that she cannot remain for long in this place of solace and refuge.

She must keep moving.

She can, and she will, keep moving.

Her pursuers do not know it, but they have selected unlikely prey. If there is anything that Janelle James knows, it is how to survive.

The men have their guns and their trucks, their planes and cars and anger fueled by greed, but Jamie has her wits and her prayers for deliverance. She waits patiently, treading water in the middle of the lake until headlights begin to approach: sweeping through the distant scrub oaks, see-sawing up and down.

A Land Rover emerges on a piece of high ground and begins to drive around the edge of the lake, following behind a man who walks ahead to ensure that the soil is solid enough for the heavy vehicle. Someone in the Land Rover pans a spotlight across the top of the water. Seeing this, Jamie swims softly for shore, sliding through the lily pads, back the way she came.

As she silently slips into the shallows near shore, the sound of the frogs is almost thunderous. They rhapsodize in astonishing synchrony, creating a pulsating amphibian masterwork of chirps and whirs and strange, metallic clacks that blend seamlessly in the hot, humid air.

The air is pregnant with hostile life, thick to the touch, weighted with droning clouds of remorseless, ravenous mosquitoes that painfully pierce her silence. She sneaks stealthily from the water, her feet making small sucking sounds in the fragrant Florida mud.

As the men in the Land Rover rendezvous with others on the distant side of the lake, she is creeping quietly away, dripping muck, breathing raggedly, creeping stealthily through the weedy ditch, past the bloody Plymouth, up to the cars that are parked near the airplane in the middle of the road. There are four cars clustered around the streamlined turbo-prop and the slick tractor-trailer, but only one has keys in the ignition - due to the carelessness of its fearless, arrogant owner. The car with the keys is a tan Lamborghini.

Before the men realize what is happening, the powerful engine roars to life and the Lamborghini spins in a tight circle, blasting off into the darkness, whipping past a drug mule who stares transfixed, gaping into the oncoming headlights. The girl leaves the stunned sentry floundering in her backwash like a torpedoed shark as she rockets away down the weed-bitten, cracked asphalt byway that leads to town.

As Janelle James races down the road, a fractured mosaic of unwanted memories returns in force, painfully assaulting her consciousness. The events of this evening have been too much to handle.

She begins to feel the pain and attempts, one last time, to suppress her emotions. But the pain builds in spite of her efforts until, like waters breaching a dam, the floodgates finally burst.

With the wail of a hopeless animal, she begins to weep in desperate abandon. Her shoulders shake spasmodically; her entire body is wracked by the onslaught of grief. She cries for herself and for Johnny, for her friend lost forever. She weeps for their closeness, for the words and the silences they shared, and for the precious gift of the friendship lost. It is too much to bear . . . too much lost too suddenly, for no good reason. The pain of it almost drives her mad.

But, in spite of her tears, Janelle James is escaping.

Homeland Estates has become her private racetrack. The sports car whips past the pines and palmettos, leaving fireflies whirling in its wake. It screams down mile-long straight-aways, winding noisily around hair-pin turns as she rips through the gears like a professional, down-shifting as she approaches every bend, kicking the gas pedal down to float lightly out of each body-slamming turn.

The killers have no hope of catching her. Their prey has fled like a deer through the net, playing them all for fools.

The girl, Janelle James, has escaped.

Wise Guys

"**W**hat do you have planned for the kid?" Franco asked uncertainly. He stood on the cracked asphalt road beside the muddy Land Rover, watching as a member of their crew drove the bloody Plymouth up the ramp into the spotless steel trailer.

Franco scowled sourly as he waited for a reply, fully expecting that the answer to his question would be as stupid as the idiot who provided it. A large, 50ish, florid man in a shapeless blue suit, Franco Marcetti looked out of place standing next to the smooth young captain of his crew.

A few yards away, the shattered muscle car idled jerkily up the ramp like a wounded warrior that had been whacked with a hammer, finally down for the count. The souped-up engine throbbed deeply as the car delivered its swan song: an automotive aria filled with basso profundo angst, a mere echo of the machismo of bygone days.

As the mule drove the car up the ramp, he blinked uncertainly, struggling to see through the jagged hole in the spider-webbed windshield. There was scarcely room to squeeze the car into the steel trailer behind the wall-to-wall bales of reefer and coke, but somehow, the driver would make it fit.

Even from a distance, Franco and Joe Boy could smell the cocaine.

The fresh white blow refused to be stifled. It tweaked their noses playfully, tantalizing them with the distinctive, tangy aroma: the calling card of pure, unadulterated Colombian flake. The bitter payload, as deadly as sin, was to them the smell of money just waiting to be made.

"Pig's got big plans for that kid," Joe Boy said. "The boy is in good hands, Frankie. Pig's gonna take him up in his plane, and they're gonna have a little talk." Joe Boy wiped his nose with the back of his wrist and sniffed loudly. "The kid's still conscious, you know," he continued animatedly, "half of his forehead is missing, but he can still talk. That's good for us, bad for him." He took a lengthy pull on his cigarette and flicked the glowing butt into the dry bushes. "Pig'll make him sing like a bird. He'll play that punk like a Stradivarius."

"Too bad he won't be able to tell us where your Lamborghini is," Franco said innocently, sneaking in a jab.

"Don't remind me." Joe Boy turned away sharply, fighting the fury that surged within him. Above all that had happened tonight, he was most grieved by the loss of his tan Lamborghini.

They climbed into the Land Rover, and Franco slipped it into gear. Behind them the big rig throttled up, its huge diesel engine revving noisily. The plane roared as if in response and began a slow taxi to the north, up the long, empty strip of wild, weed-damaged asphalt.

Franco glanced over as the younger man lit a fresh smoke. In the flickering light of Joe Boy's Zippo, his smooth-chiseled, cherubic face was the very image of pride. His curly, jet black hair was slicked straight back, his mouth cocked in a permanent sneer: delicate lips, long, thin nose, olive complexion. *A face the ladies could die for . . . when they least expect it,* Franco thought. He looked away quickly.

"What you lookin' at, Frankie?"

"Just looking around, boss."

"Don't worry about <u>me</u>, Frankie. <u>I'm</u> doin' all right, Lamborghini or no Lamborghini." Joe Boy blew a heavy plume of smoke toward Franco's swarthy, pockmarked face and laughed with a brittle monotone croak, showing his tongue like a wolf.

"I'm not sweatin' it. Pig'll make that boy spill his guts. They'll dump him in the middle of the Gulf, and nobody'll be the wiser. No one will find him but the sharks. Or maybe Charley the Tuna." He laughed loudly, admiring his brilliant joke.

"You can count on one thing," Joey continued. "Before he croaks, he'll give Pig the name of the girl who stole my car. And I'm going to hunt that girl down like a dog, Frankie: like an itty-bitty hillbilly hound dog." He smiled cruelly, running his tongue across his lips.

"She'll be fun while she lasts. The nerve of that kid, stealin' my sled. That was my ride, Frankie, my ride! She's got fire, huh? What do you think?"

"She's got fire, alright," he agreed tiredly.

"Yeah, man, she's got it good. Did you see how quick she was? She ran away like some kind'a redneck energizer bunny, bouncin' through the weeds. She's a real babe, huh? What do you think?" He slapped his companion on the shoulder.

"She's a real babe-aroo," Franco answered wearily, "no doubt about it." *Poor girl,* he thought, *what did she do to deserve this?*

"Wrong place, wrong time, that's all it was," Joey replied, as if he were reading Franco's mind. "It's too bad we have to do it, right? Ain't that what you're thinkin'? You're gettin' sentimental in your old age, Frankie." He was taunting his lieutenant now, drawing him out.

"Yeah. I'm crying," Franco said, smiling tightly and raising his eyebrows, "boo hoo." Joe Boy responded with another dry laugh and pulled hard at his cigarette, illuminating the interior of the Land Rover with the dull red glow.

"Go ahead and cry," Joey said to Franco, smiling brightly. "That's an order. One of us ought to. My Lamborghini's been ripped off!" As much as he missed his car, the thought of the girl's impending demise greatly cheered him.

Frankie pulled up to the entrance of the deserted subdivision, then turned left onto the darkened four-lane truck route, heading towards Tampa. *I'm sentimental, all right,* Franco thought, *too much for my own good. But it never stopped me from doing what I'm told, no matter how down and dirty it gets.*

Looking over at his captain, who was gazing out at the darkened Florida countryside, Franco reflected bitterly on his fate. *I obey orders, like a good soldier,* he reasoned, *and so I'm stuck babysitting the Don's son, a baby-killing punk who was a wannabe wise guy when I was already a made man. Joey knows how to kill, but not how to live. He tries to be tough, but he's just plain mean. He's just a Tampa hick tryin' to sound like the wise guys from New York City. If he wasn't the Don's son, the real tough guys wouldn't give him the time of day.*

"What are you thinkin', Franco?"

"I'm thinking that you've been hanging out with Nick and Jim too much. You're starting to sound like 'em. You're from Tampa, and Tampa ain't Brooklyn, no matter how you cut it."

"Better to sound like them than to sound like some two-bit Tampa hick, paisan."

Franco scowled and focused on the road ahead. *Joe Boy talks like a hood in a cheap novel,* Franco mused. *Nick and Jim talk that way, but at least they came by it honest.* Nick and Jim were old-time wise guys from Brooklyn who had been exiled to Tampa for transgressions in their youths. They had become button men in Franco and Joey's family, the Provencentis, and Big Jim had recently become a made man.

The two New Yorkers had found a willing protégé in young Joey Provencenti. They had schooled him in the ways of the knife and gun. And Joey, an ambitious punk on the make, had diligently copied their New York wise guy accents.

As they sped down the deserted highway, a blue sign arose out the darkness and flashed past them. Except for the sign, the night was dark and empty.

"You know what I'm thinkin', Frankie?"

"No, what?"

"It bothers me that my car was ripped off. But there's something even worse than that."

"What do you mean?"

"I'm thinkin' that maybe the girl got a look at me. You know what I mean." He sat up, straightening his back. "Maybe she made me."

"Our flashlights were right in their eyes. They couldn't see a thing."

"Yeah, but you know that we didn't plan to leave any witnesses. I stepped up pretty close when I whacked that kid who was sitting beside her. She might'a seen me."

"Yeah, I guess she could have made you," Frankie replied slowly, glancing over at his boss. "You did step up pretty close to the car." Joe Boy had a point.

As they approached a small town, their Land Rover slowed, rolling up to a stoplight. Across the street in an empty gas station, a patrol car idled. It was the only vehicle in sight. The light changed and they pulled away before Joe Boy spoke again.

"That girl was sharp, Frankie. To get away from us like she did, to outrun us and steal my car . . . that took guts. Who knows, maybe she got a look at both of us."

"Okay, you sold me. You're right; she was sharp. She might have made us. Plus, she stole your car. Didn't you say that you left your wallet in the car?"

"Yeah. Don't remind me. I left 20 grand in the glove box, too."

"Well, if you left your wallet, she can ID you from your driver's license, so we can't afford to let it slide. We'll check with the Don to see if we can put out a contract, and that's that."

"That ain't enough. Not on this one. Tampa's just a hick town, and we can't count on these Tampa hicks to do the job right. I'm bringin' in the Mick." Joey said it emphatically, with his jaw set. Taken by surprise, Franco caught his breath.

"The Mick? That freak?"

"Yeah, that freak," Joe Boy responded defensively. "Sure! He's the best!"

"He's <u>one</u> of the best, maybe," Frankie said, shaking his head, "but he's as nutty as a fruitcake. He's a serial killer! What about the bodies they found before he left town?"

"What about 'em?"

"Do you remember the heat it caused? They brought in the FBI, FDLE, you name it."

"Hey, sure, I remember the bodies," Joe Boy said without concern, blowing out a thin stream of smoke. "That's why Mickey had to leave town. It was my idea for him to leave, remember?"

Like you had any choice, Franco thought, staring fixedly at the road ahead of them. Joey's father, the Don, had given the order for the hit man to leave Florida. Joey had merely been the errand boy.

Mickey O'Malley, known to his culturally insensitive criminal colleagues as "The Mick," was a homicidal sociopath of the worst kind: the intelligent, talented, and successful kind. He had once worked for the Provencentis, and there had been some trouble.

Some of O'Malley's female acquaintances had turned up in vacant lots. The matter had gained the attention of the entire nation, not to mention the local police and Federal investigators.

In spite of the fact that he was the best hit man in the Southeast, Mickey had been asked to retire. He left Tampa for the upper Midwest at the rich young age of 28, promising to stay away from major mob cities where the families might frown on murders involving the local talent.

"I'm bringin' in the Mick, and that's that," Joey repeated. "He'll get that little energizer hick, no matter what she tries to pull. And don't give me no grief about the bodies," Joey said through clenched teeth.

"I don't care if he leaves a body in every back yard in Ybor City. If he bags some freebies, we'll just call it 'latter day damage,' like the military calls it. You know what I'm talking about," Joey added uncertainly, seeing Franco smile. "You know what I mean."

That's collateral damage, you pinhead, mused Franco, enjoying the moment. *What a complete idiot!*

"I'm bringin' in the Mick, and I'm turnin' him loose," Joey added for good measure, nodding ominously. "The trouble is, Frankie, we didn't shoot the kid in Tampa. These are the boondocks. And they aren't our kind of boondocks, either. You know what I'm talkin' about.

"We don't have connections here. We don't own the cops, the judges. We got nobody. We never had a reason to have anybody way out here. And there's no way I'm going to face a jury of rednecks in Petticoat Junction over the murder of some stupid hick who poked his nose where it didn't belong."

"If you want to bring in the Mick, you've got to clear it with the Don," Franco said cautiously. "Don't go off half-cocked."

Joey answered Franco with a string of expletives, slamming his fist on the dashboard for emphasis.

"I'll be waking the Don up when I get home," he spat angrily. "Whad'ya think, I won't talk to him about this? If I let him sleep after something like this, he'll have my head for breakfast with his crab roll."

They both knew that Joey had been way out of line. He never should have left Tampa to come to a backwoods landing strip in Homeland Estates. But Joe Boy had invested millions of his own cash into the deal, and if he wanted to see the action firsthand, who could stop him but the Don himself? If the truth were known, Joey was a thrill junkie who loved to visit the scene of his crimes.

Joey sat back indignantly in the plush leather seat and lit another cigarette off the scorched remnants of the one he had just consumed. He puffed fiercely, beginning to relax, gesturing expansively with his hand.

"No scrawny redneck girl's takin' me out, Frankie," he said from the midst of a thick cloud of smoke. He used Franco's nickname with affection, for he was beginning to enjoy the idea of what lay ahead. The prospect of fresh blood never ceased to warm Joey's heart, and he lavished the overflow on his companion.

"Hey, Frankie."

"Yeah, what?"

"You ain't half ugly, for a stupid piece of garbage."

"Thanks, boss. I appreciate that." Frankie was still thinking about the boy they had shot, trying to get the picture out of his head.

The boy was up in the plane with Pig right now, undergoing unspeakable torture. Maybe he was still able to talk, even with half of his forehead missing. But more than the boy, Franco pitied the girl. *Poor kid,* he reflected. *I wouldn't be in her shoes for all the crank in Kansas.*

Franco knew what Joey Provencenti was capable of. And Franco was one of the few living souls who knew what Mickey O'Malley had to offer in the name of death and mayhem. *That girl better run like nobody's ever run,* he thought, *or she'll be toast.*

Franco looked down the empty road that stretched ahead of them: flat, empty, and uninviting. The soulless highway, a frozen, land-locked river of grit and asphalt trapped in the merciless glare of their headlights, flashed submissively beneath their tires. They were devouring the miles, hungrily hurtling toward the relative safety of Ybor City.

Poor kid, he reflected, thinking about the girl who got away. *Before Joe and Mick are through with her, she'll be begging for someone to finish the job.*

It was true.

He might as well admit it.

Sometimes, Franco didn't enjoy his work.

The Dark Before Dawn

High above earth, in the half-light of dawn, he circles and watches the wraiths of the night. A butterfly stirs and a bat spreads its wings, caught in his unmeasured clarity of sight: locked in the gaze from the high, hidden paths where he circles, and watches, and waits for the light.

In the top of a towering smoke-gray colossus, at first it appears to be only a nest. High in the sky, he focuses sharply and sees at a glance: it is no nest at all.

On the earth far below him, a once-human form is a dark, bloody blot in the top of a tree. It smudges the landscape beneath the great hawk like a thumb in the eye of such pastoral grace. Crying and wheeling, the hawk sails away from the strange, grisly scene. All is not well on the earth, far below, where misery flowers and hawks seldom go.

In the moist, misty silence beneath the tall cypress, a thick, sluggish tap is the only sound heard. This is not dew that should drop from the heavens.

A body is leaking into the moist earth. Rich crimson death drips on fresh-fallen leaves as the tree, with no options, holds the corpse to the sky . . . a reluctant offering in uplifted boughs.

Preacher

The car idled in place, straining against its brakes as the steel gate slowly swung open. A huge Crown Victoria with a powerful engine, the vehicle was more than just another pretty ride. It was an aesthetic tour-de-force: a high-powered squad car doubling as a work of postmodern art. The car was sleek and new and unashamedly glossy, a study in green and gold and black.

The driver waited patiently, accustomed to the slow pace of life in this county and a veteran of long, hard days in the oppressive Florida heat. He was a startlingly handsome officer of the law in his early fifties: a sober gentleman with a thick white moustache and jet-black hair slashed by jagged shards of white. He was dressed, as on every workday, in the dark green uniform of the Oree County Sheriff's Department.

It was evident from the man's intense expression that for him, the virtue of patience had not been easily acquired. It could be said of him, as was once said about Ulysses S. Grant, "He looked like a man who could put his head through a brick wall, and was fixing to do it."

As the gate swung clear, the car accelerated through the cattle gate and the driver smiled and waved to the boy who had opened it. He sped up to make it through the muddy entranceway and proceeded to bump down the grassy, two-rut country lane. The cruiser seemed to navigate on autopilot through the holes and over the humps, headed toward a distant, listless, black water canal. It was 8:00 o'clock on Sunday morning.

The calendar claimed that the month was October, but the weather had been ignoring the calendar lately. South Central Florida had been enduring its own uniquely sweltering version of what is typically referred to, in fairer climes, as Indian summer.

A warm breeze blew across the open pasture and ruffled the driver's hair, filling the car with the rich aroma of growing grass and the sour buzz of cattle flies. In the middle of the huge expanse of flat green pastureland to the driver's left an angus bull stood sentry for a cluster of cattle that watched the car dumbly, enjoying a morning chew as the intruder drove by. They watched as it turned left at the canal and climbed onto the road that ran along the top of the steep embankment. The black bull bristled and took a step forward, snorting loudly, upset by the shiny machine and its unfamiliar occupant.

The driver was Sheriff Thomas H. Durrance, known to most of his constituents as Tommy, or as Preacher, or as Sheriff (the titles were used without a qualifier - he was simply Preacher, as in "Preacher said hello" - or Sheriff, as in, "Sheriff finally caught that burglar"). Tommy Durrance, as usual, was responding to a call.

Although he had never been on this particular road before, he was on familiar ground. He had spent most of his life traveling the highways and byways of this rural Florida county.

The car bumped gingerly along the elevated dirt road as the Sheriff watched closely for washouts that might break an axle. At the end of the treacherously eroded road, he reached a wide, park-like area where several men were gathered, awaiting his arrival. He parked his car between the County Coroner's station wagon and a badly dented pickup truck and got out slowly, sipping his coffee as he approached the group of men who stood in an uncertain cluster at the bottom of a huge bald cypress tree.

The Coroner of Oree County was kneeling beside a badly contorted body that was sprawled awkwardly in the shade beneath the tree. The good doctor cut quite a figure in this remote location, competing for shock value with the indecorous corpse.

Dr. Gene Thompson was a tall, wafer-thin specter of a man who was dressed, somewhat incongruously, as if he were about to play a round of golf. From his red cap and turquoise knickerbockers to his appliance-white, mud-flecked spikes, the entire ensemble screamed of bad taste. He was fully absorbed in the corpse, lost in his thoughts and oblivious to the Sheriff's approach.

Taking advantage of the moment, a short, sunburned old cracker made a vector across the clearing and intercepted the sheriff, seizing his hand and shaking it vigorously in a powerful, callous-encrusted grip. He was a rancher whose brown eyes flashed intelligently from a leathery, two-toned face: tanned from chin to mid-forehead but pitifully pale and liver-spotted from mid-forehead upwards. A straw cowboy hat was clasped in his free hand, but whether it was out of respect for the dead body or for the locally famous lawman, only the bowlegged cattleman knew for sure.

"Good to see, you, Preacher," he said. "But I wish it could'a been under happier circumstances."

"Me too, Mr. Hendry. Do you know who the victim is?"

"I don't know him, but I know his name. He's Johnny Delaney, a 19-year-old boy from up north county. He's just a kid, Preacher, and a good kid at that, I'm told. I don't get it," the old man said, unable to make sense of it. "Who could'a done something like this?"

"If you don't know the boy, how do you know his name?"

"One of my hands, Billy Cloud, he used to work with the boy up near Quilting Bee." He pointed a meaty index finger at a short, dark-haired young man who was sitting a short distance away in the shade of the cypress tree. The man's clothing was soaking wet, and he was obviously shaken by what he had seen.

"What does he have to say about Johnny Delaney?" the Sheriff asked.

"Billy," the rancher called, "could you come over here for a minute?" Billy Cloud stood and walked over slowly, squinting as he stepped into the direct sunlight. "Why don't you tell Sheriff here exactly what you told me about your

20

friend?" Billy was short and stocky, dark-skinned and fresh-faced. He looked as if he could be no more than 20 years old.

"Okay," Billy replied uncertainly, shifting his weight from foot to foot. He paused thoughtfully for a few seconds, and then he started to speak.

"The dead guy is Johnny Delaney," Billy began. "I knew him, you know." He paused again. "Johnny was a good friend," he said, licking his lips nervously. "He was a good worker, too. He could fix anything, make anything, you name it. We used to eat lunch together, there at Triangle Welding Shop where we worked, up near Quilting Bee. We were both learning to weld, but we both quit because we heard that there were health issues.

"It's bad for your eyes, you know," Billy added, glancing furtively at the corpse. "Bad as all get out." *Not that it matters now,* he did not bother to add.

"Was Johnny from around here?"

"No, sir. He's from Jacksonville. I mean, he was born here, you know, but Jacksonville is where he's from." He hesitated for a moment, looking lost. Then, he gave it another try. "His mother's from Quilting Bee. His natural mother, I mean. Johnny was adopted by some people from Jacksonville when he was just a baby. I met them, once. They were really nice. I think they probably loved him. He had a sister, you know, in his adopted family. Her name was Crystal." He paused as the Sheriff and the stocky rancher waited for him to continue. When Billy remained silent, the Sheriff spoke up.

"So, your friend came to Oree County looking for his natural mother?"

"Yeah, about two years ago. Right after he graduated from high school. His folks wanted him to go to college, but he wanted to come here to find his mother. He wanted to work with his hands, too. Johnny was really smart. He used a lot of big words, but he didn't like school. He never met his mother, you know. He wanted to meet her, and that's why he came here."

"So, what happened when he got here?"

"She was dead a long time. His mother, I mean. But his grandmother was still alive. She's a widow woman up near Quilting Bee." He used the term, 'widow woman,' as if it were her profession. "Johnny liked her a lot," Billy volunteered. "She was a nice old lady. Last thing I heard, he was living up there. She's got a doublewide on some land in Quilting Bee. It's real nice, and the yard's decorated with all sorts of country stuff. You know, wooden cows, wagon wheels, stuff like that."

"Thanks for the information," the Sheriff replied, shaking his hand, "I might be in touch with you later for more questions, okay?"

"Okay," replied Billy. He shook hands with the Sheriff limply, as if he did not trust his grip to the older man's care. Then he turned and slowly trudged back to the body of his former friend. He sat down across from the body in the shade of the ancient bald cypress.

The coroner raised his face to the sky and blinked once, twice: returning slowly to his surroundings after an exhaustive examination of the corpse. Whenever he worked, he descended into what his friends and colleagues called, 'the zone.' The zone was a plateau of concentrated examination, a forensic nether land of intense scrutiny. With the preliminary examination completed, he was leaving the zone and was climbing back into the here and now.

The coroner stood up and noticed the sheriff. He nodded and walked up to the lawman, apparently unaware of the jarring effect of his neon golf clothing, so alien to this rural setting.

Not sure of which was uglier, the coroner or the corpse, the ranch hands sneaked stares of shocked outrage at the ghoulishly contorted body and the coroner's outlandish garb. They were highly displeased with both views, so to speak, but uncertain of what they should do about it.

"Hello, Tommy," the Coroner said loudly to the Sheriff. "I'm glad you got here so quickly. This one's a puzzler." The Sheriff stared for a moment at the grisly scene.

The shattered human body at the foot of the tree had been mangled: twisted in improbable directions by an unknown trauma. The blonde corpse looked like a Playdough puppet that had served time in the hands of a sadistic child. The victim's mouth was agape, frozen in an expression of pain or remorse or dismay, as if he were embarrassed by the fact that he was missing part of his forehead.

"Good to see you, Gene," the Sheriff responded to the gangly coroner. "How'd you get here so fast? I was only ten miles away when I got the call, and it looks like you've been here for a while."

"Oh, I could have walked here. My new house is in Settler's Glen, just past the entrance to this pasture. I was just leaving for the country club when I got the call, and I turned in when I saw the kid at the cattle gate." He flashed a quick, awkward smile.

Dr. Gene Thompson was a tall, narrow-faced man with nervous hands who had moved to this rural county to get away from the pace of life in Miami, where he had been the chief examiner at the north branch of the Dade County Coroner's Office. The Sheriff had tremendous respect for the coroner's forensic skills, and he had developed a genuine affection for this quirky refugee from Florida's east coast.

"What do we know so far about this situation?"

"It's a homicide," he stated without elaboration. "Mr. Hendry found the body. Maybe he should tell you the story."

Discovery Process

The coroner nodded at the liver-spotted rancher, who spat tobacco juice on the ground and began to talk.

"Well, now, uh, we was taking a look at the cattle: me and Chub, that is, just before dawn, when we seen some buzzards circlin' in the sky back over to the east. We thought they was out there over the swamp, but we drove here to see if we could get a look at what they was circlin' for. We figured maybe one of our cows had died birthin' a calf. That happens sometimes."

He paused, shifting a massive load of snuff from one cheek to the other as he began to wipe the sweat from his face with a blue bandana. While the sunburned cattleman thoroughly dried his pink, dripping face, a red-tailed hawk screamed at the men from a hidden perch, sorely displeased by their presence and their proximity to her nest.

They were standing in the middle of a pristine piece of untouched Florida wilderness. The body had been found at the edge of a dreary cypress swamp, and the tall bald cypress under which they stood was strategically positioned on the point of a long, dry piece of land between the canal water and swamp water. This particular spit of dry land had been above the waterline long before the canal was dredged from the swamp.

"Anyway, we found the boy right up there," the rancher said finally, pointing toward the top of the giant cypress that towered over them. "He was up there in the very top of the tree. When we first saw him, we thought he was an osprey nest. But the buzzards was circlin' low by then, and we took a better look. We still wasn't sure that it was really a man; it took a while to realize it. A dead man is kind of hard to swallow, if you know what I mean. So once we were sure of what it was, I called my men on the two-way radio and asked them to come out here.

"It played the dickens on us, figurin' out how to get him down from up there. It liked to have taken us better'n an hour to get the job done. Billy Cloud was the one who finally brought him down. I had some scrap lumber in my truck, so he nailed steps onto the tree and climbed up there to get him, then he carried him down on his shoulder, one step at a time. When we finally saw the body up close, we could see there weren't hardly an unbroken bone.

"That was when we seen that he'd been shot in the head, like you see, and that's when we called your office. I reckon we should have called earlier, but we were too wrapped up in gettin' him out'a the tree.

"While we were waiting for you, Billy recognized him." His voice dropped to a hushed, respectful tone. "He took it kindy hard, you know, realizin' all the sudden that this dead guy was a good friend." He whispered confidentially, pointing to the swamp. "He got sick back there, but we pretended it weren't happening. Then he hung tough, like you just saw. Billy's a good kid.

"Now, you tell me this, Sheriff," the old man asked, looking upward and waving his hat toward the top of the tree. "How did that dead boy wind up in the top of a big old bald cypress tree?"

"I don't know, Mr. Hendry," the Sheriff replied, "but I aim to find out." He leaned back and peered up toward the treetop.

Billy Cloud's handiwork could be seen running up the trunk of the tree: short pieces of lumber nailed to the broad side of the slick gray cypress like a ladder to the sky. Reflecting on what he had heard, the Sheriff turned to the coroner, who lifted his eyebrows and sighed.

"Tell, me Gene," Sheriff asked his friend. "What do you think about this mess?"

"Give me a minute," the Coroner replied. "I'm working on it."

Streetcar

Streetcar was well known in Ybor City. He was a one-man institution, familiar to cops and bums alike: well known to punks and wise guys and retirees and little kids as a friend of respectable retailers and wizened restaurateurs. Streetcar was a familiar human landmark to all of the hard-working men and women who helped to make Ybor City what it was: a cobblestone throwback in the midst of the ugly asphalt eyesore that passed for the southeast side of Tampa, Florida.

At 7:30 on a peaceful Sunday morning, Streetcar was relaxing on his bench at the intersection of a busy 22nd Street and a ridiculously quiet 9th Avenue. He was subdued and inauspicious: a tall, lean, spotlessly clean man who tried to avoid the spotlight of public attention but drew it, nonetheless, like a magnet. Physically speaking, Streetcar was a prime example of American-Mediterranean manhood: a trim, healthy man with dark salt-and-pepper hair and beard, olive complexion, and a long, Romanesque nose. But his physical appearance was only a footnote to the human equation.

On this lovely day, Streetcar was minding his business, as always. He was harmlessly enjoying the breeze, aimlessly watching an eclectic array of colorful vehicles as they raced past his inauspicious bench. He had just popped a stick of gum into his mouth when his best friend pulled his shiny red 1997 Chevy pickup truck onto the curb beside him and leaned out of the window.

"Street', ol' buddy, what's up?" his friend asked with his ebony face stretched into a familiar smile. Before he had asked the question, Jumbo Poindexter knew what Streetcar's answer would be.

"De nada, dude," Streetcar replied in his deep, husky voice, "de nada." Streetcar was not trying to be cool. He did not care to pass himself off as a latter-day beatnik, or as a nouveau-hip postmodern hipster, or even as a stylishly passé poseur.

Streetcar was a lost soul.

He had wandered into the wrong time and place, arriving in the 21st century like a bum accidentally stumbling into a formal ball. He was stranded in the present but lost in the past. Displaced in time, Streetcar was a fish out of water in the midst of a bustling, rejuvenated Cigar City.

Better than anyone else in Ybor, Jumbo knew where Streetcar was coming from. In fact, Jumbo had once lived where Streetcar was coming from. But Jumbo had left Vietnam behind him long ago.

After he had shipped out in 1969, Jumbo had looked to the future, not the past. But Streetcar, the soldier's soldier, had gotten stuck in the transition. Streetcar spent most of his days with his body in Ybor City and the better part of his heart and mind roaming the steaming jungles and burning paddies of his youth

"You got any new jokes, Streetcar?" Jumbo asked hopefully.

"Nah. The weather was foul last night. The rain kept the cops in their cars. When that happens, I get nothin'."

"The weatherman says we should get some more of that rain tonight."

"Well, I hope that's the last rain for a while. The dry weather brings the cops out. I get new jokes, they get the buzz from the street, and everybody's happy." The cops of Ybor City, like the deputies at the nearby Hillsborough County Sheriff's substation, knew and liked Streetcar, whose reputation as a storehouse of street knowledge and questionable humor was unparalleled.

"Hey, I've got to go, Streetcar," Jumbo told him, "but you hang in there, okay? I'll see you tomorrow. Just remember, you're the man, man." He winked broadly at his buddy.

"You're one bad fella yourself, Jumbo. Respectable, too. You should stay respectable. Better you than me."

"Hey, I will. And watch where you're pointin' that finger. It might go off." Streetcar looked quizzically at the tip of his index finger.

"You think?"

"See you, Street."

"Take it easy," he replied. The Chevy pickup clanked off the curb and continued down the road.

Streetcar looked around hopefully, eager to share his joy with anyone within earshot. Seeing a dignified, well-dressed woman crossing the street, headed in his direction, he smiled a greeting and began a one-sided conversation.

"Jumbo must have worked all night," Streetcar said to the matron as she stepped onto the curb beside him, apparently headed for church. She studiously avoided eye contact and accelerated her pace.

"Jumbo's my friend, ma'am," he added proudly, enjoying the sound of the words. "He's a regular, respectable workin' ma-chine. A real-life, hard-wired, hard-workin' human moe-sheeeen!" he shouted, waving his arms for effect. "Yeah, boy, that's what Jumbo is, all right."

Opening his eyes, he looked around for the woman, who had fled the scene and was gone. "Huh!" he snorted. "That was rude!" He shrugged his shoulders and flopped back onto his bench. "I didn't really want to tell her about Jumbo, anyway," he added. But he knew that he was lying.

Streetcar was a creature of habit. Every morning, he sat on the same wooden bench. Every night, he slept in a fading, antique building that belonged to Sol D'Augostino, a retired mobster trying to make penance by helping less fortunate members of his community.

Streetcar's job was to guard Sol's empty building from the vandals so prevalent in this part of town. While the job was due, in part, to Sol's charity, his services provided a benefit to Sol as well, for he took his assignment seriously. In exchange for his diligent protective services, Streetcar received some spending money from Sol and a place to stay with utilities thrown in. As he was fond of saying to Jumbo, it beat a real job.

He had not always been called Streetcar. Once he had been known as Salvatore Benuto, but that had been long ago, in another life, far away. Growing up on the streets in one of the poorest neighborhoods in New York City, Sally Benuto had fought his way out of the old neighborhood until he had left his past, like his first name, far behind him. Now he was Streetcar, a law-abiding, self-effacing, very private and very independent citizen: the best-known street person in Ybor City, Florida.

Streetcar was a neat, tall, wiry man pushing 50 who stayed remarkably fit using the old exercise equipment in the defunct athletic club that served as his home. He lived a simple life of few vices and modest tastes. On this particular day, he was dressed in a frayed but spotless tee shirt and clean antique jeans as he leaned against the back of the bench, enjoying the cool morning light.

If the truth were known, Streetcar was neither an alcoholic nor a bum, and was not at all lazy. He was unfailingly polite, given to cleanliness, and diligent in every task that he undertook. He had simply lost all vestiges of traditional American ambition.

But he had not lost his curiosity.

His favorite bench was strategically situated, facing southwest toward the Columbia Restaurant on East 7th Avenue. Between northbound 22nd and southbound 21st streets, wide spaces between the buildings afforded a relatively unhindered view of vehicles traveling south on 21st. As a result, he could oversee a rolling river of traffic on 22nd and 21st as an ever-changing metallic tide flowed in and out of the heart of old Ybor City.

On this bright Sunday morning, Streetcar noticed the tan Lamborghini as soon as it drew near, traveling south on 21st Street. The car continued toward East 7th Avenue, disappearing behind a building and reappearing immediately, traveling at a respectable rate of speed. The keen rumble of its engine was distinctly audible as it passed directly across from him, only one short block away.

"Whooo-eee!" he exclaimed to nobody in particular, "not bad at all." He knew this car well, and he made the same comment every time he saw it.

Streetcar never failed to marvel at the sheer tawny beauty of the tan Lamborghini: at the majesty of its motion as it moved along the road. This car did not merely roll down the street. It flowed over the pavement like a drop of quicksilver sliding across a mirror.

He watched as the car wheeled into the parking lot that fronted 22nd Street and 7th Avenue and parked beside the worn brick wall beneath a faded sign that read, "Historical Hand Painted Tile." Two minutes later, the car door opened abruptly.

A young woman with long burgundy hair climbed out and hurriedly crossed 7th Avenue. Turning left, she passed in front of the Columbia Restaurant, increasing her speed as she approached the pay phone at the intersection of 7th Avenue and 22nd Street. Streetcar had no way of knowing that earlier on this same morning, the young woman had endured unspeakable trauma. He did not know why she was here or what crime she had witnessed, and he could not begin to guess why she had not gone to the police with her story.

But Streetcar knew what he saw with his own two eyes. And even from this distance, he could see that the girl was crying.

Surprise, Surprise

Inside of B's Coney Island Diner, two respectable-looking gentlemen were paying their bills and purchasing breath mints at the counter when they noticed the car. As soon as they saw the Lamborghini through the window, the alarm bells went off in their empty stomachs, releasing a flood of adrenaline and an untimely acid overdose.

The lean sports car in the parking lot was, quite unmistakably, the pricey ride that belonged to their esteemed colleague, Joseph Provencenti Jr., also known as Joe Boy, Joey Pro, or, when his back was turned, Super Freak. Joey was the son of the local king of organized crime, and he was the leader of his own successful crew. Joey's father was the legendarily suave, brilliant, and ruthless Joseph Provencenti Sr., Capo di Capo of the Dixie Mafia, Inc.

The two men at the counter knew that Joey's Lamborghini had been stolen only few hours earlier. They had been informed of the theft during an All-Hoods-On-Deck emergency meeting that had been held at five in the morning at the behest of a half-drunk capo with a nasty attitude. Because of the urgency of the message, they had stayed awake until this civilized hour instead of hitting the mattresses at dawn to sleep the morning away.

Because of the early hour, they had drifted over to the exceedingly informal 24-hour diner for breakfast, feeling stupid and hungry and helpless to boot. But now, they were in luck.

There it was, right in front of their faces: the object of the mob's desire. They were thrilled beyond words.

The wisest wise guys in America knew that the Tampa families dominated the Southeast. With the exception of Atlanta, New Orleans, and Memphis, the Tampa families were, in a manner of speaking, executive administrators of the southeastern quadrant (with South Florida and the Mississippi-

Alabama Gulf Coast excepted, as officially-open regions should be).

Tampa ruled the Dixie mob. And of all of the Tampa families, the Provencentis were the most prominent.

As longtime Provencenti button men, the two hoods knew Joe Boy well. Joey Provencenti was a devilishly handsome and diabolically successful crew chief.

Joey was the son of the Don, and Joey got what Joey wanted. And at this moment, Joey wanted his Lamborghini and the girl who was driving it. Like the capo had said to them earlier this morning, 'Joey wants his car returned like a new box of Cracker Jacks: clean and shiny, with the treat still inside.'

Beyond a shadow of doubt, the sleek car in front of them was Joey's. From the top of its roof to the tip of its tires, from the "I AM IT" vanity plate to the Darwin fish on the back bumper, the car was a shrine to Joe Boy's ham-handed artistic touch. This was the genuine article: in the metal, so to speak.

They could scarcely believe their luck.

JAMIE HUNG UP THE PAY PHONE and fought back the tears that threatened to overwhelm her. She quickly crossed the street and jumped into the car, firing it up and revving into instant motion.

Her phone call had been in vain.

Jamie's friend, Ellen, was obviously not at home. She knew that Ellen was a workaholic who was likely on the job, but she did not know the name of her new employer. For now, she had run out of options.

Jamie wanted to disappear. She wanted to dump this conspicuous car and hide safely in her friend's Ybor City apartment. But contact with Ellen would have to wait.

The car had been useful to get her to Tampa, but with the advent of daylight it became a deadly liability. She would have to ditch it and hide out. The thought of being stranded in public in broad daylight with such an eye-catching vehicle was, quite reasonably, terrifying to her.

Johnny was dead. Of that, she was certain. He had been her best and only friend in Oree County. Now he was gone, and she could never get him back.

She hoped that the killers had found nothing in the car to give her identity away. Her driver's license was in the pocket of the jeans she was wearing, and she had luckily neglected to bring her purse when she went out last night. While this act of forgetfulness had been a lapse that was very much out of character, it may have bought her some time. The killers might not yet know her name.

Jamie had panicked and had fled the county in a rush. She had gone to her apartment to gather minimal clothing, a purse and necessities, and had hit the road for Tampa without stopping to contact law enforcement officials. When she had been pulled over for speeding on a back road leading out of Oree County, she had found the Lamborghini's registration tucked into the visor and had waited patiently as the officer slowly wrote up the ticket.

She did not tell the officer about the violence that had occurred only minutes before. On its face, this decision appeared to be foolish. But given her personal history, Jamie's decision to keep silent was perfectly understandable. Janelle James had trusted two people, and one of them was dead.

She could not easily trust the police. Her father had been a policeman.

Jamie's explosive, abusive, and eminently respectable father had sown the seeds of watchful mistrust years ago. He had done his best to destroy her; but to his dismay, he had failed.

From the time that Jamie was born until she had turned 16, she had suffered at his hands. Her father had taken her on a sick roller coaster ride of emotional tyranny, whipsawing her from joy to terror and back again with unpredictable fits of violent rage interspersed with moments of sentimental affection and effusive charm. If it had not been for the summers spent with her loving grandparents, Jamie would have lost all hope.

Janelle's trust in humanity had never rebounded from the steady pounding she suffered during the long years she had spent under her father's roof. During that period, she had served like an abandoned soldier maintaining an outpost on a desert island: forgotten, friendless, and hopelessly lost. Year after year she suffered countless concussions that threatened to bury her in the tomb of her father's twisted soul. By the time she left home at age 16, she was like an earthquake survivor stumbling from the ruins of her youth.

Her hard experience explained why, in this time of trouble, she trusted only one living person on the face of God's green earth. And for now, that person could not be reached.

Jamie was alone.

Wrapped in the rich leather interior of the incredibly luxurious car, she wiped away the tears. The racecar idled at the edge of the street as she sought to merge with the traffic.

She would keep moving. She would somehow survive the coming day.

But as for where she was headed, or how she would get there, only God in heaven knew.

Hungry Customers

Watching the Lamborghini rumble to life in the parking lot across the street, the two Mob soldiers shook off their lethargy and put the proverbial pedal to the floor of their mental mettle. They were almost comical as they tripped over one another, bailing out of the restaurant and scrambling to get into their car. They tumbled into their full-sized luxury sedan and followed the sports car onto 22nd Street, leaving an acrid puff of scorched rubber in their wake.

The delicate cloud of burnt rubber slowly drifted across the filthy pavement, wafting over lipstick-smeared cigarette butts and sun-bleached brown bags that rested beside yellowing shreds of broken Styrofoam. The burnt rubber added a hint of smoky mystery to the trash that identified the parking lot as an authentic part of the Greater Tampa area.

KICKING BACK on his bench only two blocks away from the action, Streetcar was taking in the sights of another peaceful Sunday morning. But as he saw the situation develop in the parking lot, an unexpected instinct was aroused, and a reaction was triggered deep within him. He found himself standing on his feet, acutely focused on what was unfolding before his eyes.

The girl was in trouble.

A suddenly invigorated and thoroughly aware former First Sergeant Salvatore "Streetcar" Benuto recognized the situation, even at this distance, for what it was.

This was an instinctive insight on his part, not the product of conscious analysis. Seeing the two mobsters as they excitedly stumbled out of the diner, he discerned immediately that they were hot on the trail of the young woman in the sports car.

He watched attentively as the Lamborghini whipped past him within touching distance, the young girl still crying as she skillfully piloted the slick sports car down the street. She was oblivious to the shiny four-door Cadillac that was running hot on her trail.

The big Cadillac was the bearer of bad tidings. It packed a devil's deuce of hungry hoods homing in on their prey like jackals after an unsuspecting gazelle. A sinking feeling filled Streetcar's stomach as he realized that, without a car of his own, there was nothing he could do to save this troubled girl.

He got a clear view of the men as their car passed his bench. Their faces said it all: hungry, greedy expressions with flushed skin and glistening eyes intent upon the prey.

She has no idea of what's coming, he thought. His mind raced as he searched for some idea, some way that he might deliver this young woman from the terrible thing that was about to happen to her. Then, just before the Lamborghini went under the interstate, she hit the brakes and wheeled into the convenience store on the corner.

Streetcar, with his willpower more tightly focused than it had been in years, began to run.

AS JAMIE WALKED into the convenience store, the two men parked their car in the alley behind it. They were deep in conversation, attempting to coordinate an effective kidnapping strategy.

"Okay now, I go into the store. Now, what do <u>you</u> do?" the big man asked.

"I wait at the corner of the building. In the alley. I watch to make sure nobody's in the parking lot, and I'm ready to come over as soon as she steps out of the store."

"Good. Okay, so if we can, we're gonna take the girl quietly, with nobody to see it," Big Jim repeated patiently. "If we can't do it quietly, we have to cancel it. That's all there is to it. If there are witnesses, we call it off. Right?"

"Right."

"Okay. So, after we grab her, what's next?"

"We hustle her into this alley and stuff her in the trunk," Nick replied.

"And what if she screams and people come running up? What if she starts to draw a crowd before we can get her into the trunk?"

"If a crowd starts to form, we drop her quick and we beat it. Then we call Marky."

"Good, Nicky, you've got it." They slammed the doors of their car and hurried through the gate that led to the driveway on the side of the store. From there, they rounded the south corner of the store. They were just a few steps away from the little wooden front door with its cobalt blue, slightly peeling paint and ancient penguin decal declaring, 'It's KOOL Inside.'

As Nick Matalona waited at the corner of the building, watching his partner walk into the ramshackle store, he had to admit it.

This was really living!

The pending ambush would be the kind of action that Nick had signed up for when he became a Provencenti soldier. And this was what his partner, Big Jim, had dreamed of when he had burned the written vow in the palm of his hand and had bound himself under the fraternal curse forever, a made man in the Provencenti family.

This was adventure, full of the titillating taste of deadly force, the power to terrify the weak, the drunken thrill of the chase, and the violent surge of pleasure when teeth sink into the prey. This was what wolves felt like when they surrounded a startled deer and closed in with their red tongues lolling, hot for the blood of the kill.

The 22nd Street Market

Big Jim walked into the fast food market with the distracted shuffle of a natural actor giving the performance of his life. There was big money coming his way if he played his cards right: big opportunities, maybe promotions. If he were lucky, today's events could rocket him up the ladder to the top of the organization.

They got it made at the top, Jim considered, *and soon, I could be one of 'em. Who knows, maybe the old man will make me a capo.* Big Jim was a positive thinker who preferred to focus on the more attractive aspects of his chosen career. He did not care to consider that the path he was on, paved with money and slicked with gore, would eventually dump him unceremoniously into hell.

With his future in the balance, and despite the pressure, Big Jim refused to sweat. He was one cool cucumber, as ice cold as the Tastee Treats reclining in the rusty old freezer that wheezed fitfully against the cracked plaster wall inside the ancient convenience store.

This store was a wood-floored anachronism. At least as old as the cigar factories down the street, it was a dumpy grocery that had been recently converted, in an act of quiet desperation, into a pathetic excuse for a fast food market.

A place like this would burn like a torch, Jim considered wistfully, *too bad we got no reason to light it up.* He was the arson specialist for the Provencentis, and he loved his work.

As Jamie dug in her wallet and found a twenty-dollar bill, Big Jim Bianamabella ambled up the middle aisle, closing in from the back of the store. Deep in thought, she handed the bill to the teenager behind the counter, trying to gather her wits as she assessed the situation. Ellen was not at home, and this had rattled her badly. She knew that she had to come up with a plan, but she did not know where to begin. The man was behind her now, towering over her, deeply involved in his reading . . . to all appearances, at least.

Big Jim whistled softly under his breath, paging through the latest Truck Trader magazine as he tried to seem inconspicuous. *Monster Mudder, 1985 Chevy frame, needs tires/shocks, 5,000.00 dollars, firm. Hmmm, not bad!* Completing her transaction, Jamie threw the change into her purse and hurried out the door.

It was a picture-perfect job.

On this slow Sunday morning, there were no witnesses except for two rusted gas pumps and one flyblown, wide-open dumpster. Big Jim hurried out of the door behind Jamie and Nick closed in from the side like a snake skimming across a rock. The two hoods swept Jamie off her feet, each taking an elbow as they scooped her up like a sack of flour.

They managed to hustle her around the corner of the building before the shock wore off and she began to fight wildly. She arched her body like a leaping dolphin, spitting and screaming and sinking her teeth into Nick's hand when he covered her mouth to stifle her outcry. Struggling mightily to control this wild and surprisingly powerful young woman whose teeth threatened to snap his fingers, Nick butted her head and bit her ear, drawing blood as the men banged through the wooden fence gate and stumbled into the cobblestone alleyway.

In the stinking brick alley, she saw the car. Surrounded by a bouquet of weeds and perfumed with rotting vegetables, the apple-red Cadillac dumbly awaited its cargo.

Having neither eyes to see nor ears to hear, the brightly polished car was a classic American icon. It squatted in its place: shiny and radiant, reigning in lifeless splendor.

It was an American idol. And like an idol from the ancient days, the car seemed to await them hungrily, eager to receive the bloody sacrifice within the open mouth of its gaping, spacious trunk.

Familiar Territory

"**S**heriff," Gene Thompson slowly replied, gazing at the horizon, "this is a complicated situation. But to answer your question, I'll tell you what I think about this mess.

"I think I've figured out what happened to this kid." He paused and cleared his throat. "Here's what I've got so far."

He straightened his back and took of his golf cap, slicking his hair back with his right hand. The coroner and the Sheriff stood in the shade at the foot of the cypress tree, surrounded by the sunburned rancher and his employees. The men pressed in closer, straining to hear the coroner's words.

"Before he died, this boy's hands were tied together behind his back and lashed to his feet. To put it another way, he was hogtied.

"The skin around his hands shows deep bruising that occurred just before his death. He was tied up tightly, but not tightly enough to bruise. There had to be another stressor that caused the bruises on his wrists.

"Of course, the most obvious question is, 'why was the boy found, broken like a rag doll, in the top of a tall tree?' According to my examination, the most likely answer to that question is that he fell from a great distance out of the clear blue sky. Or out of the dark purple sky, I should say, since it was night when it happened. He landed in the top of this tree strictly by chance.

"You served in Vietnam, didn't you, Sheriff?" Gene asked, turning to look directly at him.

"Yes," he replied.

"I thought so," Gene said, raising an eyebrow. "So did I."

"Now, tell me this, Tommy," the coroner asked. "When you were in Vietnam, did you ever hear anything about people getting thrown out of planes or choppers?"

"Hmm. There were rumors about the A.R.V.N.," the Sheriff replied, "but I never saw it, myself."

"Right. Well, I can tell you, the rumors were pretty close to the truth." The coroner turned to the gaping ranchers, who stepped closer to savor the grisly details.

"Some guys in the A.R.V.N. - the regular army of South Vietnam - used to blindfold captured guerillas and take them up in Hueys. Up in the air, they'd take off the guerillas' blindfolds and question them. They might throw one or two out the door to prime the pump. The VC would see their comrades tossed out, and it would loosen their tongues. The technique was terribly cruel, but wonderfully effective. Usually, by the second or third toss, somebody would sing like a bird.

"I was a medic back then, and I got a good look at a guy they threw out. The damage was just like what you see here with a few exceptions. One exception is, this boy was shot in the head at close range, probably well before he went up in the plane. The wound went in through the top of the brow, skimmed the membrane containing the brain without puncturing it, and took off the left side of his forehead, as you can see. This is interesting," he added as an aside, as if he were footnoting a scholarly narration. "But it is not what killed him.

"There's a bullet wound in his shoulder that caused substantial bleeding. It may have been caused by the same bullet; I don't know yet. Judging from the coagulation, it appears that the gunshot wounds were suffered at least 20 minutes before the fall that caused his death.

"My guess is, his captors were not planning to dump him here. It looks like they were torturing him: hanging him hogtied out of the door of the aircraft.

"His wrists are badly bruised from the rope, and most of the damage is on one side. The bruising must have happened when they were hanging him out of the aircraft. His hair is tangled and knotted as if he was buffeted in a strong wind.

"Look at this, Tom." Out of his garish golf shirt pocket, the doctor lifted a plastic bag. "I secured this piece of evidence for you. It was half-buried in the dirt at the foot of this tree, and I didn't want anyone stepping on it."

In the coroner's zip-loc bag was a blood-smeared pocketknife. The Sheriff glanced at the corpse and saw that a knife holster on the belt was empty, the cover unsnapped. *He probably never planned to do anything with that knife but whittle some wood or field-dress a deer.* He looked at the inert body, his eyes filled with pity.

"You guessed it," the coroner said, following his gaze. "It's the boy's knife. We're extremely lucky that it fell here, and not in the canal or the swamp. He must have had it in his hand when he hit the top of the tree."

"Tell me the rest."

"The way I figure, somebody hung him out of the door of an airplane or chopper, or whatever. His right hand must have popped free from the ropes, and that's when this gutsy kid showed what he was made of.

"See this?" The coroner pointed with the tip of his polished shoe to the boy's right hand, which had come free and was no longer entangled in the jumbled snare of knotted rope. The boy's thin wrist displayed a cruel bracelet: a morbid wreath of blue-green bruises left by his wretched ordeal. The clotted blood showed through the wafer-thin skin like a deadly bloom of infernal, subdermal algae.

"This hand was tied up, and it was bruised badly, but somehow it came free from the ropes."

"But he was unconscious by the time they hung him out of the plane, right?" Billy Cloud asked hesitantly. The coroner blinked and stared at him, not realizing that he was speaking to a friend of the deceased.

"I don't think so. He was conscious, and the pain must have been terrific. When a man suffers a gunshot wound like this, he feels like he's being burned by a blowtorch."

"I've been shot," the Sheriff replied. "I know how it feels."

"Uh, yes, of course," replied the coroner, glancing up at the sheriff. "Then you really know what I'm talking about." The coroner returned to his narrative.

"So they dangled this boy out of a plane, torturing him, and here's what happened next. Hanging from that plane, he probably knew that they were going to kill him. So he denied them the opportunity.

"Swinging around in the wind like a sack on a string, he worked his hand loose. Then he dug this knife out." He shook the baggie that held the knife for emphasis, his lips pursed, angry at the cruelty of it all.

"The kid opened the knife with his teeth. Look at the cut there, on his cheek." They all looked again, against their will, at the gaping corpse as a fly slowly crawled across the scared white face, guiding their eyes to a clean cut beside his open mouth. "That little wound on this cheek is clean, with almost no blood.

"He cut himself opening the knife, but he didn't have enough fluid left to bleed out." The coroner pointed at the baggie. "If you have excellent vision, you may be able to see the tiniest scrap of flesh here, inside the handle, stuck to the tip of this blade. I'll bet you dollars to doughnuts that scrap of flesh matches the wound on the kid's cheek." *Dollars to doughnuts - an unlucky analogy,* the Sheriff mused, trying not to think about breakfast as he studiously tried to ignore the pathetic corpse that gaped at his feet, rapidly aging in the unseasonable heat.

"So," Gene said, his voice rising, "the kid escaped from his tormentors. Knowing that he was going to die anyway, he bit the knife open and cut himself free. I guess he held onto the pocketknife out of habit. He even shut it during the fall.

"Bottom line: he ended it before they could. That's how he wound up in the top of this tree."

Nobody spoke a word as the crickets whirred in the swamp and swarms of gnats clamored in vain for their attention. The Preacher stared at the corpse again, forcing himself to study the details.

The coroner was right about the rope. The cut was obviously fresh, and the fibers had not yet unraveled. The boy had cut himself loose and as a result, had fallen into the tree.

"Sheriff," the Coroner said, shaking his head somberly, "whoever tormented this kid is one sorry son of . . . uh, well, you know what I mean." He bit his tongue, remembering the etiquette of this rural southern county. He actually felt embarrassed about what he had almost said in front of the quiet, thoughtful man. *What's happening to me, I'm from Miami!* Then he figured out a way to politely say what he was thinking.

"Pardon me, Sheriff," he blurted, "but whoever did this is one sick, sorry excuse for a human being!"

The Preacher usually guarded his thoughts, but at this moment, he had to agree. He silently nodded as slowly, from deep within, the outrage provoked by the horrible crime threatened to sweep away his self-control. His wrath grew exponentially in a slow, relentless pulse.

He was shaken to the core.

It was as if his beliefs were at risk, as if his faith were being pushed aside by a contrary force that had arisen deep within him. He was weakened and sickened by a tectonically powerful lava flow of smoldering, molten rage that snapped and popped as it pressed its heavy, smoking weight against his soul.

The flow of anger threatened to displace all that he held dear. It groaned and cracked as it strained to move his faith from its solid, unshakable foundation.

Someone around here needed prayer, of that much he was certain.

And this time, that someone was Sheriff Tommy Durrance.

A Gift from an Armenian Friend

Ellen Bromley sat at her desk and focused on the task at hand. She was cleaning up the remains of a backlog of loan applications, and she hoped to be done soon.

Hers was not an impressive place of business. It was just another bank on the first floor of another tall building in a town full of banks on the first floors of tall buildings. Neither was her workplace a hotbed of radical innovation. It was the home of mature and reliable dreams clipped close to the wing by the fiscally conservative souls who labored therein. But as of tomorrow, she was shaking off the dust of this bank. After too many difficult days and hard-working nights spent burning the job at both ends, she would be taking a well-deserved vacation.

Earlier this morning, at a sunrise service in a familiar pew, Ellen had worshipped with a small flock of elderly women. The service had been led by an appropriately pious priest: a fervent young man who meant what he prayed when he prayed it. Sincerity was a desirable trait for any priest, Ellen reasoned.

She felt clean and relaxed. Her week had not been the best, but this Sunday was shaping up to be a good one.

In two or three hours she would be free of this place. Tomorrow, she planned to drive south to the little town of Pezner, Florida, where she would surprise her best friend.

If she hasn't found someone yet, it'll be a miracle. Jamie will probably get married before me, and I'll be the odd woman out, she thought ruefully as she typed another long string of numbers into her computer, calling up yet another account from her bank's online network. She thought of her friend and smiled.

For the first time in her life, Jamie's got it made, she reflected. *And if anyone deserves it, she does.* Freed from her unfortunate past, Jamie had found a place of refuge in Oree

County.   But now, as Ellen thought about her friend, she experienced a twinge of misgiving that she could not explain.

Ellen was an extremely practical, thoroughly grounded person.   She was a smart young woman who took life as she saw it.   She was not inclined to mysticism, and she expected no unexplained ripples in her neat little universe.   But now, as she thought about Jamie, she felt a strong sense of foreboding.   She increased the speed of her typing, suddenly uneasy.

This is crazy, she told herself, trying to drown herself in her work, to forget the premonition that she had just experienced.   *As soon as I get home, I'll call Jamie, and we'll talk.   Then I'll feel better.*

For a moment, her eyes left the screen and she looked at the gorgeous crystal paperweight on her desk.   It was a gift from an elderly Armenian friend whose mother had been killed, along with hundreds of thousands of other Christians, in the Armenian holocaust of the 1920s.   The paperweight was an antique, an intricately crafted work of art that had been created with much care by a survivor of that horrible slaughter.

On the bottom of the paperweight the artist had inscribed, in Armenian, "We are not without hope, for Love has defeated the power of the grave."   When Ellen was first told of its meaning, the message had seemed trite and overly dramatic. But today, as she thought of the words, they were curiously comforting.

As she paused to stare at the beautiful work of art, she remembered the unthinkable slaughters of the twentieth century.   In their attempt to better the lot of humanity, that century's secular idealists had committed atrocities of a magnitude exceeding anything in recorded history.   With excruciating excess, the twentieth century's political dreamers had outperformed the villains of ages and inquisitions past.

The most prominent murderers of the twentieth century had numbered their victims in seven digits.   Adolph Hitler had devilishly stoked his ovens; Stalin had filled gulags and starved the Ukraine.   Tens of thousands of Tibetans had been starved or killed by Chinese communists, and three million hapless Cambodians lay dead at the hands of Khmer Rouge. The enormity of it was enough to overwhelm the mind.

If there is justice in the universe, she wondered, *how can the world survive? And yet, surely, there must be justice.* As she considered these things, she realized the futility of her own worries regarding this profound subject.

Using her finely honed skill of denial, she blotted these thoughts from her mind. Then she turned and resumed her work.

Strange Attractors

Things were not going well for Big Jim and Nick. As they battled to control a one-woman army of power-packed femininity, they stumbled into the narrow alley. They were scarcely able to move forward as each struggled to grip his assigned half of their fiercely struggling intended victim. But despite Jamie's best efforts, they managed to drag her steadily toward their goal until Big Jim bumped into the car.

"Take her," he blurted, happy to turn the girl loose as he turned to search in the trunk for duct tape. Nick immediately regretted the fact that Big Jim had let go of his end of the package.

Jamie hit Nick squarely on the nose with a sharp blow from her free hand. He saw stars as the blood poured freely down the front of his shirt in a warm, wet river of pain.

"Stupid broad!" he shouted, striking her to the ground with the back of his hand. She went down hard and bruised a knee, stunned by the blow. It was then that Nick received his second big surprise.

"Don't call her names," an eerie voice rasped behind him. "Step back and let her go." An uncannily deep voice was speaking, uttering the words as softly as if it were whispering in his ear.

The sound of the voice was startling. It was unearthly, so low in timbre that the ground beneath their feet almost seemed to shift uneasily in response to its resonance. The two men turned their heads in surprise and saw a lean, broad-shouldered, middle-aged man dressed in faded jeans and a faded tee shirt, his long salt and pepper hair tied back in a ponytail. The man stared at them with a world-weary gaze.

"Who are you?" Nick the Nose spat out angrily, dabbing at his prominent namesake with a handkerchief. His mind was racing as his hand inched toward the gun beneath his navy blazer. Big Jim, less verbal and more dangerous than his garrulous companion, stopped digging in the trunk and looked up at the man. Frozen in place with duct tape in hand, crouched over the open trunk, he quickly assessed the situation. A visual scan revealed that the stranger appeared to be unarmed.

"Step back from the car," Streetcar said, and the eyes of the mobsters narrowed. Big Jim turned around and straightened up to his full height, eyeing the newcomer warily. Nick, on the other hand, was less thoughtful and more verbose.

"Are you a cop?" Nick asked stupidly. Then a light went off somewhere deep within Big Jim's moribund mind.

"No, Nicky, this ain't no cop," Jim answered, laughing in nervous relief. "This is Streetcar. You know, Streetcar the bum. This guy is the Ybor City mascot, the dumpster-diver. We're being carjacked by the town bum!"

Jim couldn't believe it. Here they were, stopped in their tracks by Streetcar the Bum. "You don't look like yourself, Streetcar," he said, smiling cruelly. "Are you sick already, or do you want us to help you along?" To Jim, the situation was humorous.

"Go away Streetcar," Nick spat angrily, still mopping at his broken nose. "And pretend you ain't seen nothin'."

"Oh, no sir, I won't go away," the man answered, soft and low. "Old Streetcar, he ain't goin' nowhere." He stepped close: close enough to reach out and touch their flushed faces.

"Now listen, I'll give you a chance," Streetcar added, sighing heavily. "You boys don't have to get hurt. Sit down, put your hands on your head, and don't move a muscle."

"Who are you, Dirty Harry?" Jim guffawed.

"Forget it, bum," sneered Nicky, and his hand flashed for the gun tucked in his belt.

From her seat on the cobblestone pavement, Jamie was able to see exactly what happened next, but the action was unbelievably fast, much too fast for the shocked hoods to follow. If she had not been so focused, watching the scene with such intensity, she undoubtedly would have missed it.

The back of Streetcar's left hand slammed into Nick's throat in a single, unanticipated blur that was followed by the fluid whirl of his entire body as he spun like a top and planted a heel into Big Jim's chest. The heavy blow lifted the big man ponderously into the air to the accompaniment of a dull, horrifying crack.

Big Jim was propelled backwards into the trunk of the big red Cadillac. He lay on his back inside the trunk, his hands and feet flopping helplessly as he fought for his next breath, squealing like a gigantic, hairy-faced baby stuffed into a cherry red basinet.

Shaking his head regretfully, Streetcar tied a few loose hairs back into his ponytail, looking down at the prostrate, spasmodically convulsing Nicholas "Nick the Nose" Matalona. Nick was curled in the dust behind the car in a fetal position as if the open-mouthed Cadillac had just coughed him up out of the trunk onto the hard, unforgiving cobblestones.

"Now, why'd you make me do that?" Streetcar asked no one in particular.

Shaking his head, he bent down and wrenched the gun from Nick's belt. He opened the car door and rummaged in the glove box, coming out with four full boxes of bullets

"Nine millimeter Glock," he said, smiling grimly, "not a bad gun." Cheered by success, he started to sing.

"If I had a hammer," he crooned, "I'd hammer out danger." He stood up and tucked the gun into his belt, slamming the car door shut. "I'd hammer out justice . . . all over this land." Gazing down at a stunned Janelle James, he stopped singing.

Jamie sat on the pavement in shocked disarray, slowly gathering her wits. She looked up at her unlikely deliverer with no small amount of trepidation as he smiled at her gently.

"My apologies, ma'am. Those two punks should have left you alone."

"Not to worry," she said, her voice cracking as she reached up to him.

"You gave them quite a fight," he said as she climbed shakily to her feet. "They weren't expecting that." She smiled wanly.

"Now, if you don't mind," he added, looking around the alley, "I think we'd better get out of here."

The Dispatch

The Oree County Dispatch wasn't much of a newspaper. But it was the only one he owned.

Seth Greene sat behind the news desk at the Oree County Dispatch in his typical Sunday morning pose: his feet up on the desk, fresh coffee in the pot, and a wide-open Tampa Tribune in front of his face. The Tribune wasn't the New York Times, but, hey, this wasn't New York City. This was Pezner, Florida.

To the citizens of Pezner, the City of Tampa was a massive megalopolis. The Tampa Tribune was an out-of-town big city daily that was enjoyed by many Peznerites. But the only paper that excited loyalty - or intense local interest - was Seth's baby, the Oree County Dispatch.

Seth Greene was a fifth-generation Floridian, a good old boy who had learned to be content with who he was, where he came from, and what he planned to do in with his life. He had been blessed with a lovely wife and three children who had provided him with plenty of incentive to take over the family business when his parents retired, and he had seized the opportunity to settle down to the quiet life of a small town news hawk.

Every Saturday, Seth took a day off work and attended the tiny local synagogue with his family. But Sunday morning was his personal quiet time. On Sunday, he spent the morning alone in this historic building, enjoying the ambience of his glass-partitioned office in the center of the big, old-fashioned newsroom. Savoring the solitude beneath the high ceiling and slowly rotating fans, he stoically manned the news desk.

On this uneventful Sunday, Seth was immersed in his usual routine. Soon he would return home to his noisy family. But for now, he was relaxing.

He had finished his morning tasks and was enjoying the kind of peace and quiet that could not be begged, borrowed, or purchased at home. On Tuesdays and

Wednesdays, he traded places with his wife Rachel and stayed with the kids while she spent her days at the office or took some of her own private time to rest and refresh. But this was not Tuesday or Wednesday. It was Sunday morning, and Seth was savoring every minute of it.

When he heard the front door slam, he looked up in surprise to see the Sheriff of Oree County walk through the lobby, headed towards his glass-walled office.   The Sheriff always looked intense, but this morning he seemed to be particularly grim, fully focused on the matter at hand. Smiling despite himself, Seth reflected that the problem troubling Tommy was probably trapped in the grip of his mind like a scared toy in the mouth of an angry bulldog.

"Mornin' Preacher," Seth drawled as the Sheriff barged through the glass door and walked into his office. "You don't have to knock. Just barge right on in."

"Oh, yeah," the Sheriff replied absently as his expression softened and he smiled sheepishly, realizing what he had done. "Sorry about that."

"Have a seat, son," Seth said loudly, raising his foot and shoving a chair that rolled toward the Sheriff across the polished floor. "And don't ever apologize. It doesn't suit you, Tommy. Somehow, it seems unnatural." His visitor pulled up the chair up and sat on it backwards with his arms crossed on its back. *He's a man on a mission today,* Seth mused. *He missed the Sunday service for this one. It must be big.*

Seth Greene had known Tommy Durrance since Mrs. Hubble's first grade class at Pezner Elementary. They had grown up together in this one-tractor town.

In their wilder days, Seth Greene and Tommy Durrance had cut a riotous swath through the juke joints and honky-tonks in this part of the state.   Seth had stopped carousing long before Tommy did.

Seth had married well. He loved his wife, and they had a rich, rewarding relationship. Tommy, on the other hand, had managed to bring heartbreak upon his own head. He had neglected his marriage and, as a result, had spent the past 20 years trying to atone for his bad decisions.

Interrupting Seth's reflections, the Sheriff blurted out a question.

"Seth, did you check the police reports this morning?" Of course, he didn't need to ask. Seth's sole hobby was his secondary passion.

Every day, Seth delved into the obscure, arcane intricacies of police reporting. He scanned the wires, monitored the frequencies, and speed-read everything from traffic tickets to the cat-in-the-tree reports, looking for anything unusual that might catch his ear or eye. And Tommy had to admit it; Seth was a genius at gleaning a haystack and finding the needle. At almost any time of any given day, he was the Sheriff's best source of up-to-the-minute news about significant criminal activity throughout the State of Florida.

"I've checked the overnights, Tommy. That was my first order of business, as you know." Seth's powerful police scanner was connected to a voice-activated recording machine, and Seth listened to the local calls early each morning as he flipped through the arrest reports from the Sheriff's Department and the Pezner Police. By 7:30 A.M. on any day of the week he had raced through the previous evening's data, identifying items of interest that he could turn into stories for his paper. Then, like any thorough crime report junkie, he would check the statewide news wires, the all-points alerts, FDLE bulletins, and the AP and UPI tapes. After he completed this comprehensive review, Seth would open the Tribune, and his pace would slow down considerably.

Although he was known for creating a professional product, Seth Greene put together his weekly paper at a less-than-hectic pace. To him, the slowed-down style of life in Pezner was an integral part of what attracted him back to the town. It was a quality-of-life issue, no more and no less.

"When you reviewed the overnights this morning, did anything in particular jump out at you?" the Sheriff asked. "Anything at all?"

"Funny you should ask. Take a look at this." Tommy whistled.

"That's one of last night's traffic tickets, isn't it? How'd you get hold of it so early?"

"Arnetta had a slow night, so she copied the tickets for me. She's a real trooper, Tommy."

"40 years of service, and she's still scaring the life out of any rookie dumb enough to ask her for a cup of coffee," the Sheriff replied as he focused his attention on the traffic ticket that Seth had handed him. "You're right," he told his friend. "This is one strange traffic ticket."

"It's strange, all right. One of our local folks, stopped for speeding on Highway 27 North, driving a car worth a half a million dollars. That's a tad unusual for Oree County."

"Yup."

"The speeder was Janelle James, who, in case you don't know, is a teller at Pezner National Bank. She's a very nice, pretty young woman," Seth added. "She's also very friendly, in a reserved sort of way."

"Yeah, I think I met her last year. It was at the bank's Christmas party, if I recall correctly. Does she have dark red hair?"

"That's her."

"I agree with your assessment. She is a very nice young lady."

"Right. And very early this morning, this very nice young lady was given a ticket for speeding in a Lamborghini. The Lamborghini happens to be owned by a Mr. Joseph Provencenti, Tampa address. All dutifully recorded on the ticket by your diligent deputy, who dotted his 'i's and crossed his 't's, but didn't put two and two together."

"Joseph Provencenti? That name sounds familiar."

"It should. You're the cop, Tommy. Come on!"

"Oh, yeah, Joseph Provencenti. He was arrested a few years ago in Tampa for tax evasion. He got away clean. They say that he's a Mafia don."

"You're right, and he is a don from what I hear. But take another look at the year of birth on the registration," the newspaperman urged. "You're getting slack in your old age."

"It's been a long morning," he replied ruefully. "You're right, I am getting slack. The car's owner is less than 30 years old. This can't be old man Provencenti. It must be his son." He studied the ticket. "Hmmm. What was Janelle James doing in this guy's car?"

"That's the half-million dollar question, Tommy. If a slick car like that ever showed up around here during daylight hours, the whole town would shut down while folks took a look at it."

"I'd probably be right there with 'em, crowding in to see. And I expect you would be, too."

"You've got that right," the newsman replied. Intent on refilling his coffee cup, he reached toward the pot, leaning back in his chair. He craned his head and stretched, straining, extending as far as he could and beyond, rocking in hard-fought increments until he grasped the handle of a half-full pot of coffee. He was lucky to reel in the pot without dumping the whole thing on the floor.

"This is fresh Java, old pal," he offered excitedly. "I just brewed it. You want some?"

"I reckon," the Sheriff replied, stroking his chin. "Just one more thing, Seth."

"What?"

"Do yourself a favor, buddy. Get out your notepad and your pen."

"Why?"

"I've got next week's headline for you." Seth's ears perked up as Tommy continued. "I just left the scene of Oree County's crime of the decade." The newsman reached in his desk and quickly dug out a piece of paper and a pen, his face aglow with pure, childlike enthusiasm.

"Okay," he said excitedly, leaning forward with pen in hand. "Shoot!"

Trust

"Come on!" Streetcar urged, trying to persuade Jamie to leave the scene of the crime. He knew better than to touch her after what she had just been through, so he could only plead.

"Can we please get out of here?" he asked. "Pretty please?" he added hopefully. Jamie did not respond immediately, uncertain of what she should do next.

Can we get out of here? she wondered. *We? Can I trust this guy?*

"Okay," Janelle finally said, "let's get out of here." *He saved your life, girl,* she berated herself. She looked him in the eye, beginning to recover from the initial shock of the attempted kidnapping. "But I'm driving, okay?"

"Sure," he responded, "you're driving." They walked quickly out of the alley through the gate, past the little store and up to the Lamborghini. Climbing in and slamming the doors, they were immediately sealed in a remarkably silent, insular environment.

The Lamborghini was a nation to itself: bordered by bumpers, trimmed in burled walnut. The soft leather seats fit like a full body glove, wrapping them in a rich, leathery aroma. The scent of leather was fresh and luxurious, as if they had climbed into the middle of a well-bound book or a recently purchased baseball glove.

"Not bad," Streetcar commented respectfully, "a real good-looking piece of work." She looked at him swiftly, saw he was referring to the car, and cranked up the high compression engine.

Jamie practically sprayed chunks of asphalt with the smoking tires as she tore away from the parking lot and darted up the ramp onto Interstate 4. The car merged into traffic with a swift, subtle surge of refined Italian horsepower.

"Where to?" she asked.

"I've got a plan. Go north on I-75, west on Orient Street, and park at the Tampa Bay Center Mall," he said, watching the traffic nervously. "And please, lady, don't get pulled for speeding!" Seeing the speed at which she launched the car into traffic, Streetcar realized that he was in for a white-knuckle experience. This particular Sunday drive promised to be more like a roller coaster ride at Busch Gardens than a Sunday stroll in the park.

"By the way, do you know who owns this car?" Streetcar asked, trying to take his mind off the car's swift movement through the heavy interstate traffic. Janelle bit her lip as she considered his question.

"The devil," she replied calmly. "The devil owns this car." She kept her eyes on the road, changing lanes like a grand prix driver on the streets of Monte Carlo, focused on the traffic ahead.

In the parking lot in Ybor City, just before she had tried to call Ellen, Jamie had found a wallet in the glove compartment. On a laminated, laser-veneered driver's license inside the wallet, she had been stunned to see the face of the gunman from Homeland Estates. He looked pleasant and harmless as he smiled innocently at the camera. She would never forget the name that was emblazoned in large, bold print to the right of the picture: Joseph Provencenti, Jr.

She knew who owned this car, all right.

"The devil owns this car, huh?" Streetcar asked. He smiled, realizing that he was in the presence of an undefeated spirit. "Well, don't worry, me and the devil ain't on speakin' terms. And I don't like the way those guys treated you back there, either."

"If the devil wants this car," Streetcar offered, "he can have it back as far as I'm concerned. But if the devil wants you," he added with a crooked smile, "to hell with the devil." *I always thought I had more guts than brains,* he reflected, *and now I've gone and proved it.*

"I suppose he'll wind up in hell, eventually," she replied. "That seems to be the plan."

"No, seriously, do you know who owns this car?" he persisted.

"A monster."

"Well, I guess he's a monster . . . or a made mobster, at least. It's owned by the son of the biggest Mob guy in Tampa."

Seeing the sign at the last minute, Jamie whipped into a line of cars for the I-75 northern overpass. She shrugged her shoulders in response to his comments.

"It figures."

"Yep. This car is owned by a big shot in the mob."

"I always had good luck with guys."

"There's the Orient Street exit," he interjected tersely, pointing ahead. In spite of his bravado, he was terrified by the car's speed and Jamie's careless virtuosity behind the wheel.

"I know, I know," she replied, whipping the car into the right lane. She took the exit, and they made a neck-wrenching descent around the curved ramp, coming to an abrupt halt behind an idling row of sedate sedans and pickup trucks waiting at a red light.

"That was pretty impressive," he said with false bravado, trying to regain his nerve and stomach. "Could you do that again?"

"Where now?" she responded, all business. "You said you had a plan." She knew that she had to keep moving. This man's plan, whatever it was, had to better than none at all.

"Go straight ahead for a mile or so," he replied. "Turn left to park at the mall. I hate to say it, but we have to ditch this car. Do you have any plans today?"

"My only plan is to stay alive until I can hook up with my friend," she responded, and then she became quiet, not wanting to offer any more information. She had no confidence in this man who had saved her life. He didn't have to know everything about her life, after all.

"Well, okay then," he said, thinking out loud. "We'll ditch the wheels, go through the mall to the other side, and take the bus to Northeast Tampa."

"Where to?"

"To the University of South Florida library," he replied, glancing at her with uplifted brows, "it's open to the public, you know." She stared at him in surprise. "By the way," he added, "do you like to read?"

Hardwired

He does not sit down, but stands with his hands folded in front of him, coldly measuring the man seated behind the desk. The killer's gaze is flat and lifeless, his posture the picture of perfection. He is a consummate professional.

The demands of his challenging profession come naturally to him. He desires no other way of life, for his career is his delight.

He is neither tall, nor short. He is not particularly fat, nor is he more than stylishly thin. He is, by any definition, a white man. He is a whiter shade of pale: pasty-complected, with platinum hair and sky blue eyes. Faint wisps of faded hair linger, like a melting, hoary mist, above his eyes and on the backs of his hands.

He is not given to daydreams, but today he is in a reflective mood. *Struggle is all there is,* he reminds himself, staring out of the window as he ignores the heated words that slop like sour wine from the open mouth of the portly Mafia captain.

He glances down at the pontificating capo in the cushy leather chair, and he turns back to the window. *Blood and fire add steel to the will,* he considers idly, *and temper the mettle of the soul.* These are not his own words; he is recalling a quote from a long-dead philosopher. He does not believe them; he likes to toy with their emptiness.

As his mind wanders, he realizes that the bloated mob captain has stopped talking. He looks at the capo closely, sizing up what he sees: a short, stocky hood who perspires like a hippo out of water in spite of the icy temperature in the air-conditioned office. If he could feel pity, he would pity this man. *You were once a player,* the professional thinks, staring at the capo, *once a terror. But now, you're so soft it's sickening.*

"So, O'Malley. Are you going to take the job?" the captain asks.

"No."

"No?" he bristles. "What do you mean?"

"I need more information."

"You don't get it. Your friend Joey asked for you. What more do you need?"

"I admire Joseph," the professional replies carefully, "as I admire anyone who has outgrown the vestiges of social conscience." He is beginning to lose his patience. "But I need more information before I make a decision. I need everything you can get me on this street person you're talking about. This man handled your experienced soldiers as if they were little boys. Who is he? Where is from? Where does he live? Who are his friends? I need anything and everything, and I need it right away."

"What else?"

"You said that Joseph asked for me. Fine. I want to talk to him." He looks out the window again, expressionless.

"Get me the girl's name, her friends' names, anything," he adds, "and get me whatever you can on that bum."

"Anything else?"

"Yeah. The kid, the one who cut himself loose from the plane; that's a loose end. Check out the local situation. Was the body found? If it was found, it will be big news in a rural area like Oree County."

"We're on that already"

The professional smiled brightly. "Well, that's all I need. Just do whatever it takes to get me the information. If you get me what I need and if I can talk to Joseph, I'll take the job. The contract will be for one million dollars. Half in advance, half upon execution."

"A million bucks?" the fat man blurts, sweating copiously, "That's crazy."

"What did you say?" Cold and unsmiling, like a hungry hawk eyeing an overweight, elderly falcon, he fixes his gaze on the capo. The mob captain, accustomed to tough guys, experiences a surge of terror that startles him. *He looks like he wants to eat me for dinner.*

"I'll relay your terms," he stammers. *This guy is nuts.*

"If I take the job, it's my job alone. No one else is brought in unless Joseph and I agree to it. If anyone is brought in without my consent, the deal is over, and I walk with the advance, free and clear. Those are my terms. Did you get all of that?"

"Yeah, I got it."

"If you meet my terms, I'll hunt the girl and the bum, and anyone else I have to." He lights up with glee as he ponders the possibilities. Unconsciously, he licks his lips.

"Okay. Whatever," the capo replies. "My guys are digging up the information as we speak. We'll get you the skinny on the bum and the girl," the capo says, "and if Mr. Jones accepts your terms, we may have a deal." Mr. Jones was a euphemism for Don Provencenti. "Just make sure that you take care of them."

"You've got to be kidding!" He throws his lit cigarette onto the capo's lush carpet and slowly grinds it in.

One of these days, the killer muses, *I just might whack this fat little capo for free.*

"I'm not kidding," the capo replies edgily. "If you get the contract, just make sure they don't get away." *Just give me a reason to pull your plug, punk.*

"Whatever," the killer says, yawning. "I'll be here tonight to see what you've dug up." He turns to leave.

"Hey, not so fast," the captain wheezes, coming out from behind his desk, "we've got somethin' already on that bum." *Try this on for size, you blood-drinkin' freak.* He hands him two pages, single-spaced.

"This is what we've got so far. We've found out where he stays, what he does; we even dug up the name of his one and only friend. The bum's nickname is Streetcar. He's a popular guy around Ybor City, even with the cops. He's kind of a local landmark." He rubs his chin, considering Streetcar's role in the community. "He's sort of a human wreck, you could say. The respectable citizens leave him propped up on Main Street as a warning to the rest of us not to speed in the fast lane of life." *Hey, that was pretty good.*

The killer stares him, not at all interested in his clever analogy. *Homer lives,* he reflects dryly. Turning his gaze away from the capo, he studiously ignores him, reviewing the document in his hand.

"Just one more thing," the capo adds. "The bum's real name is Salvatore Benuto. He's Sicilian."

"What's that to me?"

"I don't think he's gonna be easy."

"Right," the hit man mutters, flipping through the pages. "My, my," he murmurs, his pale blue eyes flashing. "This is a wealth of information." He lingers over the documents with intense interest, intrigued by the unexpected personal details about the street bum who cut through two experienced thugs like a white-hot knife through soggy butter.

"Fabulous," he hisses softly with a smile, tucking the papers in his pocket and turning toward the door. "So, he has a friend," he murmurs contentedly to no one in particular. Walking out through the door, he feels the excited surge of adrenalin that accompanies all new jobs. He begins to whistle softly, almost silently, as he strolls down the dim corridor. This is the moment he loves. He stands on the cusp of new adventure, new sheep to slaughter, new goats to kill. This is what he lives for.

I love my work.

The Land of Wooden Cows

The sky had been crowding close all morning, or so it seemed to Major Rawlings. As the morning progressed, the last heat wave of the year had broken. Subtly at first, the warmth leached away and the heavens congealed, thickening like cooling pudding as heavy clouds shouldered one another for room, drawing close to the earth until the sky was sealed tight with dense gray mountains. The dark clouds seemed like living beings hunched over in rapt expectation, poised to unleash their pent-up power at the drip of a precipitous drop.

The Major took her eyes off the road and glanced over at the Sheriff's expressionless face. He stared vacantly at the passing live oak forests and rich green pastures, chewing his gum mechanically. *Why did I volunteer to come out here?* she wondered, *Am I a glutton for punishment?*

She slowed the patrol car and turned right onto Highway 532. The road's weedy shoulder was cluttered with signs posted by local churches and civic organizations. Towering over them all, a faded blue billboard proudly proclaimed, "You Are Entering Quilting Bee, the City of a Thousand Trees." *City of a thousand trees. That, I can believe,* she mused.

A short distance ahead, on the right side of the road, she glimpsed a trailer tucked back in the midst of a thick grove of live oaks. The streaked and rusted doublewide dream home was obscured from view by thick trees and the most bizarrely decorated, ornately festooned yard that Major Delia Rawlings had ever seen.

She could scarcely believe it.

The entire fenced landscape around the trailer was a vast country craft explosion. It was an aesthetic train-wreck of painted corncobs, quaint figurines, and macabre, grinning wooden images of animals, farmers, and freckled-faced children. The woods were packed with half-hidden figurines: a veritable kissing coven of creative country knick-knacks that were tacky beyond mind and measure. It was hillbilly kitsch with the pedal to the plywood: bright, perky, and shamelessly over the top.

And to make things worse, there was a theme. Running through the visual morass was a recurring pattern of amoebic black blobs against a faded white background.

The theme was pure Holstein. It was black and white and udderly fabulous, a twisted, bovine nightmare.

It was not enough that the brickwork around the mailbox incorporated the black and white Holstein pattern, or that the name on the mailbox, "Tremblay," was spelled out in cows' tails.

There was more. Much more.

Tiny plastic cows lined the driveway, playing handmaiden to the oversized fiberboard heifers and broadly winking bulls that adorned the sagging horse-wire fence. Why, looky, looky, there was even an algae-encrusted concrete Holstein in a makeshift fountain at the edge of the trees. The statue stood in a pool of water, dribbling a thin stream of thick green liquid out of its mouth. In an ideal world, the Major reasoned, this entire display would be a Federal offense.

"This must be the place," she said with a sigh, signaling for the turn into the driveway. "And the boys at the station were right. You definitely can't miss it."

"Mm hmmm," replied the Sheriff, still staring off into nowhere. Then his gaze fell on the country decorations, and his eyes widened. In spite of his best efforts, he smiled.

Their car wheeled off the paved road, idling past two liver-spotted milk cans. The driveway weaved treacherously past overgrown gardens filled with two-dimensional figures of horsies and duckies and farm wives streaming faded yellow ribbons. The place was a pesthole of annoyingly cheerful country gargoyles, frogs and turtles and geese and worse, standing around waiting for a canister of teargas and an order to disperse.

The vehicle continued its solemn ascension up the long, bumpy driveway, tracing a serpentine path that headed inexorably toward the rusty beige mobile home squatting coyly in the thickening gloom.

They were trapped in limbo, lost in the Land of Wooden Cows.

Faded, fantastic characters saluted them as they passed. Ancient and mildewed, they were the affable ghouls of bygone days, weeping algae and paint chips as they sagged hopelessly in the gloom, unable to wipe the foolish hayseed grins off their filthy fiberboard faces. Here was a veritable menagerie of rustic stereotypes: cartoon hicks in overalls, countrified women in sunbonnets, the Three Pigs being chased by a leering wolf.

In the tall trees, pale white milk bottles were serving time as quaint country wind chimes. These were the haunted whispers of dairies past, rustling nervously in the damp breeze. They swung like the ghosts of spotted owls hung by the neck until dead, tolling ominously in the fitful wind beneath the darkening skies.

"Don't say it, Rawlings," the Sheriff interjected sharply, anticipating his partner's thoughts. "Don't say a thing." He had worked with Delia Rawlings for more than ten years, since he had hired her out of Tampa as the force's first female Lieutenant. After all of these years, he was sure that he knew what she was thinking.

One well-placed, sarcastic line from the Major, and he would not be able to hold back his laughter. And this was definitely, most definitely, no time to laugh.

"Sheriff, you surprise me. What makes you think I would say anything about this?" She waved her hand dismissively.

"Hmmph," the sheriff replied testily. "I must be mad to have imagined such a thing. Well, as ugly as these lawn gremlins are, our visit is about to get a lot uglier."

"Tell me about it," she replied, "as if I needed a reminder." The Major understood the seriousness of what lay ahead. She had done this before.

They parked the cruiser and climbed out slowly, walking heavily up the mossy brick pathway that led to the front door. The wind was picking up as great drops of rain began to fall: first one, then another. The branches above their heads swirled as if unsure of which direction to turn while the milk bottle wind chimes tolled the remorseless clank and rattle of disaster.

The voices of the ancient milk bottles were liberated by the wind. Like mournful ghosts, they rattled brittle chains to raise the alarm of impending rain.

When the Sheriff pushed the doorbell, their arrival was announced by a long, drawn-out moo. They would have laughed if they could have afforded it. But there was nothing funny about the occasion.

The old woman who opened the door stared at them in disbelief. The tall sheriff who stood before her with his hat in his hand was the most famous person in Oree County. Beside him was the cosmopolitan Major of the Oree Sheriff's Department. Major Rawlings was a tall, dark black woman in her early forties with brown eyes that radiated sympathy toward the elderly matron who answered the door. Behind the two officers, dry leaves and small scraps of paper were beginning to swirl across the lawn, tossed by the cool wind that raced just ahead of the rain.

The woman who opened the door was grossly overweight, a fact that she desperately tried to hide beneath a tent-like purple housedress and blowsy white apron. The inside of her house smelled faintly of sour milk.

Her apron was spotted. Or rather, it was hideously poxed with the remnants of good art gone bad. Blithe geometric images of flying Holsteins and remorselessly cheerful sheep soared across the whimsical, faded fabric.

The old woman was the very picture of poor health: heavily wrinkled with a painfully hunched back, white-haired and pale. She tottered on scrawny legs that seemed ridiculously inadequate to bear her weighty eminence. Like a nebulous cloud, the gauzy skin lightly overlaid her delicate, puffy face.

The old woman's eyes opened wide as she looked at the officers. It was as if she suspected the reason for their visit. Before the Sheriff could announce himself, she cut him short with a gesture.

"It's Johnny," she said simply. "Is he dead?"

It had to be Johnny. She had no one else.

"Ma'am, can we step inside and sit down?" Sheriff Durrance replied calmly.

Her knees did not sag; they simply dissolved beneath her. She collapsed completely.

If the two officers had not been prepared, Mrs. Tremblay would have taken a vicious fall. They leaped forward in tandem and seized her before her knees hit the ground. At first, they tried to set her back on her feet. But when they saw it was hopeless, they gently carried her inside the house and put her down on the overstuffed couch.

Mrs. Tremblay could neither cry nor speak. Robbed of the ability to control herself, she sat in the corner of the couch with her head back against a cushion, her mouth opening and shutting, her eyes closed. It was as if she were in the grasp of a shock so profound, so horrifying and strong, that it was all she could do to continue breathing.

After a few silent minutes, she seemed to catch her breath. Then she leaned forward and put her head between her knotty, purple-veined hands. As the rain began to drum on the old tin roof in a thundering cascade, the frail old woman began to weep.

Home

At 5:00 in the afternoon, Ellen walked into her house with a feeling of relief. She was glad that she had caught up on all of her work and was basking in the satisfied weariness that comes at the end of an arduous task well done. Today's tasks had taken longer than expected, but at least they had been completed before dark. The thought of her upcoming vacation sent a thrill deep within her.

Ellen freed her pinned hair, tossed her bag onto a stool, and walked into the kitchen, shaking her head as she went. As the glossy black locks cascaded below her shoulders, she ran a hand absently through her hair and filled a porcelain teakettle, humming softly, deep in thought.

The water began to heat as Ellen played the message on her answering machine. What she heard shocked her.

The message, left by Jamie from the pay phone in the heart of Ybor City, was an aural snapshot of unabated terror. Ellen forgot what she was doing and focused fully on what she was hearing.

"Ellen," Jamie's voice pleaded through the small speaker, "please, please, pick up. I'm in trouble. Please pick up. Okay, okay, you're not there. Okay. Well, when you get this message, don't go anywhere. Stay home. I'll be in touch." Then, the recording ended.

Ellen was stunned. The frightened, panicked woman who had left the message was nothing like the Jamie she knew. Janelle James was the most independent, self reliant, imperturbable person she had ever had the pleasure of knowing. Something breathtakingly terrible must have occurred to bring her to such a state.

Ellen was attempting to hastily rewind the tape when three sharp knocks sounded on her front door. She froze, almost unable to move as a sudden tenseness gripped her by the throat. *What is going on here?* she wondered. She dug into her briefcase to get her cellular phone. *Well, I still have 911.* With phone in hand, Ellen hurried to the front door. Cautiously, she peered through the peephole, intent and apprehensive.

It was Jamie.

She opened the door in a rush of relief.

"Jamie, you scared me!" They hugged fiercely for a moment, and then Jamie spoke.

"I have a friend with me. Can we come in?"

"Of course, of course. Come in, both of you." At that moment, Streetcar appeared behind Jamie, looming awkwardly, with a nervous glance that shifted from her, to Jamie, and then to the ground.

The two people who stepped into her comfortable living room could not have been a more incongruous pair. Jamie, upset and weary beyond words, was dressed in a lavender two-piece summer suit over which her vivid auburn hair cascaded like a north Georgia river running through in a patch of morning light. Thin and resilient but obviously worse for wear, she looked like an elegant young cat that had been tossed high into the air and had landed, just barely, on her feet.

Jamie's companion seemed vaguely familiar to Ellen. He was a tall, rangy, tough-looking character in faded blue jeans and a baggy white button-up shirt. Clean-shaven, lean and fit, the man had a deeply tanned, sun-wrinkled face, hooked nose, and a long, salt-and-pepper ponytail. When he stepped inside the door she caught the faintest whiff of sun on clean cotton.

He was obviously not accustomed to feminine companionship. In spite of his rugged good looks, he had the unkempt, untended look of a single heterosexual male with no girlfriend, no wife, and no prospects in sight.

"We have to talk, right away; it's very important," Jamie blurted. This was not like her. Usually, she was a patient, careful speaker. Jamie was never in a hurry.

"All right, come into the kitchen. I'm making tea." As Jamie walked with Ellen toward the small, spotless kitchen, her heart swelled within her and she spontaneously hugged her friend's shoulder. Ellen smiled and glanced at Jamie questioningly. *What's wrong with her?* she wondered. *What on earth has happened?*

She set places for her two visitors on the plain white tablecloth and gave them each a china teacup and a tea bag. Then she poured boiling water into their cups and sat down. In spite of her attempt at normalcy, Ellen's violet eyes reflected her concern, showing in their troubled depths the uneasiness that she was struggling to conceal.

"Okay, Jamie, tell me," she said politely. "Who is your friend, and what on earth has happened to you?"

Impaled on the Gig

The skin yielded flaccidly beneath the heavy stick, answering the drummer's blow with a subtle boom that blossomed from somewhere deep inside the hollow cylinder. The sound began innocuously and enlarged rapidly with a surprisingly swift expansion of tone.

This particular drum featured a big sound in a small package. All of the real power was packed into the echo.

Lonzo had tuned it well. When struck sharply, the drum crept into full voice like a slick steam locomotive lumbering out of a tunnel and onto a sound stage. First the cow catcher came out, then the dazzling chrome front, then the whole whopping tone rolled into view, blowing bleary blue smoke from it's chromium smokestack, revealing more and more of itself until it had endured well past the point of redundancy.

"What a sound," the drummer's companion marveled. "First the sneaky little pop, then that big, booming echo. It's like Baby Huey climbing out of the mouth of a rubber ducky."

"Yeah, right. Gimme a joint, Ace," Lonzo replied. "Let's burn another one."

"You're loaded enough. Come on, we gotta play. It's time for the first set."

"Whoa, now. Wait a minute! I need time to set up this new tom-tom. I gotta use it tonight, man." Ace sighed and rolled his eyes.

"Lonnie, you played all your life without a fourth floor tom." The drummer smirked sourly as Ace's lecture began. Ignoring Ace, Lonzo flicked a Bic on the roach he had just fished out of his shirt pocket and began sucking loudly, hoping to drown out the static.

"Nobody in their right mind uses four floor toms," Ace continued, increasing his volume to be heard over the drummer's loud puffs. "Keith Moon didn't. Even Tommy Lee didn't go that far. Read your history, son! Now, come on, it's time to play." He kicked Lonzo's chair. "Come on!" Ace unhooked his guitar, and as he headed out of the dressing room, Lonzo reluctantly followed.

The drummer's electric orange hair, conked and wildly askew, suited his personality. It was more than a statement: it was an apparition. It was as if Lonzo's mind had leaked out through the pores of his scalp, blazing a bold fluorescent trail that loitered around his head like an electrically charged cloud.

Lonzo made faces and twirled his drumsticks as he followed Ace through the poorly lit hallway toward the entrance to the stage. "Yes, daddy dearest," he murmured, "it's time to play. Of course, daddy dearest." Popping the smoldering roach into his mouth, he swallowed it without a second thought.

They stepped out onto the stage and were immediately immersed in a smoky cocoon of noise and light and twisted, drug-addled action. Some genius had turned on the spotlights too soon, and as a result, their entrance was public domain.

The club was packed. It was a massive fish bowl filled with drifting smoke and brassy laughter and the roar of lively chatter. The dance floor was filled with couples holding onto one another, gazing at the stage in rapt expectation.

"Hot Rod Lincoln," Ace called to his band members as Lonnie slipped on his mirrored shades and crawled behind the drums.

"I don't have a fourth floor tom," Lonnie called back testily, "I don't know if I can handle it." Ace turned around to face Lonzo, but the drummer wisely preempted THE STARE by clicking his sticks together. The tune, a knocked-out jump version of Hot Rod Lincoln, was launched with a bang.

The song blasted off in the smoky air like a fiery rocket bound for rock and roll Valhalla. It was a solid wall of sound punched out by an experienced crew. The players hit their groove from the opening beat and shot straight ahead on a heady wave of exuberant sound. They were burning it up, driving right down the middle of a tightly machined, well-oiled pocket of precise, syncopated music.

'Ace and the Full House' was not just another pretty band.

It was a great band.

It was the best electric blues/R & B/jump-cum-swing band in the state. Ace knew this, and he loved it.

As he began to sing, Ace was immediately immersed in the words of the classic Merle Travis tune. He growled the lyrics into the mike with his patented rapid-fire delivery, banging the punch notes with exuberance, playing Merle's signature guitar lick with enviable dexterity.

The band raced along behind him straining at the leash, giving new life to the funky old dog of a tune. Their rendition was jazzed and revved like a supercharged Chevy 409 that had been dropped down into the body of a '53 pickup truck. The band was a howling jump jet of powerful music: a roaring rocket of unstoppable groove.

Ace smiled and closed his eyes, riding the wave of the back-beat-driven, big-band-influenced, rocked up, blown out, hillbilly-flavored crunchadelic metal sandwich. It was rock flambeau served to a hungry audience with enthusiasm and élan, piping hot on the platter.

This is the way we do it, baby, Ace thought, watching as Lonnie began a freeform drum solo. During the drum solo, Ace's eyes wandered around the room. He clapped his hands with the beat, one ear trained for the two-measure drum signal that would cue the band to come back in.

Then, he saw his brother.

Out there, in the packed Sunday night audience, Ace saw Joe Boy.

Joe Boy looked as mean as ever. He stood at the edge of the crowd, short and wiry, dark-eyed and slick and ominous, shifting his weight impatiently as he waited for the club owner to clear a table for him.

This was not a welcome sight.

Great.   Little brother comes calling, Ace mused, sobering at the thought. *But what does he want from me?*

Ace had no idea why his half-brother would come to this place. Joey was not a fan of rock and roll or of any other kind of music. But from the expression on his brother's face, Ace knew that his business was serious.   He turned away quickly, before he could accidentally catch Joey's eye, and began playing right on cue. *This is gonna be a long set,* he thought bitterly.

Ace had to admit it.

His little brother gave him the willies.

Southbound

After two hours on the road they crossed the Oree County line, headed south in Ellen's Mustang Cobra GT convertible at a teeth-clenching rate of speed. Ellen's apprehensions were rekindled as they entered Oree County.

"So, tell me again where we're going," she asked Jamie. "Remind about me about why this is such a good idea." She tossed her head nervously, casting a narrowed eye at her rearview mirror. Her mirror was not trained on the road, but on the sleeping street person in her back seat.

Streetcar had not endeared himself to Ellen Bromley, despite the fact that he had saved her friend's life. She could not bring herself to believe that this man was, somehow, the hero that Jamie said he was. *Who is this guy, really,* she wondered, *and where did he go when we were getting ready to leave? What was he doing alone, out on the streets, while he made us wait in my apartment for 30 minutes?* Ellen did not trust Streetcar, and earnestly wished that Jamie had left him behind.

"We're going to the Sheriff's Department," Jamie replied, "I believe what Streetcar said about the man who killed Johnny. He's a gangster in the Tampa Mafia. I can't stay in Hillsborough County. Some corrupt official might give him my name and address. Besides you, who can I trust in Tampa? Is there anyone at all? Maybe, but I'm not sure.

"In Oree County, I think the odds are better. The Sheriff is an honest man. Even his political enemies admit that much."

"Okay, okay," Ellen replied. "I know there are some crooked cops in Hillsborough County, and there are bound to be some crooked judges, too. But there are crooks everywhere. Why didn't we go to the FDLE, or the DEA? Or if you don't trust the Tampa FBI, why not go to the Atlanta office? Why come down here, to Oree County, in the middle of nowhere?"

"I'm scared, Ellen," she replied, the tension in her voice rising. "When I panicked, I ran to Tampa for your help. You were the only person I trusted. You know that I'm afraid of the Tampa police, and you know <u>why</u> I'm afraid. Well, I don't trust the FBI, either. You remember what happened years ago."

"Yes, I remember." Ellen had been Jamie's best friend at parochial school in Tampa. Ellen and her mother had tried for years to get the police to arrest Jamie's father, who was beating and abusing her with escalating intensity and frequency. Her father had been a Tampa policeman, and no one had believed that he could be abusing her. He was a popular local cop, a smooth liar who covered his tracks effortlessly. For years, he convinced the police, the social workers, and the physicians that Jamie was wounding herself to get attention.

Jamie had been nearly killed before the local police had intervened and taken her out of the home. Even then, after she had been hospitalized with numerous broken bones, Florida's Department of Health and Rehabilitative Services had tried to reunite her with her father. From the very first day, they were developing a plan to send her back into the torture chamber.

After Jamie suffered a climactic traumatic event on her 16th birthday, Ellen's mother had convinced a caring judge that she should gain full custody of Jamie. Thanks to Ellen's mother, Jamie had spent her last two years of high school with Ellen's happy family.

But the battle had left scars. From the time Jamie turned 12 until she was 16 years old, Ellen's widowed mother had fought to mobilize intervention by the authorities. Local officials had ignored her, and Federal agents had been able to offer her little but regret since child abuse was not a Federal crime.

"I don't want to go to the FBI in Atlanta," Jamie continued. "What if Johnny's murder isn't a Federal offense? What would we do then, drive back to Florida?"

"I don't know," Ellen said, sighing deeply. "You're probably right." She gave another quick glance in the mirror, monitoring the slumbering Streetcar. "Let's just hope this local sheriff is an honest man. There <u>are</u> honest cops, you know."

"So have I heard," Jamie replied, "and I do, in part, believe it."

"Very funny. That's from Hamlet, right? At least Sister Audrey's English class wasn't an entire waste."

"Right," Jamie replied, smiling sleepily. "Keep telling yourself that."

"So you're sure that you're doing the right thing here?"

"Ellen, we've got to take a chance. There's a risk in action, but inaction is more dangerous. Sheriff Durrance is the best chance we've got. He's old-fashioned, and I've heard that he's a Free Will Baptist preacher, whatever that means. But at least he's not a hypocrite. I met him a year ago at our bank's Christmas party. He was a gentleman. In fact, he's probably one of the few straight men I've ever met at a party who didn't come on to me."

"What, is he crazy?" Ellen asked with a sly look Jamie's way, "You take this to be a virtue?"

"You know what I mean, Ellen. How many sober <u>and</u> good-looking <u>and</u> respectful <u>and</u> sincere men have you ever met at an office Christmas party?"

"Is this a quiz? I think you know the answer already," Ellen replied. She cleared her throat. "So, he's good-looking, huh?" Jamie rolled her eyes.

"Like a movie star," she said, smiling.

"I'm beginning to see why you wanted to come back to this county." Jamie ignored her comment.

"I'm not going anywhere else, if I can help it. This is where it happened. And this is my home."

"This is home?" she sighed. "Well, if this remote outpost is what you've come to call home, I pity you, girlfriend." Ellen arched a brow as her gaze returned to the road. "What's to call home? You're out in the middle of nowhere?"

She downshifted, swinging into the left lane to pass a rusty sedan, sans taillight. It was a barnacled wreck, an encrusted Oldsmobile with the rectangular lines of a Boston Whaler driven by a desiccated retiree who squinted darkly at their car as they whipped past him. He moved his mouth, murmuring to no one in particular about nothing of significance.

Ellen sped down the highway, focusing on the two-lane blacktop unrolling before her. The road, deserted and dark, had been sliced through the middle of some of the last remaining Florida wilderness.

At the edge of the wide span illuminated by her headlights, wraithlike beards of Spanish moss fluttered in the breeze. In every direction, to the right and the left, the monolithic hammocks and forests created an unfamiliar wall of darkness that pressed close to the road. Periodically, the forests and hammocks would give way to broad, open pastures that reached to a distant, tree-lined horizon. It was ominously dark, sparsely inhabited land. Occasionally, distant flickers of light could be seen from the windows of quiet farmhouses that were set in clumps of trees, far back from the road.

Floundering in the throes of culture shock, Ellen hardly noticed when they passed a poorly lit, seedy convenience store. To Jamie, however, the broken-down store was a landmark that was as familiar as the back of her hand.

"We're almost there," she said excitedly. In the distance ahead of them, to the left of the highway, a glow on the horizon presaged the appearance Oree County's premier metropolis. This glow was from the county seat: Pezner, Florida, population 6,521 ("and counting"). Pezner, the exquisitely cultured Pearl of the Peninsula, was home to Oree County's only supermarket, newspaper, courthouse, and bank.

They rounded a bend and came upon it all at once. Awash in an island of light, they felt like storm-tossed travelers cast into a decaying wonderland of vacant parking lots, empty streets, and rusted steel buildings.

"Turn to the right," Jamie said, pointing ahead.

They turned right past the deserted, brightly lit parking lot of the Hoggly Woggly supermarket and parked in front of a clean new building of brown brick and clean glass. Above the parking spot, a sign read, "Oree County Sheriff's Department." Jamie turned around and reached into the back seat.

"Hey, Streetcar," she said, shaking the big man's shoulder, "wake up. We're here." He grunted, then breathed deeply and opened his eyes.

"Okay, okay, I'll move along. Don't worry," he rumbled, slowly sitting up, looking around as he wiped his face with his left hand. His eyes took in the street, the town, and the sign in front of the building. "Sheriff's department, huh? Good." He ran his hand across his beard and looked at Jamie beseechingly. "Do you think they'd mind if I use their bathroom?"

A Family Affair

Ace had just sat down beside Joe Boy when Lonzo, the flame-haired drummer, approached their table.   He sauntered slowly up, looking about the big room with a bleary, blasé gaze.

"You're lookin' great, Joey Pro," Lonzo said, turning a chair around and sitting down.   "Who are your friends?" he asked, nodding at the two gangsters.

"Beat it, Drumbo," Joey said curtly.   *This ain't high school, and I ain't a freshman punk anymore, bozo.*   Sensing that he was unwanted, Lonzo stood and wandered away.

Ace sipped his drink, waiting patiently.   *Come on, Joey,* he thought uneasily, *why are you here?*

"Ace Feld-mann," Joey said, drawing out the name sarcastically.   To emphasize his disdain, he pronounced the last syllable - quite incorrectly - like the word 'can.'

"Joey," Ace answered reluctantly.

"Long time no see," Joey continued, twisting his mouth into a grin.   "What's goin' on?"

"Nothin'," Ace replied laconically.   *I wish.*

"I bet you're wondering why I'm here," Joey said slyly, toying with his glass.   He frowned.   "This drink's pretty good. Hey, Jimmy!"   At the sound of his name, the thick-necked hood to the left of him stopped gazing around the room and snapped to attention

"Yeah?"

"Go, get yourself a drink."

"Sure, boss," he replied, rising and walking away.

"Mike, you help him out, okay?"

"Okay."

"And take your time," he added.   The two big men walked off together, looking around the room hopefully.   They were unusually tall for mobsters, a group most often defined not by height, nor brawn, nor brains, but by nerve: nerve and greed and the willingness to use violence as a tool of policy. And above all, true mobsters were defined by their adherence to omerta, the unwritten code of silence.

Omerta was exemplified by the story of the hoodlum on his deathbed after the Saint Valentine's Day massacre. When the police asked him to identify who had shot him, the dying gangster replied, "Nobody shot me."

All true mobsters were bound tightly by the code of omerta. True made men, those who lived and died without repentance, adhering to the code of La Cosa Nostra, carried their bloody secrets with them into grave and beyond: into the pits of hell.

Ace watched as his brother's companions left the table. He smiled thinly at Joe Boy, waiting for the message he had come to deliver.

"Those guys are dyin' to scope out the chicks," Joey told his brother. "You know how it is."

"It's the oldest story under the sun," Ace replied from behind his dark green shades.

Ace was slumped back into his seat, sprawled out like some kind of hippy beanbag that had been loosely tossed across the table and chair. His gaudy threads could have graced the cover of a rock-and-roll magazine. But for sheer, unforced elegance: for pretense, panache, and sartorial élan, he was no match for his younger brother. Joe Boy Provencenti was a poster punk who looked as if he had just stepped off the cover of Gentleman's Quarterly (Wise Guy Edition).

Lizard Act

Joey lounged in his chair like a lizard on a rock, flat and cool and edgy and more than a little bit scary. He slumped low like smoke settling toward the floor, dark and ominous with his gray silk suit, cherubic tanned face, heavy brow and lips. Joe Boy studied Ace with an expressionless gaze, gently emitting a toxic slipstream of cigarette smoke that oozed from his mouth and slid upward into the swirling beams of the nightclub's spotlights.

Watching his brother as he sat in evil splendor, sated and supine, Ace almost expected to see the exploratory flicker of pink, forked tongue between his lips. Any minute, it seemed, the serpentine organ was sure to dart out. The thought was repulsive, but fascinating.

"So, Ace, what you been doin'?" Joe Boy asked, gazing at him through slit eyelids.

"Same old same old," Ace answered, looking around the room. "What's up wit' you? What brings you to the Babylon of the western world."

"Hey, don't flatter yourself. This club ain't big enough to pass for Babylon."

For once, you're right, Ace reflected. "So, what's up, Bro?" he added hopefully. Before Joe Boy responded, he sat up and leaned toward Ace, drawing his chair closer to the table and glancing around casually.

"Mr. Jones wants to talk to you," he said conspiratorially, and then leaned back in his chair. Ace was taken aback. Mr. Jones was a euphemism for the local boss of bosses, who happened to be their father.

"Are you sure?" Ace asked, choosing his words carefully, "We haven't been in touch for a while."

"He wants to see you, Ace. That's the truth. He sent me hear to tell you." Joe Boy was starting to get hacked. There were only three people that Joey had ever respected:

his half-brother Ace, their father, and his childhood chum, Mickey O'Malley. The Don and the Mick still deserved Joey's respect, but Ace had fallen from his pedestal more than a decade ago.

To Joey, Ace had once been the ultimate cool big brother. Ace had killed his first man before he was 16 and had led a gang of grown men before he was 20. He had been a genuine mob wunderkind. On the fast track out of the box, Ace had become a made man at the unheard of age of 23. As a young punk, Joe Boy had practically worshipped his hard-nosed gangster brother.

Then, in a calamity that Joe Boy could never forgive, Ace had backed out. He had quit the mob.

The fact that their father had respected Ace's decision to quit the Family only made it worse for Joe Boy. And to add insult to insolence, after Joey's big brother had quit the family business he had slid downhill, descending to his current sorry estate.

Ace was the leader of Tampa's best rhythm and blues band, but to Joe Boy he was a loser: just another example of degenerate, pot-smoking hippy scum. In Joey's eyes, his big brother had fallen so far, from such glory and prominence, that he would be better off dead.

"Well, I told you what I was supposed to," Joe Boy said, biting off his words. "I'm outta here." He leaned forward and stubbed out his smoke, blowing a plume in Ace's direction as he signaled to his men. Without further adieu, he rose and walked away, flanked by the two flinty-eyed hoodlums.

As the gangsters disappeared into the crowd, a deeply troubled Ace Feldmann sat staring into space, seeing nothing. He barely noticed when Lonnie came up with Brett, their keyboard player, and sat down. The two men were accompanied by a strong, smoky scent, the invisible aura of recently burned Colombian pot.

"So, where's Marlon Brando?" Lonzo asked. "Did he give you an offer you couldn't refuse?" Ace sighed and took a hit from his drink. "You know," Lonzo continued, "when Joey told me to buzz off, I could almost hear the theme song from The Godfather. You know, the balalaikas, or whatever they were. What a great soundtrack!"

"Yeah, sure, whatever," Ace replied. Lonzo, detecting Ace's disinterest, was not one to give up easily.

"You and Joey are like the Donny and Marie of Hillsborough County," he continued mercilessly, beginning to sing, "I'm a little bit rocky; he's a little bit gun and knife."

"What?" Ace asked, looking up.

"Too bad you can't choose your brothers, eh?" Lonnie was on a roll, and he was not about to stop. "Tell me the truth, Ace, and don't lie to me; I'm your best friend."

"Yeah, right. What's the question?"

"Is Joey an alien? He can't be your brother."

"Lonnie, shut up!" Ace mumbled disgustedly, raising his right hand in defeat. He began to rub his eyes, trying to fend off a pending migraine.

Brett, a new member of their band, chose this moment to speak up. It was very bad decision.

"Hey, Ace, is your brother in the mob or something?" Ace looked at his new keyboard player in disbelief. Brett, surprised at his reaction, became defensive. "Well, I mean, he acts like a hood from the movies, that's all. You know what I mean, right?" he offered nervously, disconcerted by Ace's intense stare.

"Brett," Ace asked, "where were you raised, boy?"

"In Wisconsin. I grew up in Madison, actually." Hearing this, Ace shook his head and sighed.

"That's cheese country, right? Good, honest people in Wisconsin. They're the descendants of hard-working Norwegians and Swedes. Well, hello, Brett! This is the Cigar City! This is the only place I know of that's nicknamed after a carcinoma. This city is a hand-wrapped lesion on the heart of Florida, and it's definitely not benign. It's as malignant as they get.

"So remember what I'm saying," Ace said bitterly. "Be smart, and repeat after me. There is no mob in Tampa. Got it?" Taken aback, Brett weighed his words.

"There is no mob in Tampa," he breathed. "Got it."

"Good boy. Now, lets go play another set." Ace slipped on his shades and seemed to regain his usual careless bravado. He took a deep breath and asked a familiar question. "Who's the best?"

"We is, baby!" they chimed in unison. But even as they said it, they knew that something was amiss. Trouble had crept into their world, and the drink and the drugs could not mask it any longer.

"Let's go do the dirty deed." Shaking off the cobwebs of incipient depression, they rose together and strode boldly toward the stage. They were united in their desire to play, as if by a manic outburst of electro-musical energy they could blow their blues, like their brains, into permanent oblivion.

Confluence of the Anomalies

Was there something she had missed? Ellen stared down at the tiny, shriveled woman behind the desk, trying to find something, anything, that might pass for common ground. Her unintended adversary stared back without blinking, unmoved by her distress.

Vermillion Bates, the woman behind the desk, resembled a Boston bulldog, Ellen decided after careful deliberation. She was a parody of a front desk clerk, an armed and dangerous Attack Dame: a vicious pug placed like a canine crown jewel on display inside the chrome and glass cage that separated the offices from the reception area.

The lobby of the Oree County Sheriff's Department was a surrealistic setting of glaring white roof and floor, rough cypress paneling, oak desk, plaques, and pictures of awkward white males in cowboy hats. The framed photographs displayed a pictorial record of Oree sheriffs of bygone days, imprisoned in the formal agony of their Sunday clothing. Uncomfortably captured in black and white glossies, they were wrapped too tightly for comfort in their starched suits, even after all these years. To the side of this display, a painting of the current Sheriff was displayed above a photograph of the department's second-ranking officer, Major Delia Rawlings.

"No, you see," Ellen tried to explain to the woman, reading her nametag as she spoke. "Mrs. Bates, we need your help. We need to talk to the supervising officer. Please," she added hopefully, "it's important."

The ubiquitous Mrs. Bates, a venomous, mosquito-sized juggernaut clad in sheriff's green, shook her head testily, her face changing from cheap-rouge pink to an ugly red tinged with purple. It looked as if the anger in her bosom were beginning to bruise her face.

The old woman's eyes narrowed as her gaze ricocheted from Ellen to Jamie and back again. *Where did that unkempt fellow disappear to?* she wondered, searching for any sign of Streetcar in the lobby behind them.

"I told you," Mrs. Bates recited slowly, with considerable annoyance, "the Major is in charge tonight, and she's taking a nap after a double shift. Sergeant Billings is running late, but he should be here within an hour or two. Until then, Sergeant Sykes is the supervisor, but he's out at the Highway 27 Truck Stop, where they just had a terrible wreck. Now, I'm the only deputy on duty besides the dispatcher, and I've got to cover this front desk. Do you get that? So there's no one here for you to talk to. I won't wake up the Major unless we have a crime in progress."

Don't tempt me, Ellen reflected testily.

Mrs. Bates leaned forward suspiciously glancing around the room. *Where is that rough-looking man, the one who was with them? Did he step out the front door?*

"Please, ma'am," Ellen continued. "Call the Sheriff. This is extremely important. You have no idea." As Jamie listened to the give and take, she felt the strength draining from her body. She had been awake for over 40 hours, and was nearing the point of hallucination or collapse. Seeing a chair, she shakily sat down. As she did, the receptionist/bulldog leaned out over the desk, attempting to look into the corners of the reception area room.

"Where's that man who was with you?" she asked abruptly. "Did you see where he went?" At that moment, they heard laughter coming from the hallway behind her, followed by a woman's voice.

"Streetcar, you scalawag, you haven't changed a bit!"

The door behind the receptionist banged open as the usually sober and officious Major Delia Rawlings almost stumbled into the room, wiping the tears from her eyes as she fought back another outburst of laughter. She turned back toward the hallway. "You can go back in my office, Streetcar," she told her companion. "I'll be right there." She looked up at the stunned receptionist. "Vermillion, could you please show these good people back to my office?" Still chuckling at Streetcar's joke, the Major shut the door.

Mrs. Vermillion Bates gaped like a fish out of water, fighting gamely for breath. She was not one to yield ground readily in defeat, but she had to admit that the battle was lost.

"Well, I never," she said with asperity, trying to salvage a fender of dignity from the crushed wreck of her pride. Like a Disney robot, she turned and smiled blankly at Ellen and Jamie. "Please allow me to show you to the Major's office," she said calmly, with a voice as smooth as syrup on a river rock.

Opening the door into the lobby, she escorted them through the reception room and down a short hall. With a sigh, she pointed to an open doorway.

"That's her office," she offered. "And, please," she added, grinning mechanically, "have a nice day."

True Detectives

They walked through the open door into a large office with natural cypress paneling and dark teak furniture. The Major stood as they entered, coming around her desk to shake their hands warmly.

"I'm Delia Rawlings," she said as she ushered them into their chairs and sat down again behind her desk, "and I'm an old friend of your companion, Mr. Benuto." She gestured at Streetcar, who grinned and nodded. "I was once a detective with the Tampa Police Department on the Ybor City beat. Streetcar says you have something very important to tell me."

"I'm Ellen Bromley, and this is Janelle James," Ellen said tersely, leaning forward anxiously. "We do have something important to tell you. Jamie does, rather," she added, pulling back her hair as she glanced at her best friend. Before Jamie could speak, the Major raised her hand with a gesture that commanded silence.

"Did you hear that?" Delia asked after a lengthy pause. When they shook their heads, she rose abruptly from her seat and left the room. "I'll be right back," she called over her shoulder.

Ellen shook her head in disgust, as petulant as ever, disturbed by the Major's rapid exit. "This place is a zoo," she said sharply. "And haven't I seen that old woman at the front desk somewhere before? Was it on Hee Haw, or the Beverly Hillbillies?"

"Except for the Boston accent, I'd guess The Beverly Hillbillies," Streetcar murmured in reply, waxing philosophical. "But as I recall, there were no cast members from Boston. I like the idea, though." he added. "The Nob Hillbillies. It's a bold concept."

Ellen frowned. There was something about this man that, frankly, just ticked her off.

"What about the woman's name?" Jamie asked, turning quickly to Ellen, "Did you pick up on that? Vermillion Bates? Like, is that creepy, or what? So what do they call this place, the Bates Motel?" Ellen had to smile. Jamie's humor was always infectious.

"If the Major hadn't showed up when she did, she might have gone for a butcher knife." Ellen replied.

"Eeee, eeee, eee!" they cried in unison, imitating the violin music from the shower scene in Psycho, clutching their throats and making a stabbing motion.

"I hope you girls are enjoying yourselves," a solemn, womanly voice intoned. They stopped with their hands at their throats and looked up in surprise, like children caught in the act. *Oh, to be 20 again!* the Major reflected, smiling at them. "I'm kidding," she added, "please, don't let me spoil your fun. But I've got someone I'd like to introduce you too. He tried to hide from me, but he wasn't successful."

As Delia stepped into the room, they could see that her hand was grasping something in the hall, just out of their sight, and she gave that something a tug. A tall, strikingly handsome man, wearing the star and uniform of the county sheriff, grimaced as he stepped sheepishly into her office. He smiled and nodded to the three visitors.

"Okay, you got me, Major," he said, snatching his arm back. "But I don't know if this is the most dignified way to present your Sheriff to visitors from out of town." She rolled her eyes.

"We have both been working since before dawn, yesterday," she said tartly, "so I suppose that we've moved past the point of formality and into the realm of professional exhaustion.

"This is our Sheriff," she continued. "He was supposed to go home to get some sleep, but you see how far that went."

"Yeah, well," he said sheepishly, "I tried to sleep, but it didn't work." In the absence of a solid defense, he quickly changed the subject

"Would you believe that she works for me?" he asked the visitors. "You'd think that I work for her. Please excuse our informality, but the Major's right," he looked at his watch, "it's now 3:00 AM, which means we've both been up for almost 24 hours." *Just part of the job, sometimes,* he didn't bother to add.

"I've been up since 7:00 A.M. Saturday morning," Jamie replied. "That's over 40 hours, isn't it?" The room was silent as they turned and stared at her. The Sheriff shut the door and found a seat, and the Major sat behind her desk. They noticed now that the young woman who had spoken looked frail and shaken, weak and wan and wasted inside and out. As the Sheriff sat and studied her face, he had a flash of insight.

"You're Janelle James, aren't you?" he asked. *The speeding ticket. She's the local who got a ticket Saturday night for speeding in the sports car.*

"That's me," she said, sighing deeply, "and I need to tell you something important. It's about my friend, Johnny Delaney." Hearing the name of the county's latest murder victim, the Sheriff and Major snapped to attention.

When Jamie spoke Johnny's name, a flood of memories was spontaneously triggered within her. Taken by surprise, suddenly feeling the pain that reached into the core of her being, Jamie could no longer hold back the anguish.

She began to sob, fighting to control herself but failing utterly. Ellen reached out, gently putting her hand on her friend's arm, but this only seemed to increase the intensity of her despair.

"They killed him, my God, they killed Johnny!" she cried, rocking back and forth, the tears almost leaping from her clenched eyes, "They killed him." She fought for breath through a throat that seemed to close up tight. "Oh my God, Sheriff, they killed him!" she sobbed, forlorn, broken, and desperate, "And God help me, Sheriff, I saw it! I was there! I was right there, and I couldn't stop it!"

Janelle James, fighting for her sanity, pressed her hands to her face and tried, one last time, to master her grief. She had always managed to control of herself, no matter what she went through. It had been her ticket to survival: how her psyche had stayed intact.

But now, she was losing it. Her mind swayed drunkenly, and her body began to collapse. She felt her hands weaken against the sides of her tingling face. *God, help me!* her heart cried out within her, *Jesus, pray for me!* And suddenly, like an animated puppet powering up under the influence of its master, she felt her body regain its strength. Within seconds, she had fully regained her composure. She looked up at them and blinked calmly, her face bathed in tears.

Given the lack of sleep and the tremendous stress that Jamie was under, the Sheriff and the Major were more stunned by her sudden, eerie composure than they had been by her outburst of grief. They watched closely as the delicate-looking young woman took a handkerchief from her friend and daintily dried the slick path of the tears that had coursed from her swollen eyes, leaving a shiny trail down her face. Her expression was utterly bland, as if she had not been sobbing wildly mere seconds ago.

The Sheriff and the Major looked at one another questioningly. *That girl's no stranger to trouble,* the Sheriff thought, marveling at the effectiveness of her coping mechanism, *but what could have made her so tough? What could have prepared her to handle something like this?*

"Okay, I'm ready to talk," Jamie said brightly, looking around the room. And then, with a glance at Ellen and a quick, reassuring smile, Jamie began to tell her story.

Sweating Bullets

At 6:00 AM, Ace Feldmann awoke from troubled sleep to find himself covered with sweat. He lay there for several minutes without moving, slowly coming to his senses in the half-light of dawn, gazing dully at the leaves on the moss-covered branch that almost touched his open bedroom window.

The home was built in the Florida farmhouse style, with breezy porches all around and tall window casements that aptly suited the large rooms with their high ceilings of knotty heart pine. The aged live oak that pressed its tender leaves close to his second-story window had begun its life long ago, perhaps even when Jose Gaspar was ravaging the Gulf of Mexico from his lair in the heart of old Tampa Bay. In the early morning light, its leaves and moss were a familiar sight.

For a moment, Ace enjoyed the quiet Florida morning. Then, he remembered the night before.

Oh, boy, Ace thought, reaching a hand to his aching head, *Pop wants to see me.* Ace loved his father, but was worried about the reason for the request. The Don had summoned him only twice before. The first time had been when Ace was only 15 years old, when his father had solemnly informed Ace that his mother had been killed in an automobile accident. At the second summons, when Ace was 24, his father had informed Ace that his rival, Benny Scarfa, had asked permission to kill him. Don Bentarozzo had informed Ace's father of Benny's request.

The whole Scarfa affair had been an unredeemable mess. As he considered this fact, Ace remembered the Scarfa mess almost against his will. The trouble, which had begun as a romantic adventure, had ended badly before the year was out.

Ace had fallen in love with a woman from Atlanta who was the mistress of a made guy named Benny Scarfa.

Because the woman was Scarfa's kept mistress, gangster ethics held that Benny Scarfa had cause to kill Ace. But because she was not Benny's wife, Ace had the right to defend himself using any means available.

Ultimately, it did not matter who had cause against whom. Without the nod from their dons, neither man could make a move.

The heads of the Atlanta and Tampa families thought it wise to discuss the matter, and the dons, including Ace's father, agreed not to issue a contract for the murder of Ace or Benny. In the spirit of conviviality, they decided to let nature take its course. The dons issued a strict warning to the two men, commanding them not to involve anyone else in their personal vendetta. No vengeance could be taken in greater Atlanta or Hillsborough County. This made each man's home city a safe haven. If the men played by these rules, it was agreed that no vengeance would be taken if one killed the other.

A mistress was not a wife, and Ace's infraction was negligible. The dons had issued the final word from the top. The matter would be settled between the two men, or not at all.

Ace knew that Benny would scheme to catch him outside of Tampa. When Benny's former mistress disappeared without a trace from her home south of Atlanta, Ace decided to take matters into his own hands.

It had taken all of his ingenuity to whack Benny Scarfa. He temporarily left his gang and moved to Cherry Tree, Georgia, a hick town in the hills north of Atlanta. There, he gained employment under another name, disguised as an immigrant cook working in the back of Benny's favorite restaurant. Ace had stalked his opponent from a distance, biding his time, preparing for the moment when he would finally get his chance.

Ace had whacked Benny in the restaurant's foul-smelling restroom one cold January evening, an evening that he could never forget. He had used an old Smith and Wesson

.45 magnum without a silencer, loaded with hollow point shells to make a very ugly and very noisy statement. The sound in the cramped tile bathroom had been deafening, and the sight had been sickening.

Ace had barely made it out through the window before Benny's friends broke into the room, but his plan had worked to perfection. The recently reinforced restroom door had held up long enough for Ace to escape, and the fake bolts he had added to the modified window popped out like greased sausages. His number one car, parked in the back alley, had fired right up, and his number two had done the same five minutes later. He had whacked little Benny and gotten away, free and clear.

After all the planning, all the hard work preparing the scene of the crime, the moment of truth had finally come with Benny Scarfa on his knees, begging for his life. *What a mess,* Ace thought as he stretched painfully and climbed out of bed.

Ace's successful, face-to-face hit of Benny Scarfa had confirmed him as a rising star in the mob. The old time Provencenti soldiers were like proud uncles. Ace had bearded Benny 'the Weasel' in his own den and had become famous in the process. But to Ace, the ugly reality had taken the romance out of his job forever.

Because he had played by the rules, Don Bentarozzo in Atlanta put out word to confirm that further vengeance was forbidden. Ace had established his position as the young Turk to watch in Tampa, as the best and the brightest of the new generation.

He retired just two months later, plagued by dreams in which he saw his victim begging for mercy. Benny Scarfa had lost his nerve at the end. He had fallen completely into pieces right before Ace's eyes.

After the Scarfa hit, Ace walked away from the gangster life. He left the mob at the top of his game, without a shred of regret. *Except for the Scarfa hit,* Ace thought ruefully, *I don't have a single regret.*

Who could have imagined that Benny would beg like a child instead playing the man? Ace had been prepared to face a lion but had found, instead, a whimpering old man, an elderly baby who messed his pants even before he took the bullet. In the end, Benny had been a terrified toddler among the made men of this world.

Ace's conscience had awakened that day like a hurricane hitting the Florida coast. A tempest of reproach had descended out of a clear blue sky and pummeled his unsuspecting soul.

The image of Benny groveling for forgiveness had haunted Ace for weeks, until he had finally made a decision to leave the mob. Then, like a ghostly whisper of air hissing from the dream bubble of nightmarish memory, the haunting image of Benny Scarfa had slipped softly into oblivion. Now, more than a decade later, the memory returned only at times like these when Ace was confronted with his past.

So, the Don wants to see me, Ace thought, *and he sent Joe Boy as the messenger. Great. Just great.*

The old man did nothing without a reason. And, whatever the reason might be, Ace had a sinking feeling that it would turn out badly.

Morning

She woke up after 11:00 A.M. in a fresh twin bed in a clean pastel room that smelled of potpourri. It was a Martha Stewart sort of room, pressed and starched with a blatantly feminine decor that seemed at odds with the career path of their badge-bearing hostess.

Jamie blinked at the luminous beams of light that poured through the blinds, and a flood of memories returned as if they were borne on the bright rays. And with the memories came the unspeakable pain of bereavement.

She felt a primal pain, a great gash in her soul. Johnny had been a very close friend, more precious than her own breath. Shock scarcely numbed the pain, and the wound had not yet started to heal.

Johnny is dead, she thought listlessly, *but I am alive.* The door opened, and she turned to see Major Rawlings, who had come in to shut the blinds.

"You're up already?" the officer asked, surprised.

"I suppose so," Jamie responded, remembering what had happened just a few hours ago in the Major's office. After she had regained control of herself, Jamie had shared the story of Johnny's murder. After that, at the Major's request, she and Ellen had agreed to spend the night at her home.

"Give me 15 minutes and I'll be ready to go," Jamie added, shaking off the cobwebs. *Who needs makeup or food,* she thought herself, *when Johnny's killers are on the loose, free to kill again?* Deep within her, a gritty resolve was setting in. It was a pressing need to bring Johnny's murderers to justice. It had coalesced slowly at first, as she shivered in the shock of recent events; but by now, it was becoming a flinty core of unbreakable will deep within her soul. Somehow, someway, as God gave her the strength, she would see that Johnny's killers were brought to justice.

Today they were returning to the scene of the crime.

The drive to Homeland Estates took them back through town, with the Major and Jamie in the front seat and Ellen in the back. At the outskirts of Pezner, they stopped at the only downtown breakfast joint to pick up bagels and scalding coffee. Then they continued through town.

The Major had phoned the Sheriff, and he was waiting in his car in the parking lot at the Sheriff's Department. He waved as they passed and pulled out behind them, followed by a white crime scene van and another squad car. Looking into his car as they passed, Jamie noticed that Streetcar was not with him.

Behind the last squad car, at the tail of the procession, was a red station wagon with the seal of the Oree County Coroner blazoned on the door. *Where's Streetcar?* Jamie wondered. He had agreed to spend the night at the Sheriff's house, and she had looked forward to seeing him today.

"Where's Streetcar?" Jamie asked.

"Ask Sheriff when we get there," Delia replied. "He'll know, if anybody does,"

It was a beautiful day. The sky was cloudless and clear, a royal shade of blue around the horizon but pale and bleached-out directly above, where the Florida sun brilliantly illuminated the morning sky. Cooler weather had followed them from Tampa, and the afternoon promised to be warm but not scorching, providing a needed break from the unrelenting heat of an Oree County Indian summer.

Jamie looked around at Pezner carefully as they rode down Main Street, her eyes drinking it all in. The streets looked different somehow, although she had been gone for less than two days. *Saturday seems like years ago,* she thought, *but it was just a couple of days ago. Wasn't it?* It seemed that everything had changed.

"What on earth is that?" Ellen asked, pointing to a banner that stretched across the highway on the outskirts of town. "WELCOME BASS BAITERS!" the sign proclaimed, "PEZNER SALUTES THE NATIONAL LARGEMOUTH RODEO!"

"We're having a Bass Baiters tournament," Delia answered, glancing at her in the rearview mirror. "It's a big deal. You know, the people that sponsor those freshwater fishing programs on TV. It's a bunch of good old boys in their good old boats catching fish with their good old lures to make a good old pile of money."

"Say what?"

"Bass Baiters is an organization that sponsors bass fishing tournaments all over the country. They also finance those catch-and-release TV shows for bass fanatics."

"I don't know if I've ever seen one," Ellen said carefully, "and I'm not sure I want to."

"Well, my brother is crazy about that stuff," Delia replied. "He's entering the tournament and plans on winning."

"You have my sympathy," Ellen replied archly.

"Ellen hates hunting and fishing," Jamie interrupted, smiling at the Major before glancing back at Ellen. "She turns pale at the sight of hook, rod, or gun."

"Oh," replied the Major helpfully, "don't worry about it, Ellen. The Bass Baiters don't eat the fish they catch." *Although I'd eat them in a heartbeat,* she did not bother to add. "They just catch 'em, weigh 'em, and release 'em."

"Oh, it's not that Ellen has a problem with people eating fish, Major," Jamie added dryly. "Believe me."

"Please, Jamie, call me Delia," the Major replied with a gracious smile.

"I eat meat and fish," Ellen interjected, "I just don't like to see people hunt or fish or do those kinds of things. You know, we pay people to pluck our chickens, prepare our fish, whatever. So we shouldn't have to think about those things, right?" She examined herself in the tiny mirror in her hand as she spoke, patting on a little powder. "It's just so gross!" she added, closing her compact with a loud, definitive clack.

"Well, be that as it may," the Major continued, "the Bass Baiters are having their national tournaments on the Alafi River less than ten miles away from here. That's a big deal for our little town. We might even make the evening news in Tampa."

"Well, my oh my, Delia," sniffed Ellen in a faux-southern accent, "it looks like Pezner has finally hit the big time."

"Please," Delia replied pointedly, "call me Major Rawlings."

"Please ignore her, Major." Jamie apologized. "She's doing her princess act. She'll snap out of it eventually. To tell the truth, the fact that she's giving you a hard time means that she likes you."

"Hmmm. If you say so."

"Oh, if Ellen didn't like you, she'd be so polite it would make you sick. By the way," she added, "she has a sixth sense, like a dog. She always knows who she can trust. And if she likes you, how can I put this delicately? She gives you a ration of grief."

"Hey," Ellen cried, shoving her friend playfully from behind, "six senses, like a dog? Ration of grief? What's the big idea?"

As the patrol car left Pezner and accelerated to the legal speed limit of 65 miles per hour, Jamie stared intently at the right side of the highway where a small, rusted sign raised its head above the weeds. They blew past the sign and left it wobbling in their wake of their speeding squad car. It trembled gently on the wind-swept shoulder beside the rusty barbed-wire fence at the edge of a huge, emerald-green pasture.

The message on the sign was surprisingly painful to Jamie. It was brief and to the point: "Homeland Estates, five Miles."

Visiting Hours

The words above the door were singularly unobtrusive: the company name, "Worldwide Financial Services," on a discreet brass plaque with simple, antiquated lettering. As he approached the front door, Ace had to smile. *Worldwide Financial. That's quite a name, but not so accurate,* he reflected wryly. *They should call it Worldwide Cash and Coin Laundry. They've laundered enough greenbacks to stuff Tampa Stadium right up the skyboxes.* He opened the door and stepped inside.

In keeping with the style of the modest brick building, the reception area was sparsely but elegantly furnished in mahogany and old leather, tasteful but decidedly low-key. *Well,* he reasoned, *that's how they've kept out of the papers for all these years and off the FBI's radar.* Long ago, the Tampa families had adopted a modest approach that had proven to be part of a winning formula.

Over the past 60 years, since the public execution of Charley Walker, there had been no Mafia wars on Tampa turf, no photogenic, bloodied bodies of dead gangsters discovered within the city proper. The Tampa mob had been wonderfully successful in their quest for anonymity. Here in the Cigar City, La Cosa Nostra had started early, learned quickly, and stayed with an approach that worked for them.

After the turn of the century, the Tampa families had learned to be sparing and judicious in the application of deadly force, limiting their terror to the criminal community. During prohibition, local families had developed Tampa as the preeminent American import/export hub for illicit Caribbean contraband.

By the 1980s, Tampa Bay was strategically located at the heart of a pipeline that pumped booze, dope, and the fodder of assorted vices directly into the soft underbelly of mainstream America. Over the decades, the Tampa mob had run a tight ship, controlling crime by the strict enforcement of mob turf agreements and showing an iron handgun to local punks who tried to prey on the law-abiding citizens of Hillsborough County. When murder had been the best solution to vexing problems, the bodies of their victims had disappeared without a trace: burned to ashes in licensed crematoriums, compacted and incinerated in metal recycling centers, or fed to the sharks in the middle of the Gulf.

Mob royalty were numbered among Tampa's luminaries, her most respected citizens. Secrecy prevailed, and anonymity was preserved. The code of silence remained unbroken. And as a result of the mob's sound discretion, the Cigar City had served as an underground gateway to the great American supermarket for more than 100 years.

During the roaring twenties, the mob had run Cuban rum through the Tampa gateway. During the thirties and forties, the numbers and prostitution rackets had prospered under their hand. In recent decades, the Tampa Mafia had exported white slaves to offshore brothels, controlled high-end prostitution, dabbled in public contracts and utilities, and above all else, had coordinated the protection of a steady stream of lucrative cargo, including illegal narcotics.

In response to a demand that they had helped kindle, the Tampa mob had grown fabulously rich. Tampa was heart of a secure pipeline that fed America uncounted megatons of destructive pleasure: a dark ocean of heady, deadly, exhilarating drugs. Every type of imported narcotic passed through the Bay and across its docks: resin-soaked mountains of pungent Colombian reefer, gummy rivers of black tar heroin, and the seductive, deadly distillation of seduction itself: ton after sparkling ton of pure white cocaine.

James "Ace" Feldmann thought of these things as he stepped through the door and entered the dignified headquarters. He marveled at the staid respectability of the venerable building and its opulent furnishings.

Worldwide Financial simply reeked of tradition and honor. From the tasteful music to the warmly lit, rich marble lobby, it was the very picture of propriety.

The receptionist at the front desk, young and pretty and totally unaware of the company's true business, looked at Ace with a quizzical expression. It was not every day that a musician with hair below his shoulders walked into this staid, conservative financial firm.

"Can I help you?"

"Yes. I'm James Feldmann. I'm here to see Mr. Provencenti." She blinked at him, surprised that he wished to speak with the owner of the company. "You can call me Ace," he added hopefully. *Call me anything, just remember to call me.* "He's expecting to see me," he added with a crooked smile. Ace liked the looks of this girl. "Do you like music?" he asked hopefully.

While she phoned her boss, Ace smiled and gave a subtle wave to the video camera in the corner of the room. *I wonder who's watching the screens today?* he wondered. *New blood, I'll wager.* Ace had been out of the racket now for almost 15 years, long enough to be unfamiliar with most of the new crop of mob wannabes.

"James," a loud voice said enthusiastically, intruding into his thoughts, "it's good to see you." He turned around to see Brad Johnston, a prominent Tampa attorney who served as a senior consultant to his father's financial company. Johnston, an expert in international finance, looked fit and trim, tanned and relaxed in his gray silk Italian double-breasted suit. *He hasn't changed a bit,* Ace ruminated. *This guy doesn't age. He must be pushing 80, and he looks 55. He's got to be one of the undead.*

"I'm on my way out," Brad said to Ace with a toothy smile, "I was meeting with Mr. Provencenti, and he asked me to let you in." Ace shook the attorney's hand and entered the second waiting room.

The reception area, furnished with flowers and drapes and clueless receptionist, had been mere window dressing. In the second waiting room, a bulletproof, one-way mirror in an overwrought iron frame provided the first hint of the building's true nature.

A door buzzed, and a soldier in an ill-fitting suit stepped into the waiting room, gesturing to Ace. He rose and followed the man through the door, down a hallway, up a flight of stairs, and into his father's office.

In keeping with the tenor of the Tampa Cosa Nostra, the Don's office was understated and unpretentious. Plain white walls were cluttered with the obligatory tasteful artwork, and the dark, clunky furniture was a perfect choice: not old enough to be antique, but not new enough to be stylish.

Ace's father fit the room well. Balding, in an elegant suit, expertly coifed and slightly overweight, the Don could have blended into to an executive office in any American city. There was nothing about him that would raise an eyebrow in this part of Ybor City, where upscale professional offices rubbed doorposts and cornices with trendy coffeehouses, furriers, and tobacco shops. Even the Don's regional accent was nondescript, with a watered-down, Latin-flavored, distinctively southern inflection that marked him as a native of the Ybor City.

Don Provencenti was facing one of the bookshelves when Ace entered the room. He turned to them as Ace was escorted into his office. "Johnny, you've never met James, have you?" he asked the security goon, gesturing at Ace.

"No, I never have," the young hood replied.

"Well, Johnny, this is James Feldmann," the Don said brusquely, gesturing at Ace. "James, this is Johnny Truffa." The Don nodded to the young man, who turned to leave. He motioned to a chair. "Sit down, James," he said to Ace. As his son sank down into an overstuffed chair, the Don turned back to Ace's escort, who was about to leave the room.

"Johnny, why don't you take a couple of hours off. Go get a tailor to work on that suit. It fits you like a gunny sack." The hood bowed slightly to the Don.

"Yes, sir, I will do that." As Johnny shut the door behind him, the old man smiled and winked at Ace. He sat down in the huge chair behind his desk, leaning back and touching the tips of his fingers together.

"He's just a kid," he said to Ace by way of explanation, "but he's got promise."

"We were all kids once," Ace replied with a crooked smile. "At least, most of us were." Hearing this, the Don chuckled.

"Kids," he replied philosophically, "they've got a lot to learn, but what can you do?"

"Can't live without 'em," Ace ruminated, "at least, not if you want the human race to continue." His father nodded with smile and scratched his chin reflectively.

"Ace, I called you here for a reason," he began, reaching into an inner coat pocket and pulling out a cigar. He offered one to his son, who took it carefully. Ace studiously sniffed the long cigar, bit off the narrow end, and pulled out his Zippo.

"Is this Cuban?" he asked, puffing loudly as he lit the expensive stogie.

"What do I look like, a disloyal ally to our many Cuban neighbors? Do I look like I would prop up Fidel Castro by purchasing illegal Cuban cigars, which happen to be the best in the world?"

"Yes."

"Of course they're Cuban," the Don said with a wink. "What do you think, I would settle for less?"

"Not bad," Ace adjudged through a heavy cloud of tobacco smoke. *This would go well after a joint. I gotta ask for another cigar before I leave.*

"Okay," the Don said, clapping his hands and sitting up in his chair, "this is why I called you here." He paused for a moment, his brow furrowed in thought. *How should I put this?*

"Ace, you're my son," he began. "You carry your mother's last name, but you're as much my son as Joey is. I

107

care about you. I think you know that." He paused, waiting to see Ace's reaction.

Ace was not comfortable with the subject. He and his father had never been close, even though the wily old Don had subtly supported Ace over the years. Ace had always hoped that the Don had fatherly feelings for him somewhere, hidden deep within his stone-cold heart . . . or, perhaps, locked in the deep freeze behind the icy calculator of his mind. Looking up, Ace saw that the Don was waiting for his reply.

"Sure, I always knew that you cared," Ace lied, embarrassed by the question. "That's a given. Sure." *Sure you care. You care about the family dog, too. It's a matter of degree.*

"Okay," the Don interrupted, "good. But that's not why you're here."

"Son," he said, leaning forward, "I've got cancer. It's stomach and lung cancer: too much to cut out. They tell me that I've got less than a year to live, maybe six months, maybe less." He shrugged.

Ace stared at his father, too shocked to respond. "Yeah, I know, it's a mess," the Don continued dismissively, "but what can you do about it?" Ace certainly had no answer to this question.

"Listen, this is important," the Don stated forcefully, leaning forward and staring into Ace's eyes, "I'm probably gonna die pretty soon. And then, if you're not careful, you're going to have problems with Joey." Ace looked at his father carefully, listening to him, weighing his words.

"Joey's my son but so are you, and I've got to tell you the truth. He hates your guts. He knows you've got more brains that he has, and it's been eating him since he was a kid. Plus, he hates that you're a musician, a ladies' man, a popular guy. You know, Joey's popular with his crew because he makes a lot of money for them. But he's not well liked by the girls, to say the least. He's too pushy, too forceful, if you know what I mean." The old man sighed heavily, shaking his head as he considered the hothouse of unsightly passions at play within the heart and mind of Joey, his problem son.

"Joey hates that you're a hippy. He thinks you're a pot-headed ne'er-do-well," his father added, fixing his eyes on his son, "and, I've got to admit, I'm not so crazy about your lifestyle, either." He stretched his arm forward and flicked a long, gray ash from his aromatic cigar. "I mean, the girls, I can understand. But the wacky weed, that just doesn't seem to fit. I don't get it." Realizing that he had digressed, the Don returned to the agenda.

"Joey knows you could have been a capo or consiglieri if you had stayed with the family. Maybe you could have been Don someday. He hates you worse because of that." The Don leaned back and put his hands behind his head, puffing on the cigar until a cloud surrounded his head.

"Let's face it, James. Your brother has a lot going for him, but he's not the total package. He has drive, he has guts, and he has passion. He's got the nerve of a brain surgeon. But he lacks the brains to cut it with the big boys. The truth is, you've got what he lacks. You've got what he's got plus brains, too. Because of that, he hates you. He's afraid of you."

"Afraid of me? Why?"

"What do you think? He knows how you dealt with that punk in Atlanta, you know his name. What was his name? Lenny Scarpetta, or something like that. You know, the guy you whacked just before you left the business. What was his name?" The Don rubbed his brow, trying to recall the name of the punk his son had killed.

"Scarfa. Benny Scarfa."

"Yeah, that's the guy. Benny the Weasel. Anyway, Joey knows how you wasted that punk all on your own with no backup, and with his own guys eating dinner right around the corner, no less. And who's to say that you won't waste your own brother some day?" Ace was astonished.

"Me, waste Joey? Why would I do that? I'm not a player anymore. But even if I was, he's my brother, for cryin' out loud!"

"Look, Ace, I know that you wouldn't kill Joey. I know how to read people. I can tell you what people will do, and I can tell you what they won't do. But Joey, he doesn't know zip. He thinks that everybody is just like him." Don Provencenti waved expressively with his cigar and shook his head dolefully.

"I know you don't want to have anything to do with our business, and I respect you for it. Your mother, God rest her soul, she wanted the same for you. I understand your motives because I understand people.

"You and me, we understand something important about people. Everybody's different just as much as everybody's the same. But Joey, he just doesn't get it.

"He thinks that everybody's like him: always on the make, out to get whatever or whoever they can. He thinks the whole human race is out to grab all the power and cash it can, hand over fist, by hook, crook, or lawyer. To Joey's way of thinking, if a person doesn't steal and kill, it's because he doesn't have the guts. To him, most people are chumps. He thinks they lack the guts and the brains to live like he does."

The Don shrugged. "Joey's outlook isn't realistic. But, hey, what are you gonna do? That's how your brother thinks, and we have to deal with it."

Leaning back in his chair, Ace's father drew a deep, aromatic mouthful of rich Cuban tobacco. Slowly inhaling, he paused for a moment, then exhaled abruptly and began to cough in painful, racking bursts. He leaned forward, lost in the spasms as the coughs wracked his lungs like suction from an evil wind. In a minute, the coughing had subsided and he wiped his eyes, regaining his composure.

"You need to consult with Marcello. He can help you. If you use your imagination, I think you two can come up with a solution that keeps everybody happy without hurting Joey." Ace suddenly began to see where this conversation was going.

Marcello? He's consiglieri now, and I'm not in the business. Is it that serious? Marcello had once been a close friend and mentor, but he hadn't seen him in years.

"So, this is why you called me up here?" Ace replied carefully, "What do Joey's problems have to do with me?" He knew the answer, but he had to hear it, in plain English, from his father, who was the canniest fox Ace had ever met.

"The bottom line, son, is this," his father responded emphatically, "Unless you play it smart, and I mean real smart, you're in trouble. In fact, I hate to say it, but it might be smart for you to leave town for good.

"After I'm dead, Joey will come after you. And unless you can figure a way around it, I fear for the worst.

"I'm afraid you're gonna get whacked."

Window of Opportunity

Monday morning was cool and fresh. It was as if Ybor City had been aired out, chilled down, bathed and powdered dry just in time for a bright new day. The cool weather brought with it wonderfully clear air, washed clean by Sunday's torrential rain.

As he pulled up to the familiar stop sign in his bright red pickup truck, Jumbo wondered where Streetcar might be. *You can set your clock by Street,* he reflected, *so why isn't he on this corner?* It wasn't like Streetcar to be absent. *But hey,* Jumbo reasoned, *why shouldn't the man sleep in if he wants to? No kids, no family, no responsibility except to keep an eye on the place he calls home.*

Jumbo reflected on these things wistfully, wishing that he were free from the fetters of responsibility like his friend Streetcar. *The man gets a 25 % monthly VA disability check and he's got no rent or electric bill. If I was him, I'd sure sleep in!* And yet, something didn't feel right about his friend's absence.

Passing Streetcars corner, the truck rumbled softly down the street. Savoring the beautiful morning, Jumbo glided past old wooden houses and brick bungalows under towering trees with roots that had long ago cracked the sidewalk into pieces. Reaching the park, he looked to his left and smiled as he gazed across the lush green landscape where lovers strolled arm in arm and children played a baseball on a weather-beaten diamond.

Jumbo pulled in at a driveway on the right side of the road and turned his truck off. The house in front of him was a well-maintained wooden bungalow with a screened porch that faced the lovely park.

"Well, my old friend Streetcar better get his rest so he can play some serious chess," Jumbo said aloud, "or I'm gonna clean his clock." After lunch each Monday, Jumbo would walk over to the old athletic club and play chess in the back room with Streetcar. It was one of life's little rituals, one of the many generous acts that made Jumbo's life so rich. As he thought about his chess game, the front door on his house slammed open and a small boy and girl jumped off the porch, screaming at the top of their lungs.

"Grandpa, grandpa," they cried, racing to get to the man who by now was climbing painfully out of his truck. They both leaped into his arms at the same time.

"Ooooh, babies, you're getting heavy," he said gruffly, hugging them tight. Looking up, he saw his wife standing beside the front door, her arms crossed, one foot tapping the plank floor of the wide front porch. She had tried to restrain the children, but in their enthusiasm they had escaped her arms to rush their grandfather before he could even shut the truck's door. He looked in her eyes and raised his brows with a smile as if to say, "What can we do?" She sighed, shook her head, and grinned ruefully.

"Come on babies, let's go inside," Jumbo said, putting them down and taking their hands as he led them back toward the house. "I'm sure that grandma has plenty to tell me about your wonderful morning." He smiled at his wife, certain that she would be able to tell him much more than he wanted to hear about their unruly shenanigans.

"Hmmph," Betty Poindexter snorted, "I've got plenty to tell you, all right." She glared sternly at the two children, who studiously avoided her gaze and followed their grandfather inside.

Change for the Worse

Jumbo had no way of knowing that on this day, in his pleasant little neighborhood, something had changed forever. Across the street, in the house of an elderly neighbor, a stranger had been quietly watching the heartwarming family scene.

To the uninvited witness, the scene in front of Jumbo's house was neither heartwarming nor pleasant. It was repulsive: a smarmy, second-rate show of feigned affection: a pompous strut of false familiarity: an unseemly public display, utterly void of significance.

I'd rather watch beetles rub horns than watch those people interact. They sicken me, the intruder ruminated, rising from his seat beside the window. He scratched his chest and walked toward the kitchen, idly wondering whether any food or drink could be found in the musty old house.

"I wonder how many doilies there are in this house," he said aloud. "This house is foul with doilies." Without a second thought, he stepped over the small body of his most recent victim, not even bothering to glance at his grim handiwork. *What's in the refrigerator?* He swung open the rusted white door and looked inside.

"Milk, bread, cheese," he said aloud. "Why don't you old broads ever have anything good?" Needless to say, the recently deceased refused to reply.

The victim was Esther Trapp. The killer did not know her, and she had done nothing to offend him. By accident, she had lived across the street from his latest target. She was guilty of nothing except living in the wrong house at the wrong time.

Until early this morning, a soul had inhabited the small body that was crumpled on the floor. She had been a frail old woman, getting on in years, as they say: weak and wilted in the consuming breath of onrushing time. She had lived alone, scarcely leaving an impression as she passed by, even in her own home. She had been a fading whisper of genteel womanhood drifting through the house, quietly planning to spend the remainder of her days in peace and prayerful service to God and humanity.

You would not know it now, seeing her on the floor, but once she had been a dancer. Years ago, she had even been a star. She had been a classic beauty draped in silk, strong and independent, flush with health and the promise of youth. She had made her mark on the world back then, when her limbs were light and her prospects lush. The theater and its glory had been her life.

The rich blood that had nourished her for so many years had drained away quickly after he stabbed her, rippling across tacky vinyl, seeping into the dirty hardwood floorboards. The frail body, once full of the frenzied pulse and rush of youth, now lay lifeless and cold, clamped in the first stages of rigor mortis. She lay on her back, her arms twisted into impossible angles. Her face was locked into a darkened mask of horror: eyes half shut, mouth twisted downward, false teeth akimbo as if they had dropped from her gums in shocked response to her own grisly murder.

The man stood over her and stared at her face with an idle smile dancing around the corners of his mouth. Inspired by an evil thought, he returned to the refrigerator and picked out a carton of milk.

"You look thirsty," he said, light-hearted and full of whimsy. "Would you like a cold one?" He opened the carton carefully and began to pour. The thin white ribbon cascaded over her face, over her pale pink sweater and faded beige slip. "You should have dressed for rain," he commented. "It's wet in here."

He chuckled, shaking his head in bemused wonder as the clean white fluid ran into her upturned nose. *You never know what these crazy old broads will do next.*

The killer carefully wiped off the carton and dropped it into the garbage. He had poured the milk meticulously, and not a single drop had fallen onto his freshly brushed, dark brown slacks. "Okay, don't say a word," he said to the empty house. "Who asked you, anyway?" *I'd better get back to the window. I'm getting crazy.* At the thought, he smiled. The intruder stepped over the body and returned to his seat beside the partially closed blinds, casting a glance at the woman before he sat down.

"Got milk?" he asked.

In spite of himself, he had to laugh, right out loud.

Scene of the Crime

The cars pulled up and parked behind them as Jamie climbed out of the Major's squad car and looked around. She felt as if she had escaped to this pastoral crime scene from the dark shroud of last Saturday night like an athlete emerging from a tunnel onto a sunlit playing field. *Was it only three days ago that Johnny was killed?* she wondered. *It seems like years.*

The sky was clear, the air cool as a light breeze rattled the cattails in the ditch beside the road. It had been difficult for her to identify the site, but they had finally arrived, almost rolling over the top of the crime scene before she cried for the Major to stop. She was transfixed by the beauty of this place, where swaying cattails were offset by the surreal sparkle of shattered glass on sunburned asphalt.

Engines were turned off, and the silence was disturbed only by the sound of car doors opening and shutting. The officers exited their vehicles like a crowd disembarking at graveside.

A funereal hush descended upon the scene. In contrast to their silence, the breeze seemed almost noisy by comparison. It moaned as it passed in unruly disarray, rustling the tops of the weeds and the scrub oaks on either side of the worn country road.

Jamie approached the broken glass slowly, drawn as if by a powerful force. She hoped that she would see no spots of blood, but almost wanted to see that rather than nothing at all. She could have borne the sight of blood if it would bring her closer to the memory of Johnny. The shock of the past days was wearing off, and unbearable pain was beginning to set in. She heard quick footsteps behind her, but did not turn to see who was approaching.

"Uh, miss, uh, please," a reedy voice suggested, "you might want to stop right there, if you don't mind." She turned around to see a tall, thin man of middle age with a studious, concerned expression. He was dressed in a powder blue suit that, in Oree County, practically screamed, 'outsider.'

"Oh, I'm sorry," she said distractedly. "I won't go any further."

"I don't mean to interrupt, ma'am. I just have to protect the crime scene," he offered apologetically, "it's my job. I'm Gene Thompson, the county coroner."

He took off his jacket and handed it to the young man standing beside him. "Jimmy, would you please get our toolbox? This must be the place." In Oree County, the coroner shared jurisdiction with law enforcement officials when crime scenes involved murder.

"Well," Jamie said to no one in particular, "this is the place, all right."

Ellen walked up to Jamie and stood without speaking, looking around. The road was slightly higher than the expansive, flat terrain, which was remarkable only for its sameness. All around them, cattails and scrub oaks and tall, skinny pines were scattered among watery sloughs interspersed with patches of dry brush growing from pure white sand that glistened like snow. As far as the eye could see, white patches of sandy scrublands alternated with dark lakes, seeps, marshes, and swamps.

Scattered shards of glass winked brightly on the dirty, decrepit road. In the tall weeds filling the ditch to their right, Ellen noticed a break in the monolithic green curtain. At this place, the cattails had been pushed aside in the path of some large creature. *Was this where Jamie ran from the killers? Did they chase her through this disgusting ditch?*

Standing beside her friend, Jamie stared at the cattails, recognizing the place where she had crashed through the wall of weeds and plunged into the unknown. She heard a voice, and realized that the coroner was addressing her.

"Please, Ms. James, I don't mean to seem harsh," the coroner added, looking toward the Major as if pleading for help, "it's just that this area is a key part of the crime scene.

We want to make sure that the killers are caught." He turned away quickly and walked back toward the Sheriff, who was studying Jamie closely.

The Sheriff's Department crime scene investigators, Detective Sergeant Donald Waldron and his assistant, Robert "Alibi" Albritton, began to drive a stake in the weedy shoulder beside the faded blacktop. As the Department's experts, their first job was to protect, preserve, and gather every possible shred of evidence. After staking each side of the road, they would string crime scene tape between the uprights and block off the area from further intrusion.

The Sheriff turned his attention to the two investigators. *Alibi looks tired,* he thought, *probably thanks to the joys of fatherhood.* Alibi and his wife were the parents of a one-month-old baby girl.

"Sheriff," a voice called, "could you come here for a minute?" It was Ellen, standing at the edge of the crime scene tape with one hand on her friends shoulder. Jamie stood with her back to the Sheriff, staring at the broken glass. She was hypnotized by the bland appearance of the area, the surprising normality of the crime scene.

Something monstrous happened here, Jamie thought, *but you'd never know it.* She almost expected to see hideous weeds sprouting from the bloodstained roadway, thirstily absorbing Johnny's life. But there was no dramatic evidence of Saturday night's crime.

Before long, the wilderness would hide every trace of the terrible event. *Life goes on,* she considered angrily. *But it shouldn't go on this quickly.* There was nothing to distinguish this site from 100 other sun-blighted rivers of asphalt in the vast, deserted wasteland known as Homeland Estates.

"Jamie," Ellen asked for the third time, "didn't you want to ask the Sheriff something?" Ellen was concerned about her friend, who was normally so resilient. She was scared by the way Jamie stared blankly at the crime scene. She shook Jamie's arm gently, awakening her as from a trance.

"Didn't you want to ask the Sheriff something?" she repeated, desperate to distract her friend. Jamie stared at Ellen without comprehension. Then, beginning to return to the present, she nodded her head.

"Oh, yes, of course. Thank you, Ellen. I did have a question." She turned to the Sheriff, regaining her trademark composure. "Sheriff Durrance, where is Streetcar?"

The Way Back

After two unpleasant hours in Homeland Estates, Jamie and Ellen were persuaded to ride back to town with the Sheriff.

The coroner and forensic technicians were still busy as the cruiser pulled away from the scene of the crime. They crouched over the roadway like optimistic spiders foraging hopefully for the hidden remnants of dearly departed prey.

The Sheriff's cruiser slowly carried them back through the deserted roads of Homeland Estates, rocking across broken pavement and clumps of weeds as the passengers swayed in the pale autumn sunlight. Jamie was thinking about Johnny, remembering the time they had shared and the things that he had held most dear.

"Sheriff, you're a preacher, right?" Jamie asked. She was seated in the front seat, leaning against the locked door, languidly staring at the fertile rural landscape.

"Yes."

"Do you mind if I ask you about your faith?"

"Not at all."

"Do you believe that God is good?"

The Sheriff cleared his throat and straightened, keeping his eyes on the road. "Yes, I do."

"Johnny believed that God was good," Jamie offered listlessly. The Sheriff nodded. "But you see, don't you?" she added hopelessly. "You see what happened."

"Yeah. I see."

"After all that's happened, I'm having trouble believing it. Can you tell me why you believe?"

"Okay. But I'm talking to you as a preacher, not as the Sheriff of Oree County."

"Of course," she replied, waving her hand dismissively. "We're both adults. So tell me, Sheriff: why do you think that God is good?"

"I believe that God gave his life for me."

"How did He do that?"

"God is a spirit. He came to earth in the person of Jesus of Nazareth, the Son of God. Through Jesus, God proved his love."

"How?"

"Jesus was an innocent man. On the cross, he took our place, bearing our punishment in his own body. He suffered death to give us life."

"Okay," she replied. "If that is true, it's pretty amazing. But I'm not quite sure I believe it. Johnny believed it, though, and he was very real. He was definitely not a phony."

"Good for him."

"Do you mind if I ask you another question?"

"No. Go ahead."

"Why would anyone want to become a Christian?" The question cut to the point, as Jamie always did. The Sheriff considered the question carefully.

"If you believe that Jesus is the Messiah, the Christian life is the only one that makes sense. If you don't believe, it doesn't make sense at all."

"That's logical," she replied. "Only a fool would live for something she didn't believe in." She took a deep breath and exhaled, looking out the window.

In the middle of a broad pasture to her right, a tall Brahma bull stood attentively, offering them an impressive profile that could have graced a John Deere calendar. The majestic bull chewed his cud thoughtfully as his tail lashed out at the ever-present gnats. Jamie smiled, and then, unexpectedly, she winced. *It's a beautiful day. Johnny would have loved it.*

"Thanks for answering my questions, Sheriff. This was very important to Johnny." *But now, he's gone. And I'm still here.*

"I wish I had known him."

"I wish you had, too, Sheriff."

The highway stretched ahead of them, leading the way back to the quiet town of Pezner. The sky was bright blue, and the landscape was almost gaudy. In the clear afternoon sunlight, the changing rural scenery practically shouted with ridiculously vivid primary colors: four-dimensional living statuary painted by a folk-art genius.

Jamie wanted to return to the past, but the impulse was futile. Her life had changed cruelly in an instant, and Jamie herself had been altered in a fundamental, irrevocable way.

There was no returning by the way she had come. Behind her was nothing but despair.

Perhaps, in the future, she would find the kind of hope that Johnny had known. *Maybe,* she thought, *things will change for the better.*

While her body still held breath, she would not deny the possibility that hope itself, like a tender shoot, might some day reemerge from her battered, broken spirit.

Welcome to the Jungle

Streetcar's bus pulled into the station in downtown Tampa at exactly 2:30 P.M..

Welcome to the jungle, Street', ol' pal, he ruminated. *Make sure you see the snakes before they see you, and you just might get out of this alive.*

Navigating on autopilot, he scanned the crowd as he exited the bus and left the station, scarcely noticing the urban scenery behind the sea of faces: the dirty bus station, faded posters on tiled walls, elderly men playing dominos on the bench outside the main entrance. *I've got to warn Jumbo*, he told himself. Streetcar was seriously concerned about his friend. *He's the only person who knows anything about me, and the Mob ain't gonna play nice.*

Streetcar didn't have any illusions about his own safety on the streets of Ybor. When he rescued Jamie, he had crossed the Rubicon.

There was no going back to his old life: no compromise or reasonable settlement that could be purchased with blood, love, or money. He owed it to Jumbo to fill him in on the facts and to warn him of the danger at hand. From 20 years of watching and listening on the streets of Ybor City, Streetcar knew that the owner of Jamie's Lamborghini was the worst of the worst of a bad lot. Joey Pro, as he was called, would stop at nothing to capture and destroy the innocent girl who had bested him in front of his friends.

Florida was not a state in which one would wish to be convicted of a capital crime. The state had the death penalty and was known to use it. Because Jamie's testimony could put Joey Provencenti in the electric chair and because Streetcar had saved her from Provencenti hoods, Joey would be willing to pull teeth - quite literally - to eliminate both Streetcar and Jamie.

As Joey worked his will in this matter, innocent bystanders would not be safe. The old ways of La Cosa Nostra were dying fast, and the ancient Sicilian code of honor would have little sway over Joey and his companions. Women and children would not be spared, nor would innocent civilians. To Joey Pro, the slicing-edge, proto-hip mobster, noncombatants were fair game. Women and children were sport. He had to warn Jumbo immediately.

The entire Provencenti Family would move against Streetcar and Jamie. An organization that is run by fear must be feared if it is to survive, and Streetcar had struck a blow against Mob fear. The news of his victory could spread quickly on the street. Courage, like a vaccine, threatened the Mob's malignant power. To head off the threat, they would stop at nothing to see him dead.

Knowing that he could be spotted, Streetcar decided not to travel on foot. Flush with more than $20,000.00 in untraceable cash taken from Joe Boy's glove box, he decided to spring for a taxi. He would ride in style to the defunct athletic club that, for years, had served as his only home.

Gamesmanship

Jumbo had completed his chores. He was dressed and ready to go.

"Honey, I'm going to play chess," Jumbo called from front hall, with one hand on the door. He looked at his watch. *2:33. Just right.*

"You and that bum," Betty replied from her seat in the living room. "You're early today, aren't you?"

"I sure am. He expects me to be late. I want to rattle him by breaking the pattern." They were extremely competitive, and Jumbo would take any edge he could get.

"Well, take out the garbage as you leave. And don't be late for dinner!"

Thirty seconds later, Jumbo deposited the garbage bag in the can in the alley and cut through his yard to the front sidewalk for the short walk to Streetcar's home. He had no idea that his emergence would cause excitement. But across the street, a man felt the blood pounding in his ears at the appearance of his prey. Of special interest was the state of the intended victim: alone and on foot. The killer could not have scripted it any better.

Jumbo walked rapidly down the sidewalk, looking forward to the camaraderie and challenge of another Monday chess match with his quirky, reclusive friend. The sun was warm on his shoulders, and he moved them around appreciatively, working out the stiffness.

If Jumbo had turned around, he might have noticed an unremarkable stranger following him at one block's distance. The stranger was slightly above average height, dressed in nondescript clothing with a ghostly pale face and wolfishly clear blue eyes. But Jumbo was in a hurry. He did not turn around. He slouched along at a comfortable pace, breathing deeply to savor the clean fall air as he enjoyed the beautiful day.

The sun raked the sidewalk with shifting beams that flickered through swaying branches, giving a shadowy, kaleidoscopic ambience to beautiful autumn afternoon. Unaware that a predator was closing in, Jumbo began to hum.

Behind him, hungry for blood, Mickey O'Malley carefully tracked each jaunty step. Matching the pace of his prey, attentive for changes, he sensed with a keen thrill that soon, very soon, he would be able to strike.

The Ride

"Say, ain't you Streetcar the bum?" The cabby eyed his customer in the rearview mirror, surprised to recognize the face of the prominent street person. "Since when can you afford a cab?" Streetcar sighed heavily and shook his head.

"Look, I'm Streetcar, but I'm not a bum. I work when I have to, and I don't take any handouts. I've got some money. I just don't spend it all in one place."

"You sure don't spend it in one place. That's a fact," the cabbie replied, "diving in dumpsters night and day. You must have a million bucks saved up. Are you sure you can afford this ride?" the cabbie wouldn't give an inch. It wasn't every day that he had a local celebrity in his cab. He turned around with one brown arm resting on the back of his seat. "Hey, I'm not running the meter yet, Streetcar. Do you mind telling me something?"

"Sure. What?" Streetcar replied warily.

"Why do the cops love you so much? I see squad cars parked at your corner all the time. Are you giving out free donuts, or what?"

"They like my jokes. I know a lot of jokes." Hearing this, the cabbie snorted in disbelief.

"Them must be mighty good jokes, Mister Streetcar," he said, affecting an accent straight out of Gone With the Wind, "us field folk don't get such jokes as that, out here in this dirty old cotton patch."

"What do you mean?"

"I mean, you folks livin' in the house hear the best jokes, don't you?"

"You're a smart guy, aren't you?" Streetcar replied.

"Smart enough to see through you. I'm willing to bet that you're not all you appear to be. At least, your heritage isn't. That's what I bet."

"So tell me, if you're so smart. What do you think my heritage is?"

"Oh, it's as plain as the nose on your face," the cabbie replied, "You're so Italian, you make Tony Bennett look Swedish. You make Garibaldi look like the little Dutch Boy." Streetcar laughed out loud.

"But that's not all, my friend. There's more to you than meets the eye, if you know what I mean."

"Okay," Streetcar replied, "my great grandmother on my mother's side was part Caribbean Indian and part black. Is that what you mean? She was from the Carib tribe. She met my mother's grandfather in Santa Domingo. He was a tobacco trader."

"That's it. That's what I mean. So, your grandmother was from the islands, eh? Then why don't you have an honest job? You don't act like an island boy!" He guffawed, and Streetcar smiled, charmed by the man's brash opinions. He was in a hurry and the cabbie was slowing him down, but he had to admit, there was something about this guy that he liked.

"What's your real name, anyway?" the cabbie asked.

"Salvatore Benuto."

"Oh, yeah? Do people call you Sally?"

"They call me Streetcar."

"Oh. Well, I was right about your heritage, wasn't I? Benuto. That's Sicilian, right?"

"Right as rain, taxi man. My father's old man left one island and moved to another. From Sicily straight to Brooklyn."

"So I guess I hit the nail on the head."

"Okay, now you know my name. What's yours?"

"Cohen. Billy Joe Cohen." When he heard this, Streetcar had to laugh. "My granddaddy was a Jew from Biloxi, and I got his name. He was a redneck communist Jew."

"Billy Joe Cohen? A redneck Jew?"

"He was more than just another redneck Jew. There are plenty of those in Mississippi. My granddaddy was a redneck <u>communist</u> Jew. I inherited his name, his brains, and his attitude. And a lot of good it's done me."

"Okay. But tell me this. What is a redneck communist?"

"Don't ask me," Billy chuckled. "Hey, the old guy was one tough old coot. He lived his whole life in Tampa after he married my grandmother and left Biloxi. Imagine a guy like him living in Tampa during the 1920s."

"It takes some imagination."

"It took some imagination on his part to survive, and that's a fact. His life wasn't too easy, and neither was mine. You know what I mean."

"I know what you mean."

"I mean," Billy said, pausing, "hey, look, can we talk for a minute? I need your advice."

"What time is it?"

"2:35," Billy Joe replied, "how about it? It won't take long."

Streetcar looked at his watch. *Shoot, why not.* The chess game was not due to start for 25 minutes, and the drive only took ten minutes. Jumbo was always late.

"Sure. What's up?"

"Like I said, I need your advice. I have a cousin who's in trouble for murder. The thing is, he didn't do it. Now, you know the cops in this town, if anyone does. Is there a cop I can talk to? One that will actually listen to my story?"

"Are you sure that your cousin didn't do it?"

"You sound like a cop."

"I used to be a cop. So, are you sure that your cousin didn't do the crime?"

"Oh, I'm sure, all right. He had a fuss with the guy, but no more than that. I was fishing with my cousin more than 20 miles away when the guy was killed! We were way out west of town, fishing in the Hillsborough River. But the cops and the prosecuting attorneys, they won't believe a word of it."

"Did anyone see you that day, fishing on the river?"

"Just a couple of kids in a canoe and some yahoos in an orange airboat. We stopped in a store to get bait, too. But what about my question? Do you know anyone on the force who might listen to me?"

"Jimmy Bristol should give you a fair hearing. Detective Sergeant Jimmy Bristol, that is. He's a homicide detective."

"Bristol? He sounds like a cracker."

"He is."

"So, how's a cracker going to help?

"You asked me for a name. Jimmy's your man. He's a cracker, but he's honest."

"He'll hear me out?"

"Sure he will. And if he thinks you're telling the truth, he'll whatever it takes to catch the murderer. Tell him I referred you to him. He knows me pretty good."

"Hmmm," the cabbie paused, thinking about what Streetcar had said. "Okay," he replied, "I'll give Jimmy Bristol a call." He looked at his passenger carefully. "So, tell me really, why do the cops like you so much?"

"I know all the best jokes. And like I said, I used to be a cop."

"Oh, yeah. What's that about, anyway? How did you become a cop? Why aren't you one now?" Billy Joe leaned back in the seat, waiting for the answer. He was not in a hurry on this particular day. He owned his own small cab service, and was enjoying this change of pace in the middle of an unusually slow Monday afternoon.

"I went through the academy right after I got back from 'Nam. I was a cop for five years."

"Where at?"

"San Francisco."

"So why'd you quit the force?"

Oral History

"I didn't want be a cop anymore," Streetcar answered, thinking back to those years in San Francisco. "Something happened. I changed, I guess, and I just didn't care enough anymore to wake up and go in to work each day. You might could say that I lost my ambition."

"You got any kids?" Benny asked. "I've got three."

"My wife took 'em." He sighed. *This guy really knows what questions to ask.* "I guess that's really why I quit the force. She told a few lies, got a few people to believe in 'em, bribed a couple of people, then she won custody of both our kids. I didn't even get visitation."

"No!"

"Yeah. She got a restraining order and everything."

"No!"

"Yeah, she sure did."

"So, how did that happen?"

"Well, she had a boyfriend who decided to beat on the kids. They hid it real well from everybody, and the kids were too scared to tell.

"She took the kids in to the emergency room one night. When they called the cops, she claimed that I'd done it. The kids were bullied into backing up her story. When it happened, I hadn't seen her for weeks. I would pick up the kids from daycare during the week and she would pick them up on Friday.

"I wasn't even in town that week. I was out of town; I had witnesses, but nothing mattered. All I can figure is, they must have paid off the judge. He didn't care about nothin'; he issued a restraining order without checkin' anything out. Family Services wound up clearing my name, but that took months.

"While the folks at Family Services were doin' their thing, my wife used the restraining order against me in divorce court. The same judge somehow managed to get the case. He cut me off from the kids with a single whack of his gavel, like he was cutting and wrapping a piece of beef. They must have bribed him; the boyfriend was as rich as sin."

"So, what happened?" Benny asked, looking at Streetcar in the rearview mirror as he unwrapped a candy bar. This was better than talk radio.

"Well, it didn't work out so well for the boyfriend. You might say that he hit a bad patch. He slipped and fell down the stairs . . . a few times, it turns out. As a result, he had a lengthy stay in a hospital. He never hurt my kids again, let's put it that way."

"No way!"

"Oh, yeah, baby. That's how it happened."

"No."

"Oh, yeah. I even went to see him after the untimely accident. I brought him flowers and candy."

"Flowers and candy?"

"Yeah. I wanted him to remember me fondly. You know, the next time he thought about laying a hand on my kids."

"So, what happened next?"

"I quit the force and left Oakland." He paused. "I turned in my badge.

"I had to give it up. I'd lost faith in the system. And let's face it: I violated my oath when I helped that guy down the stairs. After what that judge did to me and my kids, I didn't want to a cop anymore. So I quit, and I drifted for a while. I guess I wound up in Tampa by accident." Streetcar shrugged and lifted his brows.

"What a story," said Benny Joe.

"Yeah."

"Hey, anyway," Bernie continued, fascinated by the truth about Streetcar, "so, you're a veteran, like me. You served in 'Nam, you said. Were you there in '70?"

"Yeah."

"Me, too! Where were you stationed?"

"Nowhere particular. How about you?"

"Well, Mr. Streetcar, I was in the heart of Saigon, the party capital of Southeast Asia. I ran the noncom motor pool at headquarters. Army headquarters, that is," he added, "I was the famous GI Joe you've heard so much about. I was the guy that Hendrix wrote the song about." He cleared his throat and began to sing. "Hey, Joe," he rasped, "where you going with that clipboard in your hand?"

"Motor pool, huh?" Streetcar interrupted. "What a great job."

"You ain't kiddin' it was great. So, what was your job?" Streetcar stopped, and for a minute debated whether to answer.

"I can't say," he replied grimly. "It's classified." Billy exploded into laughter.

"Can't say? Come on man, what did you do?"

Streetcar paused, considering his question. *Here we are, in the 21st century,* he told himself. *I've been back in the states for 30 years, but the training still hasn't worn off.*

Suddenly, he made a decision. The past was ancient history. He would break with his training, and would finally talk about it.

"I was in recon. Deep recon."

"No!"

"Yeah."

"How deep?"

"Too deep."

"You and your team, right? Were you Army or Marine?"

"No team. Just me. And I was an Army grunt, just like you."

"No!" Billy replied, "If it's green, it's clean. But what do you mean, you had no team? What's that about? Were you a sniper?"

"Not really. Snipers worked with spotters. They did recon and took out targets of opportunity. They disrupted command structures or enemy activity at random, whenever they could find a target. My job was different. I destroyed targets that were determined beforehand. Sometimes I sniped, sometimes I didn't. I used different methods, depending on the mission and the situations I was faced with.

"You must have had a team, some kind of team," Billy said skeptically, "come on!"

"Just the stone-crazy Warrant Officers who flew the Hueys that inserted and extracted my dumb GI carcass. Those were the only team members I had."

"What were you, one of those ninja assassins?" Billy Joe was kidding, of course. Everyone knew that the army had assassins who would penetrate far behind enemy lines to assassinate predetermined targets, but there could not have been more than a handful in the armed services at any given time.

"I wasn't a ninja. I was just a plain old American assassin."

"You're kidding!"

"What, do you think I would kid about somethin' like that?"

"Man, that's a trip!"

"Not really. It had its moments," Streetcar offered. "But in the end, it was a bummer."

"Whoa!" Billy said softly. He fell silent, looking closely at his passenger, who turned to gaze out of the window.

It was a beautiful day in Tampa, but not in the entire world. In fact, if the truth were known, the world had not been beautiful for quite some time.

Power Play

"**S**treet!" Jumbo Poindexter pounded on the door, calling his friend's name. "Open up." He looked at his watch, and saw that it was 2:35. He was 25 minutes early. *I'm going to clean his clock today.* This was the first time in all these years that he had ever been this early, and he was prepared to make the most of it.

Jumbo turned and entered a walled enclosure, returning within seconds with a key to the security gate and the rusted front door. "Okay, I'll just have to let myself in." Streetcar never missed their Monday chess match. Street' was always here when Jumbo arrived, but today, things were changing. Today he was early, and he would win the match in record time, finally settling the fact that he, not Streetcar, was the best chess player in the neighborhood.

Jumbo opened the steel gate with a clang and unlocked the deadbolt on the door. *Whatever you've got in your refrigerator, Streetcar, it's mine.* He pushed the door open without bothering to turn the doorknob, rusted solid with disuse. He swung it shut, oblivious to nearly silent footsteps behind him as the killer crept carefully toward the closing door.

Years ago, Streetcar had abused alcohol, but for the past decade he had been notably temperate, enjoying no more than one beer per day. On the days of their chess match, he usually drank his beer during the main event.

"Well, I paid for this beer, and I'm gonna drink mine now," Jumbo said aloud. "This stuff cost me seven dollars for a six-pack!"

He entered the door and turned on the light. *It's cold in here,* he thought, turning the air conditioning off, *doesn't he know that the weather's turned cool?*

Streetcar had a nice situation, Jumbo decided for the thousandth time. He had central heat and air, free rent, a little cash, and a life unburdened by responsibility. All he had to do was pay the food bill and keep an eye on this building, and he was home free *But it's a lonely life for Street' with no family, one friend, and a neighborhood full of people who laugh at the mention of your name.*

"Street!" he yelled, "Where're you at?" He walked down the hallway and into the main room. "This place is a mess." *Nothing new about that.* He went over to one of the beaten-up, over-stuffed chairs in the middle of the room and picked up the remote. *I wonder if boxing's on ESPN?* He flipped through the three channels available on Streetcar's television, made a decision on which one to watch, and turned for the refrigerator. *It's time for that beer.*

The sight of a man standing before him almost startled him out of his wits.

"What on earth?"

"Lie down on the floor, face first," the man said calmly. It was then that Jumbo saw the gun.

"Who are you?"

"I said lie down, face first" the man interrupted, speaking slowly and evenly. "Do it." *This can't be happening,* Jumbo said to himself. He felt disembodied somehow, removed from the scene as if he were watching it from a distance, watching his own body standing before the gunman, hearing his own voice as it said something that surprised him.

"I will not!"

"Okay, fine," he replied without expression, and the gun was carefully aimed. As quick as the twitch of an eye, the pistol coughed, firing a silenced round into the middle of Jumbo's kneecap.

Instantly, Jumbo was no longer removed from the scene. He was in the thick of it, plunged into an agony beyond his worst imagination. Hot waves of pain seized him; overwhelming agony rolled over him. He felt as if someone were holding a blowtorch on his knee, peeling away the skin, charring the cartilage as the cruel, rapacious fire feasted on his flesh, eating into the very marrow of his bones.

"OHHHHHHH NOOOO!" he shrieked, collapsing on the floor and reaching for his shattered kneecap. He shrieked again as he touched it.

"That's better," the man said in a steady, rational voice. "Hmmm, let me see, why did I come here? Or rather, why did <u>you</u> come here? Oh, yes, I remember now."

"Get out of here, you pervert!" Jumbo cried. "Leave me alone!"

"Me, a pervert? I'm a pervert because I shot you? You're not thinking clearly. Perverts have depraved sexual desires. Then again," he ruminated, licking his lips and smiling reflectively, "perhaps you're right. As for my leaving, however, I'm afraid that you'll have no such luck. I have some questions. Answer them, and I'll kill you quickly. Don't answer them, and I'll kill you very, very slowly." He kicked Jumbo's knee for emphasis.

"YEEAGHHHHHH!"

"Come, come, now, let's not quibble," the Mick replied, "let's talk." In spite of himself, he had to smile. *It doesn't get any better than this.*

"What do you want?" Jumbo groaned. The pain was maddening, the trauma blunt and shocking, but from somewhere within him, Jumbo regained control over his mind, fighting with all that he had, desperately struggling to remain clear-headed so he could reason with the gunman. *Jesus, Lord, help me, he's going to kill me.*

"I want to know all about your friend, the man who lives here. You know, the bum they call Streetcar. He hasn't been here since Sunday morning, and I want to find him. That's why I visited your pretty little neighborhood early this morning."

"Why him, and why me?"

"Oh," the killer replied, "you don't understand. I'm the one asking the questions."

"What did we do to you?" Jumbo moaned.

"That's my business. Now, tell me; where is he?"

"I don't know!" he shouted in reply. The pain was unreal.

"My, my, this is getting interesting, isn't it?" The killer looked around the room, brightening up when he saw a length of rope coiled neatly in the corner. He walked over and picked it up.

"This is excellent rope. The bum coiled it perfectly. Is he a sailor?" Jumbo, in the throes of agony, could barely hear the questions. *This fool shot me in the knee!* The pain was incredible, and the blood continued to leak into a widening puddle on the concrete floor. "I asked you a question. Is your friend a hangman, or a sailor? Look at this knot," he said, holding it up. "Somebody trained him well." He began to raise the gun, looking wistfully at Jumbo's other, uninjured knee. "I asked you a question. Why does your friend keep this rope?"

"He works out with a heavy bag," Jumbo gasped, "that's just some extra rope. OWWWW!" The pain was coming in waves now, indescribable billows of white hot, unimaginably intense suffering.

"Well, whatever, it will come in handy." He looked up toward the roof. "This old building has character. If you like concrete and rust, that is. Heavy steel beams. Hmmm."

"I'll talk, man, I'll talk!" Jumbo was desperately attempting to buy time. *Where is Streetcar? He should be here by now!*

"Where is your friend?"

"I don't know." The killer tossed one end of the rope high into the air, making a perfect arc over the top of a steel beam.

"It works the first time, every time," he smirked. He tied a bowline knot with professional aplomb. Slipping one end of rope through the loop, he pulled it tight, testing his weight against the rope that hung, by now, from a thick steel rafter. "There we go," he said proudly, "good work." He turned to Jumbo and smiled.

"Now, let's see about that knee."

The Stone Warrior

"Thanks for the ride." Streetcar said as he opened the door and got out of the cab.

"No problem, Streetcar. I'll let you know how it works out. Jimmy Bristol, that's the detective's name, right?"

"Right."

"Adios." The cab pulled out from the curb and headed back toward downtown.

"See ya later, Billy Joe Cohen," he called after the departing cab.

Streetcar breathed deeply, glad to be back home. *We talked too long. I shouldn't have done that. I can't stay for long in Tampa, just long enough to warn Jumbo and get outta town.* It was almost three o'clock, and he expected that Jumbo would be arriving soon.

Streetcar walked up to the steel gate that protected his door and saw that the gate had been left open. *Hmmm,* he thought, *Jumbo must be early. That's a first.*

The front door swung open effortlessly. The doorknob was useless and had rusted fast long ago, but the deadbolt was functional, as all deadbolts were in this neighborhood. But today, the deadbolt was not latched. *That's not like Jumbo,* he thought. The light was on in the hall, and in the room beyond.

"Jumbo!" he shouted, "wha's up?" To his surprise, there was no reply. *He must have stepped out the back way,* he told himself as he began to walk toward his living room. But somehow, as he walked down the hall, an instinct stirred deep within him.

Something was wrong.

He stopped in the hallway, holding his breath.

Something was wrong.

A wave of goose pimples swept over him, and the hair on the back of his neck began to crawl. *What is this, combat?*

I must be getting squirrelly in my old age. He smiled to himself and started to walk again. *30 years, and I'm still fighting the war.* But just before he reached the end of the hall, at the edge of the entrance into his living room, something made him stop again. And here, at the cusp of discovery, he listened intently.

In the acute silence, he heard someone breathing on the other side of the wall.

His heart almost stopped.

Oh, great, here we go, he thought in a flash. His mind raced. *I stashed the Glock; I got no weapon.* His eyes flashed up and down the hall, settling on the red brick that served as his doorstop. *That'll work.* He crept back toward the doorway and picked up the brick, quietly jamming it between his stomach and his belt.

Then, to even the odds, he swung the unlatched breaker box open and turned the power off.

Street Smarts

The darkness was sudden and profound. This was total darkness: the dull, aching void of a cave deep within the earth. The windowless concrete building was sealed like a tomb, with no trace of ambient light.

"Hello, Mr. Intruder," Streetcar called in a loud voice, drawing out his vowels to cover the noise as he slipped one foot onto the rusted doorknob and stood up, leaning against the wall, feeling in the dark for the rafter that he knew was above him. "What's shakin', pal? Hey, hey, hey! What's up, wise guy? Did you drop by for a beer? Come, on, share it with me. How was your day?"

Streetcar was in the rafters now, leaning his head down low, so his voice seemed to be coming from the hallway. He had taken his position silently and efficiently, and was reasonably certain that he had not been heard. *Whoever that guy is, he has to leave by this hallway unless he's found the back door.* Streetcar just wanted the intruder to leave, right away, any way he would.

Suddenly, to his dismay, a flashlight flicked on in the next room. *Oh, no.*

"Let's get it on," a male voice whispered earnestly.

Streetcar was silent, praying that the man would not shine his light upward. He carefully leaned over and swung the front door open, allowing daylight to stream in briefly, then he pulled the chain to slam it shut. *There! I just ran for the hills, Mr. Intruder. What do you think about that?*

Suddenly, a burst of action occurred so quickly that even Streetcar had trouble following it. The flashlight rolled across the floor, shining down the length of the hall as a man rolled into sight, firing a fusillade of silenced rounds that punched through the solid steel door as if it were a cheap tin can. After firing the burst, the man swept the hallway with his light and, finding it empty, sprang to his feet and raced toward the door.

He moved so quickly that Streetcar almost missed him with the brick.

As the man snatched open the door, Streetcar unleashed his solid projectile of hard-baked, time-hardened mud. His aim was true, but the target was quicker than Streetcar imagined. Instead of slamming squarely into the man's head, the brick pounded his disappearing back with a glancing blow that struck between his shoulder blades.

"What?!" the man cried in surprise as his momentum carried him through the doorway. Streetcar landed on his feet in time to see him grab the doorframe with his left hand. What he saw next showed that the intruder was an amazingly powerful man.

At the last split-second before he blasted out through the front door, the killer tossed his gun into his right hand and latched onto a steel pipe beside the doorframe with his left. His left hand took the full force of his weight, and his feet left the ground as he was slammed to a sudden halt. The killer flipped the gun back into his left hand just in time to see the door slam on his arm, pinning his gun hand inside the darkened hallway.

Streetcar grabbed the gun as the killer began to fire. With all his might, jamming his weight against the door and wrestling with the gun barrel, Streetcar could barely keep the gun turned away from him as the door was slammed with blow after blow and the twisting arm struggled mightily to get free, firing round after round that smoked the air around Streetcar's head.

Then, Streetcar had an idea.

He suddenly took his weight from the door and jerked the gun as hard as he could. As if in slow motion, the door banged open, disgorging its contents into Streetcar's face. As the would-be killer flew towards him, low to the ground with his pale face registering disbelief, Streetcar slammed his left knee into the man's body with all of the strength he could muster. He nailed the killer in the left shoulder with a blow that spun Streetcar sideways, and he heard the man's collarbone crack like a rifle shot as the gun hit the ground and skidded down the hall.

Even this did not slow the man down. Momentum drove him past Streetcar, who whirled like a matador. The man tumbled and came up with another gun that Streetcar instantaneously kicked out of his right hand.

This last blow, finally, stopped the intruder in his tracks. Staring at Streetcar in shocked astonishment, grimacing in pain, he looked as if he could not believe what was happening. But the would-be predator was an exceptionally talented animal. He instantly adapted to the new environment.

The killer sprang to his feet and fled toward the back of the building, pursued hotly by his intended victim. He was fast, too fast for the middle-aged Streetcar, who had lost a step as he aged in spite of rigorous daily training. The man blasted through the living room and darted out the open back door, slamming it in Streetcar's face.

Before Streetcar could follow him out the door, something cut through his battle fog. Something stopped him cold.

It was a sound of sorts, a pitiful mewling sound like a kitten caught in a trap. It sent shivers through Streetcar, and his spirit sank toward the floor.

He had heard that sound before. He was afraid that he knew what it was.

Streetcar turned around to see a sight so inhuman, so grisly and shocking, it literally took his breath away.

A man was hanging from a rafter by a single, bullet-riddled leg with a knee the size of a basketball. The lighting was indirect, and Streetcar could not immediately make out the details. Refracted fingers of light from the open front door slipped over the top of the living room wall and slid through the steel rafters, slicing through the clouds of dust and burnt gunpowder. The shaky light was scarcely adequate, yet it revealed more than Streetcar ever wanted to see.

The victim was his best friend, Jumbo Poindexter.

Jumbo swung from the rafter like a side of beef twisting over a slaughterhouse floor, his body covered in red fluid that flowed, ever-so-slowly, into his soaked hair. The warm blood dripped on the concrete floor with excruciating regularity as drop after precious drop joined the dense puddle beneath his inert body. His chest rose and fell irregularly as he fought for breath: unconscious, yet struggling to survive.

For now, at least, Jumbo was alive.

911

At 3:25, the ambulance pulled away from the curb and turned on it's lights and siren.

The parking lot was full in front of the run-down concrete building that Streetcar called home. At least ten squad cars were parked in the street or in his lot, bubble lights flashing an array of intense, unnatural blues, oranges, and reds that competed with the slanting rays of autumn sunlight.

Streetcar sat on the front step with his hands cuffed behind his back. Towering over him was Officer Henry Sharps, a recent addition to the Tampa Police Force. Officer Sharps was, as they say, on the management track. He had been hired from the University of South Florida, where he had excelled in the nascent field of Law Enforcement Administration.

"So, tell me again about this intruder," he said, edgily addressing the handcuffed man who sat at his feet.

"I told you," Streetcar repeated. "I don't know anything about him. Just that he was one of the best at his trade that I've ever seen."

"What was his trade?"

"He was a stone killer," Streetcar replied. "I told you that already."

"Hmmm."

"What about Jumbo's family? Did you contact them?"

"An officer has been dispatched to tell them about Mr. Poindexter's injuries," he answered, eyeing Streetcar suspiciously. "Can you tell me why you think his family might be in danger?"

"I don't know. I've just got a sneaking suspicion," Streetcar replied. "It doesn't hurt to be safe, does it?" He looked up to see Detective Sergeant Jimmy Bristol approaching. "Hey, Sarge," he said, trying to smile but failing in the attempt, "I was just talking about you to a cabbie I met today."

"Hey, Streetcar." Jimmy's face was dark and menacing as he turned to the young officer who loomed over Streetcar. "Why is this man handcuffed?"

"Procedures, Sergeant," replied Officer Sharps.

"If I am correctly informed, this is the citizen who reported the crime. Is that correct?"

"Well, yes. He's the one who called it in."

"Has he hindered the investigation? Has he threatened anyone in any way?"

"No, sir."

"Do you have any reason to believe that this man was the perpetrator? Is there any evidence, testimony, or anything else that would provide grounds for reasonable suspicion?"

"Uh, well, I guess not. Nothing concrete."

"Nothing concrete, huh?" Detective Sergeant Bristol replied, ducking his head and rubbing his temples. "Okay," he added, "then answer this. If this man been wearing a suit, would you have cuffed him and forced him to sit like this?"

"Sir?"

"Let me rephrase that question. Given the fact that this man is the citizen who phoned in the crime and the complete lack of reasonable suspicion, why is this man handcuffed? Is it because he's a street person?"

"Uh, I don't know how to answer that, Sergeant."

"Take off the bracelets," Jimmy Bristol said flatly, "and see me when we get back to the station." As the rookie detective began to do as he was told, Streetcar caught the younger man's eye.

"Don't worry, kid," Streetcar said with a knowing smile. "We've all done some boneheaded things in our time." Released from bondage, he stood up and shook his hands, rubbing his wrists briskly. "The kid's just fired up, Jimmy. Like you and me used to be, when we were his age." Jimmy took the toothpick out of his mouth and flicked it into the street. He nodded in response to Streetcar's comment.

"So, Streetcar," he began, "they tell me that somebody assaulted your best friend and that you broke it up. Is that what happened?" He watched Streetcar carefully, waiting for his reply.

"Yeah, that's it. The best I can figure, the guy must have broken into my place and surprised Jumbo. He messed him up bad, Jimmy. Real bad." Streetcar paused and raised his hand. "Oh, man, give me a second." He bowed his head and bit his lip. It finally hit him.

Streetcar had been so pumped by the rush of combat that the full effect of Jumbo's injuries had not registered until this moment. *Jumbo might die,* he realized. He wavered on his feet for a moment, staggered by the realization. Seeing this, Jimmy put a hand on his shoulder.

"So, somebody broke in and attacked him when he arrived?" the detective asked. Streetcar nodded in reply, fighting back the flood of tears. *If I crack now, I'm good for nothing.*

"Yeah, it must've gone like that." He dried his eyes quickly with his thumb, looking away. "We always play chess at three o'clock every Monday. Jumbo's always late. But he was early today, and the guy must have been waiting inside."

"Do you have any idea who might have done it?" Streetcar did not answer immediately. When he did answer, Streetcar changed the subject.

"Jimmy, why are you here? You're a homicide cop. This isn't a homicide." Detective Bristol's eyes shifted to the ground as he searched for the correct response. How could he tell Streetcar that his only friend would almost certainly die from his injuries?

"Oh," Streetcar breathed, answering his own question as he read the officer's expression. "Never mind." He was shocked: too shocked to fully accept what he had seen with his own eyes.

The detective studied Streetcar's clouded brown eyes, noting how he stared vacantly into the distance, dull and unresponsive. The lights were on, but there was definitely no one home.

Jimmy Bristol sighed and looked around the crime scene. "Does anybody have a cigarette?" he asked to no one in particular. He had quit smoking four days ago, but suddenly, the toothpicks just weren't getting it.

The detective had known Streetcar since the famous street person had first hit town. The colorful street person had made a big splash in those days, like a melon lobbed onto the windshield of the fast-moving Ybor City business district.

Early in his career, after Streetcar had provided a tip that ended a series of burglaries, Jimmy had run a background check on the peripatetic street person. Detective Bristol had been shocked by the details of his past: a spotless, decorated service record, a meteoric rise in the San Francisco police force as a brilliant young officer, and a sudden resignation after a bitter divorce.

During the divorce proceedings, allegations had been made that Streetcar had abused his children and his wife. He had lost custody of the children as a result. After the divorce, he had been cleared of all allegations. Several months later, the same judge who had ruled on the divorce had been convicted of bribery and influence peddling in an unrelated case.

Detective Bristol had spread the word about Streetcar's past, and he had eventually become an honorary detective of sorts, a ready source of information for the many cops who had learned to like and respect him. From his corner, Streetcar had watched for years without blinking as the drama of Ybor City unfolded. He knew the streets: what was up, what was down, who was in, who on the outs. Best of all, he was willing to share his cornucopia of street buzz with his many friends in blue.

Detective Bristol had never been close to Streetcar. After all, he reasoned, the man was a street person, notwithstanding his impressive past. But the detective sincerely liked him. Streetcar had once been a cop: a good one, and Jimmy Bristol respected him for this as much as for his independence and character. In his 20 years of residence in Hillsborough County, Streetcar had not so much as jaywalked on the streets of Ybor City. In his own, quirky way, he had been a model citizen.

"Do you have any idea who might have done this terrible thing?" the detective repeated. As he watched, Streetcar's eyes switched off as if a shade had been drawn across his inner light. His body tensed with a suppressed jolt of nervous energy, hit by a silent surge of hidden power. Then, the light returned to his eyes and he smiled with a certain, practiced serenity.

"I wouldn't want to speculate," he replied smoothly, as if he had rehearsed the sentence. *Oh, great,* the detective thought, *he knows something, or thinks he does. And he isn't going to share it.* If there was anything Jimmy Bristol did not want on his beat, it was a marginally socialized former member of U.S. Army Special Forces with a major score to settle.

"Well, if you get any ideas about who the perpetrator might be, let us know, you hear?"

"Yeah, sure."

"So, tell me again, what happened here?"

"I already told the kid everything."

"I know. Humor me, okay?" Unnoticed to Streetcar, Jimmy had pulled out his notepad and pen.

"My bus got to the station at about 2:30. Here's the ticket," he said, holding it out without looking, as if his thoughts were elsewhere. "I hailed a cab, and the cabbie wanted to talk. He must have talked for 20 minutes. The cabbie saw me get off the bus. That ought'a make your job easier."

"What's the cabby's name?"

"Billy Joe Cohen."

"Billy Joe Cohen?"

"Don't ask." Normally, he would have smiled, but for the time being he had lost the ability. Streetcar looked worn and wan, a mere shadow of his jovial self.

Jimmy decided to back off for now. His instincts told him that Streetcar was not involved in wrongdoing. Streetcar's story could be easily checked out. *He's a victim,* the detective reasoned. *This was his only friend.*

"Don't do anything stupid," the detective warned grimly. "Talk to us if you remember anything. Let the law run its course."

"I hear you," he answered, smiling at Jimmy. *I hear you,* he thought, *but I won't tell you nothin'.* Streetcar liked and trusted Jimmy Bristol, but his heart was set on revenge.

Jumbo's assailant was a hired hand. He was an instrument, a human weapon that had been sent by the most powerful Mafia family in the Southeastern United States.

Because Streetcar had delivered Janelle James from Provencenti hoodlums, the deadly weight of the entire family had fallen upon the head of Jumbo Poindexter. Jimmy Bristol was an honest cop, but the family was well beyond the reach of one zealous Tampa detective.

The Provencentis were a cornerstone of the Southern mob, a venerable family of experienced wise guys from the old school. After more than a century in power they had grown as subtle as serpents and as tough as brass tacks. The family was scarcely troubled by the law or by the threat of legal penalties.

"Jimmy, can you do me a favor?" he asked the detective.

"I hope so."

"Let me take another look at the crime scene." The detective wasn't pleased with the idea.

"It's a sealed crime scene. You know that. You can have your house back when the technicians are through."

"Come on, Jimmy. Let me take a look; I'll be with you the whole time. Just let me into the front hallway. I can help you guys," he added truthfully. "It's not my first crime scene. I was as close to the perpetrator as we are right now. I might be able to point out things that will help."

"Okay, okay. We can go in to get you some clothes. But you can't touch anything, okay?"

"Sure."

The detective turned to his team's junior member. "Detective Sharps, we're going in to get some of Streetcar's personal items."

"Sure thing, Jimmy." Streetcar and the sergeant turned and stepped gingerly past a forensics expert taking photographs of the door and another crouched at the front step, photographing shell casings. As he approached the doorway, Streetcar paused and addressed the two men.

"See there, on the doorpost, that blood spot?" he asked, "You guys make sure you get a good sample of that blood, okay? That's the perp's blood. I slammed his arm into the door pretty good." The men looked at Streetcar quizzically and turned to Jimmy Bristol, who raised his eyebrows and shrugged.

"And leave that brick for me when you're through, okay?" Streetcar added. "I use it as a doorstop." As gingerly as two cats circumventing a puddle, Jimmy and Streetcar approached the doorway and stopped at the threshold.

"Here's where the guy made his move," Streetcar offered, pointing to the end of the front hallway. "He cleared the front hallway like a pro. One smooth dive and roll, just like he practiced it every day, and he came up barfing steel. If I'd been standing where we are now, he'd have gotten me."

"If you weren't in the hallway, how do you know how fast he was?"

"I was up there," Streetcar replied, pointing toward the roof. Jimmy lifted his head and looked at the exposed steel rafters.

"How did you get up there?"

"I boosted myself up on the doorknob. The hardest part was doing it quietly."

"So, how did you get away from guy? If he was so good, why didn't he get you?"

"When I first came in here, I knew that something wasn't right. It felt squirrelly, like it gets sometimes before the action starts in combat. I walked to the end of the hall, and something stopped me short. That's when I heard him breathin'."

"You heard his breathing?"

"Yeah. I told the kid all of this stuff, already. By the time I got to the end of the hall, I had doped it out. Something wasn't right."

"Okay. Then what?"

"I heard him breathing, and I knew I was in for it."

"Good ears."

"Yeah, I guess. But it scared the daylights out of me. So I slipped back here, cut off the power, and made a lot of noise, talking loud to cover the sounds. I stood on the door handle, grabbed a rafter, and climbed right on up."

"The handle's pretty rusty. What if it dumped you?"

"You would'a had two victims."

"Sounds like it."

"Make sure the forensics guys bag the guns right. I'll bet the only prints you'll find are on those guns. This guy was a pro." He looked idly at the handgun near the front door. "A nine millimeter Glock," he said, thinking aloud. "What is it with these guys and Glocks?"

"What do you mean by that?"

"Oh, I saw a show on TV the other day about crooks and Glocks," he lied. *Way to go, Bozo,* he berated himself, *don't give him anything!* Streetcar was bound and determined to keep what he knew to himself, but he was slipping up in front of one of Tampa's best homicide detectives.

"Okay, so what else do you want to tell me?" *Whatever you're hiding, I'm going to get it out of you, buddy.*

"Can we go outside for a minute?" Streetcar asked, gathering some clothing from his dresser and stuffing it into a bag, "I think I'm gettin' sick."

They retreated carefully, avoiding the evidence. When they reached the front curb, Streetcar paused and looked up at the bright blue sky. For the moment the clouds had passed, and the day was sunny and clear. It was exceptionally beautiful. *Except for Jumbo,* Streetcar thought, *it's a beautiful day. Except for Jumbo.*

"Hey, Streetcar," a short, fat cop called from a squad car. Streetcar turned and smiled, forgetting his troubles for one brief moment.

"Clark, is that you? Or is it your ugly twin?"

"It's me, you sleazy bum. Come over here." Streetcar left Jimmy Bristol for a moment to walk up to Officer Clark's squad car. "Hey," Clark said, becoming serious, "I heard about your friend."

"Yeah?"

"We'll get the punk who did this, Streetcar. Don't worry about that."

"I'm not worried about it."

"Good."

"Whoever did this," Streetcar added, "they're the ones who should be worried."

"They? I thought there was only one perpetrator."

"I was just talkin' in general. You're right, it was just one guy."

"Well, I'm awful sorry, old buddy. Maybe your pal will be okay."

"Yeah, maybe." *He may not die,* Streetcar thought hopelessly, but deep within, he was beginning to lose hope. He had seen life-threatening wounds before. He had zipped up more than one body bag.

"Well, the punk will pay, we'll make sure of that."

"Yeah, sure. Hey, Clark, I gotta go, okay?"

"Sure, Street'," the officer replied, "sure." Streetcar slowly walked back to Jimmy Bristol, who was finishing up his notes. Jimmy looked up with concern.

"Streetcar, you've been through the wringer." *He looks like death warmed over.* "Do you have a place to stay?"

"Yeah."

"Why don't we take a ride down to the station? You can give us your official statement, then I can give you a ride to wherever you're staying." He looked over at Detective Sharps, who had temporarily stopped to listen into their conversation. "Detective Sharps will be personally responsible for safeguarding your possessions. Won't you, Detective Sharps?"

"Right, Sergeant."

"How long do you think it will it take us down at the station?" Streetcar asked.

"I don't know, a couple of hours, maybe. Are you sure you've got someplace to stay tonight?"

"Yeah, thanks, I've got a place."

"Well, if you change your mind, we've got a room in the back with a couple of cots. We crash there sometimes when we're pulling double shifts. You can sleep there for tonight, if you want to."

"No kiddin'? What will the brass say?"

"You can crash there until about 4:00 A.M. The Captain comes in early some days, so it would be best if you were out by then. We can wake you."

"What more could I ask for?" Streetcar asked, smiling brightly. "A personal wake-up call!"

Detective Bristol looked at him with pity. *This poor guy's losing it,* he thought. *What did he do to deserve this?* Streetcar was known to be a totally harmless, friendly fixture on the streets of Ybor, a benign and popularly tolerated presence. He was a staple, like the bell ringers at Christmas time. Who would harm this guy, and who would torture his friend . . . a poor working stiff who had never harmed a soul?

"Okay, let's go to the station and have our little talk," Streetcar said. They climbed into the front seat of the detective's unmarked car. The engine fired up, and Jimmy adjusted the rearview mirror.

"Do you guys have coffee and donuts?" Streetcar asked hopefully. Detective Bristol sighed and shook his head as the car lurched away from the curb.

Chrome and Circumstance

As the musicians slid off the stage and headed for the parking lot, the wrung-out country crowd wandered from the dance floor, chatting at the top of their lungs. The cumulative effect of noisy conversation from hundreds of overheated mouths was a solid wall of sound rivaling the volume of the band's last set. Tonight was Ladies Night at the Silver Spur, the biggest and baddest country-western nightclub in town and the only fair-sized juke joint within three counties.

A foul cloud of smoke hung heavily in the air of the oversized, faux-rustic roadhouse. The gritty fumes were thick enough to cut with a chainsaw, or with a feloniously honed Buck knife attached to a colorfully inlaid redneck belt.

As the noise continued at a deafening pitch, the jukebox in the corner began to thump out "Hello, Walls," and the dance crowd surged back toward the floor. At the other end of the room, leaning against the polished oak of a long, narrow bar, Donny Hawkins and Ralph Spurlock were deep in conversation.

Donny and Ralph made up a mismatched pair. Donny Hawkins was a conspicuously tall, broad-shouldered cowboy who lived and worked on a remote ranch, while Ralph was a short, wiry jack-of-all-trades who had not yet found his niche in his hometown of Pezner. They were both graduates of Pezner High School, but the resemblance ended there. Donny held a degree in Agriculture from the University of Florida, while Ralph professed a notable degree of independence that was free of the taint of higher education.

"Yeah, it's terrible mess." Donny shouted above the jabbering throng, "Billy Cloud told me they found Johnny's body in the top of a big cypress tree." He straightened his black cowboy hat nervously as he talked, looking around as if he expected trouble to descend on them out of the clear blue smoke: the way it must have descended on their friend, Johnny Delaney.

"A big cypress?" his companion asked, gaping incredulously. "You can't climb a tree like that. You've got to be kidding!"

"Kidding! Do you think I would kid about this?" Donny was devastated by what had happened to his friend and was not in the mood for foolishness.

"No. Of course not," Ralph replied, gazing up at his friend. "I didn't mean it like that. He was my friend, too, you know."

"Yeah, I know." Donny took another swig from his Mountain Dew and looked around wonderingly, as if he didn't recognize the room and couldn't make sense of it all. "I just don't get it." Distracted for a moment, he thought he saw one of his high school girlfriends at a table on the other side of the room and craned his neck to get a look.

"Well," Ralph asked impatiently. "How did Johnny get up there?"

"Huh?"

"How did he wind up in the top of a cypress tree?"

"The coroner thought that maybe he fell out of a plane. I don't know, it sounds kind'a crazy."

"He fell from a plane?" Ralph marveled. "What would Johnny be doing in a plane? He was scared of flying."

"I don't know what he was doing," Donny answered curtly, worn out by the questions and the traumatic news of his friend's death. "You tell me what he was doing. Maybe he got over his fear of flying by sky-diving without a parachute."

"There's no need to get hyper," Ralph replied. "I was just wondering."

"Sorry. This stuff has gotten to me. Johnny's dead!" Donny looked pale and shaken, as if he had donated a quart of his own blood to an unworthy cause. "We were planning to go hunting next weekend down at Fish Eatin' Creek. Who could have known this would happen?" He gazed sourly around the room, sipping his soda. "I can't believe it."

Donny had come here to enjoy the music at the only juke joint in the county that had a live band. He hadn't expected to run into Billy Cloud, but it had happened, and as a result, he had heard the miserable news about Johnny Delaney.

"Hey, Donny, come outside with me," Ralph said, changing the subject. "I want you to meet Uncle Ray."

"I met your uncle already."

"You met Uncle Rick from North Fort Myers. Uncle Ray's from Collier County, down south of Naples. Come on, before he leaves."

"Okay," he replied with a sigh, "let's go see your Uncle Ray." They fought their way slowly through the raucous crowd, navigating through the stale smoke and colored spotlights that cast swirls across the faces and backs of the patrons, pressing forward until they had worked their way out into the cool evening air.

The parking lot was packed with cars: late model sedans, aging muscle cars, and pick-up trucks drunk on testosterone, decked out in overwrought accessories that dripped chrome and wretched excess. The pick-ups were simply outlandish: pumped-up, preening metal peacocks larded and pasted with mirrored metal, bristling with roll bars, lights, winches, and other dangerous-looking accessories. They proudly dominated the other vehicles: sitting pretty, jacked up and impressively wide, their headlights held high above the muddy crowd.

The massive tires on these pick-ups belonged on tractors. Squatting atop gigantic, deep-treaded rubber doughnuts, the pick-ups were the leaders of the pack. They were steely quarter horses riding herd on an assortment of clunkers, road hogs, hot rods and assorted rust magnets.

Some of the vehicles seemed to crave anonymity. In less prominent parts of the lot, a faceless hodge-podge of oil-burning bombs from the sixties and seventies huddled among the weeds and patches of clay. These were massive anachronisms from a conspicuous past: former superstars, as wide as a house and notably long in the tooth. They seemed ashamed, almost, to be seen in public.

In one obscure corner of the lot, beside the two-lane highway, was an antique, dark 1952 metallic-red classic pickup that had been restored to its former glory. Sitting on the tailgate, a huge, bald man in his forties was engaged in lively conversation with another man who appeared to be at least 80 years old. The bald man was Uncle Ray.

The old gentleman conversing with Uncle Ray was the archetypal Florida cracker: short and wiry with scaly skin as burnt as blackened redfish. He was seared and crusty on the outside and red on the inside, baked tough and tasteless by the unrelenting heat of too many summers in Florida. The fine wrinkles on his sun-beaten face outnumbered the cracks in the dusty clay.

"Ralphy, I was just talking about you," called Uncle Ray, without rising from the tailgate. "Come on over, boy. You know Yip Farley, don't you?" Ralph walked up, coughed conspicuously into his hand, and extended it toward Yip for a handshake.

"Yip Farley, you old rascal, what's up?" Yip smiled broadly, his missing teeth gaping from a wrinkled mouth that resembled nothing so much as the open maw of a beakless octopus. Yip was a wry, diminutive redneck elf in a checkered cowboy shirt, looking for trouble and certain to find his fair share.

"I ain't shakin' yer hand, Mr. Ralphy, if that's what ya want," Yip replied jauntily. "You kin play that trick on some other fool, you low-life rascal. I weren't borned yesterday." Yip grinned at Donny and winked broadly.

"Mr. Farley," Donny said, nodding respectfully at the older man. "How are you doing tonight?" He was unprepared for Yip's spirited reply.

"Man, I'm ready to go!" the old man cried, sweeping his fist through the air as his left foot swung upwards. "I tell you, boys, I'm ready to go! How about y'all?" Ralph and Donny looked at one another, trying not to laugh. Yip Farley, when he got wound up, was one of the most comical characters in Oree County.

"We're straight, Yip. We're straight."

"Yeah, well, you'd better be. It's better to be straight than drunk, I always said. You'd better <u>stay</u> straight, too." He squinted harshly at Ralph. "By the way, young man, I don't like it when you talk that danged hippy talk." Yip snorted in disgust. "You hear me, Mr. Ralph Whitehall?"

"Yes, sir."

"You'd better hear me, boy. I knew you before you fell off the turnip truck. I knew you when you were knee-high to a flagpole."

"Yes, sir," replied Ralph, wondering what on earth Yip was talking about. He turned to his uncle, politely attempting to steer the conversation in another direction.

"Uncle Ray, have you met Donny Hawkins?" His uncle stood up politely. As tall as Donny was, Uncle Ray was that much taller. Although Donny was some inches above six feet, Uncle Ray towered over him. He stood close to seven feet tall.

"No, I don't believe I have. Good to meet you, Donny," he offered. The big man smiled as he shook Donny's hand.

Uncle Ray's gigantic paw, as rough and calloused as a horse's hoof, swallowed Donny's hand like a squid devouring a starfish. "Any friend of Ralph's is a friend of mine, irregardless," he offered, looking at his nephew and cocking an eye. "So, what are you after tonight, Ralphy? You're always after something."

"Uncle Ray, would you mind showin' Donny your dog?" His uncle shook his head uncertainly.

"I don't know. The dog's had a big day, and I reckon he's tired."

"Oh, come on, Uncle Ray. Do I have to beg?"

"When did you ever stop begging?" The big man winked at Donny. "Oh, well, shoot. Let's see if that dog is awake." He looked around slyly. "Boozer, Boozer, WHAT'S THAT?"

Like a rocket launched from a catapult, a massive dog soared out of the cab of the bright red truck, vaulting cleanly through the open window without even touching the door. The quivering canine landed on the ground at stiff-legged, steeled attention: his tall ears cast forward, tense and poised. An ominous rumble rolled from deep within his barrel chest.

Faster than a rattlesnake's strike, the canine's shiny black head flashed to the right, then to the left. He leaped into the air and spun in a tight circle, executing a perfect 360 that left him precisely in his original position with his head cocked, awaiting his master's command.

He was a Doberman the size of a mastiff.

"Whoa," Donny breathed respectfully. "What a dog!"

"Down, Boozer," the big man barked. The transformation that occurred upon his command was startling. The dog palpably relaxed, sitting in the dust and blowing air through his lips. He yawned and began to scratch himself slowly, nonchalant and unconcerned.

"Give him a tomato, Uncle Ray."

"Oh, all right. Hey, Boozer!" The dog instantly stood up, his ears perked excitedly. "Let's eat a tomater!" The great beast bounded about like a puppy, quivering with excitement. Uncle Ray reached into the bed of his pickup. "This is his fourth one tonight," he said dolefully. "I hope he doesn't get sick." From a box in the truck's bed, he pulled out a massive green tomato. "You know that I bought these for Marvella to fry, Ralphy. I love her green tomatoes."

"Yes, sir."

"You'd better appreciate this."

"I do, Uncle Ray," Ralph replied, "and so will Donny. He's never seen it."

"Boozer!" the rancher boomed. "Stand up!" The dog instantly stood on his hind legs, straight and tall with marvelous balance. He neither quivered nor wavered, but stood at full attention, as still as a graveyard on a foggy night.

"Turn around!" In response to his command, the dog turned slowly in an elegant pirouette.

"Now, Boozer, CATCH!" He pitched the tomato high into the air. The dog dropped to all fours as the green prize soared almost out of sight, waiting patiently for its return. When the tomato was 15 feet from the ground and falling fast, the big dog sprang like a coiled rattler. He snagged it in the air, six feet above dusty parking lot.

Boozer landed on his feet with the trophy in his mouth. When he hung his head and bit down viciously, a fountain of bitter juice fired from his jaws in every direction, leaving a circular spray pattern in the dry orange dust.

It was an impressive display. Until this moment, Donny had never appreciated the amount of water that was stored in a large, green tomato.

"Whoa!" he said, laughing. "What a dog!" The sight was hilarious: the heroic dog expending such focused energy to snag a garden vegetable. He continued to laugh as the dog wolfed down the succulent morsel, chomp by juicy chomp.

"You better stop laughin' before he notices," Uncle Ray averred with a wink. "He gets a little cranky when his feelin's are hurt."

At that moment, the sound of squealing rubber was followed by the deep punch of metal heavily crunching against metal. The commotion caused their heads to swivel in one accord toward the highway. In the middle of the road, a mere 50 feet away, they beheld the accident that had caused the noise.

A brand new Sheriff's car had just shaken bumpers with a 70's era Oldsmobile 98. Needless to say, the patrol car had received the worst end of the bargain.

"Ain't that a sight," squeaked Yip. "It's a wreck! And durned if that ain't Sheriff hisself drivin' the patrol car."

The accident was more than a fender bender. In fact, if both cars had not been heavily armored tanks on the highway of life, someone could have gotten hurt. While Ray shut his dog in the truck, the other men hurried to the site of the wreck.

"Is everybody okay? Are you okay, Preacher?" hollered Yip, excited and solemnly officious at the same time. The Sheriff was already on the radio, calling the accident in.

"We're fine," replied the Sheriff. In the other car, however, the driver was slumped against the wheel. Donny ran up to the open drivers window and leaned in, then pulled away and grimaced in disgust.

"He isn't hurt," he called. "He's drunk as a skunk."

The drunken driver scarcely knew what had hit him. Having rendered his unfaithful disservice to family, country, and county, he proceeded to fall soundly asleep.

As he began to walk back toward the patrol car, Donny saw something that stopped him in his tracks. It was Jamie.

Seeing her in the back seat of the Sheriff's car, he recognized her as a teller at the local bank. But it was as if he had never noticed her before.

As Jamie stared at him, wide-eyed, Donny looked back, astonished by her beauty. *She is beautiful, just beautiful,* he thought, surprised that he had never noticed this fact. *What is her name?* He searched his memory for her name, but could not recall it. As he thought these things, Yip stepped up to the side of the Sheriff's car

"Looky here, boys," he crowed ebulliently. "It's that famous, newfangled female lawman, you know, the Major, the one that some folks don't like because she's a woman, or for other reasons they won't admit out loud because they're big fat hypocrites." He looked into the car, radiating concern. "Are you okay, ma'am? Kin I help y'all out?"

Delia Rawlings shook her head wearily. Her eyes met the Sheriff's, and they both smiled, sharing the same thought. *I sure hope he shuts his big mouth!*

"Put a cork in it," Delia whispered softly to no one in particular. Yip, however, was just warming up. He leaned into the car through Delia's window and perused the passengers in the back seat.

"Say, ain't you Janelle James, the new girl in town? You work at First National Bank, right?" Seeing their discomfort, Donny Hawkins came up behind Yip and put a hand on his shoulder, hoping he would back off.

"Miss James has lived in town for more than two years, Mr. Farley," Donny offered discreetly, trying to make the old coot look a little less foolish than he actually was. *Yeah, that's her name,* Donny reflected, *Janelle. They call her Jamie.* Donny had done business at the bank, and had talked to her more than once. *Why didn't I notice her before?*

"Why, looky there, boys, in the back seat. Look who it is," the old timer said loudly. He turned around to broadcast the news to the throng of onlookers. "It's Red Johnson! Red, you old hoot owl, what's brought you back to Oree County? I thought you was a big shot in Tallahassee with the Florida Department of Law Enforcement. Are you here on business? Why haven't I heard about you comin' to town? Don't nobody tell me <u>nothin'</u> no more!"

At this point, Donny could not restrain himself. He laughed aloud until, seeing Yip stiffen, he managed to suppress the outburst.

The old-timer turned around slowly and looked Donny up and down. A pained expression was etched on his tanned, leathery face.

"Donny, I always thought you was a good old boy, even if you wasn't too old," Yip rasped. "But now, I ain't so sure.

"I hate to say it," Yip continued, "but I think you're the one who laughed at me. Now, I didn't see you laugh with my own two eyes, so I can't swear that you're the guilty party. But irregardless of the truth, I've got to say it. It ain't right t'laugh at your betters, even if they ain't, and even if you wasn't the one who done it!"

Up to this point, Jamie had fought valiantly to hold back her laughter, but hearing Yip's words, she finally surrendered. She howled with laughter, forgetting her woes for one happy moment. Her glee was contagious, tickling the funny bone of the people who had gathered at the scene. Gales of laughter swept over the throng like springtime rain over a cabbage patch.

Hearing the crowd, Yip Farley blinked in surprise. He looked around at the laughing faces, trying to figure out what was going on. Then, he joined in heartily as if he actually understood what was happening. The laughter continued for several seconds without any indication that it might eventually subside.

As he sought to still his guffaws for the sake of his aching ribs, the Sheriff admitted that he had plenty of reasons to quit laughing. His star witness had been seen in public with a prominent official in the FDLE. The wrong people might catch wind of it, and their soldiers might show up in Oree County, ready to kill his star witness.

The evening had not gone according to plan.

The Sheriff stopped laughing, sobered by the realization that this untimely accident might come back to haunt them. And judging from the way things had been going as of late, the prospects for failure were definitely looking up.

Decision Point

For four years in the steaming jungles of Southeast Asia, the enemy had been expendable. To Streetcar, the enemy had been as alien and unloved as the pests that invaded the shabby little huts that were scattered like dung beetles across the face of the fertile land.

He had walked through those years and the horror of that war with The Mission enthroned in the center of his soul. The Mission had been his god: a lifeless, fickle, and unforgiving deity.

The Mission had given him a reason to live. It had offered justification for his hatred, a cloak to hide his lust for vengeance. The lure of The Mission, the drive to succeed at all costs against a brave and resourceful foe, had consumed his every waking moment. All the while, through the pain and the joy, through the good times and the bad, The Mission had ruled transcendent. Barriers to The Mission were circumvented, avoided, or destroyed.

The jungle heat was unbearable, but he learned to endure it. The coldest he had ever been was in 1970, during the first rain of the monsoon season when the temperature had dropped 30 degrees in a single hour. But even the calamity of that sudden monsoon had not deterred him from accomplishing The Mission.

Soaked to the bone in the monsoon rains, shaking so hard he could scarcely hold his weapon, he had hastily erected a small waterproof shelter and had broken out his emergency thermal gear: a thick, dry newspaper sealed in plastic. Stuffing the dry newspaper inside his wet clothing, he slowly regained his warmth and self-control. Above all else, he had survived to complete The Mission.

In those early years, at the formative cusp of young adulthood, he had learned that there was a time for everything under the sun. There was a time to avoid conflict and a time to engage: a time to attack and a time to run: a time to pass by and a time to strike: a time to preserve and a time to destroy. And there was a time, a perfect time, to utterly lay waste . . . a time to remorselessly, utterly destroy.

This is such a time, he said to himself. *This is a time to destroy.*

Questions Without Answers

At 11:00, a reluctant Detective Sergeant Jimmy Bristol ended a lengthy interrogation of Salvatore Benuto. Frustrated and unable to dig out badly needed information, the detective was compelled, nevertheless, to release him. He had no reason to suspect Streetcar's complicity in the terrible crime. There was no hint of wrongdoing on his part, now or at any time in the past.

The facts of the case, from Streetcar's rock-steady alibi to his 20-year history in Ybor City, cried out that he was a victim. But something was nagging at the detective. He was certain that Streetcar was hiding information, but he did not know how to squeeze it out of him. He would think about this for a while, consult with a couple of associates, and get back with Streetcar for further questioning.

Detective Bristol looked skeptically at the man who sat on the other side of his desk, slumped too comfortably in the heavy leather chair. The detective shrugged, stood slowly and stretched, his knees cracking as he took a long pull on his cigarette and launched a plume of smoke in the air above Streetcar's head.

"Well, I guess that's about it. A sketch of the perpetrator will be posted in every cop shop in Florida, you can count on that." He offered his hand. *After all, he is a former cop, and they say he was a good one.* After they shook hands, the detective handed Streetcar his business card. "Let me know if you think of anything you want to share with us, okay? Anything at all."

"Sure, Sergeant, okay," he replied with a bleary grin, "no problem."

"Is there anything else you'd like to say?"

"What, are you kidding?" Streetcar replied, avoiding a direct answer.

"I think there is something."

"Oh, man, I'm tired," Streetcar answered. "Thanks for offering a place to crash, but I don't think I'll stay here tonight. I gotta go."

"But, your home's still taped off. It's a crime scene."

"Don't worry, Jimmy. I know a few places to sleep. Do you think after 20 years on the streets, I don't have a place to crash?"

"Okay, well, stay around town, okay? We might need to follow up with another interview. And remember what I said. If you want to talk about it, give me a call."

"Sure, Jimmy. Sure." Streetcar turned and walked out of the room, escorted by the detective. As they walked down the hall on their way out, they encountered a woman in a red suit wearing a badge on her belt.

"Hey Sarge, aren't you assigned to the break in and assault at 22nd Street and El Camino Way?" the woman asked.

"Yeah." It was no coincidence that Streetcar lived in the area for which Jimmy Bristol was responsible under the Tampa Police Department's modified 'beat' system. They had become well acquainted because of that very fact.

"We've got a change of status on that case." Jimmy stopped in his tracks. *Oh, great, here's bad news.*

"Yeah, what is it?" He glanced at Streetcar, watching him closely.

"The victim died. Now, it's a murder. I guess they knew he couldn't make it. That's why you got the case, eh?"

Streetcar froze.

It was as if he were locked in ice: suspended, as it were, in time. Not a hair on his head stirred as he took it all in. Not a muscle twitched. Then, he blinked twice and swallowed slowly. He turned toward the detective, stiff and wooden.

"I gotta go," he said in a clear, calm voice.

"Yeah. Look, Streetcar, I'm awfully sorry."

"Gotta go," he interrupted, brusquely. "See you later."

"Okay. I'll see you, Streetcar."

"Yeah," he replied. He turned and slowly walked through the front lobby, past the marble entranceway and out through the big double doors. The evening was turning cold, and Streetcar paused on the steps, buttoning his shirtsleeves and turning up his collar.

His calm exterior did not reflect what was happening inside, where grief tore at his soul, flaying his open heart like a whip on a beggar's back. He felt dismembered, shorn not of just a friend but of a limb, as if his arm had been chain-sawed off. He was trying to orient himself, to understand what had just happened. Turning away from the station, he looked down the street, forcing his mind to shut down. And slowly, as he regained his equilibrium, he began to consider the details of The Mission that was now laid out before him.

Okay, it's a done deal, he told himself, mechanically. *Those pukes are goin' down.*

He began to walk swiftly down the deserted sidewalk, ignoring the traffic and the occasional squad car that cruised past, headed for the warmth of the station. The cold wind stirred dirty scraps of paper in the gutter and cut through his thin shirt, but by now, he did not care.

Streetcar had a mission. He had a reason to live for.

He had a reason to die for.

It was not a good reason. But for now, it was the only one he had.

Consiglieri

"Marky!" exclaimed the long-haired musician as he walked into the sedate, richly-paneled office. "Long time no see."

"Ace, what are you doin' down here?"

The question was not only figurative; it was literal. They actually were 'down here,' so to speak, in the luxurious, eminently practical underground warren that served as the clandestine headquarters of the Provencenti Family.

Ace had entered by his favorite back entrance, as he had done routinely for so many years. He had taken a short drive down 20th Street, parked in the protected lot behind an adult video store, walked down the steps beside the entrance into the office, and made a quick right turn into a gated vestibule. From there, he had used his key to pass through the gate and his old code to enter through the locked steel door. He had walked down the stairs and entered the heart of the Provencenti headquarters.

Of the several entrances into this complex, he preferred the one that he had just used. He never failed to feel a keen thrill when he climbed down the steps, opened the gate, and gained entry through the heavy steel door. The sleazy, run-down entryway reminded him vaguely of an old television show in which the central character, an American secret agent, would walk through a dry cleaning establishment to enter a palatial underground government building filled with spies, reeking of adventure.

If the FBI were informed about this place, they would never believe it. Under an entire city block of old Ybor City, hidden beneath a diverse set of antiquated buildings owned by mob companies and friends of the Family, was a labyrinthine operations center straight out of a John LeCarre novel. Built in the 1920s, 30s, and 40s, refurbished in the 70s and the 90s, the headquarters featured everything that an up-and-coming wise guy could need, from a conference room to workstations to recreation areas and a complete clinic for those awkward, embarrassing wounds from a stray bullet or knife.

Once upon a time, this headquarters had been Ace's second home. But once upon a time was long ago, in a former life that he wished he could forget.

Try as he might, he had not been able to put his past behind him. The past had reached out and touched him, and here he was, returning to the scene of his crimes.

"Please, come in, Ace," Marcello Betonini said warmly, rising to shake his hand. "Sit down. I haven't seen you in a month of Sundays." Ace took the seat and smiled as Marky shut the door and sat across from him, on the other side of an elegant tea table.

He hasn't seen me in a month of Sunday's? This guy slays me, Ace thought with a grin. *He's half Tampa hick, half old-style gentleman hood.* Ace, after spending the earliest years of his life in his mother's refined world of high art and sophistication, had never become accustomed to Marcello's curious blend of old country ethos, urban sensibility, and homey southern charm. In Marcello, Ace's one-time mentor and enduring friend, southern hospitality had seamlessly melded with Ybor City ambition and a dollop of Sicilian savvy.

The office was huge, befitting Marcello's official title as Consiglieri of the Provencenti Family. 'Marky,' as his closest friends called him, had done well. He was at the top of his game, a cagey survivor, fit and trim and flush with rude good health, a tall man who resembled Tony Bennett on steroids: lean and mean and as tan as an old boot, cut and ripped like a professional body builder. He wore his surroundings well, as if the entire underground mansion had been tailored to his design, made for him alone.

"You want a drink?" he asked, raising his eyebrows.

"No, thanks."

"So, what brings you here?" Marky asked as he lit a cigarette. He always was like that, cutting to the chase and moving on when he had learned what he needed. Ace scrutinized the Consiglieri, smiled and shrugged. *I might as well come right out with it.*

"To put it politely, my posterior's in a sling," Ace said. "Pop thought you might be able to extricate it."

Preparation

In the corner of a park, within a chain link enclosure, a sturdy shack squatted in ignominious isolation. It was a humble structure: a rusted and blistered steel building that sheltered pumps connected to three of the city's wells. Behind the squat pump house, in an area surrounded by impenetrable hedges, Streetcar found the pry bar exactly where he had left it. Two minutes later, he was extracting weapons from a hole beneath a nondescript concrete slab.

First out of the hole was the Glock, so recently taken from the hoods that had tried to kidnap Jamie. He had left Ellen's apartment and stored this particular gun while Ellen and Jamie were packing for their drive south. *Was that only yesterday?* It seemed like a lifetime ago.

Beneath the Glock, wrapped in several layers of plastic and parachute nylon and cotton cloth, was the AK-47. Like a 19th century archeologist uncovering a precious mummy, Streetcar carefully unwound the layers of material until he revealed to the gory glory of the classic weapon. It was his baby, a dependable tool for all-purpose assaults that had rested undisturbed, immured in grease since 1974. Cleaned and reassembled, he had no doubt that this particular souvenir would shoot as well as it ever had. Beneath the AK, packed in canvas, was a Colt .45 semi-automatic complete with five unused silencers, and beneath this weapon was pay dirt. Here, dressed in slick, pale-green wrappers, was the deadly core of his cache: pound after pound of C4 plastic explosives arrayed in square blocks, packed in neat little rows like soldiers prepared to march upon command.

As an ex-CIA field operative of the highest order with two classified Silver Stars on his record, Streetcar had managed to smuggle a cache of deadly ordnance into this country when he had returned from Vietnam. He had kept the cache for all these years, saving it like a hole card. "Some day," he had told himself over the decades, "some day, I might need this stuff."

Some day had finally arrived.

'Some day' was now, on this miserable night in this miserable place. Streetcar, the man who had observed Ybor City from street level for 20 years, now knew what to do with his cache.

Because he often suffered from insomnia, Streetcar had walked the empty streets of Ybor City on many a lonely night. He had seen things that few had heard of, things that even fewer would believe.

Streetcar knew the location of the Provencentis' hidden headquarters. He knew where the mobsters went at 3:00 AM, slipping into lightless doorways to disappear into darkened buildings. He knew which dignified brick landmarks fronted for the Provencenti Family snake pit.

He would devise a way to insinuate his deadly ordnance into their hidden nest.

He reflected that, as he had suspected for years, the war was not really over. It would never be over while predators crept through the cities of America like anonymous guerillas, like VC dressed up as American worker bees, humble and industrious with street clothes hiding their black pajamas, bland faces fronting for souls grown hard with greed.

The good old U.S.A. had become like Southeast Asia in the 1960s. It was swarming with traitors who were eager to destroy the peace. They waited until you relaxed, and then they struck.

You were resting in the clear sunshine, crossing a beautiful rice paddy, and they hit you out of the blue. That had happened to his unit in Vietnam.

They had been ambushed when they least expected it, and the day had turned out badly, to say the least. Just weeks after that fateful ambush, which had effectively eliminated his A team as a fighting force, he had been recruited by the CIA.

Streetcar remembered the day of the ambush with remarkable clarity. He could still smell the mud and the ripeness of the field full of rice, the faint hint of pungent smoke from a fire in the village more than a mile away. He could still hear the high-pitched laughter of children and the buzz of insects flying through the tall grass.

Journey to the East

As Sally Benuto's 12-man A team emerged from the jungle on that clear, sunny day, they heard workers chattering happily in the distance. There were two groups of workers in the field, one group harvesting rice on each side of the huge paddy.

The locals in this part of the South had a reputation as loyalists, but you never knew about these things. His team kept an eye out in every direction. They stepped out of the steamy shade into the hot sunlight, beginning the long walk down the narrow road that ran through the middle of the field leading back to their duty station.

The sun-baked paddy was bursting with life. It was a rich profusion of green and brown, filled with bizarre buzzing insects and flitting birds and arrow-straight muddy ridges adorned with ripe rice that glistened in the bright sunlight, rustling in the hot breeze. It was a particularly fertile field, wrenched from almost one square mile of wilderness: more than one-half mile wide and over a mile long. With blood and brutal labor, the field had been carved out of the voracious jungle by untold generations until it had assumed its present form as a pancake-flat, manicured paddy of steaming, ripening rice. From the air it was a neatly striped grid: straight, green rows of rice interlaced by hot black ditches filled with water.

The burning sun singed the air, tainting it with a yellowish hue that wavered tremulously above the horizon. Rising from the broiling mud in wave after wave of steam and earthy fragrance, the heat seemed intense enough to melt plastic. But for all that, it was a beautiful day.

Streetcar could still see the field full of rice and still hear the squishy trudge of boots. He could still feel the sting of a horse fly and the swat of his hand against his unshaved face.

The field stretched out before them in every direction as they drifted out into its vastness. It was surreally shapeless save for the redundant sweep of elevated paddies punctuated by hot, watery ditches. Far ahead to the right of the trail, he could see the only geographical feature of note. It was a single, solitary island of dry land, 20 feet tall and barely 50 feet across, overgrown with dense, low foliage.

If more than 100 soldiers had not passed down this path less than one hour ago and if this area had not been renowned for its lack of guerrilla activity, they would have approached the elevated island with greater caution, for their team was accustomed to adversity. But their radioman had confirmed that they were following a large group of soldiers, which meant that the field and everything in it had been swept for hostile presence.

To be safe, the Captain sent a man ahead to scout the hump of high ground in the middle of the field. After a time-consuming inspection, the scout reported that the hump, like the rest of the desolate paddy, appeared to be safe.

Streetcar was walking point at the front of the column. The Captain was behind him in the middle of line of men strung out in a straggling row. Streetcar's best friend, Wally Hamilton, was near the back of the group. He was a westerner, a fourth generation Montanan who would someday inherit a vast family ranch. For now he was just another Special Forces puke trying to make it back to the states in one piece.

As deadly as their past months had been, it was comforting to know that they were deep in the south in an area renowned for its relative safety. This was supposed to be a place where men could actually walk across a field in peace, where a team could conduct exercises without a sudden jolt of on-the-job training. Near the border with the North, where they had recently been stationed, their training had proceeded from the barrel of a gun. Today's was an easy mission designed to maintain a public presence in this rural, peaceful area.

Life had been slow and easy in the past few weeks, and they had savored the rest and recuperation. Their last duty had involved several months of deadly patrols and reconnaissance missions run out of a hell-breathing fire station - manned by his team, 12 A.R.V.N. special forces soldiers, and 700 montagnard tribesman – that had overlooked fertile mountains and valleys hiding part of the Ho Chi Minh trail.

As they slogged across the field, it was Richie Collins, the new kid from Philly, who first noticed the woman. The clarity of the day brought the distant scene into focus as the woman crept away from the small group of harvesters. She staggered heavily as she tried to distance herself.

"Look, Captain, check out the broad. She don't want to work, I guess," he said, puffing away at the unfiltered smoke dangling from his lips. "It looks like she's headin' our way." The Captain, a mere kid himself - but older than these grunts at 22 years of age - squinted and placed a hand over his brow to gaze at the faraway sight of a lone woman leaving the company of the workers.

"Hmmph," he said noncommittally.

"Don't worry, Junior," said Gary Turnbull, a hick from Louisiana, "she's just takin' a break. She's in a family way."

Streetcar had looked at the woman with minimal interest until he saw her bow down over a dry hill of rice. Somehow, he knew what was coming next.

"She's about to give birth," Sergeant Salvatore Benuto observed.

"No," Richie replied, "you're kiddin', right, Sally?" They continued their patrol, each of them turning methodically to cover every angle, scanning the workers and the horizon for signs of trouble.

"No, he ain't kiddin'," Gary blurted, "she's havin' a baby! Look!" The men stared at the sight, continuing their march across the paddy as the woman gave birth. Within five minutes, she had delivered her child. She stood up shakily, wrapping the baby in a piece of cloth.

"I'll bet that ain't her first baby, Cracker," Richie claimed. "That's what we call air mail. A woman's first delivery, it's almost always slow freight."

"How do you know that kind of stuff?"

"My mama is a nurse in a maternity ward. Shoot, I could tell you some stories that would curdle your hair."

"Don't ask me," Gary responded with his strong Cajun accent. "I don't know nothin' about birthin' no babies." The men laughed. The team enjoyed the continual crossfire between the Philly ghetto kid and the Louisiana Cajun who had become, surprisingly, best friends.

"Knock it off," the Captain said. "Keep your brains in gear." He had been around long enough to know that trouble often came when least expected. He was determined to ensure that this would not happen to his team.

"You heard the Captain, knock it off," echoed the Lieutenant. He was new to combat, but was not shy about asserting the Captain's authority.

"Hey," called Richie again, "what are those people doing?" The workers in the woman's part of the field had seen her, and they were gathering around her. An elderly man took the tiny, squalling baby from its mother and held it up for all to see.

"Ain't that heart-warmin'," said the Captain bitterly. "They're havin a baby shower. Eyes to post, men. Stay alert."

Several seconds passed without further comment. Sally Benuto was the next to sneak a peek at the woman and her fellow villagers. What he saw shocked him to the center of his soul.

At first, the sight was curious but innocuous. The old man was standing knee deep in water between two rows of rice. His bowed back was visible in the painful clarity of the bright sunlight, even at this distance. Stick-like arms were extended toward the earth, and his hands were hidden from sight, buried in the water between the rows.

Sal puzzled deeply, wondering about the significance of this strange tableau. Then he noticed that the mother was being restrained, held back by her fellow workers, and the baby was nowhere to be seen. The mother's desperate scream, piercing and poignant, wafted across the steaming paddy.

"They're drowning the baby," he stated matter-of-factly, scarcely believing it, even as he heard himself speaking the words.

"What'd you say, Sally?" asked Richie.

"I can't believe it!" he blurted. "The old geezer's drownin' the baby!" The whole team stopped and stared, unable to believe the cruelty of the moment in which a mother's joy had been turned to unspeakable horror and grief.

Surprise Party

Sometimes, even after you have grown accustomed to death and destruction, you don't expect it in certain situations and it catches you by surprise. That's what happened on that day. They were distracted by the unexpected execution of an innocent, newborn infant, emotionally caught up in the calamitous drama being acted out a mere sniper-shot away.

"No kiddin'," Sally breathed softly, totally unaware of what was taking place behind them. "They're really killin' the little guy." The idea crossed his mind that he should rescue the child, but somehow, he felt rooted to the spot.

The Viet Cong had done their job well.

One of them had persuaded a cousin who lived in the nearby village. As a result of his efforts, his entire armed cell had been invited to help the locals during the rice harvest. 'Extra hands to help,' the villagers had thought happily, promising to give a fat cow in exchange for several days of back-breaking labor. They had no idea that their visitors were guerillas, but they were about to find out.

No one from the village had seen them hide their weapons in the field, preparing for this very moment. The VC had been dreadfully clever.

Because of the relative safety of the area, soldiers at the local base returned from their patrols through this open field at the same, predictable time of day. The first group to pass by had been too large for the guerillas, so they had waited for a smaller patrol, continuing to harvest as they moved closer to where their weapons were hidden.

Now, realizing that their prey was distracted, the guerillas picked up their weapons and carefully assumed firing position, awaiting word to fire. The command, delivered with a single hiss, would come soon enough.

Sally's team, on the other hand, was transfixed.

One can train for an ambush, and one can sense an ambush. A team can be properly armed, deployed and alert, and in such a manner, prepared for an ambush . . . or as prepared as possible, given the nature of an ambush, which is built on surprise. But at this exact moment, the A team was more distracted and less alert than they had ever been on any patrol, anywhere, at any time in the past.

The sight of the dark blue, dripping baby and the hysterically weeping mother was dreadfully hypnotic. For the moment, they were captured by the event's bestial power.

The Sergeant had just turned away when the VC fired their first volley. A high-velocity bullet hit him in front of his left shoulder, blowing out through the middle of his back in a cloud of fine red mist as his body flopped loosely to the ground like a scarecrow severed from a pole.

As quickly as thought, the air was filled with the scream of projectiles and the bloody slap of steel upon flesh. A crackling sound arose in the distance and the entire A team dropped to the ground. Most fell involuntarily, bitten by an evil missile of fiery, hissing steel. Others hit the dirt instinctively, seeking cover where none existed.

Sally Benuto, diving to his left and rolled over the top of the rice hill bordering the main trail, dropped straight down into the hot, muddy water. Pandemonium erupted in the paddy as a mixture of cries, curses and prayers rose up toward the heavens.

Sally had been terrified many times during his tour of duty. But this time, strangely enough, he was unafraid.

He entered the dream realm common to people in shock. He felt no pain, and he knew no dread. He had a dim awareness of distant gunshots and a powerful, overwhelming rage: a burning anger beyond his anticipation and understanding. He burrowed down behind the hill of rice, hiding beneath the deadly swarm of screaming bullets.

"Who can fight?" He shouted at the top of his lungs. "Who can fight? Come over here!" From around him, hidden in the reeking paddies, he heard outcries. But in the wild clamor, he could not make out what was being said. Looking down the flooded ditch, he saw no one moving. Bullets ripped the air above his head, and the deep pop of more than a dozen AK-47s sputtered surreally in the distance. Although it was only mid-morning, the water was unbearably hot.

"Medic, medic!" called a voice close to him.

"Ohhh . . . " moaned another.

"Who can fight?" he screamed, raising his head to sneak a glance at the trail that they had just abandoned. On the trail he saw four bodies, none of them moving. *There's Gary,* he observed idly, looking at a body with the head twisted around and jammed underneath. *He bought it.* He marveled at the awkward position of the corpse. *How'd he wind up like that?* He could imagine no circumstance that could cause a man to fall in that particular contorted position. But war was full of surprises. He ducked his head and focused on the task at hand.

"I'm here," he shouted again, raising his gun above the row and squeezing off several rounds in the direction of the guerrillas. "Who can fight? Come here if you can fight." A bullet ricocheted off the stock and barrel, almost jerking the rifle from his hands. *Who are these guys, Olympic marksmen?* he wondered. *How many of our men are hit?*

He heard a splash, and looked up to see Vickers, a tough, skinny kid from Brooklyn. "You okay?" he asked the kid.

"Yeah. I lucked out."

"Did you see Wally?" Sal asked.

"Yeah. He took one in the leg; looks like it hit the bone. When I left him, he was behind cover putting on a tourniquet."

"Did you see anyone who can fight?"

"Everybody I saw was hit. Those guys can shoot, Sally. They shot the radio right off the Lieutenant's hip. Blew it to smithereens. The Lieutenant, too."

"They can shoot, all right," Sal answered. "They hit my rifle while I was waving it." *Great, trapped by super snipers with no radio.* A series of deep, heavy sloshes grew louder, and another soldier crawled up to them. It was Richie, the inner city kid from Philly, looking scared but game

"I can fight, Sally," said Richie. He was panting heavily. "I got this off the Turk. He bought it." Straining mightily, he slung a machine gun off his shoulder, dragging it up onto the side of the row of rice that was serving as their bunker. Looped around the other shoulder was a shoulder strap connected to a large can packed with a heavy ribbon of deadly ammo. Richie had somehow managed to drag both behind him until he reached his two friends.

So, the Turk is dead, Sal thought. The Turk had been a huge Mid-Western farm boy of mixed German and Turkish descent, six feet four inches tall and as wide as a barn, with 350 pounds of pure, power-packed muscle. He had always insisted on carrying an M60 machine gun, complete with a stand and box of ammunition, whenever they went out on patrol. While team members carried extra ammunition, the Turk refused, as a matter of pride, to allow anyone else to bear the burden of the gun, even when they were up to their armpits in steaming Vietnamese slime.

"I don't know how he lugged this thing around all day with the ammo. It's pretty heavy, you know."

"Give it to me; we're in luck. I have the other can." He pointed to a mud-covered ammo can among the greenery beside him. "Come on, get the ammo, let's get going," Sal added, feeling a wild jolt of adrenalin. *We're dead if we don't move out.*

"Where we goin', Sal?"

"We're going straight up this row; just make sure you stay down so they don't see you. I'll tell you as we go. Let's beat it!" They slogged low through the water and dense mud as Sally gasped out his plan.

When they reached the cut-through, they paused. In this gigantic paddy, a cross-flow canal cut across the field, flowing under the roadway through a huge terra cotta pipe. The canal cut through the long rows of rice mounds and flooded ditches, assuring an even distribution of water throughout the field. At the edge of this canal, they waited while Sal finished explaining his plan.

Desperate Measures

"**O**kay, you got it?" Sal asked hurriedly, looking desperately for a glimmer of awareness in the dull eyes of the two soldiers crouched beside him.

"Yeah."

"What do we do first?"

"We go underwater," Richie replied, "through the pipe, three rows up, then right. We come up out of sight behind the row, catch our breath, then go the rest of the way, two more rows, then right."

"What else?"

"We move fast. You take the big gun, and we take the ammo cans. We stay underwater as long as we can when we're in the cut-through canal, because Charley may be covering it."

"Right," he said, "now, pump it up, let's go." They took several deep breaths and slipped under the hot water.

In the still, quiet water, surrounded by relaxing warmth and surprising quiet, it was hard to realize that a moment ago, they had been at war.

No rifle fire was heard beneath the surface, no mortar round shattered the peace as they swam forward through the lightless murk, feeling past rice mounds of filthy mud and irrigation ditches until the pain and pressure and the hunger for fresh air were unbearable.

THREE!

They came up under the weeds at the edge of the third mound, quietly gasping for air. Here, above the water, the rifle fire was still crackling, including the familiar pop of an American M-15 assault rifle. *We must have a couple of survivors, anyway,* Sal thought grimly.

"Three more rows, okay?"

"Two more," gasped Richie. "It's only two."

"Yeah, he's right. It's two," added Vickers, fighting for wind.

"Okay, two more. Ready?" He paused briefly as they took deep breaths. "Go!"

Thirty seconds later, they emerged again behind a paddy, fighting to regain their wind and composure. They were at the base of the only raised piece of land for at least one-half of a mile in every direction. Over the years, as trees had been felled to build the rice field, the island had been spared by the local farmers, perhaps because of its hard-to-remove residue of powerful stumps and tough, springy roots. It was a steep little hill, rounded on the top and covered in brush, thorns and brambles.

Salvatore Benuto was confident of one thing: with no radio call for help and precious little fire being returned by his decimated team, the VC would move in to finish them soon like a tiger closing on a wounded deer. And as they moved in, part of their plan would be to take the high ground . . . this very hill.

Streetcar's Last Stand

Patches of pale, shaky light sifted through the heavy foliage as Streetcar came to himself.

It was late night in Ybor City. The air was cold, and the stars were beginning to come out from behind the heavy clouds.

Streetcar looked at the AK-47 in his hands. He had already finished cleaning it with the oil and the bone-dry cloths he had buried in plastic so many years ago. The dim streetlight, over 100 feet away, provided poor lighting for the job, but he did not need much light. He could clean and assemble this particular weapon in the dark. *It was a long bus trip 20 years ago from 'Frisco to Tampa carrying the AK and the C4 in my bag, but it was worth it,* he thought. For the task at hand, he needed his most dependable tool. The M-15 was a good gun, but for sheer, dumb reliability, nothing compared to the AK.

The M60 "Pig" air-cooled machine gun had been a dependable weapon, one of the best in the U.S. arsenal. A barely-portable cousin of the M2 heavy machine gun, it was almost as dependable as the bloody AK. Pausing for a moment as he cleaned the gun, Streetcar let his mind wander again to the stinking rice paddy, so many years removed from the alien, postmodern America in which he now lived.

In the sunny paddy that day, at the foot of a little hill in Da Nang province, Sally Benuto had quietly pushed the M60 up onto the dry land and climbed out of the hot water. Water poured out of the barrel as his men emerged from the ditch, panting and gasping for breath.

"You're in the Captain's place now," Richie whispered, his Philly bravado tempered by straightforward American courage. "Your plan'd better work."

"Come on," Streetcar hissed, "and look sharp for VC. If we make it to the top, keep your heads down until I signal you." They crept as quietly as they could, slowly dragging the big gun and the rock-heavy ammo cans. The brush was custom made for them, with thick bramble overhead and a two-foot gap underneath, perfect for crawling underneath without making the bushes sway. At the top of the little hump, Sal peeked carefully over.

"Oh, man, this is perfect," he whispered excitedly, "thin enough to see through, thick enough to hide us. Give me the ammo and go find a position." Carefully bellying over the edge of the ridge, he set the gun stand on the rounded hilltop, looking greedily across the field. Through the evenly spread, thin-leaved foliage, he could see the VC drawing closer. They dove over the paddies with smooth rolls, alternately pausing and firing as they covered one another in turn, leapfrogging ever closer to their prey, sliding down the ditches between jumps so no shooter could cue in on their position. *These guys are good.* He locked the Pig onto the stand and hissed to his men, who crawled back toward him.

"Both of you guys cover the gun. Don't worry about anything else. They must be on their way already. I'll take care of them if you protect the gun."

Richie looked around with a slight smile. Looking around the vast field, he could hardly believe that they had gained the high ground so easily. The VC must have decided that the risk of hiding someone here was too great, since every American team scouted this hill before crossing the field.

Like them, the VC must have been short on time, or they would have dug a hole and buried someone here. *Their mistake, our break.*

"This is perfect," Richie sighed over the distant, throaty pop of the AKs, "like Coney Island."

"What d'ya mean?" Vickers whispered.

"This'll be like shooting ducks in a Coney Island shootin' gallery." He crawled back to a level spot well behind the big gun, sheltered by a big root that provided a perfect rest for his rifle. "I'll keep an eye on the front door," he whispered hoarsely to Vickers, "you take the back." He pulled out his ammunition, and set it beside him, ready for quick use. The quiet click of shells sliding into the gun seemed oddly comforting. Richie glanced over at Vickers and noted that he had found a good spot to protect their back door.

"Okay, you guys," whispered Sal, "eyes and ears open. This is the high ground, baby."

"You got it," Vickers whispered softly.

"Okay," hissed Sal quietly, squinting down the big gun's sights. "When I fire," he added, "shoot at will. Nothing until then unless you have to." The VC were getting closer.

The fire from the American side had slowed to a faint sputter, and the enemy was taking advantage of the lull. They rapidly closed in for the kill as Sal waited patiently.

When the center of the group of VC was directly across from them, so close that he could throw a rock and hit everyone in the group, Streetcar squeezed the trigger.

Bloody Coney Island

Richie was right. It was like blasting ducks in a barrel, like Fire Island and Coney Island and every other gun-crazed vacation resort squeezed into a bloody, brain-rattling shooting gallery. The guerillas, concentrated into two rows directly in front of him, were as easy as targets on a shooting gallery shelf.

The compact deployment of the guerilla group proved to be its undoing.

Sally Benuto started the squeeze with the muzzle pointed to his right. He cut through the man on point and swept the fire rapidly up the row, then swung back to his left, see-sawing the gun up and down through the watery ditches, spraying deadly steel up and down each row. His first victims spun like tops and flopped like rag dolls as the rounds smacked into them. After the initial shock the survivors hit the water, desperately trying to hide in the shallow puddles or crawl behind unhelpful hills of rice.

They hid in vain. Sal swiftly and methodically panned the M60 up and down, wiping them off the earth with a profane outpouring of burning steel from the scorching muzzle.

To Sally Benuto, events unfolded at a painfully slow pace.

Time seemed to crawl out of the burly M60 like cold molasses poured thick from the barrel in a slow stream of smoking bullets that were sluggish enough to catch in his hand. Around Sally and his men, a fiery hailstorm of incoming rounds whined like riotous killer bees, chopping away at the underbrush that provided their cover. A few brave VC, realizing their desperate situation, charged the little hill in slow motion, but their efforts were in vain.

Sally mowed them down like targets in a shooting gallery: little human rubber duckies, faces contorted with pain and terror. But unlike rubber ducks, they refused to pop up again from their watery graves. They dropped on impact like men from a gallows after the pin is pulled: collapsing instantly, their limp legs useless to break the fall.

Sal burned through an entire can of 7.62 mm cartridges, mopping up the paddy until there was nothing left to mop. The bodies of fallen VC were scattered on the earth like fertilizer, splayed out in disarray, filleted and parsed by his own deadly hand. His ears rang and his eyes ran water from the gunpowder and dust, but he felt like a million bucks.

Sally was soaring on an adrenaline high. He was so pumped up, so invigorated by the hammering thud of the smoking gun, he did not hear or feel the ground-shaking bang behind him as Vickers, outgunned and outmanned, gave his all to protect their flank.

VICKERS HAD CRAWLED TO THE EDGE of the hill, covering the most obvious egress to the backside. His vantage point overlooked the watery rows that wound around the hill, close to the main canal.

The first clues that tipped him off were the ripples. The guerillas were approaching underwater. They struck surface at the foot of the hill, hidden by an impenetrable barrier of small, thick brush.

Vickers, guessing where they had surfaced, squeezed off a burst that was immediately answered by the dull pop of several AKs. If Vickers and his companions had not been lying on their bellies, they would have died. As it was, the relatively broad and level hilltop saved their lives. The bullets flew overhead, clipping the bushes, hissing like fire snakes as they passed.

A metallic clunk sounded to his right, and Vickers saw a grenade. He rolled over twice and came up with it, tossing it back down the hill, but the VC heard it coming and ducked into the water. As soon as the grenade detonated, their AKs began to fire again.

A second grenade sailed up toward Vickers. In a flash he saw that it would pass over his head and land practically on top of Sal and Richie. He lunged to his feet and jumped, catching it as a bullet hit him hard in the leg. His knee exploded and he fell forward, rolling down the hill, losing his grip on the grenade, out of control and unable to stop. He prayed and clutched at his chest as he tumbled down the steep slope, grasping desperately and pulling hard.

As he knew he would, Robert James Vickers rolled into the middle of the enemy. There were five guerrillas in all. The VC, superbly conditioned fighting men, instantly trained their rifles on him. But for some unexplained reason, they did not pull the triggers. They smiled, as if greeting an old friend.

"You die," whispered the leader, sticking his rifle to Vickers' head.

"Look," said Vickers. He opened his hands.

From the fingers of both hands dangled large steel rings. Straight pins stuck out from them, waving as if for attention. Vickers exhaled shakily.

"We die," he said, squeezing his eyes shut.

"AHHHH!!!" they cried, grimacing as four American grenades ignited on Vickers' chest with a flash and roar and a horrific explosion that blew shrapnel and Vickers and the five brave VC all over the surface of the muddy canal and the bloody little hump of land.

A Bad End

After loading the second ribbon into the gun and pumping more steel into the fallen bodies, Sergeant Salvatore Benuto paused for a while and carefully studied the remains of the guerillas. When he saw no motion, he grabbed his rifle and stood up.

"You stinkin' losers!" he shouted, falling back into the vernacular of Hell's Kitchen, "We killed you dead, didn't we, tough guys?" He laughed aloud, exhilarated by the sweet taste of victory. "AAAGH!" he screamed at the top of his lungs.

"We did it, didn't we Sally?" asked a weak voice beside him. Sal looked down to his right. It was Richie, lying on his back with a lost expression on his face. On the left side of his shirt a small fountain of blood welled out of an open chest wound.

"Oh, man!" Streetcar dropped to his knees, pulling out his bandanna and mashing it into the hole, attempting to stop the river of blood. The bandana sunk into the bloody hole and practically disappeared.

"Vickers!" he shouted, "Vickers, come help me! Richie's been shot!" There was no answer from Vickers, so he glanced over his shoulder and saw, with a jolt, that Vickers was not with them at the top of the little hump of land. His eyes flashed down a wide path, freshly beaten though the brush on the west side of the hump. The thorny shrubs were knocked down and blown apart, as if a log had rolled down the slope, and the bottom of the hill had been cleared with dynamite.

On a pile of dirt the foot of the dirty hump lay Vickers, or what was left of him. His lacerated body was half in and half out of the bloody water, mingling with the remains of the five dead guerillas. Vickers' chest resembled a concave platter of raw, shredded beef, strewn with bloody tatters of red and green cloth. Obviously, he had served as ground zero for the explosion that ended his life and the lives of the men around him. The rail-thin greaser from the Big Apple had died as he had lived: the bravest man in the battalion.

Vickers is dead, Sal reflected, stunned to the core of his battle-hardened soul. *He got himself killed. Great!*

Sal wrenched his attention away, averting his eyes. A lump swelled in his throat, and he choked it back with all his might. *Don't crack, Sally boy.* The heat of the sun swirled the colors together as sight, sound and smell mingled in an unholy symphony of discriminate slaughter.

The sky bent down and wrapped like smoke around the thorn bushes. It was a sun-hardened sky, oppressive and domineering, battering him with oppressive heat.

In spite of himself, against his will, Streetcar drank it all in: the day, the deaths, the loss of his friends, the rich brown earth stinking of gunpowder and blood, the sweat in his eyes burning like ice and coals of fire, the distant cries of the villagers insinuating themselves into the outermost realm of his hearing.

He was done for.

His face, hands and feet throbbed and tingled. They swarmed with the multitudinous pin-pricks of heat prostration: jangling nerve endings that waxed and waned, crashed and ebbed like waves on a beach, wave after relentless wave coursing through his burned-out body and mind.

He came to himself as if from a dream. He was on his knees, pressing powerfully against Richie's chest with his own, wadded shirt. He watched as the khaki fabric in his hands slowly bled through to crimson.

His mind retreated into shock. It all seemed peaceful now, as if it were happening to someone else. He was too stunned to think, too numb to feel pain but, mechanically, Sally Benuto was taking the right steps to save Richie's life.

Vickers, along with Wally Hamilton, had been with him from the beginning when he had first shipped into Vietnam. Richie had been a gutsy kid, new to the team but learning fast.

To Salvatore Benuto, the loner from Hell's Kitchen, these men were the best friends he had ever had on the face of God's green earth.

He did not notice the familiar thump of the Hueys as they passed overhead. The sound of the rotors was the heavy, mechanical heartbeat of this beautiful and horrible country: an essential pulse, but one that was often unnoticed. He did not know when the Huey's landed, did not realize that help had arrived or that the remnant of his lacerated unit was being evacuated.

A bird colonel was kneeling beside him, gently shaking his shoulder and speaking. After a minute had passed, he heard the colonel calling his name.

"Sergeant, let him go," the officer was saying. "The medics are here."

Medics? Streetcar thought numbly, *he might live?* He looked up to see two medics kneeling beside Richie. One was gently trying to pry Sal's hand off the bloody clump of cloth covering the wound that, for now, had stopped bleeding.

"Sergeant, we'll take care of this soldier," the medic said. "Your work is finished here," he added forcefully. Sal dully gazed up into the colonel's face. Standing behind the man was an unfamiliar-looking Special Forces captain, his expression as grim as death itself.

"Do you hear what we're saying, Sal?" the colonel asked again, "Do you hear us?"

He stared at the two men blankly, unable to speak as he slowly released his grip.

Refuge House

Janelle James stared at the Sheriff, the Major and the detective from FDLE. It had been a long and eventful day, and the excitement had not ended yet, although it was well past midnight.

She could not believe what she had just heard. Jamie leaned toward the Sheriff, shooting a nervous look at Ellen.

"So, you're telling me that you <u>have</u> to notify Federal officials? I thought that wouldn't be necessary. I've done all that you asked." *And I'm tired,* she didn't say. *If we hadn't had that accident in front of the nightclub, we'd have been in bed hours ago.*

Jamie was not paranoid, but she did not relish the idea that, thanks to their automobile accident, many more people would know of her whereabouts. With an entire mob family about to be impaled on the horns of her testimony, it was a bad time to be seen in public. Considering Jamie's comments, the Sheriff looked at Red Johnson and smiled tensely.

"Well, technically speaking," Sheriff Durrance offered, "our responsibility to contact Federal authorities is contingent upon the commission of a Federal crime. So it all depends on how our investigation pans out. But based on the evidence we saw today and your eyewitness account, it's safe to say that a Federal crime has been committed. That brings Federal law into play." Ellen put her hand on her friends arm.

"Look, I was in favor of involving the FBI from the beginning," Ellen said sharply, "but Jamie isn't in favor of it, and that's what counts. She's been through enough. She's the victim here. She ought to be able to determine where she lives, and where this case goes to court. She doesn't want to go into a Federal witness protection program." The Sheriff nodded.

"Florida has laws protecting victim's rights. Even if we didn't have those laws, I would take every possible step to ensure your safety. But don't worry about the Federal government," he added. "We have a sovereign jurisdiction, just like them, and a capital crime was committed in our jurisdiction. While we're holding you in protective custody, if that's what you want, it would take an order from a Federal judge to force you to leave. At this point, the evidence of narcotics trafficking is very weak. We have almost no physical evidence confirming the importation of illegal drugs, and we only have one living witness. Even if the drug evidence was strong, we have two exceptional lawyers running our State's Attorney's office. They're as good as anyone the Feds can throw at us.

"In the absence of solid evidence to support a trafficking charge, the state charges give us a compelling argument to retain jurisdiction. Florida's statute for capital murder is as tough as they get. All of these facts can help us if it comes down to a battle in the courts. I give you my word that we won't yield jurisdiction without a fight."

"Please fight, if you have to," Jamie replied. "I don't want to go anywhere else. I feel safe here. At least here, in Oree County, I'm pretty sure that nobody is on the payroll of the Tampa mob.

"Delia, don't take this wrong, I know you were on the force in Tampa, and I know that Tampa has a lot of good cops. But it would only take one bad cop to do me in." She looked around the room. "Since I have to trust somebody, I'd rather stay here. That's all I have to say." The Sheriff and the Major looked at each other with raised eyebrows.

"Well, you chose good people, if you have to trust somebody," Red Johnson said, clearing his throat, "Major Rawlings has a great reputation, and Tommy is a straight shooter, no matter what I say behind his back." He smiled, but nobody smiled back. They were too affected by the pathos of Jamie's situation. The Major glanced at Red Johnson.

"I suppose it's safe to say that nobody is on the mob payroll in Oree County," Delia observed dryly. "There's no money in it."

"But they're smuggling drugs through this county," Ellen said, glancing at Jamie nervously. Delia shrugged, a bitter smile playing on her lips.

"They don't need to bribe anyone to smuggle dope through this county," she replied. "It's just too big to cover effectively. With our small force, we can't cover one percent of the roads. And there's a lot of vehicle traffic on the truck route for cars and trucks to blend into. If they can get past the coastal radar, the rest is easy. They just fly it in and drive it away."

"Thanks for the encouraging words," Jamie said, smiling in spite of herself. "I feel safer knowing that the Oree County Sheriff's Department is uncorrupted due to lack of opportunity." She sighed heavily as her mind returned to more serious matters. "Look, please, just do whatever you can to keep me here."

"Yes, ma'am," the Sheriff replied. "We'll try our best."

"I'd settle for that, if I were you," Red Johnson commented. "I've known Tommy since grade school, and his best is usually good enough." Jamie was suddenly so exhausted that she could barely keep her eyes open.

"Okay, I'll settle for that," she said with a sigh. "I guess some people can remember grade school, so I'll take your word for it." Her wandering eyes settled on the Major, who was watching her quizzically, attempting to fathom the meaning of her last statement.

"You had to be there," she said. *I don't remember grade school,* she thought.

Listening carefully to her friend, Ellen understood what Jamie meant. *She must be exhausted,* Ellen considered, *to say something like that.* Her friend was normally obsessively private, slow to share any details about her life with anyone, at any time, for any reason. Ellen knew that Jamie remembered little of her life during her grade school years. The abuse from

Jamie's father had been so pervasive, so brutal, that her mind had locked out most of the memories.

Over the years of their friendship, beginning in middle school and continuing through high school, Ellen had put the picture of Jamie's younger years together from a mosaic of her own experiences with Jamie's father and a few confidential conversations. Now, seeing her friend's state of exhaustion, Ellen spoke up.

"Look, everybody, it's late. Let's all get some sleep, and tomorrow we'll feel better." The Sheriff rubbed his eyes, fighting back a yawn.

"Good idea."

"No, wait a minute," Jamie interjected. "I can't stay here much longer. Delia, you're a wonderful hostess, but this is too close to town. I may be in danger, and that puts all of you in danger. I need to drop out of sight. Way out of sight." The Sheriff, Major, and the FDLE detective looked at one another.

"We were talking about that earlier today," Tommy Durrance replied. "This case is big: too big for comfort. It's one of the worst crimes we've ever had in Oree County, and your testimony could damage the future of a major Mafia family. We've got to find you a safe place. A place where they'll never be able to locate you, no matter how hard they try."

"I think I can help with that," Red began slowly. "My wife's cousin, Burt Jenkins, is my best friend. He's got a house out in the middle of nowhere, and I mean nowhere. It's on cattle land that used to be owned by his wife's mother. There's no hunting lease, nobody out there at all but the cows and the hawks and the deer and maybe a stray turkey or two. I think you'd like it, and I don't think a whole army of hoods could find you out there. All I have to do is ask, and Burt will give me the key."

"Does it have running water?" Jamie asked hopefully.

"Oh, yeah, it's got everything, water, electric, central air, satellite TV, you name it. It's an old ranch house on a canal, close to a big lake. Burt's in-laws lived there until they got too old. When his father-in-law died, the old lady moved into town. She loved Burt to death. She signed the whole ranch over as a gift after their first child was born. He's renovated the place and kept it up.

"He uses it as a hunting cabin and a party place for his family and friends. Several times a year they have a cookout with big-time fireworks, barbequed hogs, the works.

"Anyway, he won't be there this year." He paused and began to scratch his chin, remembering his old friend. In the silence that fell on the room as they waited for him to continue, the hum from the refrigerator in the kitchen was the only sound. Ellen looked at him skeptically.

"How do you know he won't be there this year if this place is so nice? It's a hunting cabin, and you people hunt animals, right? Won't he use it for hunting?"

"He's gone to Paris to study art," Red replied breezily. "It was always his dream, but he gave it up after he got married. Now, his children are grown up and his wife ran away with a used car salesman. So last month, he flew to Europe. He's going to spend a year in Paris."

Red paused, looking around at them, conscious of the apparent absurdity of the situation. Yet in spite of himself, he was fascinated by his friend's artistic vision.

"He's says he's going to paint the redneck Mona Lisa," he added, looking around to see if anyone would respond. "He's going to call it the Minnie Lee."

The Sheriff glanced at Jamie. Seeing her suppress a smile, he decided to say what was thinking.

"Ah, Paris in the springtime," he intoned somberly. "Now, that would a place to hide."

A Vacation from R & B

"Okay, we can talk," replied Marcello, "wait just a minute." He shut the door to his office and returned to sit in an overstuffed chair beside an ornate Italian coffee table. "So, the Don sent you here? What a coincidence; he told me to expect you. So tell me, Ace, what is this all about?"

"It's about Joe Boy," Ace replied casually. "It's about the fact that he wants to whack me to make sure I don't rejoin the family business." Marcello did not look surprised.

Ace glanced toward the door and lowered his voice. "It's also about the fact that the Don has cancer, Marky, which might clear the way for Joey. It's like a bad play set in classical times. You know: ascension to the throne, blood and dishonor, all of that stuff."

"It definitely sounds like the formula for a classical tragedy. The Sicilian variety, that is."

"Yeah, that's the problem. If Shakespeare was alive, he'd be spinning in his grave," Ace replied ruefully.

Marcello weighed the message behind Ace's glib comments. He had been dreading this conversation since his last talk with the Don, and the moment had turned out exactly as he had expected. *Great. If I help Ace for the Don's sake, then, out of gratitude, Joe Boy whacks me after the Don dies.* He darkly meditated on the odds against them. *I guess that loyalty has its rewards . . . namely, a bullet in the brain.*

If Ace were not so cagey, Marcello might have considered setting him up after the Don's death. But Ace was too smart and suspicious to be set up, even after ten years of playing music in rock and roll joints, passing himself off as hippy scum. At this point in his life, Ace did not run with wise guys and had no reason to be around them. He would see trouble coming and would not be taken by surprise.

If Marcello wished to side with Joey, Ace would have to be killed by an outsider, and the killer had better be one of the best. But this approach was problematic. It would cost a fortune, and it might blow up in their faces. Better than anyone else, Marcello knew how dangerous Ace could be.

There was no safe bet in the coming battle. Marky wished that he could opt out of this conversation, but he could not. The Don was too smart, and he was counting on his consiglieri to help Ace come up with a non-violent solution to Joe Boy's deadly threat. The Don wanted both of his sons to live long and prosper.

The difficulty of this task was monumental. *I should whack them both,* Marcello reflected wistfully, *that would solve the problem.* He remembered how Alexander the Great had once solved an ancient riddle by cutting the Gordian knot in two. Perhaps that approach should be applied to the current problem.

Ace and his brother could benefit from such a cut.

But, in spite of these happy thoughts, Marcello still liked the two brothers. He had known them since they were pimply-faced adolescents, back when he was an up-and-coming wise guy admired for his stone-cold nerve and his appeal with the ladies.

"So, Ace, do you have a plan?" Marcello asked. Ace appeared to be irritated by the question, but he was simply preoccupied. *That's how Ace always looks with his game face on,* Marcello reflected.

"I don't know. A plan would be nice," he replied wistfully. "What do you think, Marky?"

"I think you've got two options. You can play, or you can fold. You can walk away from Florida, maybe go to a place where you could be safe. And somethin' tells me, that's what you really want to do."

"You've got it," sighed Ace. "I don't want to whack my brother, even if he is a pig. And I won't be safe around here if I don't. You know Joe Boy. He's never gonna change. He'll never trust me, and he'll always think I'm out to claim the Provencenti throne."

"So, what do you want to do?"

"Just what you think. I want to pull up stakes and make a clean cut. Move to another city with no major family presence. Maybe a small retirement community, a city in the Midwest; I don't know. Somewhere so far away, so out of the mainstream, that even Joey will realize that I'm out of the game."

"Where to?"

"I don't know." Ace scratched his chin fitfully, lost in his thoughts.

"So, what's the plan?" Marcello asked. Ace smiled at his former mentor. The elder gangster knew him well.

"Before the Don dies, I want to completely vanish. I need your help to disappear without a trace. The Don will approve it, and I'll see to it that Joey never guesses a thing."

"He'll know we've talked."

"No problem. You meet me tomorrow, 10:00 A.M. in the Don's office, and we'll work out the details with him. We'll make it look like you're offering me up, only nothing will come of it. I'll slip the trap and disappear, and it'll look like me and my wise-guy instincts saved the day. You'll be on Joey's good side for setting up the hit, and I'll be in the clear.

"Joey knows I can't hurt him if I'm not here in Tampa to shore up my old alliances. I've been out to pasture too long. Even Joey can be convinced that I'm not a threat if I'm not living in Tampa.

"I'll be gone, everyone will be happy, and the Don will smile on you because you solved the problem like a good consiglieri. No muss, no fuss, no blood on the floor."

"You malevolent little creep," Marky said, smiling broadly. *He's still got the touch,* he thought, surprised by the fact.

"Fix me a drink," Ace replied jauntily, "and I'll sketch out the details. Then, I gotta go. My band's playing the second shift at Dead Eye Dick's." Ace put his feet up on the table. "Maybe you could drop by. It's right down the street. Do you remember a girl named Toni Bartello?"

"Sure, who could forget her?" Marky asked, his eye's widening, "She was the ultimate fox."

"She still is the ultimate fox, and she's gonna be there tonight," Ace said. "She's my best girl's best friend. You might ought'a drop by, Marky."

Marcello smiled as he remembered the times he had spent with Ace, back when he was younger . . . much younger. "I don't know. Maybe." He lifted his brows. "I thought that maybe you were considering a vacation from the rhythm and blues, coming down here to talk. I thought maybe, you were considering a return to the family business." He smiled conspiratorially.

This was a bold move. The unspoken message was clear: if that's what Ace was considering, even with all that entailed, Marcello was signaling that he would be on Ace's side. In the complex world of the La Cosa Nostra, however, this could be a false offer. It was possible that Marcello was stalling to persuade Ace to remain in town so he could offer him up to Joey after the Don's death.

Whether Marcello was throwing his hand in with Ace or making a gambit on Joe Boy's behalf, it was of no consequence to Ace Feldmann. He had covered his bets, come what may. Ace had no intentions of ever, for any reason, returning to the family business. To make this clear, he acted as if he didn't understand the implications of Marcello's offer.

"Nah, not me, I can't come back into the business. I've retired to a life of leisure, and it's spoiled me rotten. Just give me that drink, Marky, so I can fortify myself before I go."

Underground Tampa

It had been a long shift, a double shift, in fact, and Pete Zachagnino was ready to sleep. But instead of sleeping, he was noisily slurping his seventh cup of coffee, preparing to endure at least four more hours in front of the flickering video terminals and glowing controls of the security room.

This was the hub. This was the nerve center of the security system that monitored the center of Provencenti family life. No expense had been spared when the family outfitted this room with every security gizmo known to humanity, or to the lack thereof. The room was filled with the best hardware available in U.S. spy shops. It flashed and whirred and beeped like a bad nightmare after a good techno-movie.

Pete was monitoring a bum in the doorway. It was 2:15 A.M.

The bum had been sitting against the front door for at least 15 minutes, busily ignoring street etiquette. It was commonly known that bums were not allowed to sleep in doorways in Ybor City, especially the Provencentis' richly marbled doorway.

Pete was annoyed with the vagrant and bored by the long hours he had spent in this darkened electronic womb. But in spite of all that, he knew enough to keep a low profile. He wasn't about to roust the guy without a good reason, and he was definitely not about to call the cops. *The cops mind their business, and we mind ours,* he reflected, smiling grimly in the flickering light of the monitors.

But now, as Pete watched the screen, the man on the street took direct action that was guaranteed to provoke a response from the most discreet racketeer. The man stood up, staggered slightly, and began to urinate on the front door. In the monitor, Pete could hear the man mumbling as he doused the expensive door with its burnished brass and

Indonesian mahogany. Petey sat up with a jolt and grabbed the microphone, punching the button.

"Could somebody go to the main entrance, right away? There's a bum whizzin' on the front door." Downstairs, a wise guy in the middle of a game of Go Fish threw down his cards in disgust and stood up. It was Nicky the Nose, a. k. a. Nick Matalona.

"Jimmy, if I didn't know any better, I'd swear you were a card mechanic," he rasped roughly to his partner, Big Jim. "You get all the good hands, and we get nothin'." *Oh, man!* he thought, reaching for his neck and grimacing, *It hurts when I talk!* Nick's throat felt as if it were on fire. When he tried to swallow, it was like gulping down a prickly pear.

"I'm out'a here," he whispered, ignoring the pain, "I'll get rid of the bum." He shrugged on his trench coat and picked up his hat. "I'm going to the store while I'm out. There's nothin' to eat around here." *Nothing for me, anyway,* he reflected ruefully, *no oatmeal or ice cream, or anything you can eat through a straw.* "You guys want anything from the store?"

"Yeah. Women. And one of them has to like big, stupid hoods with noses the size of Dominican plantains." Jim was still game for an argument, in spite of three cracked ribs that made every word a painful experience.

"Hey," Nick rasped angrily, "watch who you're calling stupid!" *Ouch!*

"I wasn't talkin' about you, Noser," Big Jim replied. "I was speaking theoretically."

"Right!"

"Well, you gotta admit, you've got a whale of a nose there on your face, Nicky. It's a classic: the schnozz that launched a thousand Kleenex." Jim started to laugh at his own joke, but the pain from his broken ribs cut him short. *Ouch! Man, that hurts!*

"Same to you," Nick whispered, "wise guy." His eyes watered from the pain as he turned to walk up the stairs. *I'll handle that bum in the doorway. Maybe I'll make him pay for the sins of his fellow bum, the one who hurt my throat.* Nick burned inside, remembering how Streetcar had taken away his reputation and his pride. *Oh, yeah, this bum is gonna pay. He's gonna pay big-time.*

Nick had been released from the hospital less than 12 hours ago. He could barely swallow, and could only speak in a whisper.

In the central security room, Petey Z was fit to be tied. "Hurry up! The front door is an antique," he said over the intercom. "It cost thousands of dollars." He was incensed at the vile desecration of such a door. To Pete, a worshipper of material goods, it was as if someone had defiled an altar. "What a lowlife!" he cried passionately. "What a bum!" In one of the monitors, he saw Nick climbing the stairs, headed toward the front entrance.

Petey smiled as Nick waved at a security camera. "That's a good man for the job," he told the empty room. "Hey, Nick," he said, punching the button on the intercom, "nuke the bum, okay? Nuke him good."

Nick saluted the camera and felt in his pocket for the blackjack. *Here it is,* he thought with excitement, hefting the heavy, flexible sapper. *This is gonna be a good night, after all.*

Nicky loved to hit people in the head.

Awakening

At 2:17 AM, Jamie fell asleep. Within minutes, she had begun to dream.

Jamie was standing in the middle of a cloud. Around her, a diffused light illuminated the dense vapor in every direction. She could see the smoke clearly, as if it was backlit by the sun, but she could not see through it. In every direction, the strange, radiant fog swirled slowly in the light.

Permeating the fog was an unspoken peace, a sense of mysterious serenity. In the midst of the cloud she felt strangely secure. But then, as is often the case when peace arrives, the troubles of her heart arose like splinters emerging from deep within her soul. She began to recall the events of the past few days.

The images cut her soul like shards of glass working their way out of her memory: Saturday night's trip to Homeland Estates, the lights in the road, the gunshots through the windshield.

Johnny was dead.

"God, why?" she said aloud, "Why Johnny?" A cool breeze began to blow, lightly touching her skin. A halo appeared above her as the mist was stripped away to reveal her surroundings.

She was drifting high above earth, sailing among the stars, safely hidden at heights that no man could approach. The halo that had appeared above her head was the crescent moon, shining through diaphanous clouds. She experienced a marvelous, soaring sensation as she drifted free and easy through the clear evening sky.

Beneath her feet, one mile below, the lights of downtown Tampa winked and glimmered. The city was beautiful from up here, high above the suffering and despair. She remembered Johnny's death and tears began to run down her face in spite of the beauty of her surroundings.

Words from the recent past returned to her mind as they had when she was hiding in the warm Florida lake. The words were a remnant of her parochial education, simple words of faith: a prayer that she thought she had forgotten long ago. "Jesus help me. Christ my Savior, deliver me." she murmured aloud, turning over in her bed.

She awoke in a room without walls, in an area defined by whiteness. Ahead of her she saw Johnny approaching. He stepped across a red line in the floor, a division of some sort between their world and hers, and walked up to her.

Seeing him in front of her, she was overwhelmed by the memory of her loss. As she hugged him, she began to weep uncontrollably.

"Johnny, I miss you. You were my best friend. Come back, please, please Johnny, come back." Johnny alarmed by her grief, turned to look behind him. Jamie felt a light touch on the arm that was wrapped around Johnny's back. She was filled by a rich, wonderful peace: beyond anything she had ever known, or ever knew could exist. Her sorrow, her pain, her fear rolled from her like a physical weight lifting from her shoulders. In place of the pain was a deep and powerful peace.

Johnny was safe. She knew that, somehow. No one could hurt him, ever again.

A memory returned to her. She recalled a night when she had driven to the coast with Johnny. There on the beach, they had walked and talked until dawn, and had spoken about life and death. Johnny had shared his views on the Christian faith, a faith that he had rejected early in life but had recently returned to. She had been glad for him, glad that he had something to believe in. She wished that she had been so lucky.

Johnny was gone. But somehow, she knew that he was safe. He had made it into the heaven of his faith.

Torn with grief and crying uncontrollably, Jamie saw a man standing behind Johnny. She almost recognized him. Unexpectedly, she saw tears rolling down the man's cheeks.

He's crying with me. He's hurting because I am, she thought. She was shocked by the realization. The man gazed into her eyes with a look of immeasurable love and untold understanding.

With a flash, she recognized the man who wept at the sight of her pain. It was Jesus Christ.

"Oh God," she gasped, "have mercy on me." She bowed her head in awe mingled with sorrow as the tears poured down in an unstoppable deluge.

In spite of it everything that had happened, she realized that God was good. What had happened to Johnny was not God's doing.

God was innocent, totally innocent, totally caring, profoundly concerned. He had given Johnny's killers the gift of free will, and with their freedom had come power: power to do good, or to do evil. It was they, not he, who had murdered Johnny.

Jamie felt another touch, and she opened her eyes and looked up. Ellen stood beside her bed, shaking her by the arm.

"Jamie, wake up," Ellen said softly. "You were talking in your sleep." She did not have to add that Jamie had been crying. Jamie stared up at her friend with tears coursing down her cheeks.

"Ellen, I saw Johnny," she gasped, "I saw him. He was with Jesus." A rush of emotion surged within Ellen as she struggled to comprehend what she heard.

"It's his faith," Jamie breathed, "Johnny told me about it, and now I understand."

"Jamie," Ellen sighed, "what do you mean?" She was beginning to wonder about her friend.

"Johnny believed that God wants to give us a better life. And after this life, He wants us in heaven with Him."

"Johnny was a great guy," Ellen said noncommittally.

"Ellen, I didn't believe him. But now I do."

"Jamie, it's okay," she said, "I understand. You've been through a lot. It was just a dream."

"No, really," Jamie said, sitting up and drying her eyes, "I saw Johnny." Realizing what Ellen must be thinking, she looked at her friend with pity. *Ellen doesn't believe me.*

"It was just a dream," Ellen said carefully, "I'm glad it was a good one."

"Yeah," Jamie said smiling. No matter what Ellen might say, Jamie was comforted beyond measure, wrapped in the warmth of that dream and of the memory of its grace. All the skepticism in the world could not take that grace away. "It was a good dream."

"Good. Well, you'd better get some sleep," Ellen said. "We're leaving before dawn to move you into your new home," she reminded her friend. Jamie stared out the window, remembering her dream and how the evening sky had looked over Tampa.

"Yeah, we're leaving before dawn," she mumbled sleepily. "You go on to bed, Ellen. I'm okay." Her friend turned around and, with a backward glance, left the room and quietly shut the door.

Jamie rose and softly crept to the window. Opening the curtains, she looked up into the cold, cloudless night sky. In this rural part of Florida, the stars shone so clearly they could be counted, if one had the time and could count that high.

They dazzled her from the deep of the void. They were shimmering clouds of light, silent swarms that glittered with heavenly prominence. Each star, unique in its light, openly declared the depth of the creativity behind its design.

"Thank you," she whispered silently, treasuring her awakening faith. "Thank you for loving Johnny."

She did not fully understand why Johnny's murder had been allowed. She knew that God could have intervened to stop it. She could not fully discern why such evil was allowed to exist, but she made a conscious decision. She would not require a reason.

She would take it all on faith.

"Jesus, I believe that you are the Savior of the world." It was an intensely personal moment. She was alone with the stars and the One who had long ago severed the day from the night. She did not know what her decision entailed, but she knew that God would show her what to do. *He that believes on the Son shall not see death, but has already passed into eternal life.* Where did she hear those words? She recognized their truth and thrilled to their meaning.

She would see Johnny again. Though the heavens melt and the earth pass away, she would see him face to face. Life, exploding in joy from an earth that could not restrain it, had long ago left death in its wake. In due time, death would become the forgotten plague of a past that could no longer cause pain.

On that day, its merchants would be shocked to discover that there was no future in death, after all.

Alas, Poor Nicky

Nick the Nose was surprised by the blast of ice-cold air that greeted him when he opened the front door. *Man, that's cold,* he thought, *it must be close to freezing. It's a good thing I wore my trench coat. Too bad I didn't put in the liner.* Nicky never paid attention to the local weather forecasts, and tonight he was living to regret it.

He looked around for the bum. The covered entranceway was empty, but an acrid aroma hung in the marble entranceway like a skunk at a dinner party. He could see the steam drifting like evil smoke from the painted ceramic tile at his feet, to the left of his expensive Italian loafers. *Great. The Don's gonna be happy about this. I wonder who gets to clean it up.*

As Nick considered the sheer, witless nerve of this particular wino, his blood boiled. The thought that he and Jim might be called upon to clean up the mess on a cold night like this made him even angrier. *I'm gonna find that freak, and I'm gonna hurt him.* He pulled a two-way radio out of his pocket.

"Petey, can you hear me?"

"Yeah, I can see you, too," replied Peter Bono from security central. "Oh, no, Nick!" he cried in panic, "What's that giant lump hangin' off your face." There was a pause. "Oh, gee, sorry, man. It's just your nose!"

"Hey, you don't know me that good," said Nick, edgy and dangerous. "Don't push it." His reputation for murder was earned the hard way, and his comment sobered up Petey Z immediately.

"Sorry, Nick. I was just kiddin'"

"Yeah, right, whatever." He fought back a sneeze, knowing that if he gave in to the sensation and let it go, the pain in his damaged nose and throat would be almost unbearable. "Now look," he whispered into the radio, barely able to force the words through his damaged larynx. "I'm gonna make this bum regret his choice of lifestyle, then I'm coming back in. Don't make me wait at the door, neither; it's cold out here. You got it?" It was bitterly cold, and Nick wanted to put a sweater under his trench coat before he walked to the all-night grocery store.

It's a good thing I'm wearing my hat, or I'd be freezing. Nick was not exactly an arctic adventurer. He was nothing if not warm-natured. In fact, he was as thin-skinned and cold-blooded as a North Sea shark. He hurried out of the doorway onto the street, eager to finish the job at hand.

He looked down the street to his right and paused for a moment, listening. Nick heard something behind him and turned to see the street person swaying in a doorway down the street, humming and rocking as he swigged at a bottle of cheap wine. The bum's back was turned.

This bum is a real loser, out here in the freezin' cold in his bathrobe, Nick reflected. *This will be fun.*

He crept up softly like a lion at a waterhole, inching closer step by predatory step as he silently slipped the blackjack from his pocket. He was primed for action and ready to strike

But a funny thing happened on the way to the waterhole.

A scrawny little kid grew up in the toughest part of Brooklyn. He became a man, made his bones, got into some trouble. As a kid he won a few fights, lost a few wars, joined a gang, hijacked a few trucks. Then he got unlucky and fell under the influence of older, wiser thieves.

When he turned 21, he got into some trouble and was farmed out to the Provencentis. Arriving in Ybor City, he cut his teeth in the Southern rackets, learning discretion, obedience, and fidelity to his Don. He became a man, in a sense. Along the way, he made some bad choices, including the worst he ever would make.

He never turned back. He stayed with *La Cosa Nostra*. He stayed, and he prospered, and he became the right hand companion of Big Jim, a made man in the Provencenti Family.

This was what damned little Nicky Matalona. It was not his choice to use violence and not the violence itself, as bad as that was. What damned Nick was his impenitent refusal to change. It was the complete absence of faith nurtured by a refusal to seek the will of God. He had laughed at the very idea of turning from his chosen path. And on this day, at this very moment, his time for turning around had run out forever.

As Nicky raised the blackjack to smack the bum, something happened. It happened so quickly, so smoothly, that his mind could neither track nor make sense of it.

Something seemed to explode in front of his eyes. He spun like a gyroscope that had lost its center, spinning into a darkened alcove as the brick and tile and glass whirled around him. Landing on the back of his skull with a crunch and a sickening thud, he felt an agonizing pain in his head but nothing from the neck down.

It was as if his head were a balloon: untied from his body, lighter than air. Was he floating? What was happening to him? He smelled the stench of the street: the stale urine, rotting garbage, dirt on the cobblestones, cigarette butts.

The scents were crisp and sharp in the cold autumn air. *I must be lying on the sidewalk. But where am I? What's happening to me?* Nick had awakened on the sidewalk more than once during his checkered career, and the aroma was not totally unfamiliar.

A face floated up next to his. He recognized it immediately.

"Streetcar, you stinkin' bum," he tried to say, but managed only a painful sigh.

"It's me, you puke," said Streetcar. "Do you recognize me?" Nick's eyes widened in fear and recognition.

"I just broke your neck, you stinkin' puke. That's the way we do it in Hell's Kitchen. That's in the big city, you stinkin' hick!" Streetcar cleared his throat and spat in Nicky's face. "That's for killing my friend, you scum. You're a disgrace to your people.

"This one is for me." He pulled back a fist and smashed it into Nick's limp face, breaking his jaw and ejecting three bloody teeth in a single explosive blast of pain that shot through Nick's mind like sparks of agony from the furnace of hell. The blood welled in his mouth as Nick Matalona struggled to breathe, choking on his own vital fluid. "You want vendetta, you got vendetta," Streetcar hissed.

"I'm killin' you now, you puke. I'm killin' you dead. Then I'm puttin' your coat and hat, and then I'm gonna visit your pals. Thanks for wearing the trench coat. I can hide an armory under that thing."

The pain and terror on Nick's face troubled Streetcar. His victim looked like a teenager who was losing a schoolyard brawl: small and terrified, shaking like a leaf, like a scared little squirrel trying to race out from under the wheels of a rapidly approaching tractor trailer. This was not what Sally Benuto expected or wanted to see. *I gotta do it now, or I'll back out.*

"Say good night."

He struck a sharp upward blow at the base of Nick's nose, driving the bone into his brain.

The sight of Nick's death was unspeakable. It was beyond sickening. The black blood welled out and poured across Nick's face, covering it like an executioner's hood as his head banged on the pavement spasmodically and the flickering light faded from horrified eyes.

Streetcar rolled over and threw up, his sides heaving involuntarily until his nose burned and his eyes poured tears of hot, dirty water. *Don't think about it,* he said to himself. *You still have work to do.* But he could not forget the lost look in Nick Matalona's eyes. He felt sick inside: violently sick.

He looked just like Vickers. But Vickers had been one of his own men.

Vickers had been a stand up guy on his combat team. This dead gangster had been something else entirely . . .

hadn't he? *This guy was the enemy,* Streetcar told himself unconvincingly.

This was wrong. This was a sin. The vendetta should end now.

It felt wrong. It was wrong. There was no getting around that fact.

But like Nick Matalona, Sally Benuto had made up his mind. Turning from life, he chose revenge with the full knowledge that, for him, revenge could prove to be a blood-slicked superhighway to hell.

This was not business; it was personal. It was bitterly, cruelly, and unrelentingly personal. Revenge was what he hungered for, a dish best served hot: an evil offering poured over a stone-cold soul. He ached for revenge, unmingled and uncut: pure and simple and bitter as hell itself.

This was not an eye for an eye or a tooth for a tooth. The Provencentis would pay with a head for each eye and a life for each tooth.

Jumbo had been the best. And now, remembering his friend, Streetcar deliberately hardened his heart.

He would punish them. He would destroy them using all of his skill, all of the training of his past. They were the enemy; they had earned all of the dishonor and the bitter disgrace that he could possibly dish out. He would hurtle them into the burning mouth of hell . . . even if it cost him his breath, his life, and his only immortal soul.

Static

In the downtown headquarters of the Provencentis, Ace Feldmann was sharing a drink his old friend Marcello. They had heard the announcement about the incontinent street person and glanced at each other in amusement. Ace raised his eyebrows.

"Who'd'a thunk it," he began. "A bum has left his mark on the front door. It's a crime against humanity. This isn't gonna go over well with the Don."

"Oh, no problem," replied Marky with a wink, putting his feet up on the coffee table. "You know he won't take it seriously." In spite of his words, they both knew that Ace's father was as fanatical about cleanliness as he was about security. 'The Bountiful Don,' he was sometimes called behind his back due to his affinity for Bounty paper towels and his propensity for straightening up every room he entered. Don Provencenti left no table unwiped, no ashtray undumped.

"The Don would have a conniption fit," Ace quipped. "He'd probably revert to his youthful ways and waste the guy right on the spot." The thought cheered him up considerably. "What do you think, Marky?"

"He'd have a conniption fit," Marcello said, "but you gotta love the Don."

"Of course, you <u>gotta</u> love him."

"He's a generous man."

"Downright bountiful."

"He cleans up every mess."

"He's the quicker picker upper," blurted Ace, saying what they had both been thinking. They shared a hearty laugh, forgetting, for the moment, the deadly circumstance of their reunion.

Beginning of the End

Petey Z watched the video screen and smiled, taking a loud bite out of his crunchy garlic bagel. *Veggie cream cheese is the best.* He pushed the button and leaned toward the microphone.

"What's the magic word?" he asked the slouched figure in the front doorway.

"Maledictum," a deep voice rasped in reply. "Maledictum doloros."

Maledictum, Petey smirked. *What's that?* He buzzed the door, and the figure in the hat and long coat stepped into the front lobby of the citadel. He was buzzed past two more security doors as he walked down the steps to the first sub-level.

The man moved brusquely. On the small black and white monitor, he looked like a figure from an early silent film moving swiftly and jerkily, resolutely hustling down the hallway. *What's with Nicky?* Peter wondered. *When did he start to move like Charlie Chaplin?* He flipped the switch to the microphone and cleared his throat.

"The coast is clear, men," he announced to the boys playing cards in the basement. "The chemical assault on our fortress has been halted, and our dignity has been restored. It is now safe to leave the bunker." He smiled and leaned back in his chair, not surprised to hear pounding on the door. *That's Nicky. He's gonna give me grief.*

Petey was only half right.

To tell the truth, Petey Z enjoyed it when Nick the Nose gave him a hard time. Almost anything was better than the soporific boredom that he endured night after night after night, alone in this gloomy room. Hearing a knock at the door, he leaned back in his chair and hit the entry switch.

The figure in the coat backed into the room, crouched over to appear smaller than he actually was. He appeared to be carrying some kind of container.

"Sure, whatever you say," the man whispered, as if addressing someone in the hallway as he put the container on the floor. "I gotta go now." As he backed into the room, Peter recognized the container as a plastic gas can. *Did Nicky run out of gas? What's that about?*

The man hung his hat on the rack, unbuttoned his coat and turned around, reaching into his waistband and raising his arm. With disbelief, Petey realized that the man straightening to his full height in front of him was not Nick Matalona at all. It was Streetcar, the bum who had given them so much trouble lately. Beneath his trench coat, Streetcar was dressed in well-worn combat fatigues. In his hand, held loose and low like a card about to be dealt from the bottom of the deck, was a large stainless steel combat knife.

With a sickening adrenaline rush, Pete realized what was about to take place. He reached for the gun beneath his chair as Streetcar's hand whipped upwards. The blood in Petey's ears pounded once, twice, and seemed to pause.

Petey's hand was halfway to his pistol by the time the knife left Streetcar's hand, headed in his direction. The knife turned lazily end over end as Petey's fingers wrapped around the butt of his gun, and he began to pull it out of the holster.

As the heavy combat knife drew closer, Pete's mouth began to open. Then the knife rammed into his heart with excruciating power, bringing a jolt of pain beyond any he had ever imagined. The shout of warning stuck in his throat and ended in a strangled gurgle, bring with it a light, foaming froth of hot crimson blood.

It was as if a chainsaw had spit Peter's chest and a bucket of molten lead had been poured into the wound. He could not breathe. His eyes lost the ability to see as an incredible weight crushed his chest unmercifully, squeezing the life from him. The roaring fire of agony washed over him completely, carrying him away from this beautiful earth: far from the fair blue planet lit by its luminous sun. The bitter flame of death carried him into another realm.

Peter awoke in the home of darkness. Here was a palpable sense of separation from all that is good. Here was isolation: immeasurably profound aloneness that could be felt and touched, if touch were possible in such a place.

He sank like a stone into the torrential depths in the midst of a lightless, flaming sea.

STREETCAR WATCHED as his victim fell. He kept the gun trained on the man, but he knew that a bullet would be unnecessary. His aim had been true, and the corpse had barely twitched as it hit the floor.

He wrapped Nicky's muffler around his right hand and walked over to the corpse, planting his boot on Petey's bloody chest as he pulled out the knife. Blood gurgled from the wound like oil bubbling out of the earth, sheeting across the chest to join the growing puddle beneath the forlorn form.

Streetcar straightened up and wiped the knife and his hands thoroughly on the muffler. Pulling a small handheld cassette player out of his shirt pocket, he placed it beside the microphone on the control console and hit the "send" switch. When the sound was amplified through the speakers that were strategically placed throughout the complex, the tiny cassette player had surprising quality and depth of tone.

It was Hank William's rendition of his most famous song, "Your Cheatin' Heart."

Cold, Cold Heart

"Your cheatin' heart," the song blared, "will make you weep." Taking off his gun vest, Sally Benuto reached into the large back pocket and pulled out block after block of green C4 explosives: eight blocks in all. "You'll cry and cry," the country crooner wailed plaintively, "and try to sleep."

Last out of Sally's vest were the timer, the wire, and a battery wrapped in plastic. He carefully assembled the C4 and wired it together, setting the timer for 15 minutes.

"But sleep won't come the whole night through," Hank insisted from the depths of his being, "you're cheatin' heart will tell on you."

The words and accompanying music faded from Streetcar's attention as he concentrated on the task at hand. He examined the neatly wired package, inspecting his handiwork and nodding in approval.

Sally Benuto stood up. Pausing for a moment, he looked at the gun in his hand and smiled. It had taken a remarkable feat of engineering to silence the blast of a U.S. Army issue Colt .45 semi-automatic handgun, but the nerds in the CIA labs had been up to the task way back in the late 60's when his silencers had been manufactured.

The silencers in his possession were still state of the art, as good as the best available on the black market. They downsized the ear-numbing blast of the Colt to the austere, muffled cough of an English butler with a cold.

He carefully walked down the hall with his handgun raised and the AK slung across his back. The rifle was a weapon of last resort that, he hoped, would not see action in the early hours of this dark and wasted autumn morning.

IN THE LOWEST LEVEL of the complex, two men smiled as Hank William's song of unrequited heartache blared from the speaker hidden in the ceiling. Marcello took a long pull on his cigar, savoring the moment.

"Now, that's real music. For an Alabaman, old Hank wasn't half bad. What do you think, Ace? You're the musician."

"He was the best in his field, Marky, and the theme is timeless. But the production values on that cut leave plenty to be desired."

"Old Petey must be bored to tears to pipe that stuff in over the intercom. He's a paint-by-the-numbers guy. But what a great idea! Hank Sr., a'la Provencenti. Bona sera!"

"Salud!" Ace exclaimed, raising his cigar in a mock toast. They both grinned from ear to ear.

"It's not a bad idea, pipin' in some real music instead of that elevator junk," Ace ruminated. "Hank goes well with a good cigar."

"But it is surprising for Petey to do something like this," Marky replied. "He's usually not very imaginative, you know." He smiled and took a sip of his drink. "But I guess he's not afraid to take some initiative after all."

In the hall at the bottom of the steps, Streetcar paused and carefully peered into the recreation room. There he saw a suitable scene for a slaughter.

Two men were shooting pool while two others watched. This would be like shooting ducks in a barrel: Bloody Coney Island all over again.

Two of the four men were made members of the Provencenti Family, and the other two were trusted soldiers who had served with the Family for years. They were at ease, talking loudly and smoking incessantly as they relaxed in the heart of their family's empire. One of the players, a great, looming lout, was Big Jim, full of pain medication but still moving slowly around the table due to his broken ribs.

"I didn't know that Petey liked country music," Big Jim averred as he sized up the next shot, pretending that he felt no pain. *Four ball in the side pocket.* He was dressed formally, having attended a wedding reception earlier in the evening.

"Well, I don't like that stuff," grumbled the other player, leaning against the wall with the rubber end of his cue resting on the ground, spinning the stick in his hands. "Country music is for hicks."

"You mean hicks like me?" Jim asked warily.

"No Jim, of course not. Everybody knows there are no hicks where you come from." His companions snorted with laughter.

"That's why they made him leave," another man said, and they laughed loudly.

Hearing the outburst of laughter, Streetcar smiled. His victims were like unsuspecting goats: wolfish babes in the woods. They had no idea of what was coming next.

Surprise

Glancing at the clock on the wall, Ace was surprised. After 15 minutes he and Marcello were still laughing, sharing stories as if he had never left the business. It was almost like old times.

"I gotta tell you something," Marcello said to Ace, as he blew another smoke ring that drifted slowly across the room. "Your father asked me to tell you this when you came by here to see me."

"What's the good word, Consiglieri?"

"It's about Joe Boy. He really stepped in it this time." Marcello rubbed his eyes with his right hand. "Not that he's a stranger to trouble, you know. But this is the worst."

"And, the trouble is?"

"Joey visited the site of an unapproved drug importation last Saturday night. It was way out in the boondocks. In Oree County, no less."

"What was he doin' way out there?"

"It was Joey's dough that financed the job, so he went along to see the shipment. He did this without the Don's knowledge, of course."

"Joey always was as dumb as a stump."

"Well, you know how Joey is when he's playin' with his own money. Anyway, there he is in Green Acres with a couple tons of primo pot, several bales of cocaine and some Mexican crank on the side, and who should drive up but a couple of kids: local kids. It was Beaver Cleaver and his girlfriend. You know the type."

"So, what happened next?"

"Joey and Franco were both there."

"Franco was with him? I thought he was too smart to go along with something like that."

"Yeah, what can I say? The Don told Franco to stick with Joey no matter what, and he didn't know about the shipment in advance, or he'd've told the Don. Don't tell this stuff to anybody, by the way. If Joey knew that Frankie's been acting as the Don's wet nurse, he'd go nuts."

"Omerta," Ace replied with a somber wink.

"Omerta," Marky replied. They paused for a moment, smiling wryly at each other.

"So what happened next?" Ace inquired.

"Like I said, they were in the middle of nowhere, and the two kids drove up. Joey could've just bluffed 'em away without letting 'em see anything, but that's not his style. He tried to whack 'em both."

"Tried to?"

"Yeah. He didn't finish the job."

"That was real smart," Ace said, shaking his head. *Man, I'm so glad I quit the business!* "So, what happened?"

"Well, one of the kids was too quick for him. She's pretty much a street kid; we've done some research. She grew up here in Tampa with a bad cop for a father, a real waste of space. He was on the pad with the Family until he double crossed us a couple a years ago."

"Not a good move."

"No, it wasn't. We arranged his communion."

"May he not rest in peace." *There's one for the sharks.*

"Yeah. So, anyway, Joey shot Beaver Cleaver, but the girl got away. She was out of the car like a rocket, before they could even blink. And that's not the worst part." Several loud thumps in the next room interrupted Marcello, and he pressed a button on his desk. "Hey, I told you guys, no horseplay," he said. "If you damage anything, you replace it." He smiled sheepishly at Ace. "What can I say? The guys play rough sometimes."

"Anyway, the story gets worse. As she's gets away, this kid rips off Junior's Lamborghini."

"What?"

"Yeah, she rips off Joe Boy's car with his ID inside, 20 large in the glove box, you name it. And on top of it all, Joe

Boy is now saying that he thinks the girl can ID him as the shooter. But meanwhile, back at the scene, the mules take the boy - minus part of his skull - up in the plane for a ride. They figure he'll talk and they'll dump the body in the middle of the Gulf. Only, as soon as they dangle him out the door to loosen his tongue, he gets out his redneck pocketknife and cuts the rope. So much for dumping the body over the water. Now, there's a body on the ground in the middle of the Sunshine State."

"No kiddin'. What a story!"

"Wait, it's not over. It went downhill from there. We just heard that Beaver Cleaver's body has turned up. Now the FDLE is involved. The next thing you know, the Feds will get into it, for sure.

"But back to the girl. Your father, the Don, put a contract on her. It's bad, but it has to be done quickly before the Feds get her. Now that the boy's body has turned up, it's even more important to get the girl, post haste. Once she's with the Feds, all bets are off. We don't own any judges in the Southern District. We can count on our Miami friends to pull strings, but if she testifies in Federal court, it's all over. The Feds have been licking their chops for years, trying to bring us down, and this is just what they've been waiting for.

"This is not only vital to the future of the Provencentis. It has far-reaching political implications up and down the east coast. Your father wants to make sure the job gets done. So, we've brought in the Mick."

"You're messin' with me!"

"I'm afraid not."

"But, he's a psycho!"

"Yeah, I know. But it was the Don's call, so we gotta stand by the decision. The Mick may be psychotic, but he's the best hitter in the business. He's been freelancin' in the open cities on the west coast, and he's still sharp as a scalpel. The bottom line is, our family has hired Mick the Ripper, and now he's skulkin' all over Ybor huntin' the street bum, Streetcar. You know who I'm talkin' about, right?"

"Streetcar? You've got to be kidding. Sure, I know him. Our recording studio is a block away from that ratty old building he watches for Mr. D'Augostino."

"Well, don't go to your studio tonight unless you want a police escort. The Mick whacked the bum's best friend today, right there in the old athletic club."

"No, man! That's terrible! Why'd he do that?"

"He was trying to get some information about the bum. You know how he does business."

"Man, that's sick. What's he got against Streetcar?"

"You remember the girl who got away?"

"Yeah."

"On Sunday morning the girl drove right up to the Columbia Restaurant in Joey's Lamborghini. Nicky and Big Jim were in B's Diner, so they followed her and picked her up down the street when she stopped to get gas. They had her right in their hands when Streetcar arrived.

"The bum beat 'em up like street punks. The girl got away with the bum. So now, the Mick thinks the bum knows where she is." Ace was flabbergasted.

"How did Streetcar handle Nick and Jim? They're gettin' old, but they're two tough old buzzards."

"We've dug up some info on old Streetcar. He's a former cop, a Vietnam vet with a classified record. His service record is so classified we haven't been able to get it yet, even with our connections. We're still working on it. This means that the bum was probably a spook who specialized in wet work."

"A spook?"

"He was in the CIA." Ace was scarcely able to accept what he heard. He shook his head unbelievingly.

"Man, this is weird."

"You think that stuff's weird, check this out," Marcello said, waving his hand casually as he leaned forward. "I've got something that will really surprise you." Ace leaned forward expectantly, awaiting the next piece of information.

Then, in a moment of time, everything changed.

Marcello appeared to wince as the right side of his head exploded and blood showered into the air. Flesh and bone blew across the desk and rained down loudly upon the carpet, and his body collapsed like a marionette with cut strings.   His broken head, shattered like a rotten egg, fell forward and bounced once, twice on the shiny coffee table as the blood flowed out freely as if it were being poured from a bucket. Frozen and speechless, Ace turned in an instant that took forever, rotating his head slowly until he saw the figure standing in the open doorway.

It was a man.

He was dressed in combat fatigues with his face painted black, his eyes empty and lifeless but hungry and quick as they scanned the office, the body, and Ace. He lowered his gun.

"You're my messenger," he said, staring at Ace. With a start Ace recognized the gunman.

"Streetcar? Streetcar, what are you doing?" Terror surged through his body as he realized what had just happened. How did this man get in here? Where were the soldiers, the men who had been playing pool in the next room?

"Your friends are dead," Streetcar said softly, "all of them.   I swept the nest clean, and you're the last little cockroach. But you, I'm sparing. You're my messenger."

"What?" Ace gasped. "What the . . . ."

"You tell the Provencentis that this is just the first shot. Tell them that my name is Sally. Salvatore Benuto. Tell them that I'm Sicilian. Tell them I understand vendetta. Tell them that they shouldn't have killed Jumbo Poindexter. He was a good man, worth more than every soldier in your family. He was a good man!"

"He was a good man," Ace repeated breathlessly, "yeah, okay, I'm sure he was. Listen, Streetcar, it's me, Ace. I'm your friend, remember?" As if awakening from a trance, Streetcar gave a start as he recognized the gregarious musician.

"Ace! What are you doin' here?" His eyes narrowed suspiciously. Ace watched Streetcar's face carefully, saw his finger tighten around the trigger.

"My father is the Don of the Provencentis, Streetcar. He's Joseph Provencenti. He asked me to visit, and that's why I'm here." His voice was shaking. "I quit the family business ten years ago." This was beyond strange.

Ace had known Streetcar for years. He passed Streetcar's corner almost every day as he walked to the market to shop for cigarettes, beer, or rolling papers. He always said hello, always smiled no matter how busy he had been. Now, the street bum had turned into a homicidal maniac who was holding Ace's life in his hands.

"Okay, Ace, you just caught a break. I'm burning this place down, but I need a witness. Your job is to tell the Provencentis who did this. Tell them that this is just the beginning. Do you understand what I'm saying? This is just the beginning of what I'm gonna do to them." Ace listened, then made a decision. He was sick of the mob, sick of what he had done, years ago, even sick of his own life. He was through compromising.

"I won't tell them, Streetcar. I won't do it."

"You won't?" Streetcar was taken aback, genuinely surprised by his statement. He squinted and waved his pistol with the silencer attached, a grim reminder of the matter at hand. "You're making me kill you," he threatened half-heartedly.

"I won't tell them."

Streetcar glanced at the body, the blood on the floor, and turned to look through the doorway at the four bodies in the other room. They had gone without a peep to their eternal destination: one by a knife thrown from Sally's left hand, three by the silenced .45. The Glock and AK had not been needed.

"So, you won't tell the Provencentis who did this? You're sure?" he asked one last time.

"I'm sure." Soon enough, the family would learn who had done this, of that Ace was certain. They did not need his intervention to figure it out. They were Sicilian, after all.

"Whatever," Streetcar said, sighing heavily. He stuck the gun in his belt. "Now, go on, get out'a here."

"What?"

"You heard me. Scram. Beat it." Ace crept past Streetcar and edged sideways through the doorway. Salvatore Benuto stood still for a moment, mired in a web of tangled thoughts.

As Ace ran past the pool table and charged up the stairs to the back entrance, he had to dodge the slippery pool of blood surrounding four slain soldiers. They had died with their shoes on and their pool cues in hand, true-blue wise guys to the end.

Ace was certain that Streetcar had killed or gravely wounded all the men in the compound. If any were to live, they would need a doctor immediately. He was headed for a phone booth where he could place a call to 911.

Streetcar wandered back into the middle of the bloody recreation room. *I shouldn't have done it,* he thought, staring around at the carnage. *It wasn't right.* He wondered if he should stay here until the timer went off and the C4 ignited. Time was running out.

He was suddenly ashamed of what he had done. All the men in this fortress were dead, but the thought gave him no satisfaction. *Oh, well, I might as well finish it.*

He knew that he should lay down his guns, but the memory of Jumbo's murder goaded him on. He hurried back to the gas can at the foot of the stairs and began to pour it around the room, slopping it on the walls, the carpet, and the fallen men.

When the can was empty, he crept up the back steps at the other end of the long room and opened the door at the top of the stairwell. At the top of a shortened staircase, Streetcar opened a door and stepped through, glancing around the corner carefully. He was behind the X-rated video store, just down the street from the front entrance to the Worldwide Financial building. He smiled grimly. *Now, let's see if this event makes the evening news.*

Stepping out into the cold air, Streetcar struck a match and lit the matchbook on fire. He watched it burn for a few seconds, then flipped it down the stairwell and slammed the steel door shut before he ran up the cold stone steps.

The heavy *whoompf* of the ignition rattled the door as he began to walk quickly across the filthy asphalt, his collar up, his hands in the deep pockets. A single car was parked in the weed-strewn lot. In the tall bushes beside the back wall he traded the trench coat for an oversized bathrobe.

No one saw the ragged street person in the dirty bathrobe as he staggered away from the scene of the crime, disappearing down a narrow side alley. Finding an empty wine bottle, he picked it up and began to sing softly to himself, the perfect picture of a homeless alcoholic.

But Streetcar was nauseas and clammy, filled with a sense of impending doom. He had changed tonight. He had become what he hated to destroy what he most despised.

The taste of victory was anything but sweet. The thought of what he had done burned his conscience like napalm, and the taste was like gall to his soul.

He had become what he most hated. He had killed in violation of the laws of God and man, not out of patriotic duty but to satisfy his thirst for vengeance. Where could he go now?

Should he destroy himself?

But as Streetcar considered the possibility of suicide, something stopped him.

He remembered Jamie.

The kid is in danger. They killed Jumbo, and I wasn't there to help. I won't make that mistake twice.

Streetcar made a decision. He would go south, to Oree County. Whether Ace delivered his message to the mob, or not: whether Ace talked to the police or kept silent, Streetcar did not care.

He would go south. He would watch her stealthily, as only he knew how. And if he could help it, if his skills could prevent it, the Provencentis would not lay a finger on Janelle James.

Not a single, murderous finger.

THE DISPATCHER was unable to get the name of the caller. The number was traced to a phone booth, but there would be no witnesses to the call and no fingerprints on the telephone. The message to the emergency number, brief and unequivocal, received an immediate response from the Tampa Police Department. Cruisers were dispatched to check out the report that there had been a shooting in a basement below the Worldwide Financial building. No suspect had been named, but the caller claimed that the building had been invaded, its inhabitants assaulted.

As the first squad car rounded the corner, within sight of the historic edifice of brick and ornate wood, the building exploded before the driver's eyes.

A brilliant flash blinded her for an instant as the C4 ignited, sending a vast shower of concrete and bricks bursting upwards into the cold autumn sky. The blast rocked the car, and she felt the heat through the windshield. Then, out of the brightly lit sky, bricks began to shower down, returning noisily to earth. The car shook violently as a particularly large chunk of the Worldwide Financial building, falling from a great height, split the hood and embedded itself in the engine, blowing out both front tires. As the heavy rain of time-hardened bricks ceased falling from the sky, the officer scrambled out of the car, speaking rapidly into the radio attached to her collar.

"This is unit 956 at the corner of Main Street and Burnett Boulevard. There has been an explosion, and we have a fire. Repeat, there has been a large explosion, and we have a fire. Send backup immediately. I repeat, send backup immediately." The officer spoke calmly into the microphone, as if this were just another cat up a neighborhood tree.

"Are there any injuries?" asked the dispatcher.

"Unknown. Send fire trucks and all the cars you can."

"Can you give us any more information?"

"Tell them Ybor City is on fire."

A Ride Among Fiends

After calling 911, Ace drove straight home. Traumatized by the sight of Marcello's bloody murder, he was almost delirious. *Streetcar killed Marky . . . killed Big Jim . . . is there anyone he missed?* In a daze, he cruised the neighborhood slowly, trying to sort it out. He heard the blast in the distance as the Worldwide Financial building exploded, but he scarcely lifted his head to glance in that direction.

Ace parked in his driveway and climbed the stairs to his apartment where he dropped, exhausted, into bed. *What should I do?* he wondered, staring at the ceiling before he fell asleep. Ace was in a quandary.

To go to the police with information about Streetcar was unthinkable. Such action would violate the code he had lived by all his life, including the formative years of young adulthood when he had served as a Provencenti soldier. But to hold his tongue completely, to withhold information from his own father, broke another part of the code of honor he had been weaned upon. His silence could be seen as a betrayal of the family. But still, he was torn.

From what Marky had told him about recent events, Streetcar had sought vengeance in a manner that the Provencentis would approve of, if they stood in his shoes. *Here's a guy who isn't involved in the rackets, or in any kind of crime. He rescues a girl and as a result, his best friend gets whacked. So he declares vendetta. If anyone should understand this guy,* Ace reflected, *the Provencenti Family should.*

As bad as his current lifestyle was, Ace was not a murderer: at least, not at the present. But if he told his father what he knew, it would be akin to murdering Streetcar. *The killing ought to end,* he thought, rolling over restlessly.

He did not hear the feet that crept carefully up the old wooden stairs, and he did not when faithful family soldiers stealthily opened his door. A hand roughly shook him as another pressed against his mouth.

"Ace, wake up; it's me, Frankie."

Ace awoke with a start, his heart racing. A hand, reeking of cigarette smoke, was slowly lifted from his mouth as Ace looked up to see three men looming above him: one at the door, one peeking out the window, and one standing with his hands folded in the corner of the room. "Come on, Ace, we're gettin' out of here." It was Franco.

"What's up, Frankie?" Ace asked with his emergency reserve of cool kicking in. *I'll play it by ear. Maybe they don't know anything.* A chill, a tease of the pores like fur rising on the back of a cat, ran swiftly down his spine.

"Come on, let's get out of here. I'll tell you on the way." Ace rose, slipped into his jeans, shirt and boots, and grabbed his black leather jacket. They hurried quietly down the stairs and walked out to the car, flanked by two tough young hoods whose black eyes flashed in every direction like Secret Service agents protecting the President. They entered the car swiftly and smoothly, as if the operation had been rehearsed, and as they sped off in the late model Lincoln, Franco leaned back with a sigh. He looked old, his face spotted with unsightly blotches against pale, wrinkled skin. His large frame sagged within his ill-fitting blue suit, shapeless and soft.

"Oh, man, I'm glad we got you, Ace."

"What's this about, Frankie?"

"Didn't you hear anything a couple of hours ago? Sirens, trucks, a big boom in the distance?"

"Nothin'. I was drunk last night, and I've been asleep. What happened?"

"You slept through it? You must have been mighty drunk." *And stoned out of your gourd, I'll bet,* Franco thought, but did not say.

"What happened?"

"Somebody blew up headquarters. They took out the whole city block: Worldwide Financial, the clothing store, even part of the porn shop. It definitely killed anybody who was in there when it went off. We haven't been able to reach Marky and some of the other guys."

"What?" Ace gasped, turning pale, "Who could'a done it, Frankie?" Ace was scared witless. *They must know that I was there. That's why they're here!*

Franco looked at him with concern. *Gee, he's takin' it hard. The kid really cares. Too bad he didn't stay in the family business. He'd have made a good Don.* "Don't worry about it, Ace. We'll find out who did it. Maybe the security cameras got something we can work with. The trouble is, they say the fire's so hot, its probably burning everything, even the fireproof stuff."

"Oh, man," Ace breathed. Relieved, he broke out into a sweat, "that's terrible." *Thank you, thank you, thank you!*

"Yeah, well, we're gettin' you outta Ybor City, anyway. The Don's orders. Until we know who's after our family, you're goin' to a safe location."

"What do you mean?"

"We have connections all over, kid. The Don's gonna see that your band gets booked in New York for a few weeks. You're flying up tonight, after you meet with the Don. We'll send the guys in your band after you. Don't worry; it's an R & B club, the biggest in Brooklyn. They'll love you to death up there."

Bad choice of words, Ace reflected.

"So, you'll be up in the big city, chasin' skirts in the Domella's territory. Don Domella will treat you like family, and his boys will show you the town. Wha'd'ya think?" the gangster asked, gamely trying to turn the negative into a positive. "Not bad, huh?"

"Yeah, Frankie." Ace answered, sighing deeply, "not bad at all."

Headline News

Seth Greene was savoring his first cup of coffee, lost in the early edition of the Tampa Tribune. Yesterday had been big.

The printing of his weekly edition had coincided with the murder of Johnny Delaney, and his normally late Monday night hours had continued until midnight - well into the second half of the Monday Night Football game. As a result, he had missed the better part of a key game between the Dolphins and the Patriots. This, to Seth, had been a cataclysmic event.

His grief at Miami's overtime loss had been overshadowed by the surprise he felt minutes ago when he read the wire service report about the explosion and fire in Tampa. At 2:37 AM, a terrific explosion had destroyed a historic building in old Ybor City. The fire had consumed almost an entire city block.

With one ear cocked for the sound of his police scanner, he heard the knock on the front door immediately. Seth rose and walked to the door with his footsteps echoing in the high-ceilinged, dusty old office building.

It was Tommy Durrance. Through the glass door Tommy looked lost and forlorn, as if the weight of the world had fallen onto his shoulders. Seth turned the key and opened the heavy door.

"Tommy, come on in," he said effusively, "I was hoping you'd drop by."

"Hey, Seth. Good to see you." Without another word, Tommy walked past him, through the darkened newsroom and into his friend's well-lit office. Seth Greene followed him and sat down behind his antique roll top desk. Seeing that his friend was deeply troubled, he held his peace, handing him a fresh cup of hot coffee and returning to his desk, leaning back and putting his feet up on a comfortably padded chair.

They sat in silence for several minutes, sipping the coffee thoughtfully as Seth browsed the Tribune's sports and local sections.   Eventually, Tommy sighed deeply and sat forward, running his fingers through his hair.

"Seth," he began slowly, "I need your help."

Colonel Pow

The big 18-wheeler rolled into the Oree County Truck Stop at 5:30 AM, rippling past the streetlights, bristling with sinuous power. It was a lithe steel dragon emerging from the mist like a monster from the age of dinosaur trucks returning to a neon lair: an oil-stained relic that belched black clouds of oily carbon and hissed testily as its massive tires ground to a halt, pummeling the asphalt.

A rangy dark-haired man with a salt and pepper beard slowly climbed out of the passenger side of the big rig, glancing around the oil-stained parking lot as he descended the steps. When he reached the asphalt, he turned to wave at the driver and, hoisting a duffel bag to his shoulder, began to trudge toward the restaurant. But he did not go inside.

He walked past the restaurant, past the dirty gas pumps and the brightly lit signs, past the 'One Stop Truck Shop' and the long rows of parked rigs with diesel motors idling and drivers sleeping inside. He walked past the farthest reaches of the lot and ambled up to a store that he had noticed just before the truck turned off the highway.

The small store squatted like a hopeful poacher beside the huge truck stop. It was almost hidden behind a large, well-lit neon sign that declared, "Terminator Gun, Rod, and Needle – Army Surplus, Survival Gear, Live Bait, and Crafts." A sign in the window featured a large smiley face with the word, "Open."

As he approached the front door, Streetcar smiled bitterly at the serendipitous fortuity of it all. When he had asked to be dropped off at the next truck stop, he had no idea that such a store was located here. It had appeared before his thirsty eyes like an oasis, almost too good to be true.

He opened the door and was greeted by a wild clamor of high-pitched barks and yaps. At his feet, a hairy gray schnauzer and a spindly Chihuahua frothed and squealed and snapped their teeth in lively disapproval. He stopped short, bemused but unsettled, wondering whether his next step might cause his ankle to become the center of a two-dog tug-of-war. Lounging in an overstuffed recliner behind a dilapidated counter, the shopkeeper looked up at his dogs and grimaced in disgust.

"Killer! Meathook!" he shouted. "Leave the man alone! Go to your room!" They stopped barking and hung their heads mournfully. "You heard me, go to your room!" With a doleful expression, the dogs slunk pitifully to the rear of the shop, trotting past the teeming worm bin and through the open doorway that led to the back room.

"Good morning," the man growled. "The coffee'll be ready in a minute. It's cheap, but it's bad." The shopkeeper felt like dirt, like he did every morning when he first opened his shop. At this early hour he always wondered, *Why on earth would a guy like me buy a survivalist bait and ammo shop?* And every morning he had to admit that there was no reasonable answer. He must have been out of his mind when he had sunk his life's savings into this precarious business.

The owner was a large, pasty faced, woefully obese man who shivered in spite of his heavy sweater and the excessive warmth of the store. He opened his morning paper and began to read, adjusting the dense black-framed glasses that kept slipping down his wide, shiny nose. The story behind today's headline surprised him. *An explosion and fire in Tampa,* he read. *Wow!*

"Hey, did you hear about what happened in Tampa?" he asked. Waiting for a reply, the shopkeeper glanced up from his paper and squinted at the tall stranger who was busily filling his shopping cart with items from the shelves. Streetcar paused for a moment, gazing up the craft aisle with its country theme and bright yarn, then decided to move past this particular part of the store. *Some questions are better left unasked,* he reminded himself. He glanced at the shopkeeper as he passed by the front counter.

"No, I didn't hear about Tampa," Streetcar answered. "What's up over there?" Streetcar was distracted, engrossed in a major survival-shopping experience.

"A whole city block blew up in the old part of Tampa. It just blew right up. The fire burned a big part of the historic district to a crisp. What do you think, was it a gas explosion, or did a terrorist do it?" Streetcar looked closely at the man.

The shopkeeper was a balding, middle-aged clerk. He presented the very picture of poor health: a doublewide body and bleached out face with narrow eyes blinking in rheumy dismay from behind light-bending spectacles. The dismally thick lenses on the shopkeeper's face belonged in the business end of a telescope, not on a human being. In full, he was a picture of hairy, unhealthy, self-absorbed angst: an unsightly collection of unfulfilled dreams wrapped around a heartache, intellectually imbedded in the story of the day.

He gazed up earnestly at Streetcar, who was moved by a sudden wave of compassion. But such an impulse was against his character, and he rejected it post haste. *Why should I pity this guy? Where did that come from?*

"Do you think terrorists blew up part of Ybor City?" the man repeated. "And if they did blow it up, why did they do it?"

"I don't know, maybe it's the anti-cigar movement," Streetcar answered, turning away quickly to escape the man's pleading expression. "Or maybe it was a disgruntled worker. Who knows?"

"Yeah, maybe it was a worker, some little guy they stomped on, only now he gets even. Maybe some executive fired him, and he just couldn't take it any more." The man smiled as he considered the possibility.

Streetcar carefully walked down the aisles, busily ignoring the strange little man as he gathered together a treasure trove of survival gear. Into a rusted shopping cart went water purification tablets, dried food, a compass, a topographical map of the county, fishing line, hooks, foul weather gear, camouflage paint and clothing, a top-quality knife, compound bow with hunting arrows, watertight tarps, hat, cigarette lighters, blankets, heavy coat, string, several quarts of insect repellant loaded with DEET, a jungle hammock, three dozen pairs of socks, detergent, soap, bleach, and three pairs of jungle boots. He picked up two Vietnam-era perimeter monitors, state-of-art night-vision goggles, and an abundance of fresh ammunition. Come winter, summer or sudden assault, he would be prepared.

The store was a survivalist's wonderland, a smorgasbord of militaristic delights that dovetailed perfectly into Streetcar's plan to blend into the wilderness of this rural county. And he would have to blend in very well, and very soon, if the Tampa police began to suspect him in last night's bombing.

He was determined to protect Jamie from the predators on her trail. In this rural county, with so much undeveloped land and so little civilization, he could hide out for months while keeping an eye on her, especially if she chose to hide out in a remote area.

"You think that maybe one of those militia nut cases blew up Tampa?" the man asked, pulling a powdery doughnut out of a crumpled bag and sizing it up for a bite. "You know, a member of that vast, right-wing conspiracy?" He looked up suddenly at Streetcar, blinking in dismay.

"No offense, pal, if you're in a militia. I know a couple of militia guys, and they're okay. It's just that some of those folks, not all of them, mind you, just some of them, are - you know - as nutty as a squirrel's stash." Streetcar almost smiled.

"No kiddin'," he answered. *Some militia members are flaky? This is news! But I'm as sane as you, and that really is scary!* "You'd never expect something like that in Tampa."

"Yeah, no kiddin'," the man replied, "but what am I doin', rattlin' on like this? Here, let me help you with that stuff." With a gargantuan effort that was almost painful to watch, the man threatened to rise from his padded recliner. As he leaned forward, the veins popped out on his neck, turning his face dark red and bulging dangerously like high-pressure water mains ready to blow.

245

"No, stay there, please. I'm okay," Streetcar replied. "I've got all I need." As he rolled the heavy cart up to the counter, the man took a bite out of his doughnut and grunted heavily.

Then, they heard a curious sound.

"Pop!" went a sharp thump to Streetcar's left. His whole body jerked at the sound, and he turned swiftly to locate its source.

At the end of the counter, behind a display of artificial lures, was a dirty little aquarium. In the bottom of the rectangular glass cage, prone atop piles of wood chips and shredded paper, a brown and white guinea pig stared up at Streetcar. The rodent's pale pink, dewy nose twitched cautiously as it studied him through a pair of dim onyx eyes.

"That's Colonel Pow. He must really like you, buddy." As the man spoke, the guinea pig rose unsteadily to his feet, backed up as far as he could, and made another run at Streetcar, ignoring the heavy glass in front of him. The creature's eyes were locked securely on the prize: the tall, bearded stranger who stood before him.

With a loud pop, the guinea pig hit the glass barrier and collapsed again, twitching gently as he lay on his side, panting rapidly. He lifted his head to stare at Streetcar and blinked dimly: once, twice. Streetcar gaped at him, shocked by the gross stupidity of it all. The guinea pig's whiskers moved rapidly; his nose twitched as he searched the air for scent.

"Yep, he really likes you," the man said, finishing the doughnut in a single massive bite to the accompaniment of small grunting sounds. "The little guy almost never bangs the glass anymore. He used to do that when my nephew was around. The kid played with him all the time. But my brother moved to Maine with his family, and he's been moping ever since.

"Is it normal for a guinea pig to do that?"

"Oh, shoot no. But it's normal for him. That's why my nephew named him Colonel Pow." He grinned knowingly. "My brother's a colonel in the army."

At this moment, a rattling sound to their right distracted the men. They turned to see the tiny Chihuahua reentering the shop through the back doorway. Like a cartoon canine begging for a bone, he rolled across the floor in front of the counter and continued rolling until he disappeared down an aisle.

"Killer, go to your room! To your room, Killer, to your room!"

The dog returned in grand fashion, rolling back the way he had come until he disappeared through the open doorway that led to the back of the shop. "He must've smelled the doughnut," the shop owner offered apologetically. "Sorry about the interruption."

Streetcar began to move his extensive stockpile of survival goods from the cart onto the counter. The shopkeeper's eyes bugged, and he struggled hastily to his feet. He could hardly believe his good fortune and, considering the rough appearance of the stranger, began to wonder if this were all a set-up.

"It'll take a lot of money to buy all of that gear, mister," he said edgily. "I don't take credit cards. You're not going to stick a gun in my face, are you?" Sweat sprang from his brow as he pulled out his handkerchief to wipe off his red face. *Man, where did I hide that pistol?*

"Here," Streetcar replied absently, throwing a roll of bills on the counter, "I think I can afford it." Seeing the fat roll of hundred dollar bills, the man's eyes bugged out like the Chihuahua's, and he cleared his throat respectfully. *So, this isn't a robbery.*

If this was not a robbery, then it was his biggest sale, ever. He hastily began to ring up items as Streetcar stacked more on the counter in row after neat survivalist row.

"Is that truck parked in front for sale?" Streetcar asked, referring to a street-legal 1962 Dodge Power Wagon that was at the edge of the parking lot. It was a tall truck perched on massive tractor tires – a practical necessity for off-roading in the soft Florida mud. For anyone with knowledge about trucks, the old hulk positively reeked of mud-encrusted class. It was a classic, flush with the promise of optimum off-road performance.

"Uh, yeah, sure it's for sale. I was goin' to put the sign on it this morning."

"Does it run?"

"Does it run? Man, it purrs like a kitten. It's one hot wagon. The whole thing's been rebuilt.

"A kid in town put an overhauled Dodge Road Runner engine in it, a modified 483: a real fire-breather. It's got hardened pistons and cylinders, a rebored block, new headers, twin four-barrel carbs, the works. No tellin' what the horsepower is. The kid put a two-ton truck transmission in it. It pulls like a semi when you use the granny gear. It ain't pretty, but it'll put a hurtin' on you. Everything works: the power winch, spotlights, you name it. That thing's a redneck's dream." At this, Streetcar had to laugh.

"I'm not a redneck."

"Well, we don't discriminate around here, mister. We love rednecks, Yankees, foreigners, hippies, anyone who pays cash. We even like running dog capitalists and media elites."

"How much for the truck?"

"Eight thousand dollars."

"I'll take it," he said, throwing a second bundle of cash onto the counter. The man added this to his subtotal and quickly finished his calculations.

"Don't you want to drive it first?"

"I don't need to drive it. I'll take your word. Is the canoe out front for sale?"

"That little sweetie is priced at 600 dollars. It's like new."

"I'll take it."

"All right, we have a sale," the storekeeper bleated, exhaling sharply. "All of the items you've got here with the canoe, plus the rebuilt Power Wagon. We'll make this three separate purchases, if you don't mind," he whispered conspiratorially, "I have to make a report to the revenuers if you pay more than $10,000.00 in cash. We don't want to do that, do we?" He winked.

"No, we don't," Streetcar whispered. *Why are we whispering?*

The man tore the receipt from the adding machine. "That's $4,221.24 for the gear, plus $600.00 for the canoe. And $8,000.00 for the truck, including tax." He smiled coyly, "that's a special seven percent cash discount. I'll put on the title that you paid $100.00. That's more than I paid for it." He winked. "It needed some work."

"It's a smart man who don't pay taxes," Streetcar lied, testing the man.

"Well, then, I guess I'm smart. I hate the revenuers almost as much as I hate the Feds."

"Why?"

"Shoot, they came after me once after some con claimed I sold him a machine gun. I hadn't done it. Not that it mattered to them. Several thousand dollars later, my lawyer finally got 'em to leave me alone."

"Man, that stinks." *That's good for me,* Streetcar reflected, eying the man. *You'll probably keep your mouth shut when the Feds start askin' around about me.*

"It stinks all right," the man replied bitterly.

"Hey, uh, can you take care of the title for me? What about the tag?"

"Don't worry, I'll take care of the title. You just sign. And you can use one of my disposable commercial tags 'till you get insurance."

"Okay." Streetcar threw his fake ID on the counter and began to scoop the items on the counter into plastic bags as the man greedily counted his money.

The papers to transfer the title had been signed when a chugging sound distracted them. It was a rhythmic puffing not unlike the hiss and surge of a tiny steam locomotive.

Streetcar looked up to see a bedraggled schnauzer in the open rear doorway. The shaggy pooch scooted across the threshold on his posterior, puffing like a steam engine struggling to make it up a hill.

"I won't ask what his problem is," Streetcar said, turning his eyes away from the unsightly spectacle.

"That's Meathook, mister. He has a glandular problem, and the medicine just ain't gettin' it." The shopkeeper shook his head and smiled as the dog puffed and scooted across the carpet. "Isn't that cute? He sounds like the 'Little Train that Could,' doesn't he?" He pulled out a dirty handkerchief and dabbed at his moist eyes as Meathook the Schnauzer huffed and puffed out of sight. "I don't know," he added. "Maybe he sounds more like that guy in Kafka's Metamorphosis. You know, the one who turns into a giant bug."

"Hmm," Streetcar replied, not sure of how to reply. *Kafka who?*

"Isn't that cute?" the man asked, sighing deeply. His voice trembled with emotion.

"Oh, yeah," Streetcar replied scrupulously, "very cute." He wondered about this man's sanity. "Well, I thank you very much. I'd better get on the road."

"Thanks, mister. This is a red-letter day for me."

"Good. By the way, do you know where can I buy a cell phone around here?"

"Just before you get to town, on the right side of the road, there's a place called Pezner Networld and Satellite. That's the place. It opens early, too." The shopkeeper turned and flipped through a jumble of keys hanging from hooks on a weathered pegboard.

"Here are the keys for your truck." He whirled and tossed the keys at Streetcar without any warning.

"Thanks," Streetcar said, catching them and hastily gathering his merchandise. *I've gotta get out of this nuthouse.*

"Oh, I almost forgot to tell you something. We got a problem critter." The man caught himself and stopped. "Well, it's no big deal. Uh, well, maybe it is." He wiped his forehead with his sleeve, suddenly nervous. He mumbled something unintelligible, then looked up at Streetcar with an anxious expression on his broad, pasty face. "It's a cat, mister. I guess I better tell you about him, just to be safe. Watch out for the cat."

"Watch out for the cat? What cat?"

"The big old mean rapscallion. The Maine Coon Cat." He pulled out a handkerchief and thoroughly mopped his face, vainly attempting to stem the tide of rampant perspiration triggered by a bad case of nerves. *What if this guy gets mad at me? Where is that gun?* He struggled to get a grip.

"It's no big deal, probably," the shopkeeper added sheepishly. "He's just an old stray tom that's been hangin' out near that truck you just bought. He doesn't let anyone near it except for the kid who did the mechanical work. He liked the kid. Go figure.

"Anyway, the cat sleeps in the tree above the truck, and he guards it like a watchdog. You'd think it was his best friend. I've never seen anything like it. But I don't have the heart to call animal control, and I've been feedin' him when he'll let me. Uh, you can have the cat, by the way." He smiled hopefully.

"Yeah, right," Streetcar replied brusquely. "Well, thanks for everything, and don't worry. I'll keep an eye out for the kitty."

"You do that, mister. He can be, well, you'll see what I mean. Or maybe you won't. Maybe he's out hunting, and you won't have to mess with him."

"Yeah, maybe. Okay, thanks." Streetcar shook his head glumly, considering the man's words. *Watch out for the cat? What's he gonna do, use my legs for a scratching post?* He bent over and hoisted the duffel bag to his shoulder, gathering several plastic bags full of merchandise as he did.

As Streetcar turned to go, the man pulled out another doughnut. That was the final straw that broke the pooch's back.

The sound of the rustling Krispy Kreme bag was too much for Killer. The little dog came back into the room, rolling down the middle aisle of the store like something out of a circus.

Streetcar gingerly stepped over the tumbling Chihuahua and swiftly strode toward the front door, bravely attempting to ignore the unsightly display. But his discretion failed for a moment, and he turned back for one last look. In the open doorway to the right of the counter, Meathook the schnauzer was beginning to chug down the tracks.

Meathook was, indeed, the Little Dog that Could. Raising his head high, seated firmly on the rough carpet, the hairy pooch scooted rapidly across the rear doorway, furiously laboring in a vain attempt to ease his permanent itch.

Streetcar stepped quickly through the door, abandoning the pet nuthouse to the accompaniment of an unlikely farewell salvo: rolling Chihuahua, snorting schnauzer, and one last, percussive pop from the hopelessly romantic Colonel Pow.

Stupid Truck Tricks

It was just before dawn, and the darkened parking lot was windy and cold. The big Dodge Power Wagon seemed to beckon invitingly from its spot on the pavement beneath a huge mulberry tree. Streetcar felt a surreptitious thrill at the prospect of driving the old warhorse. It was similar in appearance, except for its age, to many trucks he had driven or ridden in during his first tour in Vietnam.

With his right hand, he picked up the lightweight aluminum canoe and approached the truck. Up close, he could see that it was covered with dents and blotches of poorly applied camouflage paint. *So much for the body.* Seeing that the tailgate was down, he swung the short canoe into the rear bed of the truck and tossed his duffel bag between the two aluminum seats. The weight of the bag would help keep the canoe in the truck during the ride down the windy highway.

Thankfully, the dreaded renegade cat was nowhere to be seen. Streetcar hastily unlocked the door, stuffed his shopping bags onto the spacious right floorboard, and climbed inside. The familiar steel dashboard and the oil-scented interior evoked powerful memories.

He turned the key in the ignition, and it roared to life with a chest-thumping rumble. The engine was superbly tuned. It had the timbre of a kettledrum, guttural and deadly serious. The interior lights and the heater worked well, and all systems appeared to be working.

Streetcar relaxed and sighed. Pulling a Slim Jim out of his pocket and peeling off the wrapper, he savored the moment. *Dried beef and preservatives: yum, yum, yum,* he thought idly as he took a large bite of the skinny, shriveled sausage treat. It tasted marvelous.

He turned on the headlights and pushed in the clutch. And then, to his great surprise, Streetcar learned that the storekeeper had not been exaggerating.

At this very moment, he came face-to-face with THE COMBAT CAT.

It was a huge feline by any standards, more like a bobcat than a tabby. *That thing's almost big enough to hunt deer!*

As it dropped onto the hood from the mulberry tree, the old truck was rocked with the weighty thud of unrequited wrath. The gargantuan tomcat faced Streetcar though the windshield, his mouth open wide. He yowled in a fit of fanged fur, spitting and scowling and screaming like an eagle as he cast off hot sparks of perilous feline anger. The tom radiated danger like a downed power line, arcing and snapping across the hood of the truck.

In his eyes was a fearful, pained expression, as if he had been tricked and betrayed. "HSSSSSSSS! RRRRRRR!" he squealed, waiting for a response from the man in the cab.

Whoa, Streetcar thought, *it's a good thing that he's out there, and I'm in here.* As fearless as he was toward men, Streetcar bore a childhood dread of enraged pets. And he had a special respect for a wild and wooly cat of this size and ferocity.

"Git!" he shouted, "Go on, git outta here!" The cat hissed and spat and bowed its back like a crescent moon, trying every weapon in his arsenal. He was terrified that he might lose his only companion, the rusty old truck. Streetcar turned on the wipers, but this only enraged the beast further. Then, Streetcar had an idea.

Rummaging through one of his bags, he pulled out some pepper spray. "This ain't always effective on people," he said aloud, "but it ought'a discourage a cat." *Don't hit the cat, just shoot the spray out the window,* he said to himself, *they've got good sniffers, like dogs.* He cracked the window, pushed his hand through, and fired a short puff of toxic pepper into the morning breeze. As if he had been scalded, the cat leaped from the hood with a howl.

Seizing the moment, Streetcar popped the clutch, and the truck surged into the parking lot headed for the highway. Behind him, he heard a sound that chilled his bones.

It was the big cat, yowling in terror. He shrieked in agony, as if he were about to lose its best friend. *Oh, great,* Streetcar thought angrily, *you had to go and do that, you stinkin' cat!*

He hit the brakes, slammed the truck into reverse, and skidded to a stop. With a scowl, he threw the door wide open.

The cat stared at him from other side of a dirty puddle, illuminated in the shaky light of the bright neon sign. He was surprised and confused by the strange man who was stealing his metallic soul mate. He hissed half-heartedly and raised his brows, cocking his head as he tried to understand.

"Hey, Fluffy, hey, Kitty, whatever your name is, do you want a ride? Do you want to ride in the nice truck?" Streetcar couldn't believe that he was doing this, but somehow he couldn't stand to leave the cat bereaved of its only pal, even <u>if</u> its only pal was a lifeless steel hulk.

"Hey, Boots. Morris, Garfield, whatever," he called, snapping his fingers, "come on! Get in!" Streetcar was running out of names. "Kitty kitty kitty?" he added hopefully, but received no response.

"HEY, CAT!" he yelled impatiently, slapping the seat loudly, "LOAD UP!"

In a single leap, the big Maine Coon cleared the puddle and landed on the seat beside Streetcar. He looked up at the big man, startled and more than a little afraid.

"Hey, don't be scared, big guy," Streetcar said unevenly, unsure about his next step. He swallowed as he took in the sheer size of this cat. "Uh . . . here, Cat. Have a Slim Jim. That's a good kitty."

The cat took the food daintily from his hand and began to devour it with vigor. "Okay now, Cat, I'm gonna shut the door. I ain't gonna hurt you, okay?" He leaned past the gray-and-black cat and hooked the door handle, pulling it shut with a bang. The big Maine Coon scarcely glanced up from its meal. "Great. That's a good cat. Now, let's get outta here."

He let out the clutch and pulled onto the highway, heading down the road toward town. When he mashed the petal to the floor at 50 miles per hour, both four-barrel carbs kicked in and they were slammed backwards into the seat. Streetcar smiled contentedly, put on his baseball cap, and began to whistle softly.

The sun was beginning to color the edge of the horizon. The stars still burned brightly, as if they knew their time was short and were determined to make the most of it. They feebly illuminated the hushed stillness as the land and its creatures paused, waiting for the dawn.

Speeding down the highway, Streetcar cranked the window down and turned on the ancient AM radio. A country song crackled out of the tinny speakers as he breathed deeply, savoring the cold morning air: fresh, clean and exhilarating.

"Hey, Cat," he growled. "Your name is Cat, right?" The cat, beginning to purr loudly, laid its massive head on Streetcar's thigh. "Okay, 'Cat' it is. That's a nice Cat. A good Cat." He stroked the cat's heavy fur. *Man, this guy don't belong in Florida with a coat like this. He must burn up during the summer. Burn up . . . what a great choice of words.*

"We're gonna park up here in the woods. We'll wait for the stores to open. You'd like that, right?" The cat rumbled a happy reply.

Streetcar was trying to forget what he had done in Tampa, but he could not drive the memory away. Even if he were never associated with the crime, the fact remained that he was guilty of a monstrous act. He had slaughtered Provencenti soldiers like cattle, violating the laws of God and man. He had almost killed Ace, and Ace was an innocent man. Streetcar knew him to be a gregarious, generous musician. Ace was one of the few people, besides the cops and Jumbo, who had ever taken the time to speak to Streetcar as if he were a real human being and not a freak of nature.

Ace's story had the ring of truth. He was not a mobster; he was related by blood to the head of the family. Had he killed any other innocent men – men like Ace - last night?

Even if every victim had been a blooded Provencenti soldier, if they had all been as guilty as sin itself, it had not been his job to play the executioner. What he had done was simply inexcusable.

If justice existed in the universe, if God and goodness ultimately prevailed, his bloody crime cried out for justice. He had not taken vengeance on Jumbo's murderer; he had punished the murderer's family. The hit man who killed Jumbo was still on the loose. And that man was too smooth, too highly skilled at his craft to be caught unprepared, like the soldiers last night.

His hand unconsciously clenched the cat's fur tightly, and it began to purr more loudly. Hearing the sound, Streetcar let go and began to pet the big cat. He sighed heavily and turned up the brainwave-free, manic rock music, hurtling down the dark highway toward town.

The Promise

"So, that's the story," the Sheriff said, sighing deeply and leaning back in his chair. "What do you think?" Seth Greene considered carefully before giving his reply.

"Well, Tommy," he began, "I appreciate your confidence. I'm glad you leveled with me. Our newspaper has reported Johnny's murder, but as far as the circumstances of the girl's involvement and details you've given me, I'll sit on the story. There's no way I would place one of the victims at risk." He sipped his coffee thoughtfully.

"It sounds like Janelle James has been through enough to break most people. From what you've said, she must be an extraordinary young woman."

"She is. You never really know what a person is made of until they go through the fire. Before this mess, I had spoken with her maybe a half-a-dozen times. She seemed like any other decent kid. Who would have thought she could land on her feet after something like this?"

"It's pretty remarkable."

"I just hope we can keep her safe."

"Don't worry, Tommy, I won't tell a soul until you think we should go public. Who knows, maybe the James girl can put that Mob kingpin away for good."

"This is going to be a mess, Seth. She didn't want us to bring the Feds in, but I told her there's no way around it. Of course, the Palm Beach office will run the Federal investigation in Oree County. But whatever the Feds decide, the fact remains that a capital crime has been committed in our jurisdiction, and Miss James is the only witness. We're going to keep her in Oree County as long as we can. I think we have solid legal grounds to keep her here until after completion of the trial for capital murder. The physical evidence to support a Federal charge tied to drug trafficking is pretty thin."

"You're the expert," Seth said, rubbing his chin. "But whatever happens, be sure to hide her well. She's up against the wall."

"Don't worry," Tommy said, "we'll hide her where nobody can find her."

"I don't doubt that," Seth replied, smiling grimly. "Tommy, it looks like you've bitten off a big chunk of trouble. No more than you can chew, I hope."

"I don't know, Seth. That remains to be seen. When I leave here, I'm walking over to see the Chief. He'll want to know everything. But at least he can be trusted."

"Well, good luck, Tommy."

"Thanks, I'll need it. After the Chief, I'm meeting with Clay. He'll put me through my paces on this one." Clay Calhoun was the tough-minded, thirty-something state's attorney for their jurisdiction, renowned for his fishing prowess as much as his legal skills. The Sheriff stood jerkily, scraping his chair on the floor. *He's exhausted,* Seth thought as his friend turned to leave.

"Tommy."

"Yeah?"

"Once you've hidden that girl in a safe place, you get some rest. Do you hear me?"

"I'm busy, Seth."

"Promise me, right now. Promise me you'll get some rest as soon as you can."

"Okay. Once the girl's hidden away, I'll get some rest."

"Oh, shoot!" Seth blurted loudly, slapping his forehead, "I almost forgot to tell you. There was a big explosion last night near downtown Tampa. It took out most of a city block. They're saying it might have been arson."

"No kidding."

"Yeah. It was at a financial center on the edge of the Ybor City historic district."

"No kidding," he repeated dully.

The sheriff was truly exhausted, unable to respond in his typical, animated fashion. Seth looked at him and scowled, shooing him away with his right hand.

"Go on, get out of here. Hide that girl.' Tommy turned and began to walk out.

"And, Tommy," he called after him.

"Yeah, Seth?"

"You get some rest, you hear?"

"Quit naggin' me!" He scowled and shook his head.

"I mean it!"

"Okay, okay!"

As the Sheriff stormed out and slammed the door, Seth leaned back and smiled. He continued to lean back, precariously tilted in his chair, stretching behind him until he retrieved the coffee pot. "He's a stubborn old mule," he said to no one in particular as he poured the bitter black liquid into his cup and took a long, careful sip.

Rest Stop

Outside of the small, web-nouveau office of 'Pezner Networld and Satellite,' Streetcar sat in his truck and dug through his pockets. He carefully fished out a crumpled business card and, using his new cellular phone for the first time, dialed the number on the card and waited. According to his new watch, it was 8:05 A.M. He was almost certain that the person he was calling would be in his office.

"Bristol, crime scene investigations, homicide team," a voice answered brusquely.

"Hey, Jimmy, this is Streetcar. I was wondering if you had any leads yet."

"Oh, Streetcar. Hey, how're you doin', buddy. Let me check on that. Just a second." There was a pause while he went online and checked the case status. "Okay, here's where we're at. The prints on the gun didn't match anybody in our database. We've forwarded them to the FBI and FDLE. Maybe they'll get a match.

"Everything we've found so far confirms your version of events. The place was clean: there were prints on the gun, but nothing anywhere else. The killer was fastidious. Maybe he was a professional, like you said. If you hadn't showed up during the crime, I doubt that there would have been any evidence at all.

"We got some blood off that brick you tossed. You must have hit him pretty good. We have your description, the prints, and blood for DNA evidence. We'll submit the blood profile to all available databases after we get the DNA fingerprint. But for now, we don't have a positive ID. To be frank, we don't have any idea yet who might have done it." The detective was sharing a lot with Streetcar, but he was not worried about the niceties of policy or protocol. Streetcar used to be a cop and a good one, at that. *Florida has laws guaranteeing victims' rights,* the detective mused, *so let's just say that I'm fully compliant.*

"Okay, Jimmy. I've got a phone now. Do you have caller ID on your phone?"

"What do you think? I'm in my office at the station downtown."

"Well, add my number to your list. If you need me, give me a call." *At least, you can call the number for _this_ phone.*

The phone that he was using had been purchased under his real name. But on his way to Oree County, at an all-night Walmart Super Center in Lakeland, Streetcar had purchased another cellular phone: under an assumed name using foolproof fake identification that he had purchased years ago and maintained ever since. The number of that other phone, with its service for an entire year, would not be divulged to anyone under any conditions.

"Okay," Jimmy Bristol replied. *Streetcar has a cell phone?* Somehow, that did not add up to the detective. Streetcar had never shown an interest in the conveniences of the microelectronic revolution.

During Streetcar's years in Tampa, he had lived a static life, relatively unaltered by technology. His existence had been simple and straightforward. He had been as dependable as the sun, rising every morning to sit on the same bench, on the same corner, wearing the same goofy hat, which was replaced every few years by the next goofy hat. But the detective understood what could happen when people were exposed to the extreme trauma. He knew that many people would suddenly change life-long routines under that kind of pressure.

"I'm in Oree County," Streetcar told him. "I read in the Tribune yesterday that they're having a fishing tournament down here. You know, for bigmouth bass. I thought I'd check it out."

Largemouth bass, the detective thought, *not bigmouth. And since when did you fish?*

"So, anyway," Streetcar continued, "I thought, why not? I used to fish in the Pacific Ocean when I was out in California, so I figured, why not take a vacation to check it out? I'm glad I came down. With Jumbo gone, there's nothing in Tampa for me." He said this matter-of-factly, without any taint of self-pity.

"Yeah, well, okay, Streetcar. If we get anything, I'll call. Listen, I've got to go now."

"Okay."

"Hey, did you hear about the explosion last night?"

"Explosion? Where?"

"You must have heard about it."

"I hitchhiked down here last night. I haven't read today's paper." Streetcar lied. "What happened?"

"It's a real mess. Early this morning, something caused an explosion at an investment firm in the old part of Ybor City. It took out most of a city block. They weren't able to put the fire out until a while ago. They're still hosing it down. They don't have any idea what might have caused it at this point. I've got to go down there once it's cool enough."

"Well, I hope nobody was hurt." *You sneaky lying weasel,* Streetcar thought, berating himself for his own duplicity.

"Listen, Streetcar, if you think of anything else, anything at all, give me a call. We really want to catch that guy. Some of the guys down here knew Jumbo."

"I will," Streetcar replied. *Later, maybe, when I know that the girl is safe, maybe I'll tell you then.* Streetcar marveled at how easy it was to lie, even after years of scrupulously avoiding the slightest mistruth. The deceptive words rolled off his tongue like honey as his conscience winced from the unfamiliar abuse.

"Okay, I gotta go," the detective interjected brusquely.

"Later."

Streetcar turned off the phone and leaned back with a wan smile. The cat was still purring beside him, gnawing on its fourth Slim Jim and still going strong.

"So, Detective Bristol doesn't suspect me," he said to the cat. "If Ace talked, he didn't talk to the cops. That means I don't have to hide, Cat. Not yet. The Tampa cops won't know about my run-in with the mob unless they contact Oree County. Even then, they may not put it all together for a while."

Streetcar decided to take a chance. He would stay above ground for a few more hours. If Ace Feldman had talked to the Provencentis, they would not report the matter to authorities. The mob presented an altogether different type of problem.

Mayhem was headed in his direction. Trained killers would soon be on his trail. Yet at this particular time, the police posed the greatest danger to his plans. If he became a suspect in last night's murders, his ability to protect the girl would be directly threatened.

For the time being, Streetcar could still maneuver freely. He decided that he would contact the Sheriff to see if he could learn where Jamie would be staying. At that location, he could set a trap for the predators who would surely come sniffing after her trail.

Sally Benuto had lost his best friend to the Provencentis, and he was determined not to lose Jamie. *Maybe I deserve to be killed, but Jamie never hurt anyone. She's like a lamb surrounded by wolves. And I know how to deal with wolves.*

He did not romanticize his mission. He was a world-class murderer who had recently crossed swords with the best of the local talent. He was a fitting foe for the Provencentis, able to match them evil for evil.

He glanced down. The warmth of cat was strangely comforting to him. On the highway ahead of him, in the slanting light of a clear autumn morning, the streetlights began to turn off in the growing daylight. The appearance of streetlights beside the highway meant that the town of Pezner must be near.

"You like those Slim Jims, don't you, Cat?" The cat purred loudly in reply, rumbling like a washing machine filled with ball bearings.

"Let's get some breakfast up the road somewhere. Then we can visit the Sheriff. Is that okay with you?"

The big Maine Coon stretched out on the seat and closed his eyes. He languidly clawed the air and yawned as the truck rolled down the potholed road, headed for the rumble at the end of the rainbow.

The Honey Bee

The Honey Bee Restaurant was packed to the gills. A bus full of high school students on their way to a state band contest had just disgorged its contents into the old-fashioned eatery, and the high-spirited children were boisterously packed into every nook and cranny.

Streetcar found an empty spot at the counter and sat down. Although he had briefly scanned the room before sitting, he did not notice a man who sat at a small table behind a flamboyant silk plant. The man was John Dicella, a prominent member of the Provencenti family. John had been sent to reconnoiter the county in order to determine whether the girl, Janelle James, had returned to the scene of the crime. The girl was a witness who could decapitate the Provencentis, and whoever executed her contract would gain great prestige in the Tampa mob.

John Dicella was a brilliant, subtle man who could have been a success in any profession. A detail-oriented analyst and a wellspring of practical information, he was also a man of action. The current assignment had been handed to him because he was, with the demise of Marcello and the exception of the Don, the cleverest man in the Provencenti family. As such, he was the one most likely to blend into the boondocks and gather information without drawing undue attention from the local constabulary. But John Dicella, like all made members of the family, was a stone killer. He would whack his own brother at the command of the Don.

Due to the importance of the mission, John had not been called back to Tampa after the disaster. The news had been stunning. It appeared that Marcello, the Provencentis' consiglieri, had perished with several other soldiers in the terrible explosion in Ybor City. The news had startled John, but he could not afford to dwell on it. From Orlando, where he had been vacationing, he had been dispatched to this county to serve as the eyes and ears of the Provencentis.

When Streetcar walked into the crowded restaurant, the canny Mafioso responded immediately. He recognized the prominent Ybor City street person and buried his face in a newspaper, marveling at his luck. But the coincidence that John Dicella marveled at was really no coincidence at all.

Given the diminutive size of Pezner, the odds were favorable that any visitor to town would see every other visitor on any given day. This was especially true in John's case, since he was eating at the larger of the two restaurants in the greater Pezner area.

Carefully peeking over the top of his paper, the mobster watched as Streetcar sat at the counter and ordered breakfast. *I guess this seals it; the girl is here.* He would have left the restaurant immediately, but he wanted to take care of some unfinished business.

The nerve of this clown, this stinking bum, was unbelievable. He had defied two family soldiers, enabling the girl's escape. This simply could not be tolerated.

If word of Streetcar's triumph got around, the family would lose respect. This would encourage other rebellions, making it more difficult to control crime on Tampa's seedier streets. *He doesn't have any idea that I'm here. Maybe I can even the score.*

After ordering his eggs and sausage, Streetcar rose and headed for the restroom. He was unaware that he was being carefully and meticulously followed by one of the Tampa Mafia's most talented killers.

Sometimes, good habits pay off in remarkable ways. As Streetcar approached the restroom, he glanced in the convex mirror in the corner of the room and noticed something awry. It was something that he could not quite put his finger on.

He paused for a moment at the condiment stand, scrolling a toothpick from the steel holder and picking up a used newspaper, browsing the front page auspiciously.

267

Turning the page, he sneaked another peek in the mirror. There was nothing particularly suspicious, at least nothing that he could identify.

What's wrong with this picture? he wondered, putting down the paper and continuing toward the bathroom. *Am I jumping at shadows?* Whatever it was that had unsettled him, perhaps it would come to him. He glanced around as he left the counter.

John Dicella followed Streetcar into the restroom casually, as if he were taking a Sunday stroll on Davis Island with his own dear, departed grandmother. Walking past a battery of sinks, he rounded the corner and saw what he had hoped for. It was a sight that exceeded his cruelest dreams.

At a urinal in the right corner of the room, Streetcar stood alone, unmistakable even from behind in his outsized black leather jacket and vivid salt-and-pepper hair. The mobster stepped up beside his victim, unzipped his fly loudly, and stuck the gun hard against Streetcar's temple.

"Don't move," he said in a soft voice, "or I'll kill you in your tracks." He spat in Streetcar's face. Seeing no reaction, he shook his head dolefully.

"So, Streetcar the bum, you thought you could steal our witness, beat up our soldiers, and we wouldn't find you?" In reply, out of the mobster's sight, Streetcar's hand slowly pressed through the side of his loose leather jacket until the mobster felt the end of a gun barrel mashing securely against his ribs. It was aimed for his heart.

"Oh, yeah," Streetcar replied, "I knew you'd find me. But I figured, so what? Why not go for it? Your boys couldn't stop me, even when I told 'em what I was gonna do. And to you, my name ain't Streetcar. It's Salvatore Bellocio Benuto."

"So, what, so you're Italian? I am, too. That's nothin' to me."

"Whatever. But I'll tell you what ought to be somethin' to you. If you shoot me, my finger will spasm and I'll kill you dead as a doornail." He smiled brightly and his eyes rolled to his left, looking at the gun, then into his assailant's eyes. *Can I take this guy?* "Isn't that a 9mm Glock?" Streetcar added with a flip serenity that sent the gangster into a rage.

This man is an idiot, the mobster thought. He was beginning to shake with anger and dread, experiencing a sickening inner cocktail of fear, wrath, and unadulterated annoyance.

"Yeah, it's a Glock," he spat. *Why do I get stuck with the nut cases?*

"What is it with you guys and Glocks? That's my question. I'm packin' a Glock too, by the way. I took it off one of your boys. It's balanced good, shoots good, but it ain't my kinda gun. "I like the old Army .45. One shot and they drop like a stalled ox. You know that song, "If I had a Hammer?" Well, the Colt .45 is exactly what they were singing about. That's a hammer, baby. You can almost outrun the bullet, but the slug weighs a ton and carries a ton of impact. Your target stays dead.

"I took this little Glock off the ugly guy, the one with the big schnozz." He looked the gangster up and down. "You hang around with bad company," he continued, "no class, no brains, too slow, no luck. What're those guys names, the ones I took out?"

"That's not a gun," John offered, nonplussed. "You don't have a gun. You're bluffing."

"Yeah, right, whatever," Streetcar replied with a laugh. He flushed the urinal and winked broadly. "Whatever you say, Einstein."

"Okay, you've got a gun. We have a stalemate."

"Yeah, it's a stalemate. If you pull the trigger, maybe my finger spasms as I die, and vice versa."

"Maybe not. Maybe you just drop."

"Yeah, maybe so, maybe no. It's Sicilian roulette, and we've both got our hands on the wheel of chance. Who spins the first cylinder?"

"Maybe I kill you right now," John Dicella hissed, beginning to lose it, almost blind with anger, "that's all. Maybe you just die"

"Maybe so," Streetcar replied, "maybe no." His finger began to tighten on the trigger as his temper started to uncoil, evil and deadly cruel. "Do you want to find out right now, wise guy?"

He felt exhilarated and fearless, sailing so high, so fast and unchained on such a wild, twisted wave of adrenalin that it didn't matter anymore; nothing mattered; it was all just a sick joke. *Maybe I will pull the trigger, just for fun.* Then his high spirits crashed to earth.

He heard the voices of children.

Laughing and pushing one another, two teenaged boys came into the front part of the restroom, just around the corner from the tense standoff. John Dicella and Streetcar stared at one another, and Streetcar shook his head.

"Put the gun away, right now, or I shoot and take my chances," Streetcar hissed.

The mobster swallowed hard. The tables had turned, and at this point, he had to believe that the raging bum meant what he said. His gambit had failed, and it was time to cut his losses. He did not want to leave two living witnesses, and it would be too messy to kill the children.

Confident that his opponent was too much of a boy scout to kill him in front of the kids, John Dicella put his gun in his belt and pulled his sport coat shut, buttoning it to show that he had no further plans. Streetcar hastily stuck the pistol in his waistband and zipped up the leather jacket.

The two kids barreled into the main part of the restroom, bumping into the two men as they tried to leave. They were big, beefy youths with the look of rude good health and arrogance common to some high school athletes and athletic wannabes. They ran directly into the men and stopped in their tracks, overcome with annoyance.

"Hey, give us some room," the taller boy said testily. "Jerks," he hissed, elbowing abruptly past them as he headed for a stall. Outside the restroom, the mobster stopped and turned, staring curiously at his foe.

"Tell me one thing. How did you make me?"

"What'd'ya think? Don't you know that we're the only guys of Southern Mediterranean ancestry in this whole hinky town?" He clucked in mock asperity like a disapproving professor surveying a wayward student.

Streetcar had worked hard to repress painful memories in the past hours, and had largely been successful. But now, as he saw the gangster walking away, he remembered Jumbo and the anger pounded hard against him. His jaw clenched. *If I could, I'd waste you right now.*

Streetcar walked stiffly into the restaurant, struck by the significance of what had just occurred. *This man is spying for the mob,* he reflected, *and he's seen me. Now, they'll know that Jamie's here.* As he stood, absorbing this revelation, the two teenagers barreled out of the rest room. They bumped into him again and stared narrowly as they passed.

"Hey, Carlito, out of my way," hissed the shorter of the two.

"Yeah," the bigger boy said with a sneer. "It ain't Carlito's way around here, it's our way, see?" They laughed. Streetcar ignored them, preferring not to consider the idea that these two youths had not been worth saving.

The danger of his encounter had temporarily disoriented him, but he was now beginning to make sense of it all. He felt wounded, as if he had betrayed Jamie's trust.

I can't let this guy report what he's seen. I have to take him out, he thought desperately, with a terrible, sinking feeling. Vengeance had lost its savor. The prospect of further slaughter turned his stomach, but he felt his options narrowing. He was convinced that this man had to be stopped immediately, at all costs. Streetcar quickly scanned the crowd, seeking his target in a state akin to panic. Not finding his quarry inside, he hurried out the door and scanned the crowded parking lot. But despite his efforts, the merchant of death was nowhere to be seen.

Face Down, Jig up

Streetcar stood outside the front door of the busy restaurant and considered his options. He turned slowly, scanning the horizon for motion, for any clue. Then, he walked slowly back into the restaurant.

"Excuse me, sir," the cashier said. "The man you were talking to left this at the counter." She held up a pair of sunglasses. "Is he with you?" she added hopefully.

"In a way," he answered. "Did he go out this way?"

"No. I just saw him headed in that direction." She pointed toward the rest rooms and, beyond them, toward a narrow glass door that led to an alley.

"Okay, I'll give 'em to him." He took the sunglasses and tried them on for size. *Not bad. I forgot to get shades at the survival store.* As he slipped them off and headed back toward the restroom area, a waitress entered through a swinging door at his left. She was heavily armed with a ton of breakfast: a fully loaded tray packed with delicious, grease-soaked eggs and bacon and steaming coffee that was strong enough to wake the dead.

One glimpse through the swinging door revealed a surreptitious means of exit. At the other end of the kitchen, a rectangle of sunlight illuminated the edges of a partially open steel door. The whole layout beckoned to him, as if it had been planned for his benefit. *This is too easy.*

Streetcar walked boldly through the swinging door into the kitchen, headed straight toward the back door. The cooks barely glanced up as he strode past the hot grill packed with bubbling chicken embryos and snapping pots of Georgia ice cream, that snowy-white, molten tar also known as grits. In this part of Florida, grits were the viscous mortar that held the bricks of local culture together. He paused at the steel door that led out of the restaurant, unzipping his jacket discreetly.

The door opened quietly. It could not be said, however, that silence was essential to his progress.

An ancient air conditioning unit in the back of the building was producing a roar that overwhelmed every competing sound. Looking to his left, Streetcar saw the back of the gangster who had confronted him in the rest room. The killer was calmly smoking a cigarette, waiting for Streetcar to walk into the parking lot. With an unimpeded view of the freshly painted lot, the location offered the promise of a clean and seamless hit.

The mobster didn't see him. He did not sense Streetcar's presence until the gun was pressed against his liver and a voice whispered softly in his ear.

"Bad timing," Streetcar said as he reached around and took the custom-made pistol from beneath the gangster's coat. "The jig's up, pal."

"The jig's up? Gimme a break! Nobody says that anymore," scoffed John Dicella, a wise guy to the end.

"Shut up. Put your hands on your head, and kneel. Do it now!" The gangster knelt slowly as Streetcar stuffed the gun in his belt and frisked him with his left hand, finding the Glock in a holster behind his back.

Streetcar placed the second pistol in his pocket and pulled out the first gun for a look. It was a long-barreled pistol with a scope, a hybrid designed for concealment and accuracy. Staring at it in appreciation, he whistled softly. Then the noisy air conditioner shut off, interjecting an eerie silence into their strange and violent world.

"Some gun you got here," Streetcar said, biting off the words. The blood began to surge in his ears, an oceanic, tidal pulse that almost drowned out the words coming out of his own mouth. He was sick with anger, grown queasy with the hateful taste of it, but he stubbornly refused to let it go. He saw no way out, no turning back from a descending spiral of death, a sickening whirlpool of blood and vengeance with hell at the end of it, gaping wide, eager to engulf him in its bottomless abyss.

"Say goodbye to mother earth, you freak." Streetcar started to say. A loud slamming sound interrupted him, and he turned to see a skinny kid toss two garbage bags into the dumpster a mere 30 feet behind them. The garbage bearer was a restaurant employee in colorful uniform wearing a radio on his belt and thin plastic earphones. He rocked ever so gently to the compelling beat, his eyes half-closed with the rapture of it all.

"Oh, no, another kid!" cried the kneeling hoodlum, overcome with sudden glee. "Put up the heat," he cried joyously, "you'll traumatize the punk for life." He stood up and dusted off his knees. "Go on, put it up, you know you're not gonna whack me now. Not in front of the kids, right?"

"Shut up," Streetcar replied half-heartedly.

"Hey, kid," the mobster yelled as loudly as he could, "hey, kid, over here!" The target of his efforts stopped tossing bags into the bin and looked around in surprise as Streetcar tucked the gun away and zipped his jacket. Now that he had the boy's attention, the mobster walked quickly in his direction.

"Could you tell me how to get to Tampa?" he asked the befuddled teenager.

"Uh, yeah," he replied, "no problem. It's that way." He pointed northeast.

"No, I mean, would you come over to my car and show me? I've got a map there. I'd really appreciate it," he added, smiling broadly and winking at the stern Streetcar.

"Sure," the teenaged life preserver said to John Dicella, "just show me the map. No problem." Glad for a reprieve from his lowly garbage detail, the kid dropped the last trash bag and began to follow the gangster toward the cars.

"Stay here, kid," Streetcar said to him. "We don't need your help." He put his hand on the young man's shoulder, stopping him temporarily.

"Come on, let's go," said the hood, grabbing the boy's arm and tugging him past Streetcar. "Don't listen to my cousin; he's the one who got us lost." Smelling a possible cash reward, the young man ducked around Streetcar and followed John Dicella across the asphalt to his red Lexus coupe.

Racked with regret and desperate to prevent the soldier from contacting the Provencentis, Streetcar nevertheless saw no way to stop him. He tagged along like a helpless child, watching as John Dicella got into the driver's side of his car, made a public show of getting directions from the teenager, and gave him a generous tip. The gangster burned rubber as he rocketed away.

Streetcar considered chasing him, but knew that it was helpless. A chase would undoubtedly endanger the innocent citizens of this sleepy county, and any attempt to catch the nimble coupe would likely prove futile.

He had to inform the Sheriff quickly, and Jamie would have to be moved to safety immediately. Any cushion in the time window had been erased by the fact that the mob now knew that she was here. *It's looking more and more likely that I'll wind up as gator food,* he reasoned uncomfortably. In his confrontation with this latest killer, Streetcar had been checked - almost checkmated - and his confidence had been badly shaken.

They beat me this time, he reflected ruefully. *The next battle I lose might be my last.*

Not Like Old Times

"**M**ajor, there is a man in the lobby who wants to talk to you," sniffed Samantha Jenkins as she strode into Delia's office. "He says he knows you." Samantha was the department's receptionist and self-anointed Controller of Public Access during the day shift.

Her expression displayed a profound disapproval bordering on disappointment. She seemed saddened by the possibility that such a disreputable citizen might be a friend of Major Rawlings. "His name is Boxcar, or something like that," she added distastefully. The Major looked up over her glasses, gazing past the stacks of paperwork that covered the top of her desk.

"Streetcar," she replied patiently. "His name is Streetcar, not Boxcar. Walk him back to my office, Samantha. Please." Ms. Jenkins pursed her lips as if she had been asked to bring in a sack of garbage.

"Yes, ma'am," she said testily, spinning on her spike heel. One minute later, Salvatore Benuto was seated across from Delia, fiddling nervously with the brim of a baseball cap. The colorful label on the tan cap read, "Kiss me, I'm Anglo!"

"Nice cap."

"Oh, uh, this ol' thing," he grinned sheepishly, "I got it a while ago." He cleared his throat and leaned forward, turning the cap in his hands. "It doesn't fit."

"It looks like it fits."

"Not the size. The message."

"Oh."

"Uh, Major," Streetcar began carefully, "you've heard all about what happened in Tampa on Sunday, with Jamie and me, right? I was gone yesterday, so I don't know how much she told you."

"I know everything. You did a great thing, saving her life."

"Yeah, well," he scratched his nose and looked around furtively. He felt out of place in such a clean, well-decorated, and relatively pristine environment. More than 20 years on the streets of Ybor, with the last ten spent living in the abandoned athletic club, had conditioned him to dust and cobwebs and the smell of rotting vegetables splattered on cobblestone. The scent of Delia's cinnamon potpourri almost gagged him.

"It was no big deal," he answered off-handedly. She did not reply, allowing him time to settle down as she studied him closely.

"Are you okay?" Delia asked.

"Yeah. But, listen, you know those mobsters, the guys that tried to kill her?" He paused for a moment.

"Yes?"

"I just saw a guy at a restaurant, and I'm sure he's one of 'em. He recognized me, but I couldn't stop him. He got away. You can bet he's called home by now, and they know that I'm here. So now, they gotta know that Jamie's here, too."

"Are you sure he was one of them?" she asked, feeling the muscles tense in the back of her neck.

"I'm sure. He confronted me, and I confirmed it. This was less than ten minutes ago. He got away clean, and I couldn't stop him."

"Listen," she said bluntly, leaning forward, locking her eyes on him. "You aren't a cop anymore. Don't try anything crazy. Call us, and let us do our job." She said it sternly, brusquely. "Do you hear me, Mr. Benuto?"

"Loud and clear. But I can't promise that I won't help you out, if I get a chance." She shook her head and sighed.

"This happened ten minutes ago?"

"Yeah."

Taking it all in, Major Rawlings stared distractedly at Streetcar, adjusting her plan to include the new facts. She leaned forward in her chair.

"What was he driving?"

"A red Lexus coupe, a CS 400. That's the one with the V8. He might be out of the county by now."

"Did he utter a direct threat to your personal safety?"

"Yeah, I guess so."

"Do you have reason to believe that he is armed?" Streetcar smiled in a secretive manner. *She's a good cop.*

"Oh, I don't know, he may have a rifle in the trunk. But I'm willing to bet that he's fresh out of handguns." He did not say how he knew this to be a fact.

She looked at him curiously. *What did he mean by that?* She picked up her phone and punched a button that connected her with the dispatcher.

"Bill?" she asked, staring at the pencil in her hand, "Put out a stop and search on a red Lexus coupe, probably leaving the county on U.S. 40. Male driver, possibly armed. Tell them to look for weapons. We have a report of a threat." Streetcar was waving at her, but she ignored him. "Call me on the mobile if they stop him." She looked up at Streetcar and smiled thinly. "What do you want?"

"Uh, I don't think you could prosecute this guy for threatening me. At least, you couldn't without getting me in trouble, too."

"What did you do, Streetcar?" she asked, sighing deeply and scowling.

"You could say that I threatened him."

"You could say?"

"I threatened him." She instantly waved her hands, shut her eyes and turned her head aside.

"Don't tell me anything that I don't need to know. Was there any property damage? Was your threat made in self-defense? Were there any witnesses?"

"No, yes, and no," he answered, suddenly deflated at the memory of what had happened. "He got away from me, Major. He got clean away."

"Don't blame yourself. It wasn't your job to stop this guy. You were eating breakfast, for goodness sake. Jamie wanted you to come back here, anyway. She's been through a lot, and she doesn't know who she can trust. But she trusts you." She stood up.

"Jamie will be leaving this morning with her friend to go to a safe location. She'll be hiding at a place where we believe the chances of discovery are almost nil. She asked us to let you know where it is." Delia marveled at the clarity and intelligence in the man's eyes as he listened closely, taking it all in. *To think that I wrote this man off as a bum when I worked in southeast Tampa. He was a nobody, like a street sign you get familiar with.*

"Okay. Well, if you can tell me where Jamie's gonna be stayin', maybe I can go say hi." He suddenly rose, wiping his hands on his pants.

"I'll take you there, Streetcar. You can go out there with us when we take Jamie."

"No, please," he replied anxiously, "just tell me where she'll be. I'd rather find it myself." She studied his face.

"It's in a remote area."

"I like remote," he offered. She paused again before replying.

"Suit yourself," she said finally. "Just don't let anybody follow you or get wind of what you're up to. It's not good for a stranger to be seen in the area. The locals know everybody."

"Where is it?" In response to his question, Delia sat back down in her comfortable leather chair.

"I'll draw you a map," she replied, pulling out pad and pen. "It's on a canal beside a lake in one of the most remote parts of the county." She began to write quickly, her tongue slightly protruding from her mouth. "Nobody goes out there but a few hunters, fishermen, and cowpokes. The mosquitoes are as big as songbirds."

"What kind of land is it? Swamp? Forest?"

"The cabin is on a 700 acre spread. There are 500 acres of swamp and oak hammocks and 200 acres of improved pasture." She finished writing, tore off the page, and thrust it toward Streetcar. "Here you go. Good luck.

"Thanks, Major."

"Streetcar, we are not going by the book here. The Sheriff is convinced that you're to be trusted. He thinks that you're an asset, and I have to say that I agree with him. We've done some checking up on you, and you've got a pretty impressive history. Just keep it between the lines, and everything will be fine."

"Thanks," Streetcar replied, "I'd better go." He stood abruptly, carefully folding the map and putting it in his pocket.

"You're sure you don't need a ride? How will you get out there?"

"I'll make it fine. Thanks," he concluded, and abruptly turned to leave.

"Be careful. Stay in touch."

He glanced back at the Major with a sad, mysterious smile. *I don't think I'll be in touch,* he reflected, *but you might hear from the Tampa Police, or maybe the Feds. And what they're gonna be tellin' you,* he reflected, *ain't gonna be what you want to hear.*

Bad to the Last Bone

The charred ruins smoldered and radiated brow-singing heat. Arrayed before Detective Sergeant Jimmy Bristol in supine, smoking splendor was a bed of coals as big as a football field. The dismal spectacle belched dense, foul clouds toward the heavens like futile regrets oozing upwards from the mouth of a dying dragon.

The smoldering ruins sizzled loudly as the rain began to fall. All but one fire truck had left, and the hoses had been turned off to preserve the integrity of the crime scene.

They had not expected the rain.

Almost an entire block of Ybor City had been laid low, and news crews from all over the world had showed up to capture the morbid eye candy for consumption by the world's hypnotized masses. It was now past noon, and some of the news vans were rolling away like sated sharks swimming from a bloody shipwreck. They had gorged their cameras with obligatory crime scene photographs and uploaded their data to the mother ship. Tonight, they would swap stories and pathologies as all disillusioned hedonists do: bound and determined to eat, drink, and be cynical.

On the south side of the building, under a broad black umbrella just inside the bright yellow crime scene tape, Jimmy stood with a colleague and stared into the twisted wreckage. In front of them, above the tangled pile of rubble, was a clear view of the street to their north. The walls had collapsed into the basement.

Arnie Williams, the leader of Tampa's best arson team, popped another stick of gum in his mouth and pointed to his left for the benefit of the detective. "That burnt-out shell over there was the adult book store," he told the detective. "I spoke to the owner. He said the store was empty at the time of the explosion. He was closing up for the night, counting his money, and the blast knocked him over. But he made it out with all of his cash."

"I feel better already."

"Yeah. Anyway, the rest of this block was the finance company and related properties. They weren't open at night, so we don't expect to find any bodies. But you never know who might'a been working late, eh?" Jimmy Bristol stared at the mess in front of him.

"Let's hope it was empty," he said glumly. "It was pretty late."

"Yeah, we can hope." The arson investigator was a short, stocky man under a broad-brimmed fedora. He looked like a gray-haired refuge from The Untouchables, not at all like a 21st century forensic specialist. But he was a craftsman, a scientist and artist who excelled at the obscenely difficult task of reassembling burnt-out crime scenes, sifting through carbonized evidence until a pattern of truth emerged. "Hey, did you hear who owns this building?" he asked the detective.

"No, I'm not officially assigned to this case yet. They had a 911 call about a shooting here last night, but the evidence is in that hole, if there is any. I don't know why they sent me down here while it's still smokin'. I'm a homicide guy, and we don't even have a victim."

"Well, maybe I've got your answer, Jimmy. The Provencentis own this building. They own the whole block. You know, Joseph Provencenti and company." Detective Bristol whistled softly and squinted at his colleague skeptically.

"No kiddin'?"

"Yeah, no kiddin'."

They had heard the rumors that Joseph Provencenti was the top Don in Tampa. But the rumors had never been proven in court. Mr. Provencenti was a successful empire builder who had meticulously avoided brushes with the law since the callow days of youth. He was a popular figure in old Ybor City, where locals had long held a "don't ask, don't tell" attitude toward organized crime.

In Tampa, Florida, the days of bloody bodies turning up in car trunks were ancient history. Nowadays, unexplained disappearances were the preferred means of enforcing mob rule. No obvious mob hits were necessary, given the fear that La Cosa Nostra wielded over Hillsborough criminals. Close proximity to the Gulf guaranteed an evidence-free shark fest for the Tampa Mob's few, carefully chosen victims.

Tampa families, through judicious use of terror management, had managed to minimize unregulated crime along with the body count. It was all very good for business. Crime was tightly controlled, and the mob was respectable, like a rogue uncle that you admire while ignoring the obnoxious neighbors he grinds up to fertilize his magnolias.

"Well," said Jimmy, "that seals it. If Joseph Provencenti owns this block and a homicide occurred here, I'm gonna retire tomorrow."

Arnie laughed, but Jimmy did not smile. The thought of a potential homicide case was appalling. As the senior detective in his unit, he was invariably assigned to high-profile mayhem, and this case would have the highest profile of all. *If there's a murder, my job is to catch the perpetrators. Will I have to defend a mob family to do my job?* The very thought was galling to him.

He tried to imagine what a body would look like in the smoldering mess before him, and he stopped before he got sick. He had investigated arson murders before.

The sky opened and the rain began to dump on the city in earnest. The rainfall was beyond torrential. It was as if an icy lake had suddenly decided to drop down for a little visit.

"Great," Arnie said bitterly, "this'll really help with the investigation." They stared where he was pointing to the street north of the wreckage. On the other side of the building, a broad gash in the sidewalk led downward from the edge of the street. Through this rift, storm water was beginning to cascade onto the twisted wreckage of the Worldwide Financial building.

"It looks like we'll be wadin' through a pond in a couple of hours." He frowned.

"Just don't ask me to join you."

"Oh, don't worry," Arnie replied, "if we need your help, we'll call your boss, not you. This is bigger than both of us. Your boss, he's the guy that'll ask you to join us for a swim in the new Lake Ybor recreational center."

"Thanks for the thought, Arnie, but this is your show. You don't need any help from me." The arson specialist smiled.

"You're right, we don't need you. But in that mess, maybe there's a body that could." Arnie Williams frowned as he gazed down into the smoking heap of twisted tie rods and broken bricks.

When he turned again to speak to Detective Bristol, he was alone. A dangling chunk of concrete flooring broke off and rattled down into the pit as the arson expert carefully wrapped his gum in a Kleenex and slowly walked away.

Safe House

"You can sit up now," the Major said. "We're here." Jamie raised her head from the back seat and sat up, looking around swiftly, drinking it all in. The front passenger door swung open as Ellen climbed back into the car, scowling and brushing off her hands.

"That cattle gate was filthy," she said disapprovingly. "Are they all like that?" In response to her question, Delia nodded knowingly.

"How do you like the place, Jamie?" Delia asked.

"It's remote enough." She said, visually scanning the wild land that surrounded them.

The trail-worn Jeep began to crawl across the huge pasture: a garishly green carpet of grass embellished by grazing cattle that gazed up in dull curiosity. The cattle began to walk in their direction as if they were expecting something. As they realized that the Jeep was not familiar, they stopped and chewed reflectively, with wet blades of grass dribbling from glistening lips. Expecting the familiar molasses truck, they were surprised that a strange SUV had invaded their home turf.

Beyond the pasture to their left, the land rose in a majestic sweep of low hills studded with rich hammocks crowned with sprawling live oaks. Spanish moss dripped from the broad branches, swaying gently in the cool breeze that had sprung up as a revitalized cold front crept into South Central Florida.

To their right, the green pasture sloped downward until it merged into lowlands marked by a wall of ancient cypress, hoary and silent. The cypress trees were the monarchs of an impenetrable, ancient swamp. Their home was a hotbed of snakes, cruel-fanged wild hogs, and alligators of untold girth and length, waiting in the steaming mire for any poor creature that might walk their way.

"Well, it certainly is remote," Jamie said. "If you're a Sierra Club member, this would be seventh heaven."

"Which, I take it, you're not?" Delia replied, glancing back over her shoulder.

"Not exactly. I like my nature in theme parks or on television."

"This is a theme park," Ellen said ruefully. "This whole county is a theme park. It's Cracker World: like that movie, The Truman Show. Only nobody's watching."

"Let's hope that nobody's watching," replied Jamie. The venerable Jeep Cherokee chugged along a barely-visible two-rut roadway, rocking and bumping its way toward the oaks in the distance. Ahead of her, Jamie could see the place where the road entered the hammock and disappeared from sight. She leaned back in the seat and allowed herself to relax.

Unexpectedly, a memory returned to her. It was Johnny, screaming in surprise to the accompaniment of the smash and rattle of glass, the dull hammer-blow of the gun, the sounds of shouts as she ran through the ditch, ducking low, weeds whipping her face, sticks cutting her ankles in the hot, shallow water.

She remembered the lake and the peace it afforded. She recalled her exit from the lake, how she softly swam to shore and climbed out soaked to the bone, shedding tepid lake water as she crept back toward the scene of the crime, slipped into the Lamborghini, and blasted away. And with the return of these memories, the pain of Johnny's death roared back into her life.

The pain swept through her soul like a firestorm. She could not cry out, for it was too severe. She could not weep, for she was cut too deeply. No cleansing blood flowed from the wound; no healing flow of grief purged the poisonous memories embedded in her mind. No fountain of tears washed the jagged splinters of remembrance from her wretched, miserable soul.

She choked back a sob and wrenched her mind away, forcing her attention back to the present. *I must survive.*

Suddenly, she realized that someone in the car had spoken. She looked up at Ellen, who was staring at her.

"Did you say something?" Jamie asked. Ellen lifted her brows and nodded encouragingly.

"Yes."

"Do you mind repeating it?"

The Water Weasel

His grandchildren were going nuts in the spray kicked up by the Water Weasel. In the midst of the cascading water, to the accompaniment of an obnoxious, high-pitched whir from the popular toy, the children were oblivious to the steamy mid-afternoon heat.

Here in the quiet Hernando County countryside, on his daughter's fifty-acre estate, the Don was able to relax. Here he could enjoy himself despite the recent litany of bad news. He was dressed garishly today, ablaze in a canary yellow Hawaiian shirt and sky blue shorts, looking deceptively like a well-tanned retiree.

Don Provencenti took a sip of his gin and tonic and sighed deeply. He watched with interest as the tanned waifs jumped in and out of the wobbling pattern of spray put out by the shiny yellow Water Weasel. These children, his daughter's offspring, were his own flesh and blood.

He loved them for it.

Yesterday's cool weather had been answered by hard morning rain that heralded the arrival of a heat wave edging in from the Gulf. By late afternoon it was unseasonably hot in the Tampa Bay area, an unexpected reminder that they were in Florida, after all. The warm front had stalled over the Tampa Bay area, triggering storms in surrounding counties without denting the cool weather that remained in the rest of the state.

"All is well with you, I hope?" his father asked Ace, who was seated uneasily at the Don's side. Ace, in his torn jeans and tee shirt, looked out of place in this upscale poolside cabana.

"Okay," Ace replied.

His father nodded as if he understood every nuance of Ace's reply. Ace had never visited this house before, because he had never received an invitation. Ace was, after all, the

Don's illegitimate son. He had never been treated as a full member of the family. But on this day, the Provencenti nuclear family was gathered together in appropriate solemnity: Ace, his sister Bella, and their hot-tempered, hair-trigger brother Joey.

"You aren't doing so well, are you, Ace? Well, join the club, kid. None of us are doing well right now." The Don pressed a button hidden in his pants pocket and received a dose of morphine that cut through the pain from his cancer. He took a sip of espresso from a tiny porcelain cup. The cup was an expensive antique: delicate as a flower, azure as the sea. Pulling out his handkerchief, he wiped his forehead slowly, clearing his throat and his mind.

"Bella," he said solicitously, "you don't mind if we talk business?"

"No, pop. You don't mind if I don't leave, do you?" She was insolent as always, leaning back in her chair and fanning herself. Bella was enjoying a break from her annoying husband and was in no hurry to return to the house.

"Suit yourself," he replied, shrugging his shoulders as Joe Boy rolled his eyes in disgust. *He's getting soft in his old age,* Joey reflected. He was right, of course, but in the wrong way and for all the wrong reasons.

The Don ignored his son's fit of pique, preferring to cut straight to the chase. "Ace, we all know why you left the family business," he said. "It's a tough life, and it's not for everybody. We believe in our business. But you didn't, and you left. That's okay. You had to follow your heart." Joe Boy shifted uneasily in his chair, hostile and uncomfortable. *It ain't okay with me, big brother.* But Joey nodded deceitfully, as if he agreed with his father.

"You don't like our business, but to be honest, you gave the Family more than you took away from it. You were a made man at an early age, and you earned it the hard way. You served us well. You believed in the Family. We saw that when you were a kid, the way you used to fight side-by-side with Joey," he smiled at the memory. "You were a couple of tough little rascals!"

Joey frowned. *The old man's gettin' senile.*

"We were brothers," Ace said cautiously. "We stuck together."

Ace was sure that the Don could not know he was in the headquarters when it was invaded. Even if videotape from the security cameras had survived, the coals were still hot. No one could have viewed it yet.

Where is this heading? Ace wondered. He thought he knew the answer.

"Here's where we're at, Ace," the old man said, leaning forward and resting his large, wrinkled hands on his knees. "Marcello is missing, probably dead. Since this concerns us all, I thought you might be able to contribute something, to share your thoughts. This is a family thing."

Ace listened in surprise and leaned back in his chair, picking up his drink to hide his emotional reaction. *How can I turn you down?* In the core of his psyche, he ached for the love and respect of the father who had always been so distant . . . this aging man who was beginning to die before his eyes.

"Back when you were running your crew, we thought you might eventually be our next consiglieri. You looked like it, and you acted like it. None of our guys could dope out a scheme like you. Remember when that cop ran for councilman, the ladies' man? The big guy? What was his name?"

"Ross. Carl Ross.

"Yeah, Ross. You figured him out before any of us. We had no idea he was on the Francescas' pad. Even I didn't get it. You figured it out, and we persuaded him to withdraw from the race. That saved us plenty of money, kid. Imagine a Francesca man representing Ybor City. Charlie Walker would've had the last laugh from his grave."

The Don's comment was apropos. In the 1930s, Charlie Walker had been appointed by Tampa's civic leaders to keep an eye on Ybor City's crime families. After many years spent dodging death, culminating with bewildering testimony before the Kefauver Commission on organized crime, Charlie Walker had turned up in the trunk of a car, ventilated like an aluminum screen. This had been the last blatant mob hit in recent Tampa history. Charlie Walker's murder sent a clear signal: the Italian gangs of Ybor City would never be controlled by Tampa's civic elite.

In northwest Tampa, it had been a different story. The Francescas, those sniveling pen pushers, had made an alliance with the respectable backers of Charlie Walker. The alliance gave them entrée to Tampa's old money, and they had mingled for decades with the city's leading lights.

"Yeah, I guess I doped that one out," Ace replied. "I can't believe we almost got fooled by Carl Ross. What a lox that guy was." Something had bugged Ace about that guy, and he had dug around in the dirt until he had extracted information that confirmed his suspicions.

Ace looked at his father, sizing him up. He liked what he saw.

Burning intellectual clarity still lit up the old man's eyes, and he still had a knack at cutting to the chase. He looked good despite his cancer, despite what had happened to his headquarters less than 24 hours ago. Maybe the old man would beat the reaper, after all.

Bella stood, taking the pause in the conversation as an opportunity to escape what was, to her, a boring conversation. She was a tall woman, taller than the Don, who was of less than average height. She rapped her yellow beach towel around her lavender swimsuit and tossed the hair out of her face.

"Enough business, already!" she said petulantly. "Daddy, do you want any more nachos?"

"No thank you, Princesca," he replied with a smile.

"Then, excuse me, please." She gave him a hug and walked away. The Don turned back to his sons.

"It looks like we lost some soldiers today," the Don said. Ace nodded somberly.

"Franco told me." The death of Marcello and other made members of the Family was a severe blow. This was serious business, and Ace treated it as such. "It's a terrible loss. Marky was like an uncle to me."

"We're pretty sure that he was in the building when it blew up. We think we lost Nick and Big Jim, maybe more. We've got seven men who haven't contacted us. They may all be toast." As if to emphasize his point, the Don picked up a piece of toast from the elegant tray and began to spread jam on it. "The kid in the security booth, Petey Zach, he's either dead, or he's the one who sold us out. Either way, I don't think he'll be in touch." He took a noisy bite out of the toast and jam and began to chew.

"It's pretty bad." He stopped chewing and stared at the table, deep in thought, then shook his head as if dispelling a cloud. "This is bad for business. Word gets around."

The Don leaned back, basking in the sun. He pulled three cigars out of his shirt pocket, handed one to each of his sons, and fetched out a gold cigar clip.

"Let's smoke some Cubans."

"No, Pop," Joey said with a sly smile, "the Cubans are our friends." The joke was out of place, but Joey knew his father well enough to predict its effect. The Don laughed heartily: a loud, staccato burst that ended as abruptly as it began.

"You're one sick kid, Joey. Just like your old man." They smiled at one another, acknowledging their shared depravity with pleasure.

Ace wondered at his father. What kind of hardened heart and deadened nerves would allow someone to shrug off the murder of a life-long companion? The Don had been Marky's Godfather. He had stood by as Marcello was christened; yet now he joked with Joey as if nothing had happened. Ace, on the other hand, was falling apart inside.

Ace, a gifted poker player, was very good at the art of deception. In fact, he was too good for his own good, and he was well aware of this fact. He slid the unlit cigar slowly under his nose, sniffing the intoxicating, earthy aroma. *Only the best for the Don.* As they clipped and lit their smokes, the brothers focused intently on their father.

"So, Ace, what do you think? Who hit us?" the Don asked abruptly. Ace, expecting the question, was still taken aback.

"Not the Francescas," he replied cautiously. "They're too sedate. Old man Francesca has a heart like a machine, but it's a high-powered cash machine, not a killing machine. Little Davey is just like his father. They're both totally predictable. And they don't have anyone capable of this kind of mayhem." His mind raced, running along paths that he had not visited in more than a decade. "At least, I don't think they have anyone. Is there any one new in the Francescas, anyone who could have done this?" His father and Joey looked at one another and shook their heads.

"They got no one," Joey replied contemptuously. "They're racketeers, not gangsters. They pay the pad, keep the judges happy, control the bookies and prostitutes, and farm out white slaves to the islands. That's about it. They're a bunch of clerks, pimps, and pen pushers. They've got no stomach for war."

"Is there anyone else with a motive?" Ace asked.

"Of course," the Don stated emphatically. "Envy is a terrible thing. We're the top Tampa family. We've have always shown the rest how it ought to be done. We work behind the scenes, we play smart, and we don't leave any bodies behind. We live by omerta. What we do, nobody knows about. Those we can't accommodate or buy off, we either go around 'em, or take care of 'em in our own good time.

"I know the parents of Petey Z, the kid handling security last night. They're good people, and he's always been a responsible, loyal kid. I don't think he was in on this. More likely, they'll find his body in the rubble." He scratched the side of his face, deep in thought.

"This was a stupid play. It's too public. I can't think of a family that would pull a stunt like this. We're no threat to them, and we make money for everybody. We stay on our turf, and the other families stay on theirs. We avoid the open cities because we have enough business at home, right here in the Tampa Bay area.

"The only ones with the juice and the guts to do what was done are the big families in New York and Chicago, maybe Memphis or New Orleans. But it just doesn't make sense to me that any of them would do it. We move plenty of their product through Tampa. We have the local resources, the local connections. There's no angle for them to try and take over. The costs outweigh the benefits." He smiled wanly. "It's a tough one, Ace. That's why I brought you in. What do you think?"

"I don't know. I need more information."

Joey, growing impatient, spoke up abruptly. He was angry that his brother had been invited into this council and wanted to show off his knowledge of the family's business.

"We've got no reports of any outside talent visiting Tampa, and we would know if anybody showed up. The five families give us respect, and we return it.

"The Italians in Tampa have been at peace with one another for more than 75 years. My crews stay away from the Francescas. I don't do anythin' without the Don's okay."

The Don was upset with Joey's last comment. He waved his cigar in the air impatiently.

"That's a load of bull!" he barked. "Who okayed your recent trip to the boondocks? Who okayed drug trafficking?" The Tampa mob did not directly traffic in drugs. For a Provencenti to deal directly in drugs was a major breach of family etiquette.

Joey stopped talking, and his face turned white. He averted his eyes while shock and rage tried to best him. He had been treated disrespectfully in front of his illegitimate brother, but there was no recourse. He would have to take it like a man. Nobody, not even Joe Boy, was stupid enough to take on the Don.

Don Provencenti winked at Ace, amused at his son's ill-concealed anger. *So much like me, the feisty little rascal.* He continued speaking to Ace as if Joey were not there.

"Joey went to the boondocks last Saturday night to watch his mules bring in a load of dope. Of course, he did this without my approval. It didn't turn out like he expected. Two local kids drove up while they were offloading. Joey tried to whack them, but one got away. A young woman."

Even though he had already heard the story, it still surprised Ace that Joey had been stupid enough to violate of two of the cardinal principles of the Family: never visit a crime scene unnecessarily and never, ever, kill without the permission of the Don. The latter was a Mafia tradition that was as old as the Black Hand of Sicily itself.

In Mafia families, only a Don could authorize murder. This was a means of focusing and controlling the mayhem that gave the mob its power. Violation of this particular tradition was punishable by death, for the strength of the mob came not from violence alone. Much more could be accomplished through the fear of death than by death itself. Death released its captives when it claimed its ounce of flesh. The fear of death, on the other hand, could hold souls in bondage for a lifetime.

"The young woman that got away," Ace asked, "did she get a look at Joey?"

"We think she got a good look at him. What's more, she stole Joey's Lamborghini: lock, stock, and barrel. His wallet was in it, his photo ID, you name it. There was even 20 large in the glove box." Ace looked at his brother, who was seething with embarrassment. "Then, it gets worse."

"Worse?"

"That morning, the girl came right into Ybor City, and Nicky and Big Jim saw her. But when they tried to pick her up, she was rescued."

"By the cops?"

"No. By Streetcar, the bum."

"Streetcar? The bum?"

"Yeah, you know, the guy who hangs out on the bench at the old athletic club."

"That guy?" Ace repeated to himself, feigning astonishment. "Unbelievable!"

"Yeah. He beat the stuffing out of Nick and Jim, and got away with the girl in Joey's car."

"What are we gonna do about it?" Ace asked his father.

"We're researching his history, and we've got some of our best talent assigned to the job."

"The girl has gone back to Oree County. The local Sheriff is in charge of the case, and we don't own him. But we've extracted a few details. We don't have any idea where the girl is hiding, but we think it's just a matter of time." He sighed heavily. "This is not the way to do business. When I was younger, this kind of thing would have driven me up the wall. But what can I say? I've mellowed.

"Joey is my son," the Don said. "He defied me, and he's in trouble up to his ears, but he's still my son. I love him. What can I do about that?"

Ace was surprised. All his life, the Don had been reserved with his children: breezy and amiable, but untouchably remote. He had changed, and the change bothered Ace deeply. *I guess the Don's brush with death has brought out his sentimental side,* Ace reflected.

"Well, it's good to know you're not gonna waste me, Pop," Joey said, beginning to recover from embarrassment.

"Hey, I didn't say that," the Don replied, smiling mischievously. Ace dearly wished to change the subject, to somehow turn the attention away from such a display of paternal sunshine. This was the kind of fatherly warmth that he had heard of, but had never seen.

"So, what are you gonna do about the explosion?" he asked. The Don took a huge draw on his cigar, causing the tobacco to crackle and the ashen tip to glow hot red. He leaned back and blew a stream of smoke upwards, gesturing broadly.

"Who knows?" Behind them, the French doors that led to the pool deck opened, and Ace' sister Bella called loudly for her children.

"Ferry, Lonny, come in," she cried, clapping her hands, "it's time for a snack." Expecting something sweet to eat and cool to drink, the children abandoned the Water Weasel and raced for the house. Taking it all, the Don smiled magnanimously.

"I'll tell you what I'm gonna do, Ace," the Don said calmly. "I'm gonna do like one of those lawn machines on TV, what do they call it, the Weed Whacker. I'm gonna find out who did this thing. Then, I'm gonna whack 'em like weeds. I'll whack 'em, bag 'em, and burn 'em. And you, my dear Ace," he said, exhaling a lungful of Castro's finest, "you're gonna help me do the job."

Street Machine

At 3:00 P.M., Streetcar walked out of the tiny ramshackle office, looking at the key and the padlock in his hand. He turned back and waved at the old man who clumped down the walkway from the small office to a ramshackle house without so much as a backward glance.

Streetcar whistled softly and tossed the key ring into the air, trying to catch it on the open padlock hasp. Missing, he bowed down and snatched it up, then broke into a trot, headed toward the Power Wagon. He fired it up, marveling again at the powerful voice of this street-savvy mud machine as he wheeled it into a narrow alley between two long yellow buildings.

The sign on the rural highway read, "Storage City." The heart of the business consisted of two storage buildings, elongated rectangular structures in the classical Southern "shotgun" style. They were cheaply built, durable concrete block units crouched beneath bug-speckled streetlights.

The red doorways to the storage units ranged in size from narrow steel entryways to massive, reinforced garage doors that rolled up to allow access. Streetcar had rented the deluxe model, a 14 by 20 windowless concrete cavern built to endure a nuclear blast.

"This is where we start walking," he said to the Maine Coon Cat, stroking his long fur. "I hope you don't mind." He drove his truck up to a huge red door and climbed out, letting it idle as he opened the padlock. "That'll do," he said, jumping into the truck and gunning the engine, idling it into the room. He turned off the key and climbed out, gently picking up the cat, which hissed at him softly in displeasure and dug long claws into his arm.

Streetcar had spent most of the day searching back roads in Pitman County, 20 miles and two counties north of the Oree County line. His supplies, along with the canoe, had been cached in dense underbrush beside a wild creek a mere half-mile away from this storage center. The map showed that this creek flowed 30 miles to the south and east before ending in a vast lake near Jamie's new home.

Streetcar grabbed the door with his right hand as the cat, sensing that something was awry, began to struggle. Suppressing the cat's movement, he quickly swung the door to the storage room down and turned him loose.

"Ow! You crazy cat, that hurt!" He sucked his pierced finger as the cat hissed at him, shocked and surprised by the sudden disappearance of its boon companion: the weathered Dodge truck. Streetcar smiled. He was prepared for this moment. Reaching into his pocket, he pulled out a Slim Jim, peeled off the wrapper, and bent over to the cat, waving it in the air. "Here's something you like, Cat." The cat paused and tested the air, his nostrils flaring suspiciously. His eyes looked almost human as he considered his dilemma: should he abandon his strong but unresponsive steel friend for this new acquaintance, the tall man with a treasure trove of delicious Slim Jims?

After securing both padlocks, Streetcar once again addressed his feline companion. "I don't know about you, Cat," he offered, "but I'm cutting through that woods over there." He pointed to his left, past the end of the storage building.

"On the other side, there's an orange grove. And on the other side of that grove, there's a creek with our canoe and supplies. And along that creek, there's a big chunk of wild land that's just waiting for us to explore it. That's where I'm going. How about you?" He turned and walked quickly down the narrow alleyway. With a final, seductive flourish, he casually waved the Slim Jim in the air.

Daintily, as if he had planned to all along, the big cat turned and followed Streetcar. The Maine Coon trotted quickly past him, and then glanced back over his shoulder as if to say, 'can't you keep up?' Soon they were out of sight, lost behind a wall of towering trees.

The Weasel Whacker

"So, that's why you're here, Ace," the Don told him, "to help us figure out which weed to whack."

Ace had been afraid of this. He was torn between his desire to protect his family and a deep-seated desire to protect Streetcar, who had been, after all, a harmless victim of Provencenti greed.

Past the poolside cabana, on the perfectly manicured lawn, the Water Weasel continued to shriek eerily, firing tightly wound streams of water into the clear afternoon sky. A light mist, the faintest hint of its liquid blow-by, began to drift their way, pushed by an errant breeze. Joey frowned at the Water Weasel, plainly irritated. Without the children to blunt its spray, the noisy toy sent up a Texas-sized gusher to accompany its annoying whine.

"So, what about this mess with the girl?" Ace asked. "How are we gonna handle it?"

"We're on it. Joey brought in that crazy friend of his from St. Bonaventure High. You know, the Irish kid."

"Mickey O'Malley."

"Yeah, that's the kid. I was against it, but Joey persuaded me. He's a sick character, but he's the best mechanic around."

"Yeah."

"We learned something interesting from the guy yesterday," the Don said, pressing the morphine button again, fighting the brutal pain in his stomach. "You tell him, Joey."

"Mickey says hi," Joey began with an evil smile. He knew that Ace and the Mick had always hated one another. "So, this is what happened yesterday.

"Mickey wanted to use the bum to get to the girl. He went to the bum's crib, only he wasn't there."

Joey Pro paused and leaned back with a blasé expression, puffing out a perfect smoke ring. *If the old man can relax at a time like this, so can I,* he reasoned. Slumped in his chair, Joey glanced over at the old man. Beholding the Don's stern expression, he immediately straightened up and continued his narration.

"Mickey went inside the bum's place to wait for him, but an old guy showed up who happened to be of the black persuasion. It turns out that this guy was the bum's best friend. So the Mick decided to take advantage of the opportunity. He was interrogating the guy when the bum showed up."

Ace was riveted by this description, drinking it in. *So that's how it happened.* He was determined not to reveal what he knew about Streetcar, but torn by a deep desire to help his father.

At that moment, he reached a decision. Any security video had been likely destroyed in the fire, and it was too late to tell everything that he knew. For this reason, he would stick to his original plan. He would not offer Streetcar up right away. But if they provided him with enough information to put two and two together, he would finger Streetcar as the probable perpetrator.

It was a pragmatic decision. He would cover for Streetcar to a point. He would not provide cover at the risk of his own life.

"The bum showed up and surprised the Mick, who tried to ambush him," Joey continued. "But somehow, the bum figured out that he was there. He doused the lights, pretended like he had left the building, and tricked him. Mickey barely got away with his life."

Ace was startled by this new information. He should have known that Streetcar could do such a thing. He had seen him kill Marky and had witnessed the killing floor at Provencenti headquarters, but it was still hard to believe. That a local street person could exceed Mickey O'Malley in the fine art of mayhem . . . such an idea defied logic.

"What is it about this guy?" Ace wondered aloud. "First he handles Nick and Jim, then O'Malley. This is unbelievable." Ace despised Mickey O'Malley, but he respected him as a man might respect a ten-foot rattlesnake. He remembered how Mickey had practiced, since childhood, the martial disciplines he had planned to use in the service of death.

"The Mick said that this bum is the best he's ever seen," Joey said. "The best, can you believe it? A bum!" This galled Joey, and he did nothing to hide his disgust. Their father leaned forward and knocked his cigar in the ashtray, disgorging a large chunk of ash. He waved his hand to stop his son's narrative.

"Just before you boys got here, I got some new information on this guy," the Don informed Ace. "This new stuff explains a lot." He reached into his pocket and, unfolding a sheaf of papers, put on his glasses to read.

"Salvatore Benuto, a.k.a. Streetcar." He paused and gazed over the top of his lenses at his sons. "Sicilian, born and raised in Hell's Kitchen, New York City. His father was a cop who married Salvatore's mother when he was 40 and took her out of the old neighborhood. Salvatore was born one year later.

"When the kid was three years old, his father was killed off-duty trying to stop a hijacking. The crooks were well connected, and they didn't serve a day for the crime. The widow was left with nothing. The death benefit was denied, and she had to move back to the Kitchen. Old man Benuto had been a crusader who stood up against fellow cops on the pad, and they hated him for it.

"The boy was raised by his mother. She died when he was 12. He had no other family, and lived on the streets after his mother's death.

"Salvatore Benuto enlisted in the Army in 1969 at age 16. A local wise guy liked him and got the kid a fake birth certificate in his real name, so he could enlist. He served four years in Vietnam, where he quickly rose to first sergeant. He could have gone higher, but he turned down officer's candidate school.

"It took our best connections with the Feds to get his service records. They're protected to the nines, but we got 'em, anyway." Joey and Ace looked at each other with the same thought. As always, the old man had probably seen the need for this information before anyone else. He must have started pulling strings as soon as Streetcar had assaulted Nick and Jim. The Don removed the top page and put it on the table.

"Here's a summary of his service record. I won't bore you with the details, but the bottom line is that Sally Benuto was trained to be a killing machine par excellence.

"During his first tour, he started out on a long-range reconnaissance team. After most of his team was wiped out, he was recruited by the CIA into the Phoenix Project. This was the program where they sent small squads to wipe out villages of VC sympathizers. The Phoenix guys were pros who did the whole job: men, women, children, even cattle. They left nothing alive. You may remember Mai Lai? It was done by Phoenix wannabes.

"The real guys, they did their work at night or under dense cover. When they left a village, they left nothing but charcoal. They'd drag the bodies into the huts and call for a three napalm strikes, one after the other. Bidda bing, bidda bang, bodda boom. Burn, baby, burn. Clean work, everything carbonized, nothing for nosy reporters to dig up."

The Don pulled heavily on his cigar and exhaled the rich smoke luxuriantly. "Man, is this good." A breeze was beginning to toy with the oscillating gusher from the Water Weasel, pushing a heavy mist their way. Joey scowled at the source of the cool drizzle, the anger rising hotly within him.

"So, our friend Salvatore, he was pulled from Phoenix after less than a year. He was put into the most elite program the CIA had. He became an assassin."

"A sniper?" Ace asked, aware that sniper teams had reeked havoc during the war, taking out targets of opportunity behind enemy lines.

"No, he was a real, solitary assassin. He was a red, white and blue Sicilian-American assassin who stood out like a sore thumb in Vietnam or Laos or Cambodia . . . if you saw him. Only you didn't see him. His missions were to stalk a specified target, whack him, and make it out alive. And he did it, time after time. He won two silver stars, both classified, before he was 19 years old. The General in charge of the program wrote that he was the best soldier he had ever served with. This is all in his official, sealed service record.

"So the bottom line is, this street bum was the top mechanic in the U.S. army. At the time, he was maybe the best mechanic in the world." Ace's eyes widened and Joey's narrowed at this new revelation.

"He came back to the states in 1973 and became a cop in San Francisco. He won a medal for bravery after stopping a jewelry heist. He married, had kids, and went through a vicious divorce after his wife hooked up with a rich society guy. They tricked up some phony charges, and he lost his kids. That's when he became a bum.

"He drifted across the country and wound up in Tampa, where he blended in with the riff raff. He obviously stayed in good physical shape, probably out of habit. He didn't become a drunk. He did enough work to pay his bills, minded his business, and became Ybor City's favorite bum. Then, something happened.

"He saw a girl in trouble, and a switch was turned on. The trained killer kicked back into action. He found a new mission.

"This was our bad luck.

"Now, the bum is standing between us and Joey's runaway girlfriend. And I hate to admit it; this guy is a force to be reckoned with." He sighed and shook his head. "We have to take him out. And that won't be easy." He smiled ruefully. "Oh, one more thing. He almost whacked Johnny this morning."

"Johnny?" Ace asked, "How'd he manage that?" John Dicella was subtle and cagey, not the type to go down easily.

"The bum was eating in a restaurant. He recognized Johnny as a wise guy, and he didn't let it show. When John tried to take him out, he turned the tables. Almost whacked him, but Johnny got away.

"This all happened in Oree County. We know the girl is there, too, because where Streetcar is, the girl is bound to be." It was strange hearing their father naming a street person as a serious threat, but in a strange way, it made sense. As a Sicilian who understood vengeance and retribution, the Don gave respect to the bum whom nobody had really known, the human cliché who was not a cliché after all. The Don respected Streetcar, but was nonetheless determined to kill him.

"So, that's enough about your brother's youthful indiscretion. Let's get back to that explosion in Ybor City." He clamped his cigar in his jaws, ignoring the smoke that streamed up in front of his face. "Ace, who do you think did it?"

Ace looked intensely at his father, recognizing the look of piercing intelligence that was so familiar to him. *He knows who did it. He's testing me.* Ace let out a deep breath that he hadn't realized he had been holding. His reply was brief and to the point.

"It has to be Streetcar. He did it."

His father smiled wryly and nodded as the front legs of Joey's chair slammed down onto the painted Italian tile. Joey was incensed.

"What, are you crazy?" he asked hotly, seething with indignation, "You think a bum got past all of our security and whacked our guys?" He looked at his father, at a loss. "Maybe he was a killin' machine 30 years ago, but he's an old man now. He couldn't have done it!"

"Ace is right, Joey," his father interjected wearily. "I was thinkin' the same thing. I just wanted to see what Ace thought." The Don stared at Joey glumly. *How could my own flesh and blood be so stupid?*

Pop wanted to see what Ace thought? Joey was shocked and dismayed. *He respects Ace's opinion more than mine?* The idea almost drove him mad. Joe Boy stood instantly, drew his handgun, turned, and fired three quick shots at the oscillating Water Weasel.

His marksmanship was astoundingly accurate.

Three bullets hit the Water Weasel squarely, blasting it into oblivion. The first shot blew off the spinning top of the device. The second shot flipped the canary-yellow body into the air and the third beheaded it on the fly, severing the weasel right where it joined the hose. Responding to the gunshots, four men came running around the side of the house, then stopped when they saw Joey standing with an angry expression and a smoking gun in his hand. He snorted and gazed wrathfully at the shattered scraps of yellow metal.

Ringed with a jagged remnant of colorful yellow steel, the liberated hose poured a placid puddle on the lawn. Joey pocketed the gun, ducked his head, and dropped back into his seat. He was suddenly nervous, afraid that he had incurred the Don's wrath.

The Don began to smile, then began to chuckle. He burst into loud, prolonged laughter, hitting the morphine button as his stomach bounced to the rhythm of one hearty guffaw after another.

"Joey, you are one crazy kid," the Don gasped, leaning forward and rumpling his son's head. "We should all shoot as well as you." He pulled out his handkerchief and began to dry his eyes. "But if you ever do that again on your sister's property, son of mine or not, you're gonna pay, kid. You're gonna pay."

"Right, Pop," Joey replied, smiling sheepishly. If he were in real trouble, he knew that his father would not have said a word.

Evening at the Oasis

"This is really nice," Janelle James said. She leaned back against the chair and took another sip of hot chocolate.

"Mmm," replied Ellen, "mm-hmm." She leaned up against the other chair, staring into the fire.

The storms had abated during the afternoon, and Oree County had been spared the encroachments of the warm front that had stalled over Tampa. The weather was fresh and cold for late November; the temperature had dropped into the low fifties, and yesterday's downpours were long departed.

The fire was beautiful, almost hypnotic. Yellows, oranges, and reds rippled languidly across the small, well-dried live oak logs as the heat pulsed steadily from the coals, warming them deliciously. Ellen, savoring the moment, drank in the impressive quiet of this remote cabin.

It was more a house than a cabin, an old-style Florida Cracker house made of heart pine, paneled with cypress, and floored with iron-hard, hand-hewn live oak, a wood seldom used because it was almost impossible to mill. Live oak lumber was outrageously tough. It was tool-bending tough, the kind of wood that turned nails into pretzels and blunted steel awls.

The design of the house was open, with a huge kitchen adjoining a dining and living area in which they now reclined. The house had been recently converted into an urbanized nature-lover's dream. It featured all the modern conveniences, yet was located in the midst of a vast expanse of untouched Florida wilderness.

"Delia," Ellen called languorously, "this hot chocolate is magnificent. How on earth did you make it?" Delia, who had been leaning back in the overstuffed couch, roused herself and sat up.

"It's an old family recipe," she said sleepily, "real milk, a little cream, real chocolate and butter, a touch of vanilla, and a dash of fresh-squeezed cherry juice."

"Be still, my cholesterol-clogged heart," Ellen replied.

"You sound like the host of a cooking show, Delia," observed Jamie with a smile.

"Really, though, you simply must market this hot chocolate," Ellen said to Delia. "Would you consider partnering with an experienced financial analyst who specializes in entrepreneurial development?" Jamie rolled her eyes and smiled at Ellen's suggestion. *She hasn't changed a bit.*

"Sure. Fax me the details," Delia answered, leaning back into the couch. "My people will have lunch with your people."

"Seriously, when this is all over, we need to talk about this." She was drowsy, beginning to drift.

From outside, a clear, melodious sound rang out, disturbing the chorus of the crickets that had serenaded them all evening. The sound was powerful, unearthly and haunting. It was, without a doubt, the most unusual tone that Ellen had ever heard: rich and liquid and unsettlingly mysterious. She sat up abruptly.

"What on earth was that?"

Jamie was not bothered by the familiar sound. She smiled, took a pillow from the chair behind her, and stretched out on her side before the fire. The rug, a thick, well-worked bearskin, was clean and soft and exceedingly comfortable.

Feeling that she had to respond to Ellen's question to show proper hospitality, Delia stirred and replied sleepily. "That was the call of a Florida hoot owl, otherwise known as the Great Horned Owl." In the distance, another owl sounded with the same clear, bell-like tone.

"There's another one," Ellen said, not sure that she was comfortable with this concept.

"They say that the owls make that noise to scare small animals into moving, so they can eat them," Delia said. "That's also how they communicate. You should hear them when they get into an argument." *You learn a lot when you live in the middle of nowhere,* she reflected wryly.

"Turkeys hate owls, and owls hate turkeys," Jamie added. Ellen turned sharply toward her friend.

"What did you say?"

"Turkeys hate owls, and owls hate turkeys."

"Where did you hear that?"

"Johnny told me."

"You've been out here too long, girl. You need to move back to Tampa. We're gonna have to start calling you Danielle Boone."

They laughed, enjoying the moment. Ellen took a pillow from the chair and lay down on her side like her friend, facing the fire, placing her cup of hot chocolate on the warm hearth. Her ebony hair cascaded onto the rug, where it could scarcely be distinguished from the pelt of the Florida black bear.

"Johnny told me all about the woods around here," Jamie continued. "He used to claim he would imitate an owl when he was turkey hunting, just to see if there were any gobblers around. 'Gobblers challenge owls,' he used to say.

"He said turkeys will fight to keep predators away from their families." *I wonder what that's like,* she thought, *to have a parent who protects the family from predators.* In her own family, her father had been the predator, a hungry fox trying to corner his swift little dove.

Her father had devoured her slowly, piece by piece, in secret at night. The respectable predator had been well hidden behind the smooth facade of a typical suburban house in a wholesome suburban neighborhood. Jamie turned her mind away from the memories, forcing her consciousness back to this beautiful moment: the warmth of the fire, and the conversation of friends.

"That's a good story about turkeys defending their families," Ellen drawled lazily. "Is it true?"

"I think so," Jamie answered simply, "Johnny thought it was true." *Johnny was an optimist,* she thought. *But aren't even optimists right, sometimes?*

She looked over at Ellen, surprised to see that she was already asleep. Ellen's happy knack had not failed her; she could still fall asleep at the drop of a pillow. Looking up, Jamie saw that Delia was also asleep, breathing lightly and regularly.

Jamie turned back to the fire and stared into its flaring kaleidoscope. The fire snapped and popped and softly groaned as logs were liberated from their rigid solidity, hotly rushing up the chimney to radiate warmth to the world, freed from their woody prison by combustive conversion into gas, carbon, and light.

She was glad that her friends were getting much-needed rest. But for her, tonight promised to be like most other nights. Rest was a happy state that she could scarcely aspire to.

She remembered that she had planned to pray tonight, and she smiled dourly to herself. *Maybe I'll pray for a miracle,* she thought. *Why not?* Sleep promised no relief from her unrelenting nightly nightmares.

Unless she received her miracle, she would be awake for most of the night.

Four Months Later

Victory Sweetens the Pot

Bronson Drury had to admit it. Although he would never say it in the presence of his colleagues, it bore saying nonetheless: the state's attorney for Florida's 21st circuit was very good at his craft.

Clay Calhoun, a member in good standing of the Florida Bar, was a fresh-faced state's attorney who hailed from the ridiculously named town of Pezner, Florida, located in lowly Oree County. Today, much to Bronson Drury's surprise, this relatively unknown lawyer had whipped him, like an impenitent schoolboy, up and down the spacious marble halls of Fort Lauderdale's Federal Courthouse.

Clay's canny jurisprudence had led a ruling on behalf of Oree County in the case of "The People of Florida versus Joseph Provencenti, Jr." Despite of a demonstrable Federal interest in prosecuting Joseph Provencenti for drug trafficking, the State of Florida's capital case had been determined to have priority, due in part to the perceived weakness of the Federal case. In accordance with the court's decision, the Florida case would be tried before Federal authorities could prosecute.

As the hammer fell to adjourn the session, Bronson glanced over at his adversary, who smiled broadly and walked up to him, thrusting out his hand. Bronson sighed and shook, smiling wryly.

"You play a tough game," he said to the younger attorney. The smile on Clay's face turned up the wattage.

"It's a tough league," he averred cryptically. "I had to."

Bronson was envious of Clay Calhoun: envious of his youth and looks, his careless charm and acid wit. But despite his envy, he had to admit that he liked the younger attorney, and this irritated him above all else. *I'll get you next time, you smirking twit,* he thought, almost believing himself.

He was already dreading what his superiors in the Justice Department would have to say about today's case. They had put his feet to the fire on this one, demanding that he gain jurisdiction and move the Provencenti trial to Federal court, but his best efforts had failed spectacularly. To make matters worse, he had been beaten not by a highly paid team of legal gunslingers but by a pair of rube attorneys from Pezner, Florida. Clay Calhoun served as state's attorney in the state's smallest judicial circuit, and his office was located the state's least populated county. His co-counsel, Marcia Woodruff, appeared to be even younger than Clay.

Light-headed from the heady taste of victory, Clay Calhoun returned to his table, stacking papers and pushing them into a disheveled briefcase. A strong hand seized his shoulder and squeezed.

"Not half bad," a familiar voice said. He looked up to see the Sheriff of Oree County.

"Preacher, I appreciate the encouraging word. I was mighty glad to see that you made it for the hearing. I almost thought I was gonna need one of your sermons to bring the judge around." The Sheriff grinned broadly, his eyes twinkling.

"I don't think they'd want to hear a sermon from me," he said. "I can picture it now. 'Repent or perish!' They'd throw me in jail for contempt."

"Well, we won this one, so you can save that one for next case," Clay said, excited by the big win. He grabbed the Sheriff's hand and shook it vigorously. "We did it, Preacher!"

Approaching from the back of the courtroom where she had been speaking with a bailiff, Associate State's Attorney Marcia Woodruff had to smile as she looked at the Sheriff and the state's attorney, so dissimilar in appearance but so similar in character. Both were tall and broad-shouldered, quick to smile and slow to anger: the golden-haired attorney, perfectly dressed in his expensive gray suit, and the tough old Sheriff in his rumpled uniform, dark complexion and ebony hair streaked with white, nervously fiddling with his cowboy hat.

"Well, I'll see you back home," the Sheriff said to Clay, ducking his head as he turned to go. Seeing Marcia, he smiled.

"Congratulations, counselor," he said. "That was quite a show."

"Worth the price of admission, I hope?"

"Well, admission was free."

"So, was it worth it?"

"Absolutely."

They smiled at each other and the Sheriff paused, suddenly struck by her beauty. He had always known Marcia Woodruff as a brilliant attorney and as Clay's protégé. She was a legal tactician from an old family in Hendry County, a dependable prosecutor concerned with justice. At this moment, to his surprise, he noticed that she was a lovely woman in a sober navy suit: a beauty with smooth black hair, olive complexion and eyes the color of a dark summer night.

He had never noticed that before.

He had always thought of her in professional terms; he was a man who habitually resisted seeing any woman as anything other than a colleague or as a citizen to serve. The sudden realization of Marcia Woodruff's palpable loveliness, fresh and clean and right here in front of him, totally unnerved him.

"Counselor," he said to her, bowing his head and tipping his hat. Without further ado, he walked quickly out of the courtroom. As she began to gather her papers, Clay Calhoun let out a soft, low whistle.

"Did you see that?" he asked.

"What?" she asked suspiciously, half expecting a prank. She knew that Clay could become playful at any given moment.

"Did you notice the way the Sheriff looked at you?" Marcia stared at Clay in disbelief.

His words annoyed her. No, they did more than that.

To put it plainly, his comment ticked her off.

"Why on earth would you say something like that to me, Mr. Calhoun?" she asked testily, pugnaciously waiting to pounce on his reply. "Am I an esteemed colleague, or do you think I'm some kind of Babe in Boyland?"

"I was serious," he answered disarmingly. "I think he might like you."

"What, am I supposed to be happy about that? He must be 50 years old." She regretted her words as soon as she said them. The Sheriff was a kind, decent man. He had always treated her as an equal, with great courtesy and respect. Her comment seemed somehow out of place.

"He _is_ 50 years old," Clay replied, "and he's been a widower more than 20 years, since I was just a kid. And in all that time, I've never, ever, seen him look at any woman the way he just looked at you before he left this room. I thought you might want to know, even if the very thought of it disgusts you." He gazed in her eyes as he snapped his briefcase shut, miffed by her attitude.

"Oh," she said, "oh." He sighed and shook his head apologetically.

"Marcia, we've worked together for three years now. I consider you a good friend as well as a colleague. I didn't intend any disrespect. I just thought you'd want to know."

She squinted at him, puzzled. _Why does this bother him? Clay is single, like me_, she thought, _and he's straight. He's only a couple of years older than me. Could he have a thing for me?_ And then, it hit her. _He's not jealous of me, he's jealous of the Sheriff! He thinks I may have captured the heart of his childhood hero!_

Now, she understood. It was as if she had gone back into Clay Calhoun's childhood, entered the local cinema, climbed into the silver screen, and lured Roy Rogers away from Trigger with a single toss of her raven locks.

She could picture it all clearly. There was Clay, 11 years old, watching the Saturday afternoon matinee when suddenly she crashed into the movie and stole the Sheriff's heart. 'Where'd the Sheriff go?' a galoot on the screen would say. 'Oh, he's dumped all the little buckaroos across America,' a pal would reply. 'He's chasin' that glamorous outsider from Hendry County. She done went and lured him away with some of her feminine wiles!' The first galoot would look puzzled. 'What's a wile?' Marcia smiled at the scenario.

"Well, let's hope you're wrong," she said to Clay, regaining her sense of humor. "The Sheriff is a terrific-looking guy, but he is really <u>much</u> too old for me. And I don't mean this as a put-down, but he's definitely not my type."

"You don't have a type," Clay replied, grinning weakly. "You're in love with The Law, and you know it. You cherish, honor, and obey every scintilla, dash, and codicil. But, I have to say, you're the best attorney I've ever worked with." This was a real compliment, considering that Clay had cut his teeth clerking at the Supreme Court, and not the one in Tallahassee.

"Yeah, sure," she replied, hiding her pleasure. "I'll bet you say that to all the lawyers." She picked up her briefcase and accompanied him toward the exit. They waited at the elevator for a full minute without speaking.

"In two weeks the trial begins," she finally said, breaking the silence. They looked at each other with mutual trepidation and stepped onto the elevator.

They had a lot to think about, or not to think about. They were about to prosecute a capital murder with a defendant who was heir apparent to Tampa's most powerful crime family. Disembarking on the bottom floor of the Federal courthouse, their footsteps echoed through the hallways as they walked past bronze plaques and pictures of notables past and present. Deep in thought, they stepped through the wide double doors that led to the parking lot.

"Yeah, the trial is next," he replied, pausing for a moment. He let out his breath and looked down at his well-polished shoes. "That's something we don't want to miss."

"If only we could," she offered hopefully.

"If only."

They walked down the steps together, ignoring the heat of spring.

Small Beginnings

Great evil, like great goodness, can grow from small beginnings.

The town was astir with the news of next week's trial, and the sensational buzz overwhelmed the town's other prominent news. The Grand National Bass Baiter's tournament scarcely earned a comment from the regular crowd that gathered at the lunch counter of Pezner Rexall Drugs.

The popular downtown drug store was the favorite hangout for the political elite: professionals, doctors, attorneys, and courthouse hangers on. Its lunch counter was not representative of Oree County, but provided a slice of professional perspective.

To the gun and rod crowd comprising much of the county's population, the Bass Baiter's Grand National Tournament still dominated the news. The local lakes, fed by the restored Kissimmee River, were the most prolific largemouth bass waters in the world. But it was still hard to fathom the fact that tiny Pezner had been selected to host a nationally famous tournament.

For this one week, Oree County would be ground zero for the big-time bass business. Her citizens were living at the epicenter of the ultimate gathering of largemouth luminaries.

At the Oree County Truck Stop, gas station attendant Buck Trimble spoke of nothing but the coming tournament. As the week progressed, he recognized more than one famous fisherman and a few of the not so famous. More than once he pumped their gas at the self-service pumps, talking their ears off until they heartily regretted their choice of service stations.

This was Buck's lucky day. When another shiny black truck pulled into his station towing yet another fancy chrome trailer and fiberglass boat (with blue metallic flake finish), Buck quickly strode up to window and propositioned the startled driver.

"Fill 'er up?" he asked hopefully. Buck had no way of knowing that he was speaking to a world-class hunter of men, not fish.

"I though this was a self-service pump," the man replied calmly. He was a tanned stranger who had been brought to these parts by news of the coming trial. White-haired and cool, he stared impassively from behind dark, stylish sunglasses.

The stranger's tan, like his rig, was pure artifice. It was the best that money could by. But behind tan and the fancy rig, he was still the same, bad old Mickey O'Malley: friend to none, hater of all.

"The sign says Self Service," the driver stated when the attendant did not reply. His jaw muscles, flexing powerfully, provided the only clue to the extent of his irritation.

"Oh, it's a self-serve pump, but don't you worry, mister," the amiable young man said. "I'm providing an extra service for y'all Bass Baiter pros." The attendant took off his cap and wiped his shiny, prematurely balding head with the sleeve of his blue shirt. As he did, the driver noticed that the attendant's nametag featured a largemouth bass, grinning and winking. Realizing that he was in the presence of a true fan, he decided to give up the fight.

"Okay," he grated. "Fill 'er up."

"You're a professional, aren't you?" Buck asked, leering knowingly. "You're makin' the big bucks, right?"

"Yeah," the man replied, smiling discreetly. "I'm a professional." He looked at himself in the rearview mirror as he gripped it and adjusted the angle delicately. "And I make the big bucks."

The young man hastily went to the rear of the vehicle and began to pump gas, looking over the gaudy, glistening bass rig with wide-eyed wonder. When he had filled the tank, he returned to the truck window.

"That's some rig, mister. I've never seen one so new and shiny. It looks like it's never been used."

"Oh, it hasn't been used. It's brand new." The attendant whistled and shook his head, taking the fifty-dollar bill offered by the man.

"I'll get your change."

"No, don't bother. Keep it." He fired up the engine, which rumbled deeply.

"Man, what a truck. What a rig. What's your name, mister?"

"Jim. Jim Belzer."

"Belzer? Never heard that name. Do you have a handle? All you guys've got handles."

"Do you mean a nickname?"

"Yeah. Do you have a nickname?"

"Sure," the man replied with a secretive smile, dropping the truck into first gear and easing off on the clutch. "Call me Killer."

"Wow, cool. Well, I'll see you on Saturday, Killer." The man gaped admiringly as the truck sped away.

Mickey pulled out onto the highway, savoring the beauty of the morning. His collarbone had fully healed in the past months, and he was in top condition, ready for the contest that was ahead of him.

Janelle James had been hidden effectively, but that was about to end. Soon, she would have to testify in court. To do that, she would have to leave her hiding place.

The Provencentis' lawyers had developed a clever scheme that might get Joey off the hook entirely. As a last resort, the family planned to appeal the case by claiming that their counsel had been incompetent by reason of his hidden addiction to alcohol. Their attorney was a highly skilled criminal attorney who also happened to be a practicing alcoholic.

To set up their appeal, he had been seen this week in local bars, conspicuously consuming large amounts of liquor. He would be full of liquor, tight but controlled, on the day of the trial. Immediately after the verdict, he would have a one-car accident in downtown Pezner, ensuring that he was arrested for drunk driving less than 20 minutes after the trial ended.

Certain justices on the state appellate court were longtime acquaintances of the Provencentis. If their attorney pulled off the plan, the appellate court would definitely order a retrial. It did not matter if the girl testified at the first trial, if she could be prevented from testifying at the retrial. This was the key to the strategy, and its success required one simple act.

Mickey O'Malley was still authorized to eliminate the girl, if her hiding place could be found. He, and he alone, had been sanctioned to execute the contract. The Don had ordered that the hit must be done discreetly, with no collateral damage, or must not be done at all.

Of course, Mickey had reserved the right to do the job his way. He could care less about what the Don wanted.

Joey Provencenti and Mickey O'Malley had devised a plan. Their plan was risky, and was not authorized by the Don. But, except for that one, ominous sin of omission, theirs was a well thought-out strategy. The local authorities would never expect them to strike immediately after the hearing.

The street bum who had cleaned the Provencentis' clock had disappeared from the face of the earth. Agents from the Federal Bureau of Alcohol, Tobacco, and Firearms wanted to question him about a certain arson murder, and Tampa's finest, angry that someone had pulled off such a crime in their city, were also hot on his trail. *The bum's probably passed out on a pile of garbage in some alley somewhere,* the killer thought, grinning broadly. *But if he isn't, I'm ready. He can't match me again.*

Mickey recalled his conversation with the rube at the service station and shook his head. These local hicks were easy picking, he reflected, hitting the gas as he pulled out to pass a rusty white station wagon full of children.

A young woman was driving the car. She was pretty and relatively unspoiled, and he glanced at her with professional interest as he passed the car. He had heard that the hunting was good in this part of the state. The reports appeared to be true.

Just call me Killer, he thought with a smile, nodding to her as he caught her eye. The gesture was a small beginning in an unfamiliar county.

He turned up the stereo and pulled back into the right lane, easing up on the gas as he let Mozart wash over and through him, savoring the tingle of anticipation and the thrill of new horizons. *This is the life,* he reflected. *No rules, just right.*

He looked in his rearview mirror. With his 20-15 vision - eyesight beyond perfection - he could tell that the young woman was staring at him with a crooked smile on her lips.

"Hmmm, let me write down her license plate," he said aloud, pulling out a pen and writing the number onto his hand. He was always looking for opportunities to combine business with pleasure.

He sighed and relaxed, basking in the moment: awash in waves of Mozart. He began to dream of sex and gore, gore and sex. The images mingled like unholy angels, sulfurous spirits that twisted upwards through his mind, scorching his soul as they inflamed him with sick, perverted lust. He remembered the power, the sheer, wanton depravity of it all.

He lived – he loved - to dominate and control his victims, to spread horror like rain and sow seeds of terror, seeds that grew great, howling blossoms of death. The thought of it set his fevered imagination on fire.

He was beginning to like this little patch of the boondocks. There was plenty of game, and the local bipeds were unaccustomed to predators of his caliber. Who cared about the lack of a sporting challenge? Not he. *These women are like tame deer that eat from your hand,* he mused. *A hungry man doesn't care if there's any sport in the hunt, only that he fills his stomach.*

This would be almost too easy. *Hmmm . . . that's nice.* He had to admit it. Easy pickings appealed to him.

Big Night In

Just before dusk, the visitors arrived separately as the reclining sun ignited the sky with a vivid display of hyper-chromatic impressionism. The sunset was a profuse explosion of light: bold and brazen and almost overdone in scope and intensity. It was a masterwork from a vivid palette of rich vermilion and royal purple, red and orange dusted with delicate pinks.

The travelers had followed carefully mapped routes. Each had journeyed through a different route to arrive at this common destination. The cars – one per person - had begun their journey from different parts of the county, meandering down endless two lane highways that were knife-straight and utterly devoid of traffic. The deserted roads had provided a clear view forward and aft, and all of them were confident that they had not been followed.

They had been extremely cautious. They had to be.

Arriving just minutes apart, each driver paused to open the cattle gate before idling through the overgrown entranceway and bumping through the shallow ditch. One by one, the cars rocked cautiously across the fertile pasture that led toward a grove of venerable live oaks on a small hill beside the canal.

Along the way, they passed under tall trees that guarded the way jealously, threatening their progress like giants from the dreams of Don Quixote. The ancient oaks were impressive sentinels that waggled thin, scraggly beards of Spanish moss disapprovingly in the errant breeze, their mighty arms mutely outstretched toward the darkening heavens.

Shortly before nightfall, the three guests had parked their cars in the lush grass in front of the ranch house. Tonight, the frumpy farmhouse had undergone a transformation. It was decorated for a party.

An element of danger had been inherent in their arrival; they could have been followed, and were extremely careful to ensure that they were not. But now, they could relax. This remote house was like thousands of others in this huge, rural county. There was no risk that their gathering would draw killers who did not know where to begin looking.

They were here to celebrate Jamie's twentieth birthday. In the back yard, beside the path that sloped toward the canal, torches had been planted to light the way for the guests who had gathered for the gala. The torches burned with exotic flair, casting weak, fickle light that competed feebly with the powerful floodlights at the corners of the house.

On the broad lawn past the back porch, an ancient brick barbecue sent up a heavy column of smoke into the darkening sky. Chef Tommy Durrance stood ramrod straight beside the smoking pit, tall and sun-scorched and badly in need of tenderizing, not unlike the meat on the grill. He moved his brush slowly, carefully applying heavy brown sauce to a huge side of pork locked tight in a shiny steel rack. It had taken weeks to convince Jamie to allow him to cook a wild hog, and he was determined to produce a meal that would justify his relentless, shameless hype.

This party had been Delia's idea. Long months in the remote setting had left Jamie lonely for company, and the idea had been exciting. The guest list was somewhat limited, but the gathering was already showing signs of promise.

Ellen Bromley had arrived early this morning to spend two weeks with her friend. On this, her second trip to Oree County, she had adjusted to the local culture - or the absence of the same - with relative ease. Ellen was relaxed and loquacious, a valuable mood-elevating influence for Jamie.

"Sheriff," called the Major from her rocking chair on the small back porch, "leave that pig alone and come over here." Delia Rawlings was involved in a lively debate with those two prominent officers of the court, Clay Calhoun and Marcia Woodruff. As might be expected, she was having trouble winning them over, and was in need of strong evidence that could support her argument.

The Sheriff wiped his brow with a bandana, put down the basting brush and walked over. The weather was unseasonably cool, but the barbeque pit was doing its duty, radiating face-tightening heat. He was warm and ruddy-faced from his job beside the fire.

"All right, able counselors," Delia stated succinctly. "Look at this man. I ask you, does he look dangerous?" The two attorneys looked closely at the Sheriff and turned to Delia in one accord.

"Yes," they replied in unison. Delia rolled her eyes.

"You've been working together too long," she replied dubiously. "You've become your own evil twins." They smirked at each other, taking this as a compliment. Clay Calhoun and Marcia Woodruff did, after all, get along like sister and brother, and they both had a wicked sense of humor. They might well be compared to twins. They were a pair of matching anomalies: state prosecutors who shunned the spotlight, public attorneys who were renowned for their close-mouthed discretion and unfailing honesty as they performed in court with a unity that had made them an unbeatable legal team.

"What's this about?" the Sheriff asked impatiently, in a hurry to return to his barbeque pit.

"Nothing at all, Sheriff," Delia replied. "I shouldn't have let them talk me into calling you over. You may return to your pig in peace." Marcia, however, was not about to let her off the hook in front of the Preacher.

"Delia claims that you're all bark and no bite, Sheriff. She says you're the softest-hearted law enforcer in Florida." The Associate State's Attorney, normally a reserved professional, was enjoying a chance to get the best of Delia, given the fact that such opportunities were rare. "Let's just say that we doubted the veracity of her testimony on this subject."

"I'm telling you the truth, counselor," Delia interjected, cutting her off at the pass. "He is all bark. The way this man handles our problem employees, he's in the wrong line of business. He should open a Mr. Softee franchise. And his manner with suspects is basically the same. He's 'Mister Minimum Required Force.' He could disarm a stick of dynamite with a heart-to-heart talk."

"Let's contact the Associated Press," Clay offered. "I can see the headline now, 'Sheriff upholds law with minimum force.' What a yawner!"

"Well, he looks dangerous to me," Marcia Woodruff repeated. The Sheriff looked at her quizzically. He was dressed in loose black jeans and a baggy gray shirt, relaxed and happy: in short, totally out of character. The aura of intensity that usually surrounded him like a high-powered electrical field had dissipated, replaced by a placid demeanor that was more reminiscent of a happy-go-lucky beachcomber than of their Sheriff.

The conversation paused as Tommy and Marcia gazed at one other, then immediately resumed as Jamie arrived bearing gifts: a generous array of devilled eggs on a wide, enameled platter. The eggs looked and smelled delicious.

"Chicken eggs, anyone?" she asked brightly, smiling with a deliberately vacant twinkle.

"Thanks, Jamie," replied Clay, "it's reassuring to know that they're not turtle eggs or snake eggs. People eat strange things in the middle of nowhere."

"And what exactly is wrong with snake eggs?"

"That's my point, exactly," Clay answered, looking at his companions for support. "The wilderness changes people in mysterious ways."

"It hasn't changed me," Jamie assured him unconvincingly.

"Are you sure they're chicken eggs?" he asked suspiciously.

"No."

"Don't torment me; I'm hungry." He greedily grasped a devilled egg and popped it into his mouth.

"That one <u>was</u> a snake egg," Jamie said with a grin. "Didn't I tell you?"

"Very delicious," he mumbled through the mouthful. "My compliments to the snake."

"Take as many as you want," she added, smiling brightly. Clay swallowed and grinned sheepishly.

"You are simply too kind. I can't, really," he averred as he piled seven devilled eggs onto his plate.

"Come inside, you guys, the mosquitoes are starting to bite," Jamie offered. "You need to help me with this food. I've been baking for three days. You must eat mass quantities." They laughed, vowing to help as they headed toward the house.

As the Sheriff watched them leave, a lump rose in his throat and tears threatened to appear in his eyes. He quickly cleared his throat and began to walk slowly back toward the barbeque pit.

Tommy Durrance appreciated the precious nature of this evening. He appreciated the uncommon decency of these people, the rarity of sincerity in a world full of users with hearts set on money and position. He turned again to look at his friends as they began to file into the house led by Jamie, who was laughing as she stepped inside.

At the top of the steps, Marcia Woodruff paused and looked back at Tommy Durrance. Her glance took him by surprise, and he stared back at her with the intensity for which he was famous. Marcia's gaze was serious, inquiring, reflective; his was direct, unabashed, riveting. He concentrated on her single-mindedly, searing her image into his memory. The sense of sight, sharpened by a rush of adrenalin, became his only prism of focus.

Marcia's skin was smooth and dark, her face framed in glossy hair so black that it was almost blue. Her eyes were surprisingly green: oceanic in their clarity and hue, as luminous and opalescent as sunlight piercing the ocean depths. The light within her eyes was a subtle fluorescence, a dazzling swirl of life in the midst of the sea.

A faint hint of freckles showed on her cheeks when she blushed, and her nostrils flared as she inhaled sharply. A startled expression crossed her face and she was gone. The door shut tightly behind her.

The Sheriff's senses slowly returned: smell and hearing, touch and taste and a profound, unsettling sensation deep within. He smelled acrid smoke from the burning pit and citrus scent from the torches that flickered dimly all around him.

The burning citronella scarcely dented the clouds of mosquitoes that were beginning to drone like a chorus of fiery, airborne ants. He put his hand to his mouth, rubbed his chin, and felt the five o'clock stubble. He remembered how Marcia had looked, standing in the doorway.

"Whoa," he said quietly. His words were surprisingly loud in the silence of this remote setting, at the edge of the wilderness on this quiet evening in late March. He wandered back to the hot pit slowly, hearing a burst of muffled laughter from the house.

The pig sizzled and spit burning grease onto the glowing coals, spawning flare-ups that cast rays of red and amber light against the sides of the pit. Heat from the coals pressed against Tommy like an unseen hand. He slipped on his insulated gloves and began to baste, watching the rich sauce as it oozed across the surface and snapped and bubbled at the edge before dripping into the flames.

In the canal behind him, a heavy splash signaled the entry of a large alligator into the water. *He must be hungry,* the Sheriff mused, *just like me.* He thought again of Delia's conversation and smiled ruefully, shaking his head.

Me, harmless? I wish! He knew better. Tommy Durrance knew how much harm he had done in his lifetime. He had wasted his youth and neglected his young wife, carousing like a fool, staying out late during her pregnancy until a terrible automobile accident had taken her life and the life of their unborn child.

He could never repair the damage wrought during those wild, wasted years. Nor could he take back the hot-tempered times in his youth when he had used anything <u>but</u> the minimum required force. Delia was wrong. He was definitely <u>not</u> a harmless man. At this point in his life, however, he was considerably less harmful than he had been 20 years ago, and for that he was profoundly grateful.

Marcia Woodruff troubled him.

Tommy Durrance was 53 years old. He had no desire to ruin another woman's life, especially the life of a young woman with her best years ahead of her.

Over the past two decades he had avoided romantic entanglements by perfecting the art of gracious disarmament. He had deflected every advance and deftly avoided every compromising situation. With Marcia, however, he found himself taking the opposite tack against his own will: hoping to catch her eye and wishing that somehow, they could be alone. This troubled him deeply. He could not imagine that he could be anything but bad news for a woman . . . any woman.

Twenty years after his wife's death, he still mourned her passing. And yet, at some profound level, he had healed from the worst of the grief and was suffering, instead, from unresolved guilt.

With his faith in the power of grace and forgiveness, he knew that he should not be reproaching himself for behavior that he had abandoned decades ago. But this was real life, not a theoretical construct. In the real world, his practice was falling short of his faith.

He had been warring against hope for years, loathing what he had once been and despising what he had once done. He realized how perversely egocentric this was, but it was hard to abandon the habitual practice of psychic self-flagellation. He was trying to quit, but he had not yet gotten to that point.

Shaking his head to clear the cobwebs, Tommy Durrance took a long pull from his ice cold R. C. Cola. *Man, oh man, R. C. is the best cola, bar none. All I need is a Moon Pie to make this feast complete.* He looked at the pork stretched over the top of the smoking pit and frowned impatiently.

"Cook, Pig," he snarled, painting more sauce onto the top it, "cook, and stop snapping at me." The pig sizzled and snapped in reply.

"Let's make a deal," he offered, "I'll add the sauce; you add the taste. No more back talk." Pulling back his arm, he noticed that his hair had been singed.

"Shoot," he said aloud. Working too close to the flame, he had been scorched by the light-warping waves of heat.

It was a problem that he should have anticipated. But for some reason, it caught him by surprise.

Swamped

A swamp is a terrible place to live. It is a sorry place to visit and a dangerous place to traverse. But a swamp is definitely a terrible place to live.

For six long months, Streetcar had lived in a steaming cypress swamp. The weather had been mercifully cool and dry during that time, and the mosquito population had been somewhat suppressed. But with summer on its way and the weather returning to the norm, he was prepared to do battle with the full fury of the swamp: limitless clouds of hardcore mosquitoes that attacked in waves and multiplied with reckless abandon as the summer rains began to fall.

The mosquitoes that lived in this forbidding sump were dreadful to behold. They were huge, carnivorous beasts: delicate, diaphanous bloodsuckers that resembled hungry, airborne tarantulas. It was as if they had been cobbled together by an evil Gipetto from flimsy black twigs and a ravenous whisper of gauze.

Streetcar had purchased several quarts of DEET-based insect repellant months ago, and he was confident that it was effective. But if it ever proved inadequate against the coming onslaught, he was prepared to retrieve his hidden canoe and paddle out into the middle of the lake on the worst nights. He had used that particular trick long ago, on a bay in Vietnam.

During his first summer in 'Nam, his team had been temporarily stationed at an ammunitions dump at the edge of friendly territory. Vietnamese mosquitoes, like those in the cypress swamp, were vicious creatures that could penetrate two layers of heavy canvas. One hot Vietnamese night, he had slipped past a sentry and left the camp far behind him, sick of the steamy, unrelenting heat and painful bites from voracious mosquitoes that insinuated themselves through the tiniest break in mosquito netting.

He had paddled out into the huge bay on a small reed raft, making a beeline for open water. Far from shore, the ever-present droning faded away. He drifted in the warm water all night, untroubled by mosquitoes, reveling in the blessed relief as he was rocked quietly asleep beneath the stars.

When he awoke at dawn in a patch of cattails beside a mud-and-stick shack, he looked up to see an old man and a boy standing at the edge of the water: their mouths open, staring at him in blank surprise. The memory made him smile.

For a swamp, this ain't so bad, Streetcar reflected. *Once you get used to rattlesnakes on cypress knees and moccasins swimming on top of the water.*

The baby cottonmouth moccasins had surprised him. They were feisty, irritable whelps that periodically chased him through the shallow water of the swamp, slithering across the surface in his panicked wake like evil charcoal spaghetti. He fled gracelessly before them, sloshing loudly between the tall trees and the smooth brown cypress knees.

Streetcar had established a camp on a dry island in the middle of the dense swamp, and this island had become his home. Here he cooked at dusk on a dry, tiny fire, and here he rested every afternoon. His entire family lived here with him: namely, the cat that had become his furry shadow.

As much as he appreciated this camp and its hump of dry land, Streetcar did not sleep on the ground. He slept in the top of a tree.

Every evening, just before dark, he would cook his meal, eating a portion and locking the rest in his steel mess kit for breakfast. Then he would hike toward the canal and quietly scramble to the top of a huge bald cypress tree. There, just below the topmost branch, he would sling his hammock on the south side, directly across from the huge osprey's nest that dominated the north side of the treetop.

After climbing the tree and securing his bed, Streetcar would carefully roll into the jungle hammock, praying that the zipper would hold, and he would not roll out. Thus far, he had managed to stay inside. This was a great relief, considering that he was 60 feet up a slippery tree that required all his considerable skill to climb.

From the hammock, he could see the farmhouse. The house, weathered and comfortable, was situated atop a low knoll less than half mile away in a clearing ringed with live oaks. Streetcar could monitor the house and surrounding terrain from his treetop. With his night vision goggles and powerful spotting scope, he could study the canal and the pasture that surrounded the oak grove, watching for movement, listening for any sound that might tell him a car, canoe or boat was approaching. As an added security measure, if an intruder crossed the barbed wire fence that bordered the pasture, a monitoring system would alert him.

His evening meal and his climb to the top of the tree were routine by now. But tonight, as he waited on a branch near the top of the tree for darkness to fall, his schedule was rudely interrupted.

When the first car drove through the cattle gate, an infrared beam was broken. At that point, the monitoring system triggered another device that dialed the number of his beeper.

When the beeper on his belt vibrated, alerting him of the intruders, he quickly rappelled down into the shallow water and ran toward the house, ignoring the risk posed by the snakes. As he approached the swamp's border, he paused behind a tree, carefully studying the car that was bumping slowly across the pasture. He recognized Delia Rawlings' vehicle and heaved a sigh of relief.

Streetcar returned the way he had come, sloshing slowly through the darkening swamp. When he reached the top of his tree, he was pleasantly surprised to see that a party was beginning at Jamie's farmhouse. He desperately wished that he could attend, but he knew that this was impossible.

For many years, Streetcar had lived with a painful sense of isolation. An intense feeling of fated separateness gnawed at him from well below the level of intellect, deep in the very heart of his being. He had felt this way since that day in a steaming Vietnamese rice paddy when he had lost almost every man in his unit. That dreadful day had been a turning point that had led to his first medal for valor. It had also led to the CIA's aggressive recruitment of the young man who would prove to be their most talented killer.

In the service of his country, Sally Benuto had done brave, murderous work that placed him outside of the laws of all decent nations, including his own. He had been an idealist, believing that he defended the people of America by assassinating carefully chosen targets. In the execution of his duty he had sought to protect the rights of the free people who had cursed and spat on him when he returned to San Francisco. But that was then, and this was now.

And for now, Streetcar was swamped.

He was determined to hide out in this miserable wetland, for it was the only way that he could stay close to Jamie and safe from the arm of the law. To protect Jamie, he had to stay out of sight.

Once the police connected the dots of the Ybor City arson murders, the trail led directly to his door. Even if there were no hard evidence, they would want to bring him in for questioning: long, tough, and unrelenting questioning.

Streetcar had used Vietnam-era C4 plastic explosives in the Ybor bombing, and the Feds had likely traced the chemical signature by now. In Vietnam, he had ready access to such explosives. Given his rescue of Jamie, his friendship with Jumbo, and the circumstances surrounding Jumbo's murder, he had both motive and opportunity. The conclusion was a no-brainer.

In this steaming, miserable swamp, times were tough. But at least there were no tough questions under a hot light in a sweaty room full of unfriendly faces.

As he considered these things, he had no idea how apropos they were. The Federal noose was tightening. In fact, the Federal effort to capture Streetcar was a topic of discussion at this moment, less than 1,000 yards away from Streetcar's sentinel tree.

A Federal Crime

"Did I hear you talking to that pig?" Delia asked skeptically. Startled by her voice, Tommy Durrance looked up and blinked. He was profoundly embarrassed.

"Yeah. I was talking to the pig."

"Well, did it answer you?"

"Not really. It snapped at me a few times, but I couldn't make out what it was trying to say." Delia smiled and shook her head.

"Have you had a chance to contact the Feds?" she asked, changing the subject. He paused and wiped his brow. She glared at him petulantly, like a woman who was prepared to scold a recalcitrant brother.

"I've been busy," he offered inadequately. He was openly evasive, hoping to defer on the subject for now.

"They called twice yesterday. And today, as you well know, two AT & F agents waited in our lobby for over an hour to talk to you. I was barely able to pacify them by assuring them that you were out of the office and would call them tomorrow. You can't ignore this one, Tommy. It'll come back to bite you." She was reading his mind again, heading him off at the pass.

Tommy poked the pig with a long fork and frowned bitterly. Delia was not discouraged by his tactic. "Really, Tommy," she continued relentlessly, "I haven't had a chance to tell you about this stuff. Every time I try, you're too busy to listen."

"Okay." He sighed and put down the implements. "Let's sit down. Tell me everything." He reached into the ice chest and pulled out two bottles, offering her one. "R. C. Cola?"

"Sure," she replied, taking it from his hand. "What, no Moon Pie?" He smiled faintly as they sat on opposite sides of the picnic table, facing one another.

"Okay, what did they tell you?"

"The Bureau of Tobacco and Firearms is hot on this one. You remember the plastic explosives that were used in the Ybor City bombing?"

"Yeah. That's old news."

"Well, this part isn't. Last week, a Federal lab confirmed the manufacturer's lot. This week, they dug up the audit trail for that particular batch of C4. And just guess what they learned yesterday."

"What?" *I don't want to know,* he thought, but did not say.

"The explosive was manufactured in 1969 by an Army contractor and was delivered in 1970 to a firebase in South Vietnam. Part of the shipment was still at the base when it fell at the end of the war.

"The firebase that received the C4 had a heavy CIA presence. But just guess who was staying at that particular base back in 1973, between covert missions into unmentionable territories?"

Tommy sighed. The answer was obvious, but unwelcome. "Salvatore Benuto."

"Right. Streetcar."

"What else do the Feds have?"

"At the end of the war, the U.S. Army abandoned the base under heavy enemy pressure. The records are incomplete. Somebody could have smuggled plastic explosive out of the camp during the confusion at the end, but there's no proof one way or the other.

"According to personnel records, Streetcar was stationed at the base just before it was overrun. He disrupted the enemy's advance and apparently saved a number of lives. But just guess what that particular military action involved."

"C4?"

"Right. Large quantities of C4, all from the same batch used in the Ybor City bombing."

"What else do they have?"

"What else do they need? This gives them the link they were looking for." Tommy frowned uncomfortably. Before this development, there had been no solid evidence that connected Streetcar to the Ybor City bombings. But this information changed everything.

"Without more evidence or something that places him at the scene, the C4 fingerprint isn't enough to convict him," he replied half-heartedly.

"You're probably right, Tommy. But they definitely have enough to charge him and make an arrest. They used to have nothing but motive. Now they can show opportunity, and they can directly link him to the murder weapon. The jury can decide whether to convict him." She squinted into his eyes. "Right now, Tommy, he looks guilty as sin."

"You're right," he said, shaking his head ruefully. "I agree with your assessment. But do you know why the Feds are so eager to share this information with us? What can we offer them?"

"They think he's somewhere around here, Tommy. Somewhere nearby. They want us to help find him." Tommy stared Delia without seeing her, lost in thought.

"It is our job," he said, as if he regretted the fact. In the course of his career, Tommy had been nothing if not dutiful. But this was different. Neither of them wanted to take aggressive action to arrest Salvatore Benuto given the facts of the case, the unsavory nature of the victims and the apparent culpability of the Provencenti Family in the murder of Streetcar's only friend, Jumbo Poindexter.

With this last piece of Federal evidence, they could avoid the issue no longer. They sat together in silence for a while, until finally, Delia spoke.

"The Tampa Police have given us a lot of information. From what we've learned, I think Streetcar's on a one-man mission to protect Jamie. He's probably in Oree County, just like the Feds think. In fact, I'll bet he's near us, right now." Her eyes met his, and Tommy nodded grimly. He rubbed his hand through his mixed jet-black and snow-white hair and slumped as if the wind had been knocked out of him.

"Red has told us all we need to know about Streetcar," he whispered glumly. He stood and cleared his throat, stretching and gazing into the darkness. "He said that he practically had to move heaven and earth to get the guy's service records. He finally got a guy in Atlanta to show him the records, but he couldn't get any copies. He called me yesterday with the whole story. I've been meaning to tell you, but we've been to busy."

"Well, tell me. What's the story?"

"In Vietnam, Streetcar was what we used to call a one-pack," he began slowly. "He was a one-man hit team. There weren't more than a handful of those guys in the entire Army, probably less than five. One of those guys from World War II was the father of my college roommate, and that's how I learned about them. I heard some rumors about them in Vietnam, but never any details.

"Red told me yesterday that Streetcar was the best of the breed. He won two classified silver stars and a bronze star to boot. From what he told me, if the Mafia makes a move to kill Jamie, Salvatore Benuto is worth 20 deputies."

"You're right, Tommy. But it's just like you said; our job is to bring him in. Besides, the Feds are chafing against the bit that you and Clay stuck in their mouths in Federal court. They won't know Jamie's location until the trial is over. And they're not stupid. They know they can't find Streetcar without Jamie."

"Okay," Tommy said suddenly, sitting up and straightening his back. "It's our duty, so we'll pull out all the stops to help them find Streetcar.

"The trial is next week, and the Bass Baiter's tournament is about to begin. Until the trial is over, every officer in Oree County will be working overtime just to keep up with basic patrolling, given the number of people who will be visiting the county.

"The network news crews will be here in full force: CNN, the big newspapers: you name it, not to mention the bass fisherman, support teams, and fans. The population of Pezner will double. The tournament might end before the trial, who knows? After one or the other is wrapped up, we'll free up two of our best deputies to search this area."

"Two officers?"

"Yeah, two. Any more than that and we might as well send out a marching band with drums and cymbals; we'd have zero chance of finding him. But if we send out the right pair of deputies who know how to hunt, we just might get lucky."

"A two-deputy search party for a capital arson suspect? That'll make the Feds happy."

"I don't care if it makes them happy," Tommy replied with a sternness that startled Delia. "It's the only way we have a chance to catch a man with his training. Besides, it's our county, and it's our call. The Feds have their jurisdiction, and we have ours. Let's get a conviction for the murder of Johnny Delaney. In the meanwhile, as soon as we can, we'll search for the guy who blew up mob headquarters." Against her will, Delia found herself smiling.

"That sounds like a good plan."

His reasoning was impeccable. Their department was stretched too thin by far, and they would be short-staffed until the trial or the tournament ended. Given security constraints and the need to protect their star witness, they could not spare their best deputies until then. And it would definitely take their best deputies to find Salvatore Benuto, if he could be caught.

Of course, there was an obvious flaw in Tommy's plan. Given the length of the tournament, the trial was likely to end before it the final bass was weighed. After her testimony next week, Jamie would come out of hiding, and Streetcar would probably leave Oree County for good.

In all likelihood, the searchers would find nothing but a cold fire and an empty camp.

If they found anything at all.

Adventures in Muckland

A swamp is a terrible place to live. Streetcar had to admit it. But when he was at rest in the top of his tree, he could forget about the miseries of the swamp.

In the top of his tree, he would leave his troubles behind. He would rest in the hammock with his head propped up: watching the house, dozing off, and waking at the break of dawn to unhook his bed and climb down. Life at the top was not too bad. But life on the ground was another thing altogether.

Out of a healthy dread for water moccasins, Streetcar lingered every morning on the lowest branch of the tall tree, waiting until daylight before descending into the fragrant water below his perch. He hated the floor of the swamp.

The swamp's floor was a slick, flat, foot-deep mirror of dark water that hid a squishy mat of rich black muck. These badlands were neither land nor water, but were a nether region between: a place where the lake and the land had uneasily decided to cohabitate. The floor of the swamp was a veritable sump of plenty: a vast, fecund puddle of pure, earthy ooze that reeked of dank fertility beneath black water that reflected the landscape above it.

In the daylight, one had only to look down to see the reflected images of slick tree trunks and twisted cypress knees, backlit by a brilliant blue sky. The dark water provided a superb mirror image of the swamp that trembled and rippled under the influence of water bugs. The skittering bugs caused the colors of land and sky to dance and bleed together lavishly: leaves, blue backlight and overarching trees mingling mysteriously in a delicate rainbow whorl.

The gnarled cypress knees and weathered tree trunks were covered with green algae and dusty air plants that attached themselves to every spare flake of cypress bark. It was a no-man's land bursting with life, an unholy warren of bugs and frogs and moss and snakes and unrelenting Dixie chiggers that seemed determined to rekindle the Civil War, which was still called "The Recent Unpleasantness" in this part of the country.

The alligators were easy to spot. The snakes, sad to say, were more cunning. Clothed in mottled camouflage, they blended seamlessly into the stillness as they waited for prey without moving, as silent as the stones beside a path.

Sometimes the snakes slithered stealthily through the water, barely noticed as they sought out the treasures of the swamp. They slipped across the surface with the faintest of ripples, swift and relentless in pursuit of prey.

There were scads of snakes in this swamp.

These were not placid garden snakes or complacent farmhouse scavengers. These were wild, angry serpents with attitude that feared nothing and hated everything: serpentine brutes that would dance with the devil at the drop of a cloven hoof.

At the top of his cypress tree and nowhere else, Streetcar found safety and rest. This was his sanctuary. Here, he found respite from the steamy sameness of the deadly swamp.

His lofty treetop perch was the very pinnacle of the swamp. And, as was fitting for the swamp's summit, the site provided him with a surprising variety of experience.

The birds had startled him at first. Creatures of the sky, seeing him in their own native element, did not seem to fear his presence. They perched fearlessly nearby, within touching distance at times, ignoring him or watching disinterestedly as they preened and cleaned their feathers.

More than once, an osprey landed close to stare inquisitively with head cocked and one proud eye locked on the uninvited intruder. Owls occasionally lingered near the top of the tree, hooting mysteriously and scanning the terrain for movement. In the pause before dawn, he sometimes heard the distant thunder of wild turkeys coming down from their roosts.   Once, deep in the swamp, he heard two bears conversing in rich, guttural growls.

The Maine Coon cat had adapted swimmingly to his new home. With his hair thinned considerably by Streetcar's sheers, he could handle the steamy heat. All in all, he was really quite content.

The cat did not care for Streetcar's nightly excursions, or for his tall sentinel tree. He hated the water and cared even less for the owls and ospreys. But he loved, he positively adored, the little island that he had come to call home.

The Maine Coon hunted all night on the isolated hump of dry land, waiting patiently for nutria, mice, or snakes that were careless enough to cross his path. He returned to the campfire at dawn to carefully lick his whiskers and curl up against his human companion while Streetcar ate a cold breakfast and talked quietly to his only friend.

"You're not half bad for a cat," he would offer as he stuffed his face with turtle, water bird, frog legs, raccoon, possum, catfish, shell crackers, bass or bream. As the cat listened to Streetcar, he would purr like a Ferrari idling at a traffic light. The volume was ear splitting, and Streetcar never ceased to marvel at it.

"Now I know why you liked that truck," he would tell the cat. "It sounded just like you." As if in answer, the cat would kick up the volume to another level, stretching on his back and exposing his stomach as he purred like a Maserati without a muffler.

After breakfast the man would rise, pick up his arrows and bow, and stealthily creep away. Every morning he hunted, driven by the compelling desire for variety in his diet. If all else failed, he would practice archery by shooting at frogs, carefully retrieving his bright titanium arrows after each shot.

He was always searching for something different, something like - dare he dream - a turkey! The frogs were his daily fallback position, a desperate act of dietary last resort. In

343

this swamp, he had quickly learned one bitter truth. Poached frog legs soon lose their luster as a dietary staple.

As a final, hopeful act before hunting frogs, he would approach the canal and pull in his trotline. If he were rewarded, he would find a soft-shelled snapper or a catfish on one of the hooks.

If he came up empty, there were always the frogs.

Poached, boiled, roasted, hot or cold, they were as reliable as Spam and as gamy as dried armadillo. If the truth were told, they had worn out their welcome long ago. By now, to Streetcar's taste buds, the frogs were as rank as any creature that had ever croaked, swam, buzzed, oozed, or slithered across a cypress knee.

He was trying to make the best of it, but he had to admit it.

A swamp is a terrible place to live.

After Dinner Friends

"Tell her," Clay was saying, "go ahead; tell her what they called you in college." Marcia glanced at him sternly, then sighed and shook her head, finally relenting.

"Okay, okay! They called me, The Mole. I spent so much time in the library, they said I was ignoring life."

"The Mole?" Jamie blurted spontaneously. "That doesn't fit <u>you</u> at all!"

"Believe it," Marcia replied, looking daggers at her fellow attorney, "I got no respect. It's still that way, to this day." She reached over and punched Clay in the arm. "That's the down payment for telling my professional secrets. And the balance will come when you're not expecting it!" He grinned broadly, winking and grimacing.

"Just tell me, dear colleague," Clay rejoined, "was that a punch, or were you brushing off a piece of lint?"

"You'll find out later," Marcia replied sweetly, "when you're not expecting it." Jamie cleared her throat to get their attention. She had come to know them well during the past months, and knew that they would want to hear what she now had to say.

"I have a surprise for you. For all of you," Jamie began. They stopped talking and looked at her expectantly.

"I've met somebody." Seeing their surprise, she hastily clarified her meaning. "I mean, it's someone I knew before, but I didn't know him very well." Ellen sat up and looked at their companions.

"What <u>do</u> you mean, you met somebody?" she asked archly. *She met somebody, and she didn't tell me about it!* Recognizing her friend's tone, Jamie smiled.

"It happened like this. The other day, I was on the dock fishing, and a guy drifted up in a canoe. You know, it's really quiet out here, and usually I can hear something like a canoe moving through the water. But it was windy that day, and I didn't hear him. When he got close to the dock, we saw each other."

"What happened?" asked Ellen, suddenly feeling tense.

"I panicked. I dropped the rod in the water and ran up to the house."

"And?"

"He got the rod and came up and knocked. I had the shotgun ready, and I wouldn't open the door. Then, he explained who he was, and I remembered him from the bank. He used to come in almost every week. You might remember him; he was the guy at the nightclub, the one who asked us if we were okay on the night we got into the accident. You know him, don't you, Sheriff?

"Anyway, he was so quiet and polite, I guess I trusted him. I let him in the house."

"You? You let him into your house? You?" Ellen looked around wonderingly and pointed at Jamie's companions. She pointed a finger at them accusingly. "All of you are in on this. You've replaced Jamie with a double!"

"It's proof of Delia's evil twin theory," interjected Clay irreverently. The Sheriff sat up and cleared his throat.

"I know the young man you're talking about, Jamie. He's Donny Hawkins," he said.

"That's him," Jamie replied, lighting up.

"I've known him since he was a little guy," the Sheriff said soberly. "He's a good kid, the quiet type. You can barely drag a word out of him." Everyone but Jamie let out a collective sigh, relieved by the Sheriff's endorsement.

"But he's not quiet with me, Sheriff," Jamie replied quickly, "not when he's here, anyway." She caught herself, aware that she had said too much. "Okay," she added sheepishly, "he's come by here more than once." Knowing that they were obsessively concerned with her safety, she felt guilty, as if she had done something wrong.

"He came by here more than once?" Ellen asked, arching an eyebrow, miffed that Jamie had not told her.

"Well, I guess he's been visiting every day, actually," Jamie replied hesitantly, "except for today."

"Except for today?" Ellen answered testily, her head shifting from side to side. "Except today, when your best friend just happens to be visiting?"

"Ellen, please don't take it wrong. I really want you to meet him. He's coming by tomorrow. I just wanted to tell everybody at the same time. Everyone here has been so nice to me."

Jamie trusted everyone in the room. She had never had trusted this many people before, and she wanted to share the news with all of them. Perceiving this, Ellen nodded and reached out, placing her hand on Jamie's.

"I'm glad for you, honey," she said, fighting back a surge of emotion that threatened to send tears trickling down her face. "I'm sure he's a great guy." She sniffed and looked over at Delia, who was also blinking back tears.

Jamie's resiliency was amazing. Having survived a nightmarish childhood, she was spending her twentieth birthday party hiding out from Florida's most powerful crime family. And yet, for all that, she still harbored the hope that life could be good.

All of those gathered here shared Jamie's hope. It was almost painful to see the fresh, hopeful look on her young face. On Jamie's countenance, the promise of youth was mingled with wisdom beyond her years, tinged by fear of the unknown.

Jamie was graced with an innocence that was wise beyond worldliness. Her hope transcended the reach of bitter experience, flourishing in spite the odds stacked against it. Her hope had survived intact in spite of her past, escaping the demons of yesterday like a dove taking wing.

As they considered these things, the emotion in the room was almost palpable. But before their feelings could get the best of them, Delia deliberately broke the mood.

"So, you've met a guy."

"Yeah."

"The cowboy from the night club?"

"Yeah."

"I've seen that boy up close," Delia said. "He applied for a job with the road division about a year ago, and I did the interview. We offered him the position, but he couldn't take it because his father had gotten sick and he had to help out at the ranch." Delia looked at Jamie and Ellen and glanced at the two attorneys. She determinedly ignored the Sheriff, who was staring at her quizzically.

"Now, let me tell you, Jamie Jameson. If that boy is half as good as he looks, you're in pretty good shape." Jamie blushed hotly as they all laughed. She was not accustomed to such an environment: safe and happy, enjoying a special moment with friends.

She had always dreamed that life could be good, and she had secretly wondered if it were true. Now, she had an answer: life could be good, after all. *I wonder,* she thought, *does life ever stay this good for long?*

Life at the Top

Not far from the knoll on which the house sat, in the top of a tree near the canal, with senses sharpened by long months of profound silence, Salvatore Benuto could hear the laughter coming from the farmhouse. It was faraway hint of joy cascading down the hill, a soft kiss of happiness that spilled softly into his universe like the whispered blessing of a distant angel. He laid his head on his pillow and smiled at the stars, warmed by the distant sounds as if he were there with Jamie and her friends.

Months ago, he had added a window of mosquito netting to the jungle hammock directly above his head. Through this window he could see the distant stars or watch as the luminous clouds slipped in front of the moon. On rainy nights, he stretched a waterproof tarp across the branch above him, making a roof over the entire bed. But on nights like tonight, he would gaze up through his window and savor the beauty of the stars that quivered in the surreally darkened sky. They were at once familiar and strangely mysterious: too far away to comprehend, but almost close enough to touch.

At some time past midnight he fell asleep, serenaded by the faint sounds of conversation from the house. The visitors would stay with Jamie until tomorrow. For this one precious night, Streetcar would sleep soundly.

They would all sleep soundly while they could. Next week, when Jamie testified at the capital murder trial of Joseph Provencenti, Jr., none of them would find any rest. Sleep itself would be a memory of times gone by.

The Devil You Know

Joe Boy was seething as he gazed through the blinds at the main street of Pezner. *Some main street,* he reflected bitterly, *it's as dead as a back alley.*

In the dim light before dawn, the entire downtown was deserted save for a lone newspaper vendor noisily loading the Tribune into a steel and glass rack. Far down the street, Joe Boy could see the bright lights of a tiny breakfast restaurant frequented by hunters and fishermen and the leading lights of town.

The distant diner was tightly packed and noisy: a bustling glow in the pre-dawn darkness. Somehow it beckoned to Joe Boy perversely as the only action in town. Sickened by the unseemly wholesomeness of it all, Joey turned to Franco in disgust.

"Pezner!" he said, sneering as if the name tasted bitter as it left his mouth. "Frankie, do you think they named this town after the candy? You know, Pez, the candy tablets that come in a dispenser?"

"Sure," Franco mumbled, scarcely glancing up from a dog-eared copy of yesterday's Wall Street Journal.

"This town is the world's biggest Pez dispenser, Frankie. They feed live hicks in one end and spit dead hicks out the other, right into that cemetery on the hill." He pointed to his left, at the small cemetery on the edge of town. "They sure named it right. Pezner."

"Hey, I think you're onto something," said Franco, putting down his paper and leaning forward. He squinted and paused to take a deep, bitter drag on his hot cigarette butt. "They've got quite a racket goin' on down here."

"You ain't kiddin'. They're makin' money at both ends, from the cradle to the grave."

"Sweet!"

"I'll say! It's the Pezner family business. Breed 'em, fatten 'em up with lots of greasy food, and bury 'em on top of the hill. Along the way, each generation breeds another. It's like recycling."

"Just one big, happy family."

"You got that right."

"It's the first family of Florida, Joey: the Pezner Family," Franco declared with a wink. "Live by the grits, die by the grits." Joey grunted his assent.

"Right. But what are we doin' in Pezner, Frankie? We don't belong in this family. People marry their cousins in places like this."

"Wait, wait!" Franco said, not willing to abandon Joe Boy's concept so quickly. "I think you're on to something with this recycled hick thing." He snapped his fingers excitedly.

"It's, you know, like a circle. The dead hicks push up daisies; the pigs root up the daisies and eat the worms. The live hicks eat the pigs, get heart disease from the lard, and become dead hicks so they can push up more daisies. Bingo! The whole circle starts over."

Franco slapped his knee excitedly, almost leaping out of his chair. "It's the Circle of Life!" he crowed ebulliently. "Like in the Lion King."

"It's the Circle of Hicks," Joe Boy replied bitterly.

"Just like the movie."

"Speaking of the Pezner Family, the bail bondsman must be the judge's brother," Joey continued undeterred. "Two million bucks bail! Can you believe it?"

"Well, if that yuppie prosecutor had gotten his way, you'd still be in jail."

"Yeah, me in jail. Who could imagine, with my squeaky clean record?" He looked injured when he said it. As incredible as it seemed, Joe Boy was serious.

"Who could imagine it?" Franco asked facetiously. "What, you, in jail? It's unthinkable!" Hearing Franco's sarcasm, Joe Boy turned red.

"They got nothin' on me, Frankie, remember that. They got not<u>hin</u>'!"

"Right," Franco was bored by this tired dodge already. "Sure thing. Anyway, what I hate the most is that we're stuck in this hinky county. The judge was an idiot. 'BAM' with the hammer, just like that, and we can't leave the county until after the trial. Who does he think he is?"

"He's the judge," Joey suggested.

"Oh, yeah."

"But it still ain't fair!"

"What is it with these people?" Franco wondered aloud, ignoring Joey's ridiculous complaint.

"They're stupid, that's what. They're inbred, low-browed, stupid southern hicks."

"You pay two million to make bail, and we still have to stay in the county."

The two hoods were going stir crazy in their cramped quarters. The local motels and apartments had been booked for months due to next week's Bass Baiter's national championship. As a result, they had been forced to lodge in a cheesy fleabag hotel in the heart of downtown.

The thought of facing Florida's electric chair in a one-horse town like Pezner galled Joe Boy. He blamed the girl. She had refused to die, and he would not rest until he had evened the score. Full of self-pity, he stared down at the empty street and cursed the coming day.

His eye caught movement and focused just in time to see a yellow and white cat as it began to cross the road. The tabby padded daintily across the damp asphalt, gazing around carefully for cars and stray dogs. Seeing it, Joey shuddered and turned away. He had long suffered from a phobic dread of all things feline, be they great or small.

"Tell me how it happened last night," he blurted, changing the subject. "How'd they manage to give our guys the slip?"

"You remember how our connections at General Telephone got us the address of the girl's best friend?"

"Yeah.   They traced the call she made from the Columbia."

"On the morning she stole your car," Franco added with an inward smile. "Which was just a couple of minutes before Nick and Jim had their hats handed to 'em by the bum."

"That's ancient history," Joe Boy said, gritting his teeth, annoyed at Franco's flippant attitude.

"I guess," Franco said casually. *Gotcha.*

"Nick and Jim are dead now, anyway."

"May they rest in peace," Franco responded respectfully, making the sign of the cross on his forehead, chest, and shoulders.

"They're dead, you idiot!" Joey interjected hotly, infuriated by Franco's gesture. "They're just plain dead, and that's the end of it!"

"Whatever," Frankie replied defensively. *You believe what you want to, I'll believe what I want to,* he thought. *And I believe in tradition, pal, whether you like it or not.* But he did not dare say this aloud.

"You shouldn't do that stuff for Nick and Jim," Joe Boy went on. "They were stone killers, just like the rest of us. If that religious mumbo-jumbo is true, they're both burnin' in Hell right now."

"Well, maybe," Franco replied impassively. "Who knows?" Franco did not really believe in heaven or hell or any of the rest of it, but he stubbornly refused to dishonor the traditions of his family just to please Joey.

"What d'you think?" Joey continued, "Do you think that Nick and Jim got right with God there at the end, maybe in the last split second? Whad'ya call that, 'just in time deliverance?' Just before the building blew, or maybe right when the explosion sucked the air out of their lungs, they got right with God in the last possible split second? Just before they were turned into charcoal? Give me a break!"

"Well," Frankie replied, "maybe they went to purgatory." *Try that on for size!*

"How likely is that?"

"I guess it isn't," Franco admitted. *But I still ain't gonna dishonor my family tradition, you bloody freak,* he did not add.

Franco was in the wrong line of work, and he knew it. He should quit, but there was a lot of money in what he did. For that reason, he knew he would stay.

Life as a soldier in a major crime family was usually routine and boring, and the work rarely involved violence. The implied threat of violence was sufficient to solve most conflicts. But in some cases, direct action was required.

Franco would convince himself during quiet periods that his career was basically benign. This strategy would work well until the next grisly hit. The dirty work challenged his concept of loyalty, decency and honor: family values that were most often honored in the breach.

"So tell me again what happened last night, Frankie. And cut out the mumbo-jumbo."

"Okay. So, remember the girl's friend, the banker?"

"Yeah, sure. Her name is Ellen... Helen... somethin' like that."

"That's the one. She left Tampa yesterday afternoon and our guys followed her, just like we planned."

"We followed her from Ybor City to Oree County. Our guys switched cars three times, and she never knew we were there. We had a couple of other guys following the attorneys." They had known it was the star witness' birthday, and on a hunch had decided to tail some of the people who might know where she was hiding.

"But these guys were smart. Our tails had to sit way back on the deserted two-lane highways, and the people they were followin' used some tricky turnoffs and switchbacks. They lost 'em. All of 'em. We're no closer than we were before."

"It ain't over yet, Frankie."

"Nope. Not by a long shot."

They would use their fallback plan to locate the girl's hideout, and it was a good one . . . nearly infallible. Their family's best killer had set up his side of the scheme, and Franco and Joey would not foul up theirs.

Franco was thoroughly deceived, believing that their plan had the Don's approval. And while the weather held, Joey and Mickey's evil scheme was on the fast track for success.

Like all successful predators, they were willing to bide their time. Hunting was like that. You waited, and you waited, and you were about to give it up when the prey appear right in front of you, just begging to be shot.

It was always like that.

They were experienced in these things, and experience gave them confidence that in due time, the young woman would be found. She would be cornered and slaughtered and dismembered, scattered in the Gulf of Mexico as a lesson to the multitudes by reason of her unexplained disappearance. She would be, in the end, an untraceable thumb in the eye of anyone who might even think about rising up against them. She would be a tale to be told around urban campfires - a public sign to strengthen the hand of Tampa's First Family.

Jamie had surprised them the first time. But they were confident of one thing.

The next time they met, the surprise would be on her.

Q and A

On the morning after the party, Delia Rawlings and Tommy Durrance were the last to leave. They lingered after breakfast, sipping their coffee, asking questions and carefully listening to Jamie's replies.

"You seem to be doing well," Delia was saying. They had just finished washing and putting away the dishes and were enjoying a few moments of rest before their long drive to town.

"It's been nice out here," Jamie replied, relaxed and happy. "What can I say? It was horrible at first." She pushed back a long strand of dark red hair that had fallen across her face. "Johnny was all I had. I met him the first month after I came to Oree County, more than two years ago. We were close, Delia, maybe too close. We were like a brother and sister. We didn't have any friends except for our friends at work. We were together every night and apart only to sleep. We even woke one another up with phone calls in the morning. I guess I could have fallen in love with him, but the idea never occurred to me. He was my friend.

"Johnny was so nice, so decent, so moral. He drove me crazy sometimes. He could get on his soapbox." She stood, looked out the kitchen window, down to the dock at the canal. Faint smoke, rising from the remnants of last night's cookout, slowly crossed her field of vision: luminous, slowly-twisting strands, highlighted in the slanting rays of the morning sun.

"This has been a real revelation for me, living here. I guess you could say that I've come full circle. I came down here believing that there was no God. My father was a bad cop. He was a rapist and a pervert . . . what can I say? But he was a cop. He got away with it.

"When I moved down here, I met Johnny. He was a good, decent man, like nobody I ever met. He became my best friend. But then he was killed, and my life was turned upside down. And now, in spite of everything, I've come to believe that God is good. Please, tell me how that makes sense?" Delia and the Sheriff exchanged a curious glance.

"I guess you had to be there," Delia responded.

"Yeah, I guess."

"It makes sense to me, Jamie," Delia added. "And I can't explain it, either."

Glancing out the window, Jamie saw Ellen walking toward the dock, carefully looking out for snakes, mincing delicately through the tall grass. Jamie smiled, admiring her best friend's pluck. She knew it took a lot of courage for her to walk alone toward a canal infested with alligators and assorted aquatic reptiles.

"Johnny listened to me. He understood things." Her eyes narrowed, and she turned back to her companions.

"Sheriff, do you remember the conversation we had on the way back from Homeland Estates, after we visited the crime scene?"

"Of course."

"I'd like to pick up where we left off. Do you mind?"

"Not at all," he offered. She paused thoughtfully before replying.

"Okay, Sheriff, you were saying that God is good. I've come to believe that, too. But why should He bother to save us from death? And why would He offer only one way to salvation? I mean, that seems so exclusionary."

"Well, you said that you believe that God is good. Why do you believe that?"

"It's obvious," she said, looking around, waving at the wilderness beyond the kitchen window. "The beauty of this wilderness makes the point. I don't see how anyone could believe that life is an accident. This wilderness was created without human intervention, but it's amazingly complex. Everything about it is way over our heads."

Jamie raised her eyebrows. Standing in front of the sink, barefoot in faded overalls, with burgundy hair cascading

357

over her shoulders, she looked like she had grown up wild and free in this country: riding horses across these fields, climbing the hills, and wading in the narrow creek beds.

"The past winter has been a real learning experience. This is incredibly beautiful land," she continued. "It had to be created by a poet. The fact that all of us can enjoy it, regardless of who we are and what we've done . . . that's proof of God's goodness, isn't it?"

"Yes," he replied quietly.

"Then what about Johnny?" she asked, choking back the emotion. "What about death? Every living thing doomed to die, it's just too miserable. Why would God allow it?"

"That's probably one of the toughest questions I know of," he answered, sighing. "If God is good, why does He allow death? To answer that, you have to go way back."

"To Adam and Eve?" Jamie asked doubtfully.

"Yes. The truth is, human beings were created to live forever. Something inside of us cries out that we <u>should</u> live forever. Otherwise, why would we question the existence of death?

"Death is natural, but it seems unjust. It seems cruel. But if there was no death, cruelty itself would never die.

"Death ends tyranny. This much makes sense to us. We don't want Hitler to live forever. But if death happens to everyone, how can that be a good thing?

"Our instincts tell us that we should live forever, and I believe this is true. Death was not something that God desired for humanity. It was introduced after the first humans quit trusting God."

"Adam and Eve? How did they quit trusting God?"

"Satan persuaded Eve that God was trying to keep them away from the really good stuff. They both fell for it, and you know the rest.

"A long time after Adam and Eve, God had a friend in Abraham. God promised that through him, all nations would be blessed. Abraham's grandson Jacob spoke of the blessing in more detail when he prophesied of the Messiah, 'out of

Judah will come the Governor . . . binding his vine to an ass, his choice vine to an ass's colt . . . . "

"That sounds like something I've heard before."

"It's like the prophecy of Zechariah, 'Behold, O Israel, your king comes. He is meek and having salvation, lowly and seated upon an ass, and upon a colt the foal of an ass."

"That's Jesus, riding into Jerusalem."

"Exactly. Jesus was the fulfillment of God's promise to Abraham. Isaiah predicted that God's faithful servant would be 'cut off from the land of the living' and would justify those who believe in him. Jesus, God's Son, came to bless Israel first, and then to bless all nations. He came to give eternal life to all who believe."

"What a deal," she said softly. "But why did God's Son have to give His life for us?"

"Because God is good, and we're not," he answered bluntly. "He has to punish wrongdoers if He is to be just. Should He let murderers into paradise? What about liars? To satisfy justice and mercy at the same time, God took our punishment on Himself.

"We're too proud to consider that God may, in fact, be far nicer than we are. But He is. In Jesus Christ, God gave his best for us. When He rose from the dead, He defeated death forever. It's a small thing for God to raise the dead . . . after all, He is God."

Delia smiled. *Tommy has a gift at stating the obvious.*

"The sacrifice of Jesus Christ was the ultimate gift," Tommy continued. "His life was the ultimate paradigm. He exemplified kindness, honesty, and an awesome, all-powerful love. Through His sacrifice, the doors of heaven were thrown wide open."

"So, we will rise from the dead, too, if we believe in Jesus Christ?" Jamie concluded for him.

"Yes."

"What then?"

"If you love Jesus Christ, you'll believe Him and obey his words. He'll live in you and be with you, like he promised.

"His teachings are all about love. Pure love is harmless, faithful: everything good. Anyone who hates others is not an obedient Christian."

"What if I wasn't raised to believe in this?"

"I wasn't. My father was an agnostic and my mother left home when I was a baby. My ancestors aren't from Israel. But if any person, from any culture, seeks the truth from God, that person will learn the truth about Jesus Christ."

"You're sure?"

"Absolutely. God can't lie, and He promised it."

Jamie tossed back her head and ran her fingers through her hair. She tilted her head forward, frowning and gazing at the floor.

The kitchen floor looks great, she reflected. It was different from the flooring in the rest of the house. It was heart pine, durable and varied in appearance. Thinking these things, she knew that she was stalling for time by letting her mind wander. She finally gave up. She grinned sheepishly, shrugging her shoulders.

"What can I say? I heard it from Johnny, months ago. I just wanted to hear it again to see if it still made sense to me.

"I believe it. It's too good to <u>not</u> be true." She sighed. "Nothing else makes any sense to me. Nobody loves me like He does." Thinking about what Jesus had endured on her behalf, she raised her eyebrows as if to say, 'What else can I do?'

"I've always avoided this subject," she continued. "I ran away from God. I longed for His love, but I pretended it was the last thing on earth I wanted. When anyone raised the subject, I was like Br'er Rabbit, 'No, please, anything but the briar patch!'

"I can't deny it anymore." She smiled wryly, considering her past decisions. She was relieved that she had finally reached a turning point.

"Okay. I believe that God loves me. I believe that Jesus is the Son of God, and I will follow Him." This statement, the first public declaration of her newfound faith, released a tremendous tension within her. She was suddenly liberated from the dread that had descended into her life after Johnny's horrific murder.

What this would mean in the days to come, she had no idea. But she knew that it was the beginning of a monumental change.

And for now, at least, she felt fantastic.

A Convocation of Bass Baiters

It was Friday night at the Silver Spur, and the crowd was preparing for lift off. They were packed to critical mass in the cedar-beamed main room: wall-to-wall people generating an ear-numbing buzz that drove the band's recording meter past the redline with a monolithic, ever-growing, unrelenting spike of roughshod Saturday night sound.

The noise level had been increasing for the past hour as the satin-shirted, cowboy-booted, hard core and semi-authentic country-western audience revved its vocal engines like a 767 firing up to full power: throttling throaty jets to an ear-bending conversational roar, straining to launch into the wild blue beyond as they reached the end of their beer-slicked runway.

Most of the Bass Baiters were relaxing in their motel rooms, busily avoiding the singles' scene at the Silver Spur. But a few famous fisher folk had shown up, lending spice to the same old crowd of spinning dancers and sober music fans and bar-leaning alcoholics from all over the tri-county area.

Yip Farley fell into the latter category. As a respectable bar-leaning alcoholic who paid cash and tipped freely, Yip was a deeply beloved - or should we say, tolerated – character at the Silver Spur. He was particularly excited tonight due to the invasion of the Bass Baiters, and was busily regaling the famous and not so famous with unsolicited quips straight out of The Big Fish Bible.

"Well, if it ain't Howard Eliason," Yip bleated loudly as he staggered up to yet another table of strangers and singled out a tall, pleasant-looking middle-aged man with a gray beard. "Howdy doody, Mr. Eliason."

His victim nodded, embarrassed to be singled out. He was hoping that Yip would go away, but his hopes promised to go unfulfilled.

"Do you really use the Go-Go Glow Worm?" Yip bleated. "You know, the fancy worm you sell on TV?" Yip shouted this question close to his victim's ear, ensuring that he could be heard above the incessant crowd noise.

His was a burning question.

The Go-Go Glow Worm, squishy centerpiece of many an expensive television commercial, was hyped as the hottest thing to splash down since the last Apollo spacecraft. For Yip, who fished religiously, the Go-Go had been a hopeless bust. He desperately needed to know why this was so, and now was his big chance to get the straight dirt, direct from the Go-Go's inventor. He had cornered the Big Baiter of televised fishing, the world-renowned Howard Eliason.

"Uh, yes, I use the Go-Go," Mr. Eliason replied politely. "Have you tried it?"

"Tried it?" Yip asked, leaning closer as he tried to focus on the target of his inquiry as he swayed like a perturbed pendulum. "I like to have almost wore the dad-blamed thing out. I came nigh unto busting a catgut, chuckin' that thing around. In and out, in and out, jest like you said on TV. Only I didn't get no stinkin' bite! Now, ain't that a hoot?" he asked to no one in particular. Yip looked around with a pugnacious, unfocused gaze, blinking dully in the dim light and dense smoke.

In every way, Yip Farley looked to be the authentic hick that he actually was. He was as short and stringy as a toothpick whittled from hog gristle: a wafer-thin, knock-kneed, bristle-haired bottlebrush of a man. Yip Farley was an animated cartoon cowboy in scuffed boots, worn jeans, checkered shirt, and bolo tie. His sunburned, bald, dazzlingly reflective head was hidden beneath a sun-mauled straw cowboy hat that had soaked up and evaporated an ocean of perspiration in its day.

Yip was a bantam rooster out to prove something. Howard Eliason, on the other hand, was a gentle, self-effacing giant who sat hunched down in his chair. Howard acted as if he were sincerely embarrassed by the greatness that had come his way in the fishing tournament of life.

So, this is a representative of my loving local audience, the famous man considered. *Why didn't I listen to my mother and become a banker?* After taking a deep breath and counting to ten, he scratched his chin and began to answer Yip.

"When you used the Go-Go worm, did you follow the instructions on the package?" Howard Eliason asked Yip, not willing to give up on the Go-Go without a fight.

"Follow the instructions?" Yip spat back. "Shoot fire, man, instructions are for fools and id-jits. I just chucked it out there like everything else I fish. My Go-Go done got up and went-went. It kept diving down toward the bottom. I had to stick three corks on it to make it float."

"You need to read the instructions. It's an underwater lure designed to perform between two and five feet below the surface. It goes up and down with about three feet of vertical action."

"Well, I'm a top water guy. I ain't no bottom fisherman. And the Go-Go didn't catch me nothin'.

Howard Eliason tried to catch their waitress' eye, hopeful that her arrival might change the subject. But he had no such luck; seeing Yip at their table, the waitress hurried past.

"If that lure were makin' itself a livin' as a Go-Go dancer in a Go-Go Club, it would'a been booed outta the Go-Go cage, if you catch my drift." Yip was warming to his subject. "Yes sirree bobtail, that lure sure stank. And in a bad way, too, mister! It was slicker'n owl's grease on TV, but it stank in real life.

"Y'all must have used a robot fish in that commercial. Did you use Billy the Singin' Bass, or one'a them animal-tronic robots from Disney World? Because believe me, boys, there ain't a real bass in the whole world that would go-go after such a freaky little lure!"

Howard smiled wearily. "Try reading the instructions," he replied patiently. "It's not a top water lure." He turned to the woman to his right, resuming the conversation that Yip had so rudely interrupted.

"You want me to fish the bottom? Now, that ain't how a man should fish!"

Yip was confused.

He loved to watch largemouth bass angrily snatch a top water lure, blasting halfway out of the water or making a sharp pop that sounded like a hand hitting the surface. Sometimes, on a hot day, a big bass would arise to take a lure with a languorous swoosh before disappearing into the dark, acid-stained murk. He hated to think that this legendary fisherman, the famous Howard Eliason, was - heaven forfend - a bottom fisherman!

"Well, excuse me, Mr. Perfessor," he finished gamely, rising in a huff. "I guess I must'a did it all wrong. I ain't so much for readin' instructions!" He tipped his hat and stormed away in a snit.

As Yip staggered up to the bar, he brushed past a stranger who was deeply absorbed in conversation with a young girl. The man was tall and thin, with a surprisingly realistic golden tan that belied his ash blonde hair. He was not a fisherman and not a dancer; he was a hunter of lost souls whose name was Mickey O'Malley.

"I don't like the hicks around here," the girl was slurring in a rich, unaffected Southern drawl, her eyes swimming with the effects of the liquor. "And they don't like me, either." She ducked her head and took a long pull on her cigarette, tossing her light brown hair back to look at the man beside her.

He was quiet and assured, tall, broad-shouldered, and well mannered: clever and good-looking in a deliberately careless sort of way. *Things are looking up for me,* she thought, gazing up the man and smiling sweetly.

Mickey's new acquaintance was young and sweet and anything but innocent. She was a pretty young woman with long dark hair and skin as clear as cleansing cream. Heavily made up, she was desperately trying to look as mature as the jaded country-western singers she idolized.

"I'm seventeen years old," she added. "But I've been married for more than a year."

"You don't look a day over 16," he replied, smiling slyly.

"Oh, hahaha," she replied demurely, taking another long pull on her cigarette and leaning back, blowing the smoke upwards. "Yeah, I'm married, but my old man and me, we have a deal. He doesn't ask me any questions, and I don't ask him." As if there could be any doubt about what she meant, she looked at him and winked slowly.

He watched her carefully, taking another long sip of the beer that he had nursed all evening. She was vulnerable. There was hurt in her soft brown eyes, mingled with not a little lust.

She's heartbroken, he thought sympathetically. *Somebody's knocked the wind out of her sails. How convenient! I'm here to pick up the pieces. Or to scatter them abroad, as it were.*

"I don't care about my husband. He's a redneck idiot. I hate him," she slurred with her rural Florida accent. She pronounced the word 'him' as if it were two syllables: 'hee-im.'

The young woman's slender right hand shook slightly as she raised the butt to her lips and inhaled. A long arc of ash masked the glowing core of fire at the tip of the cigarette. The ash was a decaying reminder of former glory, a charcoal depiction of human folly grown as long and as curved as an acrylic nail. The ridiculously elongated ash refused to fall into her lap as she held the cigarette and adjusted her earrings. He stared at it, fascinated. *She's gifted,* he thought, staring soulfully at the distended ash, then gazing deeply into her face, lost in the brownness of her eyes.

The lights in the packed roadhouse were flashing, and the band began to play its overpowering opening number. The attention of the audience shifted to the bandstand as the man leaned forward and spoke into the girl's ear. No one noticed as the young girl left through the main entrance and the stranger left through a side door. They met at the shiny black truck parked in the shadows at the rear of the parking lot. The truck had Hillsborough County tags.

He opened the passenger door and she demurely stepped in. When he climbed in the driver's side, she was waiting for him, up close and personal.

As the truck rumbled onto the highway, she leaned her head on his shoulder. In the lights of a passing car, she could see him smile.

"Do you know where we could find some privacy?" he asked, suppressing the tremble of excitement that threatened to steal into his voice.

"There's a place up the road, to the right," she said. "No one will find us there."

"Perfect." They rode along silently for a minute, and then she spoke.

"What did you say your name was?"

"Killer. My friends call me Killer." He liked the sound of it.

They turned right onto a lonely road, passing a deserted farmhouse and continuing down the unlighted roadway that led to the shores of the lake.

After Nightfall

Late Friday evening, Jamie and Ellen sat at the end of the wooden dock that jutted out into the canal, talking and laughing about their high school days. On shore, the insect zappers lit the night with sporadic blue bolts that singed the surrounding air, adding an electrified aura to the wavering light from smoking Tiki torches. On the dock, where the women talked and dangled their feet, all was placid and calm.

Water lapped softly against the dock pilings. It was clean, dark water with a smooth, glimmering surface that belied the activity beneath the surface. The canal was a pristine ecosystem bursting with life: fish and alligators, insects and snakes, turtles and slippery, ubiquitous frogs.

They sat and listened to the sounds of the wilderness. Crickets whirred in the trees, frogs serenaded from the pond, and all was well with the world.

The cove to their right, flat and black, was silhouetted against the starlight. From its weeds came a powerful, deep grunting sound. The sound was repeated again and again, gaining in volume as a male alligator bellowed like a submersed bull, bellowing powerfully from his lily pad lair, "UMPHH-UMPHH-UMPHH-UMPHH." At the end of his soliloquy, the surprisingly loud sound ended with an abrupt "HUFFF."

"Let's go inside," Ellen suggested, rising shakily to her feet. Jamie smiled and waved at her dismissively.

"When I first got here, I used to run into the house every time I heard that sound. Finally I realized that the old bull gator was just warning me to stay away." She raised an eyebrow and gestured for her friend to sit. "We've struck a deal. I'm not going to swim in his cove at night, and he's not going to come onto my dock. So far, he's kept his part of the bargain."

"That was an alligator?" asked Ellen incredulously, "It sounded like a mad moo-cow." She sat back down as Jamie laughed.

"A moo-cow? What on earth is a moo-cow? Is it like, you know, a quack-duck or a croak-frog?"

"No, it's, you know, like a songbird or a knucklehead, you wisenheimer," Ellen replied archly, tossing her hair. "Some people understand about these kinds of things." In the distance across the canal, the wild, haunted cry of a lonely bull rang out, echoing across the watery flats.

"Okay, now <u>that</u> was spooky!" Ellen said, standing again. "Was that a banshee, or just your garden variety monster?"

"That, my dear, was a <u>real</u> moo-cow. A moo-bull, I should say."

"I didn't know that cows could scream like that."

"Only when they're lonely, or looking for a mate, or otherwise expressing their inner calf.

"Some of the ranches around here are huge. The cattle are basically left in the wilderness to fend for themselves. Donny says that sometimes, a bull gets pushed out of the herd by a stronger male. The bull wanders alone, an outcast, searching for a cow to call his own. It's very sad"

"Searching for cow to call his own?" Ellen responded dryly. "How romantic."

"Yeah, a cow to call his own. Or maybe a young heifer, a cow in waiting."

"A cow in waiting? You've been away from Tampa too long, girlfriend."

"Well, Donny said they get lonely, anyway" she responded defensively. "Maybe I'm embellishing a little."

"A little?"

Again, in the distance, the lone bull sounded. This was not a moo or bellow. It was a hopeless shriek, a long, drawn-out wail that dripped with desperation and haunted, inchoate loneliness. It was a primitive, solitary sound that quavered with emotion, saturated with unfulfilled bovine angst.

"Okay, I guess you're right; it must be a moo-cow," Ellen said doubtfully. "At the end of that last shriek, I think I heard a little moo."

"It's not a moo-cow, Ellen. It's a bull."

"Whatever! It sounds like an alien." The bull began to cry out again and again, building to a crescendo before he ended with a long, drawn out howl.

"Okay," Ellen said, smoothing her clothing primly. "What's up next, a dinosaur?" In response to her question, the liquid hoot of a Great Horned Owl sounded in the trees nearby, just across the pond.

"Hooorrrl," it called, purling the end of the tone as if it were gargling water, "Hooorrrl."

"So that really is an alien, right?" Ellen asked with her eyes widening.

"It's a hoot owl," Jamie replied. "I wonder if it's the white one?" A huge albino owl had been visiting lately, sitting high in a massive oak tree during the heat of the day. She had mentioned this to Ellen, who had been less than enthusiastic about meeting the mysterious raptor.

"Hoohoo hoo-hoo . . . hoohoo hoo-hoorr," the owl called. The owl's voice was clear and powerful, with a preternatural sonic quality, a tone as clear as a bell.

"That's a delightful sound, isn't it?" Jamie asked. "It's almost unreal."

"You're unreal," Ellen replied, "and so is the owl, if that's what's making that sound. It really sounds like something from another planet." As if in response to her comment, a huge black shadow slipped from the top of a tall tree - directly across the canal from them - and swept quietly in their direction.

As the owl approached, riding on the wind, it changed from a dark, onrushing blot to an apparition in white that passed overhead as if it slow motion, giving them a long, slow look at its powerful frame. They saw the great white bird clearly as it glided past, illuminated in the warm glow from the torches.

The owl was a pale specter with brownish pink eyes and grim, scaly talons dangling beneath a massive body: a feathered ghost with yellow beak and glistening ebony eyes, huge and powerful. The big bird swept silently past on outstretched wings armored with ivory, dusted with down that was as white and clean and seamless as fresh-fallen snow.

They stared transfixed as it sailed overhead and glided off toward the cove, turning again into a coal-black shadow as it glided soundlessly away. As suddenly as it appeared, it was gone. Jamie and Ellen stared at one another in surprise and exhaled simultaneously.

"Wow!" Ellen said softly, "What was that?"

"That, my dear, was a predator."

"A predator? It creeped me out!" She stood up. "I'm going inside," she said authoritatively, "and this time, you can't make me stay."

"Oh, don't worry about that one, Ellen. That was a relatively wholesome predator."

"Wholesome? It came and went like a ghost. It gave me the creeps."

"It moved like a ghost, you're right," Jamie replied. "The owls come and go on a whisper of wind. And it's a nightmare if you're a mouse or a bunny. But if you're an owl, at least, you're safe. That's why I said it's a wholesome predator. It doesn't prey on its own kind."

"Oh, right, it doesn't eat members of its own species," Ellen said, nodding in agreement. "There's something fairly wholesome about that, I suppose. Compared to the alternative." As Jamie stared silently into the dark, mysterious water, Ellen watched her in the fitful light of the torches, remembering the reason for her best friend's exile to this lonely house at the edge of nowhere, wrapped in the arms of the wilderness.

"Compared to some of the predators in the world," Jamie whispered, almost to herself, "that owl's as pure as the driven snow."

The Killing Shore

When the Sheriff got the call at 9:00 on Saturday morning, he was drinking coffee in his office with Red Johnson, who was visiting Oree County to testify with his FDLE forensics team at the upcoming Provencenti trial. The phone call was short, but disturbing nonetheless.

Tommy Durrance dialed Delia's extension and gave her the news. Within two minutes, the three of them were walking out of the cool interior of the building and climbing into the hot squad car for a drive to Lake Bagly. The Oree County crime scene unit was paged, and the crime van would soon follow them to the scene.

A body had been discovered at a remote site on the shore of a lake in the distant reaches of the county. For the Sheriff, it was déjà vu all over again.

Their squad car rocketed swiftly down the narrow county roads, blowing past cattle that raised their heads and chewed thoughtfully as they passed. The car scattered hungry flocks of buzzards from road-killed armadillos as it whipped past whirring crickets and cattail-lined canals.

Inside of the car, they scarcely spoke. The Sheriff drove as Red and Delia sipped their coffee and reflected, with professional dread, on what lay ahead of them.

The road that led from the highway to the lake was a faded blacktop with weeds growing out of the cracks, a narrow one-lane scar blasted into pieces by the sun. Remnants of a high, shattered concrete curb lined the narrow roadway like a miniature wall of rectangular stone blocks, choked and covered with weeds and grass and long tangles of angry sandspurs.

The terrain grew lush as the car drew near to the lake, transitioning from parched open pasture with islands of palmettos to hardwoods and dark green palms that sinuously snaked upwards toward the bright blue sky, competing to gobble the light. In this dense foliage, a bare trickle of light reached the forest floor.

At the end of the road, they got out and the car and hiked down a twisted path that led through the brush toward the lake. County Coroner Gene Thompson was the first person they saw as they arrived at the crime scene.

From his covered head to his steel-spiked foot, the county coroner was dressed in garish, Kelly green. He looked exactly like what he was: a refugee from a local golf course who had been wrenched away to do his sworn duty in a remote setting.

Gene Thompson glanced up at them absent-mindedly as they arrived after wending their way down the narrow path to the clearing by the shores of Lake Bagly. They saw no corpse, but the pallid scent of death palpably drenched the humid morning air.

"Tommy, Delia, this is a fresh crime scene," Gene said to them as they approached. He was fully absorbed in his work and did not offer any further greeting. "In fact," he continued, "I must say that we are very lucky to find these remains so soon. The victim was killed last night at about eleven o'clock." He raised his rubber-gloved right hand and showed them the proof. Pinched between his thumb and forefinger was a slim, bloody finger: Caucasian, three inches long, covered with a thin wash of dried blood and graced with two shiny gold rings. Delia frowned at Gene and waved both of her hands.

"Gene, did you have to show us that thing without warning?" she asked tartly. "Was that called for?" He did not answer. "Well, was it?" she continued. Delia was visibly perturbed. "We're your partners, Gene" she reminded him, struggling to regain her collegial composure. "Where's the love?"

"Well, the love wasn't here last night, I can tell you that, Delia," Gene replied brightly. "This is the victim's ring finger, to use the layperson's term. She was obviously married, female Caucasian." Gene turned to point at a hole in the ground behind him, then at three others at different spots in the clearing.

"The severed ring finger is what brought us all here this morning," the Coroner offered enthusiastically. "This is the digit that the dog dug up." He looked at them and noticed their bewildered expressions.

"Uh, let me start at the beginning. Earlier this morning, two local boys were fishing over there," he said, pointing to the shore. "Their dog started digging in this clearing. After a while, he ran up to them with this finger in his mouth."

I think I'm going to be sick, thought Delia.

"You see those sticks?" he asked, pointing to a series of sticks thrust into the ground throughout the clearing. "Those are the burial sites identified by the dog. The dog's owner is one clever boy, by the way.

"The older boy stayed here while his little brother ran to call the Sheriff's Department. The big brother took the dog around the clearing, marking every spot where the dog showed an interest. He says he didn't let the dog disturb anything. I've taken a look at spots that he marked. At each one, there's freshly turned earth. I suspect we'll dig up body parts under every stake in this clearing. So far, we're batting a thousand. I checked out two holes, and found two graves." He pointed to a small pile on the ground that was mercifully hidden under a sheet of black plastic.

"I dug up fingers, toes, and a couple of things I won't mention. We're really lucky that these kids went fishing here today. This body - uh, these parts - were buried about 18 inches deep, covered with dirt and loose leaves. They were well hidden. Someone took his time here last night.

"The body might have been here for months, maybe years, before anyone found it. Or it might have never been found. But we got it while the trail is fresh. Maybe we'll have a chance to catch the killer." Gene smiled.

Gene Thompson was heroic, in a sense. He was already savoring the capture of the murderer, a human so twisted and hateful that he killed a young woman and scattered her piecemeal through a clearing in the woods. On the other hand, he seemed untouched by the horror of the carnage.

Gene enjoys his job too much, mused the Sheriff, watching his friend closely as the coroner excitedly shared what he had gleaned. *How does he emotionally separate himself from this stuff?* Gene was a sensitive, caring man, but he had the unnerving ability to separate his grisly work from the tragedies behind it. The Sheriff interrupted, desperate to change the subject, if only for a moment.

"Gene, how did you beat us here?" he asked. "We came straight from the station."

"Oh, yeah," he said, smiling, "that. I was on my way to the country club when I got the call. I was less than a mile away on Highway 23. Just like the last murder, right? The kid in the tree? I beat you to that scene, too. And I missed my golf game, just like today."

"You sure did," Tommy replied.

"So let's look at what's been laid out in this clearing," Gene continued. "Look at the flags. I put flag markers everywhere the dog identified remains. If you look closely, a pattern will emerge."

Delia turned away from the coroner, who was still absent-mindedly clutching the bloodied finger. Staring at the marked spots, she was the first to recognize the pattern traced by the flags.

"It's a smiley face," she said, blushing angrily. "He drew a smiley face." Tommy and Red stared at her, then looked at the clearing again. In the light sifting down through the tall oaks and hickories, they could see what Delia meant. The coroner had excavated two holes and had meticulously marked the others. 26 thin wire stakes with bright orange plastic flags marked the graves, sketching out the rudimentary pattern of a circle containing two dots and an arc. It was, indeed, a connect-the-dots smiley face.

"Well," the Coroner replied, "I think you're correct. The killer has drawn a smiley face with his victim's remains.

"The murderer was most likely a man, since it took a lot of upper body strength to butcher the victim in this manner. And, by the way, if you didn't already know, this does not appear to be a crime of passion. This is the work of a warped mind obsessed with dominance and control.

"The cut marks where the body was divided are smooth and regular, with square edges, curves, all kinds of crazy patterns designed as part of each cut. He - or she - was a very strong person who must have used a surgical saw. It's as if the killer were deliberately deconstructing a human jigsaw puzzle."

All three officers jerked as if they had been jolted with electricity. They gazed at one another, doubting what they had heard and the conclusion that they had simultaneously reached. Tommy spoke up.

"Okay, let's seal off this crime scene immediately. Nobody should disturb the scene. Not even us, Gene," he added apologetically. "For now, Coroner, I think you should do this work alone until the forensics team shows up. Let's all try to step in our own footprints as we leave. Nobody gets in here except for you and Don Waldron."

"That's fine with me, Sheriff. I agree."

The Sheriff turned to Red and Delia. "I don't think we should stay down here. What do you think, Delia?"

"I think you're right. We can count on some major help with this crime scene, Tommy. We shouldn't walk around here anymore. I'm going to call this in."

"When you get up to the car, could you please ask Myrna to patch us through to the FBI, Palm Beach office?" he added. "I'll be right behind you." He let out his breath in a long, whistling sigh, feeling old and weak in the knees.

Red reached out to Tommy and put a hand on his shoulder. He had known the Sheriff since he was a rowdy kid in grade school, and he knew that his friend would take this hard. Tommy Durrance lived and died by the safety of his fellow citizens, agonizing over every crime, sorrowing along with every victim.

Tommy and Red carefully backed out from the crime scene and followed Delia up the bank to the cars parked beside the road. When they reached the cars, Red shook his head somberly and pulled out his cell phone, punching in a number from memory. After a few seconds, he spoke to a party on the other end of the line.

"Hey, Lenny, this is Red. I'm at a crime scene in Oree County." He paused. "Yeah, I know, I'm supposed to be fishin' until the trial, but something came up.

"Do you remember that serial murderer in Tampa about ten years ago, the one they never caught?" He paused again. "Yeah, that one. Well, I'm at a murder scene out in the middle of nowhere. It looks like the same serial killer might have been doing some business in Oree County last night." He paused as the person on the other end of the line asked a question. "Yeah, that's the one," he replied bitterly. Pausing again, he pursed his lips.

"Well, let's put it this way. The person who did the murder last night is either America's most famous serial killer, or he's a real bloody copycat. Either way, this is a big case." He paused again, for almost a minute. "Yeah, I know," he said into the phone. "How likely is such a thing in Oree County? Well, from what I'm seeing, it looks pretty likely. Suffice it to say that Tommy Durrance is calling the FBI, and he's not the hysterical kind.

"I think you'd better send a team down here ASAP, Lenny. If you don't agree, why don't you patch me through to Maureen and I'll put her in charge of this one." He looked at Tommy Durrance and grimaced, then rolled his eyes as the voice spoke on the other end. "I thought so. Okay, tell them to give me a call once they're on their way."

Down by the shore, the lake lapped gently against the sand and a small frog jumped into the water from a drifting lily pad. The beauty of the remote area presented the false impression of deep, profound peace.

A few feet from the lake's shore, in the sun-dappled clearing, ominous, wire stakes and orange flags marked miniature burial grounds. The impromptu earthen crypts below the flags signified disaster for this remote county.

More than ten years ago, an infamous serial killer had murdered several prostitutes in the Tampa Bay area. Then, without warning, the killings had ceased abruptly. Or at least, the killings in Florida had ceased. The killer's last murder in the Tampa Bay area had been his most notorious.

Two prostitutes had been murdered and sawn into curved, finger-sized pieces. Their remains had been buried throughout a vacant lot in a new housing development. A large, plastic smiley face had been placed over each buried body part. It had been eventually discovered, from aerial shots of the crime scene, that the pattern of smiley faces spelled out a name.

Over the next few years, a trail of bodies had been uncovered in the industrial suburbs surrounding Detroit, Michigan and Gary, Indiana. In murder after murder, investigators had confirmed the killer's ghoulish signature: corpses cut into kibbles, meticulously butchered like the pieces of a puzzle. But in spite of a mounting, moldering body of evidence, no suspect had been identified. To this day, ten years and more than 40 known victims later, the killer was still at large.

At the top of the hill, beside the deserted road, Sheriff Tommy Durrance watched the path that led to the lake, leaning against his squad car. He closed his eyes for a moment, waiting patiently as the county dispatcher attempted to contact the Palm Beach office of the FBI.

High above his head, a slight breeze teased the topmost branches of a giant hickory. He looked upwards. The breeze rippled through the pale green, luminous leaves, scattering spots of light and shadow on the ground below. The swirling lights and shadows danced lightly across the musty earth, the weather-beaten road, the green and white squad car, the shimmering windshield and the sun-browned face of the sheriff. He sighed and looked down at the ground.

To Tommy Durrance, the past six months had been unbelievable. First, his rural county had been shaken by an infamous murder and by a trial involving Tampa's most prominent crime family. And to top it all off, a horrific murder had just occurred – a murder that appeared to have been perpetrated by a notorious serial killer.

Why on earth would a big-time serial killer strike here? And why now? It just doesn't make sense. He struck in Tampa Bay, then in the great cities of the upper Midwest, and now in Oree County? As the Sheriff reflected on these things and waited for his two-way radio connection to Palm Beach County, the Oree County Sheriff's Department crime scene vehicle appeared. The late model van idled up to the squad car and slowly rolled to a halt. Tommy raised his hand and signaled that they should come over to talk with him.

He thought of the name of the famous killer. It was the name that had been spelled out by smiley faces in a vacant lot in Hillsborough County years ago. The very thought made him sick.

Sawbones.

There was no glory in this work. There appeared to be little chance that he could apprehend the man who had eluded the FBI's finest for more than a decade, and his own friends and neighbors were at risk.

Sawbones.

In spite of the heat, he shivered.

Surprise!

Sally Benuto felt like doing nothing.   And on this hot Saturday, which happened to be his birthday, he was up to exactly what he felt like: doing nothing.

He sat on his island in the middle of the swamp, surrounded by a vicious mist of swirling mosquitoes that buzzed him but did not land, repulsed by the DEET that he had sprayed and smeared all over his body. Slowly chewing a cold frog leg, he thoughtfully pushed the cat with his bare foot as it stretched out and sunk its claws into his pants leg.

"Are you okay, Cat?" he asked. "What's up with you?" The cat purred loudly, almost roaring.

His eye caught movement at the edge of the clearing, and he slowly rose to his feet with the cat still securely latched to his ankle.

He could scarcely believe his eyes.

Standing in the midst of the palmettos, a wild boar was busily scanning the clearing with his dense, myopic squint. The boar was taller than Streetcar's waist, a massive brute covered with a stiff, curly coat of mottled black and brown hair. Long, razor-sharp tusks descended from his open mouth in an evil, yellowed coil of aged ivory. *How did he get there so quietly?*

The hog and the cat smelled one another at the same time.

The Maine Coon flipped to his feet and arched his back, presenting a sizable silhouette to the intruder. The huge boar bristled, the long shoulder hairs standing straight on end as he snorted loudly and pawed the earth.

Because Streetcar was standing in the middle of the clearing with no climbable tree in sight, he looked about desperately for something, anything that might be used in his defense. Imbedded in a stump to his right, he saw the field axe: a broad bladed, short, slender-handled tool that he sometimes used to cut soft wood.

He reached for the axe slowly as the sweat trickled down the back of his neck and his body hair prickled, standing straight up in honor of their guest. Terror swept over him, washing his skin with electricity and covering him with thick goose pimples.

Ever so slowly, his hand found the axe handle, and he carefully rocked the head out of the wood and drew it toward him. He slid the bottom of the handle into his left hand with the heavy blade to his right, shifting his weight as he prepared for the charge. He began to ease toward the big cypress stump, hoping that, if need be, he could duck around it.

Wild boars, when angered, can be dangerous, deadly beasts. And this wild boar was nothing if not angry, dangerous, and exceedingly deadly. Earlier this morning, the Maine Coon had stolen a newborn pig from his herd, and the big boar was out for blood. He raised his heavy head and squealed wildly.

It was a deafening cry that proclaimed unequivocally that this was his swamp. The old boar was the primordial owner of this land, and he was about to prove it to the two upstart intruders. He shook his huge head powerfully, scattering strands of saliva that sent up a cloud of foul, noxious spray that smelled of rotten food and rotted swampland. The pungent cloud of saliva formed an unholy halo around the boar's weathered, filthy face.

"ROOWWRRR!" screamed the Maine Coon cat, leaping in front of Streetcar, standing as tall as he could. Sparks of anger arced from his fur as he arched his back frantically, hissing and spitting at the massive beast. Streetcar crouched low, his eyes flashing left and right, searching for a way out.

Without further pleasantries, the boar lowered his head and charged.

As swift as a striking rattlesnake, the cat streaked directly towards him, dodging his tusks and disappearing beneath the surging form. Tumbling underneath the wild boar, the cat sunk powerful front claws into his chest and was whipped around by momentum that slammed his back legs directly upward, into the not-so-soft belly of the beast. The big cat began to dig frantically, ripping away at the hairy flesh.

The boar steamed ahead, bearing directly down on Streetcar. At the last split second, risking all for victory, Streetcar sidestepped behind the stump and whipped the broad steel blade across the boar's eyes, driving the axe deeply into the center of the brute's rock-hard skull.

It was amazing how slowly time can pass when one's life is in danger. Sealed in a silent world of focused intensity, Streetcar watched in surprise as the axe blade struck the boar's head, sending a shower of bone chips and blood gushing toward the heavens. The small, angry eyes stared sideways at him in stunned stupidity, losing focus as the head jerked up from the force of the blow.

The boar flashed past Streetcar in a surreal blur of unbelievable speed and power, almost ripping the axe from his hands. Holding on for dear life, jerked around by the force, he managed to snatch it from the beast's solid head.

Streetcar's sense of hearing returned in hypersensitive glory, and as it did he became painfully aware of the hellish squeal of the pitifully wounded animal. The sound was at once piteous and horrible.

The hog tried to turn around, still in full gallop, spraying chunks of mud and leaves as his narrow hooves gouged a sloppy trench in the muck and the cat ripped into him from underneath, mercilessly spraying flesh and blood. The beast stumbled and fell to one knee with hot blood pouring from the hole in his skull.

The blood was a blinding river that ran into his eyes and cascaded to the earth, flowing hot from a fountain that pulsed wildly from the wounded beasts head. The boar tossed his head and squealed, mad with pain and anger and terror, preparing to charge again as the cat continued to rip away, tearing deeper, biting the chest and gouging the belly.

The squeal ended when Streetcar hopped up and swung the axe again with all his might, delivering a sweeping overhand stroke that severed the spine at the base of the skull. The hog's legs failed instantly and he collapsed on top of the cat, crushing him under hundreds of pounds of dead weight.

Streetcar dropped to his knees, seized the limp boar, and heaved with all his might, lifting it straight into the air. He was afraid to roll it over lest he crush the Maine Coon. His tendons popped audibly as he slowly lifted the carcass, giving it all that he could muster. Still on his knees, he hoisted it out of the mud with legs and head drooping downward, toward the bloody ground.

The cat yowled pitifully as Streetcar's strength failed. He toppled over backwards, pinned beneath the massive weight of the dead boar.

It must have weighed more than 300 pounds. The weight was crushing Streetcar, the warm blood drenching his shirt as he grappled in the soft mud, maneuvering his arms so he could escape.

"Cat, are you okay?" he called. He heard no reply as he strained to wriggle his arms into position. Finally, after driving his elbows down into the mud, he was ready to begin the most important bench press of his life.

As he began to push the heavy carcass upward, hearing tendons pop again as the mud reluctantly released the hog to the accompaniment of obnoxious sucking sounds, Streetcar felt a sharp pain in his foot and ankle. It was the cat, renewing the game that had been so rudely interrupted by the wild boar.

The Maine Coon bit his foot and clawed at it playfully. He growled low in his throat and began to purr.

"No, cat, not now! Let me go!" Streetcar shook his foot, but the cat dug in deeper.

Still straining to complete his lift, Streetcar was nevertheless tempted to laugh. He fought off the feeling but it threatened to overwhelm him, in spite of his best efforts.

Finally, with gargantuan effort, he heaved the carcass as high as he could and pushed it away. It slammed to the earth directly behind his head, splashing mud all about. The boar's stiff spinal hair covered Streetcar's eyes, and the heavy weight of the backbone rested squarely on his forehead. He could see nothing, but he could certainly feel the pain in his ankle as the Maine Coon made up for lost time, chewing and scratching as if his life depended on it. *Stupid cat!*

"Let go!" he called loudly, shaking his foot. The cat hung on, his purr becoming a roar.

Streetcar laughed aloud, long and hard: attempting to stifle the noise as he convulsed, unable to stop. He laughed until his sides hurt and the cat's attentions became simple unbearable. Then, mustering his willpower, he gave one final push and liberated the top of his head from the dead animal's heavy weight.

He sat up quickly, catching the cat by surprise. It yowled, clawing as he snatched it up and hugged it fiercely to his chest.

Streetcar began to cry. He was overwhelmed with joy, jubilation, and unexpected grief. The cat stopped struggling and gently dug his claws into Streetcar's chest. His tail stopped lashing, and he purred loudly as the man tried to stop the unanticipated flow of tears that ran freely down his face. He pulled the cat's furry face up toward his own and they looked at each other.

Covered with blood and victorious in battle, they felt not so much like heroes as outcasts. They were freaks living outside of society, unaccustomed to any kindness except their own, unloved by all except one another.

Streetcar turned his face away. The bloody fight had stirred up old memories. It was too painful, too fresh, too real. The experience was reopening wounds that were best left unexplored. As he stopped crying, he breathed deeply and began to rock the cat, hugging him closer.

The past few months had been a living nightmare.

From the time of Jumbo's murder, he had wallowed in grief and despair. The Maine Coon had been the one bright spot in an otherwise hopeless life. He stroked the cat, and the happy roar gained in intensity.

"Thanks for jumping in there," he said. "You're like me, Cat, more guts than brains." The cat licked the man's neck with his small, warm, sand paper tongue.

"Hey, what's up with that?" he asked, pulling him away to look into his bright green eyes. "Cats ain't supposed to lick their humans. Don't you know that? That ain't like you, Cat." He laid him in his lap, stomach up with the big furry legs splayed wide. He patted the soft stomach as the cat lazily took a half-hearted swipe at his hand, purring like an idling lawnmower.

"What's gonna be next around here, Cat? Can you give me hint? I don't want any more surprises, okay?"

The cat tried to reply. But purr as he might, he could not answer a single word.

Final Breadth

"What did the Don say?" Ace asked sleepily, sitting up in his bed, staring up at the man who had shaken his shoulder. It was John Dicella, nervous and drawn, looking as if he had just eaten a sour pickle.

"He just said that he wants to see you right away," John answered Ace, looking around the room. His eyes flashed across the dusty pictures, dog-eared posters of rock legends, the bookcase packed to overflowing, a jumbled pile of compact discs that shared a table with the reefer tray filled with Columbian gold, rolling papers and seeds. This was the flotsam and jetsam of a careless life, the trash of an idle existence washed up onto the beach of a rented apartment in a crumbling old house: the height, depth, and breadth of a wasted wanderer.

"My band's got a gig tonight," Ace mumbled. "How long is this gonna take?"

"Not long, Ace. Where are you playing?"

"The Jumble."

"That's right near where we're goin'," John replied. "You won't miss a thing. Just grab your guitar and anything else you need for the gig tonight, and let's get out'a here."

"Okay, just a minute," Ace said groggily, running his hand through his hair as he climbed out of bed. He picked up the phone and dialed, then picked up a faded pair of jeans and began to pull them on.

"Hey, Lonzo, wha's up?" Ace asked into the phone, pulling a faded tie-dyed shirt over his head and quickly returning the receiver to his ear. "No, I don't need a ride tonight. I got one." He tucked in his shirt and smiled and winked at John. "Yeah, it's a babe," he lied, "a beautiful babe in a big Mercedes. Look, I'll see you tonight at The Jumble, okay?"

Ace hung up the phone and picked up a joint out the tray as they walked to the door. John frowned disapprovingly and followed him downstairs.

They walked out into the sunshine of another warm Saturday afternoon. The sky had that thin-as-gruel, bleached-blue look that was common to winter in this part of the state, but the mountainous stacks of fat white clouds and the itchy humidity declared that spring was in full swing, providing a muggy preview of the joys of the coming summer. They climbed into the dark green Lincoln Town Car and Ace leaned forward, ruffling the hair of the man behind the wheel.

"Hey, Rollo! Long time no see!" he said jovially. Rolando Micci had once been in Ace's crew, where he served as a trusted, dependable utility player. He had been equally adept at hijackings and extortion, strong-arm robbery and racketeering, urban terrorism and poker.

"Hey, Ace, watch it," he said sheepishly, straightening his hair as the car pulled out into the quiet street. "I'm a respectable guy now."

"Yeah, I don't doubt that," Ace said, "I respect the heck out'a you, myself." He winked at John, who suppressed a smile.

Ace was surprised by how quickly he fell into the old ways. It was as if his footloose, drug-tainted hippy musician persona were just a thin veneer that was peeling away in the heat that had built up over the past several months.

There was plenty of heat in this car; of that, he was certain. The tension was undeniable, and there was an edge to it that he could not quite put his finger on. His mind began to work as he studied the two men closely. *Are they gonna whack me?*

"Hey, John," he asked, turning to look him in the eye, "are you guys gonna whack me?" John's face lit up, and he laughed spontaneously. From the front seat, Rollo let out a guffaw.

"Ace, you've been smokin' to much of that wacky weed. Your brain's the only thing that's gettin' whacked.

We're takin' you to meet the Don, like we said." Ace sighed and leaned back in the seat, satisfied with the spontaneous nature of their response. *Okay, not today, anyway.*

He was beginning to realize exactly what his father's demise would do to his own fortunes. Things would become very dicey after his little brother Joey - a former torturer of pets who had long ago graduated to bigger thrills - took over the family business. Unless Ace left Tampa or took drastic measures, he would probably follow his father to the grave.

"You boys don't mind if I smoke, do you?" he asked, sticking a slender joint between his lips. John rolled his eyes, and Rollo laughed nervously.

"Whatever," John answered abruptly. "Rollo, roll down the windows, would you? I don't want to be lit up like a Christmas tree when we get there."

"I do. I want to be lit up like a lightning bolt," said Ace, flicking his Zippo and taking a long, acrid hit. He held the smoke for a good 20 seconds, until it burned his lungs. Then he exhaled slowly through his nose.

This is the last joint I'll ever smoke, so I might as well enjoy it, he reasoned. *I'm not gonna leave Tampa. Joey isn't gonna have his way.*

Deep within, Ace felt a surge of anger, a deep wrath rising against his brother. Their father had been a gangster and a racketeer, a man who used violence as a tool to reach unjust ends. But throughout his career, the Don had never endorsed cruelty for cruelty's sake.

Don Provencenti had not been a good man. He had been a prominent hypocrite: a supposed pillar of the community: a killer and a gangster: a mover and shaker of men, their lives, and their dreams. Finally, during the last part of his life, he had become a diplomat of sorts, the voice of organized crime in old Dixie, respected from New Orleans to Memphis to Bogotá and Bolivia. But as bad as the Don was, he had never killed for the thrill of it.

Joey, on the other hand, was a bloodthirsty punk. Left to his own resources, he would bring the Tampa Mob back to the bad old days when broken bodies turned up in car trunks and Ybor's teenaged hookers were sold to the islands, worked to death as slaves, and buried at sea.

The Don was a bad man, a wicked man. He was a successful businessman willing to kill the innocent for the sake of business. But Joe Boy was worse by far. Joey was a mad dog: a monster who was restrained only by his dread of the Don.

As Ace thought of these things, considering that his own life was in danger from the little brother he had loved so dearly, his rage deepened.

Through childhood and young adulthood, Ace had loved his brother Joey. He had protected him in parochial school and had mentored him in the ways of La Cosa Nostra. He had saved his life once. But now, he could see that none of that mattered.

Nothing could make Joe Boy care whether Ace lived or died. Ace had helped to raise a snake that would eat its own in the nest. Mature and ready to strike, Joey seemed to lack a human heart. He was a slick serpent grown huge and powerful and hungry for blood, determined to eat those who had fed and protected him.

"Hey, Ace," Rollo said, pointing ahead of them on the busy thoroughfare, "do you see that big building on the right? That's the new Jumble. Jimmy Cogan built it. They say it cost him a fortune."

"Ace's band is playin' there tonight, Rollo," John told him.

"You're playin' there, Ace? You guys are makin' the big time!"

"Yeah, Rollo, we're makin' it big," Ace said tiredly. *Big enough for me to get whacked as soon as Pop bites the dust.* He turned and looked at John. Then he threw the burning joint out of the window. He had lost interest in it after the first toke, anyway. He pulled out a cigarette and lit it. "Johnny, can we talk? Open and honest?"

"Yeah, sure, Ace," John replied, sizing him up with hooded eyes, "what is it?"

"I'll put it to you straight. I'm sure that, by now, you're the new consiglieri." John hid his surprise, but Ace detected it. *What does he think, that I was never a player?* This type of thing was too easy for Ace. He could read the signs and navigate the political landscape better than the best of them. He was becoming bitter over the threat posed by Joey, and was ready to use all his gifts.

"I know what this summons is about," Ace said. "I've figured it out." He nodded knowingly toward Rollo, who could not see him. "I can't tell you yet because you've gotta act surprised when I tell Pop. But I'll show you what I mean when we meet with the Don. You'll see today that I know what's up, and I'm a force to be reckoned with." He pulled mightily on the cigarette and inhaled deeply, letting the thick smoke bleed from his mouth into his nose.

"The reefer that I just threw away," he continued, "was my last joint, Johnny." He tapped his nose. "I can't afford to do it any more. I'm up against it, and I've decided to become a player again.

"You know what I'm up against, and I got news for you. If you make the right choices in the next few months, you'll be sitting pretty." *You make the wrong choices, you'll burn with Joe Boy,* he did not bother to add. John Dicella was a big boy who could connect the dots.

"What you talkin' about, Ace?" asked Rollo, as obtuse as ever.

"We're in a cone of silence back here, for all you know," Ace replied. "We might as well be speakin' Sicilian. Rollo doesn't get a thing. Right, Rollo?"

"Hey, I can speak Sicilian," Rollo replied, puffing up angrily. "My grandmother was from Sicily. Whadd'ya mean?" Ace laughed.

"You're the best, Rollo," Ace replied, winking at John, who stared at him glumly. Ace had just dropped a bomb. The new consiglieri of the Provencenti Family would have to study his proposition carefully. He knew that Ace had once been revered and feared as a powerful young bull of the old school, an honorable thief who had been true to his family and crew, wise in the ways of treachery and a stone terror to all who dared to defy him.

Ace had done so well and had been so renowned for his insight and success, he had been a made man by the unheard of age of 24, on the fast track to consiglieri. But all of that had changed. Or had it?

Did Ace still have what it took? Was he ready to fight and win against his own brother? Or would he, John Dicella, find himself on the wrong end of a gun if he bit at Ace's offer? John sighed heavily and rolled his eyes.

"You're supposed to be a burnt out hippy, Ace," he said glumly. "A space cadet with no future."

"You wish. That would make your life easier, wouldn't it?"

John pulled out a stick of gum, unwrapped it, and folded it into his mouth. Reaching into his coat pocket, he retrieved a pair of reflective sunglasses and put them on, leaned back in the seat. He put his hands behind his head and kicked the front seat.

"Give us some music, Rollo."

John was a slim man, dapper and meticulous and proper to a fault, but he chewed the gum ravenously, as if it were his last meal. Rollo turned up the radio, and the powerful sound of rock and roll took over as primal guitar therapy pulsed through their bodies. It was an oldie by Joe Walsh.

"Spent the last year Rocky Mountain way," he twanged, "couldn't get much higher." The monumental guitar chops of the famous song stood in stark contrast to the singer's thin, strained voice as the stone-solid rock monolith ground hypnotically forward, propelled by a juggernaut rhythm section, throbbing bass and pounding drums.

The song was a steaming locomotive, a hard rock landslide that rumbled hypnotically forward, smoking through the speakers, tumbling into the depths of their being. Inside the car, the intense volume rendered normal conversation hopeless.

"Yeah, I wish you had stayed stoned and kept your mouth shut, so we could have whacked you when the old man died," John said to Ace, confident that his words were drowned out by the high-octane musical extravaganza. Ace leaned forward and shouted into John's ear.

"I knew that you and Joey are planning to whack me, Johnny," he said, "but I'm also aware that you don't know me. I can't blame you. You weren't ever in my crew, and we never worked together. But once you've seen what I bring to the table, you can make an informed decision." John stared at Ace, astonished, his mouth wide open.

"I can read lips," Ace shouted with a tight grin. "You learn it in the clubs." Seeing John's shocked expression, he laughed aloud. "Hey, no hard feelings. This is business. Ask around, you'll see that I never hold a grudge. I don't have time for grudges. Besides, we were never on the same crew, and I don't expect loyalty until it's promised." Joe Walsh continued to wail as the pounding rock and roll classic ground forward toward its inevitable end.

"Bases are loaded and Casey's at bat," sang the nasal rock legend, "playin' it play by play. Time to change the batter."

Leaning back in his seat, Ace turned away, staring out of the window as their car flashed past a mini-slum in the low rent part of northwest Tampa. Past the slum, the car turned left into a warehouse complex, passing a security guard who grimly waved them through. *He's one of ours,* Ace thought, *and so is the guy parked in that car over there.*

The family business had grown in the past ten years, he did not recognize many of the faces. They rode past the soldier in the parked car and continued down the road. *This is heavy,* Ace reflected. He was making a dangerous play, and he had no idea whether he could pull it off. Would his old crew stick with him? Would the new guys buy in?

The rock anthem, relentless in its momentum, thundered from the speakers. "And we don't need the ladies cryin' cause the story's sad, uh huh," whined the singer, "Rocky Mountain Way is better than the way we had." The guitar chorus kicked in with all of its mountainous rock majesty as Ace waited for an answer from John Dicella.

Ace needed John. He desperately wanted John Dicella on his side, but the new consiglieri was playing it close to the vest. Would John tell the Don or Joe Boy what Ace was up to? *If I was in John's shoes,* Ace admitted to himself, *I might turn down my offer.*

He had to admit it.

Things were not looking up.

Punks of Steel

"**S**o, tell me again, Frankie," Joe Boy said sarcastically. "What did he say?"

"He said you need to stay put, that's what," Franco replied half-heartedly. "And what can you do? He's the boss." The windshield wipers flung the water aside, but barely managed to clear the view for an instant due to the torrential flow of the heavy Florida rain. "Man, this rain came outta nowhere."

It was just after sunset. In the half-light of dusk, they were driving toward the only nationally franchised fast food restaurant in Oree County, making a desperate attempt to allay the boredom that had descended upon them like a pall. *It's Saturday night,* Franco reflected, *like it was when Joey whacked the kid. Back when this whole mess began.*

"Saturday night," Joe Boy stated loudly, "just like the night when this whole mess began."

"Hey, stop that!" Franco blurted, scared witless by Joey's recitation of exactly what he had been thinking.

"Did I say what you were thinkin' again?" Joe Boy asked innocently. "Well, hey, how was I to know? I guess great minds think alike."

"I hate it when you do that!"

"You're too easy," Joey replied, bored with this game. *So what if I said what you're thinkin'? What's the big deal?* Franco was too superstitious, Joe Boy surmised. *If Franco ever suspects that the Don hasn't approved our plan to attack the girl's hideout, he'll weasel out of it in a heartbeat. What a wimp!*

"Hey, Joey, look!" Franco said, pointing at a two cars that they were approaching rapidly in the rear view mirror. The two large vehicles of matching make, model, and color, whipped past their car and accelerated, speeding away into the distance. "Did you see those guys?"

"Feds," Joe Boy answered.

"No doubt."

"I'd bet the rent on it."

"Those guys were excited about something, Joey, speeding like that in the middle of nowhere. It's not us they were after."

"Duh. They got us already."

"I wonder who they're after?"

"Gee, I don't know. We're respectable citizens. At least, I am." Joey laughed.

"Hey, I am, too. My record was wiped clean years ago. I'm reformed, Joey. Didn't you hear?"

"Yeah, sure. That's why you're my right hand man, Frankie. You're the sneakiest weasel in Hillsborough County. If I had listened to you, I'd'a never killed that kid, and we'd all be better off." Joey smiled and winked. "I'd'a let _you_ do it on your lonesome. A solo shot." Franco refused to take the bait.

"I wonder who the Feds were after?"

"Maybe they're in a hurry to see the doctor."

"What do you mean?"

"The doc."

"What?" Joe Boy drew his finger across his throat and made a slitting sound. "You know that we've brought in our best talent to do the job on the little girl. Did you think that he wouldn't want to warm up?" He smiled lasciviously. "He must'a had a dress rehearsal. I wish I'd been there."

Franco felt his heart sink. A rush of adrenalin sapped downward within him, pulling heavily toward the earth, sickening and strong. His mouth was suddenly dry, and he licked his lips futilely.

"You had to go and get the Mick, didn't you? Nobody else was good enough."

"Quit complainin', Frankie."

"The Mick. He's the freakiest mechanic I ever met."

"Are you referring to our own dear Doctor Death?" Franco sighed and put on his blinker to turn right into the brightly lit parking lot. "When your own life's at stake, you get the best surgeon that money can buy."

"Sawbones," Frankie replied glumly, "Mickey Sawbones." Franco was one of the few men who knew exactly why Mickey had been forced to leave Tampa so many years ago.

"Hey, Frankie, you're just jealous," Joey said, taunting him. "You don't have the guts to do what he does."

Franco looked at Joey unbelievingly. How could you explain things to a guy like Joey, a guy who thought that most people didn't kill for fun because they were cowards? Joey thought that all of humanity secretly longed to be like him and Mickey O'Malley.

These two guys were dangerous together. They were punks, but they were punks of steel: talented, disciplined disciples of death, dedicated practitioners of the arcane arts of destruction.

"Sawbones," Franco repeated sourly. *Doesn't he know how this makes us look to other wise guys, in other cities? We're the Provencentis, a major, respectable family, and Joey's turnin' us into the greatest freak show on earth. We've got Joe Boy as Clown Prince and Mickey O'Malley as the official Court Molester.*

"You shouldn't have brought Mickey in on this, Joey."

"You don't get it at all, Frankie," stated Joey emphatically, waxing philosophical. "It's not enough to come out on top. You've gotta come out on top, IN STYLE!" Franco shook his head.

"I think it's a mistake. He'll draw too much heat, and we've got enough already."

"You sound like an old woman. Mick will take the heat off the rest of us. You saw the way those Feds blew right past us. Who do you think is on their minds, my trial, or the latest corpse from America's most famous mass murderer? Thanks to the Mick, we actually have some good news to share with the hicks in this inbred, hammer-browed, chicken-stealin', egg-suckin' redneck county."

"What good news?" Franco asked wearily.

"The doctor . . . uh, I mean, the sawbones," Joey replied, savoring the words, "is in!"

Redneck Rap

"So, what's it like, being a Redneck?" Ellen asked innocently, looking sideways at Donny Hawkins.

"Ellen!" Jamie interjected. "What a question!" She had long ago become accustomed to her friend's nervy sense of humor, but she was not certain that Donny would understand her playful intent.

"It's kind of like being from Miami," he replied, "only not." He smiled as Ellen laughed at his reply. He had arrived early on this clear, balmy Saturday, and they were having an impromptu party that had lasted into the evening hours.

In the background, Jamie's new sound system pounded out a reggae beat, driving the conversation along, forcing them to speak loudly to be heard. The sound system, a birthday gift from Ellen, was undergoing its first stress test.

"Miami's an interesting city," Jamie said, "I went there, once." Donny leaned forward in his chair, fully engaged in the conversation, unaware that his glass of iced tea was sweating large beads of colds water down the back of his hand. He was a big man in his early twenties who looked even younger, a youthful man-mountain capped with a crown of snow white hair: broad in the shoulders, lean in the waist, and baked brown from years of hard work under the broiling Florida sun.

"I love Miami," Donny said, nodding, "we should go down there some time for Calle Ocho, in little Havana. What a party! The paiella is out of this world." He reached forward and dipped a corn chip in the salsa. "It's a great place to visit, but it's too crowded to stay for long."

"Pezner is too crowded for you," Jamie said, a smile playing on her lips.

"Yeah?" he asked innocently, looking up, "Well, maybe it is. So?" He glanced at Ellen for support, and she shrugged her shoulders.

"So, what's wrong with that?" Ellen interjected impertinently.

"This from a woman who considered Oree County beyond the reach of civilization as we know it."

"So, I was wrong. I didn't appreciate the finer things in life."

"Okay, enough talk," Jamie responded abruptly. She stood up and took Donny's tea, setting it carefully down on a straw coaster. "Stand up," she ordered. He stood obediently, looking at her questioningly.

"Good," she stated authoritatively, winking at Ellen. "Now, let's dance."

They began to dance to the blistering reggae beat, not touching one another but totally in touch: letting the rhythm pulse through their feet, fingers, arms and legs until their entire bodies were adrift in a synchronous ocean of sound, pulsating in perfect tandem on the rippling wave of Jamaican reggae like human sea grass swaying in the shoals to the surging Caribbean beat.

The dynamic dance, which began slowly and built to a dramatic crescendo, was hilarious to Ellen. She did her best to suppress her laughter, but to no avail.

Midway through the song, she burst out laughing. Donny ignored her, but Jamie stopped dancing and scowled. She signaled with a cutting motion, and Donny stopped too, smiling apologetically.

"Okay," Jamie said, picking up the remote control and turning off the music. "Why are you laughing?" In the sudden silence, Ellen continued to laugh. She picked up a napkin and waved it at her friend in a gesture of abject surrender.

"What's so funny, young miss?" Jamie asked, her hands on her hips, doing her best Sister Serena imitation. The good Sister Serena, a parochial school teacher from their high school years, had been a living caricature of an authoritarian nun. She could be imitated uncannily by most of her former students, including Jamie.

"It's nothing, Sister Serena. I mean, Sister Jamie," Ellen replied gamely. "It's just that you guys are so . . . good." She dried her eyes with the cocktail napkin. "You are both really good dancers. I mean, you're fantastic. I knew that you could dance, Jamie, but him!" she guffawed again.

"Him? What's so funny about him?" Now, Donny spoke up.

"It's against the stereotype," he volunteered.

"That's it," Ellen said, still drying her eyes, "you're right. Could you please explain it to her?"

"Sure. What's so funny is, I'm a redneck," he began. "I mean, there's no getting around it. I'm the total package. I have the hick accent, the knife holster on the belt, I hunt, fish, I even have an "Eat More Beef" bumper sticker on my pickup truck. But in spite of all that, I dance like an urban legend. That's it, right?" Ellen nodded weakly, wrung out from the laughter.

"This is embarrassing," Ellen stated, straightening up, putting on a straight face.

"So, why is that funny?" Jamie repeated indignantly, refusing to give up, wanting an answer from Ellen herself. "A southern male who can dance something besides a hoedown? This is comical?"

"It's the whole set up," Ellen replied. "I mean, Jamie, this could only happen to you. Nothing average ever happens to you. When it's bad, it's beyond horrible. When it's good, it's beyond good. Here you are, stuck in the middle of nowhere, and you hook up, excuse me, with a cowboy Baryshnikov."

"I've heard that name. He was a foreigner, right?" Donny asked with a vacant glaze in his eyes.

"He was a Russian dancer who became a U.S. citizen," Jamie answered.

"I know who Baryshnikov is," Donny whispered, "I'm just kidding." She pulled back and swatted him as he smiled proudly. Donny had been playing dumb, an annoying habit that she wished he would break. *Why does he think that's funny?*

"Speaking of rednecks," Ellen continued, undeterred, "what is going on with this Sheriff? He is far too good-looking to be a cop. He acts like the last Boy Scout. Is he for real, or is he just a big phony?" Jamie looked at Donny, who sat back down on the frayed tan sofa and picked up his iced tea, thoughtfully taking a sip.

"I can answer that. I've known Sheriff all my life, since I was a little boy. He's for real, for better or worse. With him, what you see is what you get." Ellen gazed at him with veiled eyes, leaning back in the hickory rocking chair.

"So, what do I see? Is he married?"

Jamie sighed, tossed her hair back, and collapsed into the cushions, putting her feet up on the coffee table. *Same old Ellen!* she said to herself.

"He's a widower," Donny replied. "His wife died when he was 30 years old, and he's been alone ever since." Ellen lifted an eyebrow and gazed at Jamie.

"How did a man with his looks become a preacher? And a single preacher, at that? Is there something wrong with him?" she asked candidly. Ellen could be quite nosy, once she warmed up to a subject.

"Ellen!" Jamie exclaimed, smiling in spite of herself as she shook her head disapprovingly. *She is over the top.*

"You'll have to ask him," Donny replied. "I think he would be willing to answer you."

"I'm afraid to ask him," Ellen answered, "his nickname is Preacher. I might get a sermon."

"You might," he admitted. "Then again, it might be interesting."

"So, what's his story?" Ellen pulled out a cigarette and placed it between her lips, searching in her purse for a lighter.

Ellen's serious, Jamie thought, *but why does she care? Maybe she's just being protective. After all, here I am, hiding in the middle of nowhere, and my life is in the Sheriff's hands.* Jamie had long ago grown accustomed to her friend's overprotective nature. But regarding the Sheriff, the time for protectiveness had been months ago. *She's just being nosy,* Jamie finally concluded. *No surprises there.*

"A few years ago I heard some rumors about Tommy's misspent youth. I asked my Uncle Les, and he told me the story," Donny replied. "He said that some bad things happened a long time ago, but most folks have tried to forget about it. I don't think Sheriff would mind if I told you.

"Tommy Durrance was once the wildest kid in Oree County. My uncle knew him well. They ran around together with Seth Greene, back in their high school days. Tommy was the one who got them all into trouble. Seth was the responsible one who tried to repair the damage, and Uncle Les just went along for the ride.

"After they graduated from high school, Tommy won a football scholarship and got his degree from the University of Florida in Gainesville. He became a policeman in Orlando, then he was hired back here as the first full-time detective on the Pezner Police force.

"When he moved back to Pezner from Orlando, he brought a wife. The folks around here called her Miss Donna. She was a Blanchette before she got married, the daughter of a United States Senator from Georgia. You might have heard of him: Senator Blanchette of the Ways and Means Committee."

"Wasn't he a segregationist during the civil rights era?" Jamie asked.

"Yes, that's him."

"I read about him in school."

"Tell us the rest," Ellen said impatiently.

"Anyway, Uncle Les says that Miss Donna was the most beautiful woman who ever set foot in Oree County. Of course, Uncle Les has never seen Jamie." Ellen ignored the comment and put her cigarette down without lighting it, transfixed by the tale.

"Go on."

"So, Tommy brought his wife, Donna Blanchette Durrance, out here to the boondocks. And out here, she didn't fit in. It was like planting a hothouse orchid in a sandy patch of piney flat woods. After a while, Tommy got restless. He began to pick up on his old ways." Ellen stared at him.

"Details," Ellen said brusquely. "Give us details." Donny glanced uncomfortably at Jamie.

"It's basically the same old tale that's been worn to death by fools in every generation. Wine, women, and song, to put it politely," he continued, "and not necessarily in that order. The Sheriff's wife, Donna, heard about was going on, but she loved him too much to leave him. It was a sorry predicament, all around.

"The saddest part, according to Uncle Les, was that Tommy really loved her. But he loved liquor more, and the women wouldn't leave him alone. The combination was deadly."

"So, what happened?" Ellen scooped salsa onto a chip and shoved it into her mouth without blinking.

"What happened?" Jamie echoed, reaching for a chip, impatient to hear the rest of the story.

"Well, one Saturday night when Tommy was out drinking, Miss Donna went out lookin' for him. She stopped in at the truck stop to see if he was having dinner there. Uncle Les worked in the truck stop restaurant as a short order cook, and he says Miss Donna came in and asked if he knew where Tommy was. She was worried sick, afraid that Tommy might get behind the wheel and die drunk on the highway.

"Uncle Les said she was scared and desperate that night: as white as a ghost and frayed around the edges. She left the restaurant in a daze." He paused, and looked at them both.

"She drove out onto the highway and got hit head-on by an 18 wheeler, right there in front of the truck stop. She was killed instantly." Ellen and Jamie's mouths dropped open at the same time.

"Oh, no," Ellen whispered.

"Tell us the rest," Jamie said, tugging on his sleeve. "What happened to the Sheriff?"

"Well, to say that he took it hard would be an understatement.

"He quit the police force. He stayed to himself and basically started to drink himself to death. He was heading in that direction for a couple of years. Uncle Les said that Tommy never went out of his house during that period. He just stayed at home while the bottles piled up in the back yard.

"Then one night, a revival came to town, and Tommy staggered into the tent to see what it was all about. By the end of the service, he had given his life to Jesus. He quit drinking, and a couple of months after that, he got a job as a sheriff's deputy on the road patrol.

"It's been about 20 years since that tent meeting. The Sheriff has become the legal backbone of this county, more or less, and the conscience as well. He's got a reputation as a tough but fair lawman who believes in second chances. He never writes anyone off.

"He's forgiven a lot of folks during the past 20 years. At that first revival meeting, he forgave the truck driver who had crossed the centerline to kill his wife. Fifteen years ago, he was shot during a liquor store robbery, and he forgave the shooter. Last year, when the guy came up for parole, Tommy was a witness on his behalf. But the one person Tommy Durrance hasn't forgiven is himself.

"He still can't forgive himself for the death of his wife. I think that's why he hasn't had a date in the past 20 years." Jamie and Ellen exhaled in unison, looking at each other, then at Donny.

"That's so sad!" Ellen exclaimed.

"It is. Too sad," agreed Jamie. "I never would have thought it."

"I would have," Ellen said. "I knew there was a sad story in his past. But it's sadder than I thought."

"Well, if it's any comfort, I think Tommy's better off alone," Donny said, trying to lighten the mood. He smiled and winked at Jamie. "Women just complicate things." She sat up indignantly and shoved him.

"You worm!" He laughed as she shoved him again. "That was totally uncalled for!"

"You're right," he said. "Uncalled for. Absolutely." Ellen ignored their give and take, choosing to reflect upon the life and times of Tommy Durrance.

"He can't forgive himself," she said soulfully, "so sad." She stared pensively toward the window, deep in thought. "But, with his past, how did he ever get elected Sheriff?"

"Well, folks around here believe that people can change. In Tommy's case, it was obvious. He quit drinking, he began to work, he quit running around with women, joined a church, and became a nicer person and a better cop."

"A better cop?"

"Tommy used to have a reputation as a hard case. He was known as a cop who didn't take any flack, from anybody, at any time, for any reason. After he changed, he became more patient, more polite, less likely to use force. That's what Uncle Les told me."

"Okay, but how was he elected Sheriff? I mean, don't you need political connections for that?"

"Oh, don't you know?" Donny asked, surprised.

"Know what?"

"His grandfather owned every oil lease in Oree County. In fact, he owned most of the leases in South Central Florida."

"Oil leases? Do you mean, oil in the ground?" Now it was Ellen's turn to be surprised.

"Black gold, Texas tea," Donnie responded glibly. "Yep. A good part of this county is floating on a tidy little sea of oil. Tommy's from one of the richest families in the Sunshine State. And he was the sole heir of the family fortune."

"No!" Ellen replied, aghast.

"Yes!" he replied with a smile.

"Then," she paused, deep in thought, "okay. Help me figure this out; it doesn't make sense. Why did he become a cop?"

"Uncle Les says that Tommy and his father didn't see eye to eye. I don't know the details. I just know that Tommy was independent, and he chose his own career. To his father, that was a mortal sin.

"The family business was too boring for him, so he struck out on his own. He became a cop because he liked the action.

"He was cut off from the family as a result. Uncle Les said that, as far as he knows, Tommy's father never forgave him for making his own way in life.

"After Tommy's wife died, he ran for Sheriff to provide a public service. By that time, he didn't need the money; he had already inherited the family fortune. As a result, he was able to finance his own campaign."

"But if his father never forgave him, how did he inherit anything?"

"Tommy's grandfather hadn't trusted Tommy's father. Before the grandfather passed away, he tied up all his property in unbreakable trusts and life estates. The whole shebang reverted to Tommy when Tommy's father died."

"Everything?"

"Everything. Not that it changed his life, or anything like that. Uncle Les said he was pretty much the same before as he was after he received the inheritance."

"But, really," Ellen probed. "This man hasn't had a date since his wife died?"

"Yeah. He never got over it."

"And he's rich," she responded mournfully, "very, very rich." Jamie stared at her, her face reflecting her skepticism.

"Uh, huh," Jamie murmured suspiciously to herself. "What a coincidence."

"It's just too sad to be true," Ellen added, rousing Jamie to respond aloud.

"It's too sad <u>not</u> to be true," she replied. "The world is full of sad stories."

"Maybe," replied Ellen thoughtfully, "but even sad stories can turn out well."

"Yes," Jamie replied, smiling in spite of herself. *Ellen can be so transparent.* Jamie reached out and patted her best friend's hand.

"You think that even the Sheriff's story can turn out well?" Jamie asked hopefully.

"Yes," Ellen answered. Jamie sighed deeply.

"You know, Ellen, I hope you're right."

A Voice from the Grave

Ace was not prepared for the sight that greeted him when he said hello to his father.

Don Provencenti looked ghastly.

In spite of the much-heralded remission of his cancer, he was as emaciated and wan as a whisper from the grave, looking as if he might be swarmed from beyond and borne by ghouls across the threshold of death at any moment. The Don was a living skeleton, clothed in soggy flesh and fronted by the bloodshot fright mask that was currently passing as his face.

The skin on his pasty pale countenance hung in great, variegated folds streaked with leprous blotches of sour yellow, hot pink and dead white. The Don's once-powerful grip, when they shook hands, was weak and tremulous. Ace could almost feel the frailty of the thin bones in the strong right hand that had been so mighty. He could almost hear the tendons creak as the Don attempted – and failed - to show that he still had a manly grip.

When they let go, his father's clammy fingers clung to Ace's hand as if they had been attached with suction cups. The clinging sensation reminded Ace of a tree frog that he had once picked up.

He had been eight years old, and the tree frog had made quite an impression. The tiny green amphibian had held to him relentlessly when he tried to release it, and the delicate tenacity of its cold grip had slithered into a deep crevice in his memory, waiting to crawl out at this very moment.

"So, you're lookin' pretty good, Ace," the Don rasped, attempting a smile.

"I'm doin' okay," Ace replied: reserved, suspicious. They entered the room and sat down in the Don's opulently furnished den. It was a darkly paneled study overflowing with books that loomed over them from towering bookcases: a traditional, tweedy male hideout filled with richly grained mahogany furniture and heavy leather chairs. It was not what one might expect in the middle of a suburban industrial complex, but it accomplished the intended effect. It was a room that commanded respect.

"I visited your mother's grave this morning. God rest her soul," the Don began, his voice faltering, hoarse with age and disuse, "she was the greatest woman I ever knew, Ace." Ace was shocked. The Don had seldom spoken to him openly of his mother, and had never raised the issue with another person present. He glanced nervously at John, the only other person in the room. John lifted his eyebrows and remained silent.

"Ace . . . son," the Don said, his voice cracking, "I'm glad you came here tonight." Ace was startled again as, deep within him, surprising emotions were stirred up. *He never used to call me son.*

"Don Provencenti," Ace began, and his father grimaced and waved his hand.

"Call me Pop, why don't you, Ace? Better late than never, huh, kid?" The Don pulled three cigars out of a wooden box. He trimmed one and passed out the other two along with his gold cigar clipper, leaning forward for a light from John Dicella. He puffed loudly as the Zippo ignited his 30-dollar stogie. As his guests trimmed and lit their Havanas, the Don sagged weakly back into his chair, visibly wearied by the ritual.

"John is our consiglieri now, Ace," he stated bluntly. His son nodded.

"I know." The Don glanced at Ace sharply and looked at John, who signaled that he had not given the news to Ace. The Don smiled at Ace.

"You would figure that out, wouldn't you?"

"Yeah."

"So, if you're such a wise guy, can you tell me why I called you here?"

"I think I can." Ace was not certain, but he had an idea. He was willing to take a chance.

"Go ahead."

"The Council doesn't want Joey to succeed you as Don." Don Provencenti's eyes widened in surprise, and he shook his head disbelievingly. Even the new consiglieri was unable to hide his surprise.

"You're a smart guy, Ace," the Don stated emphatically, *smarter than I thought, and I already knew you were smart,* he did not bother to add. "How old are you now?"

"Thirty-five."

"Your band is getting famous, I hear. Jimmy B told me that a major record company in Atlanta is sniffing around. He heard they're planning to offer you a recording contract."

"We've been talkin'," Ace said impassively. "It's in the works." The Don leaned forward and pointed at Ace with his cigar.

"Okay, here's what's up, Ace. And this is for you, too, Johnny," he said nodding at his consiglieri. "I didn't tell either one of you until now, because I had to close the deal with representatives from the families. If the deal fell through, Johnny, you needed deniability with Joey and his crew. I also wanted to see if Ace still has what it takes. I brought him here today for a purpose. I wanted to see if he could guess what was up, without any hints." He turned to Ace.

"Well, I can see that you still have what it takes," he said, nodding smugly. "And you still have the guts, too." He turned back to his consiglieri. "So, Johnny boy," he said slyly, "what did Ace say to you on your way over here?" John decided to tell the truth.

"He said that he was going to become a player again," John replied, "and that if I'm smart, I'll be on his side." The Don smiled through a cloud of rich, pungent tobacco smoke that wreathed his head like a whorled vortex crowning royalty from the duchy of Hades. He looked like a prince lately come from the infernal regions, just slumming here on earth.

"That's my kid," he said to John, winking slyly. He turned to Ace and squinted.

"So, you wanna be a player again, Ace?"

"It looks like I'm going to be a player, whether I want to be, or not." Ace replied with a guarded smile. "But, yeah, I guess I do."

"Here's what's goin' down," said the Don. "The Council wants to whack Joey." John sat up abruptly in his chair, but Ace scarcely blinked. The Don smiled again and coughed deeply, again and again.

He coughed until he almost strangled, waving them away when they tried to offer help. After some tense moments, he regained his breath and composure. He wiped the saliva from the corner of his mouth and took a sip of water.

In spite of the pain, Don Provencenti was enjoying this meeting. What could he say?

He loved his work.

"The reason the Council's wants to kill my namesake is obvious. They want to protect the most important moneymaker in the whole country: the Tampa Bay Pipeline.

"About 20 years ago, back when you were just starting your career, the docks of Tampa provided the only secure entry point for cocaine and reefer. It's still the same, except that most of the pot's not funneled through the Bay anymore, and cocaine is just part of the story nowadays.

"The Tampa Pipeline has become the only secure route for Mexican black tar heroin. As you know, this stuff has become very popular with the younger set, especially the ones who like that gloomy kind of rock and roll. You know what I mean . . . scum rock."

"Grunge rock."

"Yeah, that's it. Anyway, as a result of these up and coming marketing developments, the Tampa families have become like the Kuwaitis. We sit on the tap for the whole country. And it goes without saying that we Provencentis are the royal family.

"We're in the catbird seat. We're sitting right on top of the pinch point for the biggest drug market in the world. We have the political base, the judges, you name it. Whatever it takes to keep things running smoothly, we've got it in spades.

"The Colombians and the Mexicans, they respect our power. They have to. We can make life easy for them, or we can make it hard.

"We still have the same deal with the cartels and families, just like when you were active in the Family. We protect the docks, we protect transportation, we keep the cops looking the other way, keep the Feds happy, and do whatever else it takes to facilitate their shipments. They pay us more than one billion dollars cash each year just to secure the pipeline so they can keep up the flow. And it's not even our dope.

"The dope is divided among the Eastern syndicates and Mid-western gangs. They give a big piece to Atlanta, which is the central distribution point. It's still pretty much the way it was when you were first making your bones. We maintain a hefty pad, pay some key people: a few Feds, some FDLE, key politicians and local cops in high places. We keep a low profile and the rest takes care of itself.

"Because we offer the only secure point of entry in the country, whenever the Tampa artery looks like it might get clogged, half of the U.S.A. has a coronary. So we keep it flowing and we play it cool. The Tampa families are anonymous. It's been like that since we whacked Charlie Walker and consolidated our power.

"But your brother has been screwing up the whole deal. By getting his face in the papers, Joey is endangering the livelihood of a lot of heavy hitters.

"Joey is my son, Ace" he continued, "but he did a stupid thing when he defied me. He not only smuggled dope through an unprotected route, he got caught doing it. He put our business on the street.

"When he was discovered, he whacked a citizen, a civilian. It's never good to kill a non-combatant, especially if you don't finish the job. Killing a civilian is tricky business, and these things must be done delicately.

"Along with the Francescas and the Canzanas, our family controls crime in Tampa Bay. But we don't control every single human being in the whole country. There are limits to our power. I know that and you know that, but Joey has never bought into it. So without my okay, he whacked the kid and brought on the heat.

"Then he brought in his crazy friend from high school. You know, the Pole."

"The Mick."

"Yeah," his father smiled slyly, "I know. I'm messin' with ya, kid. Anyway, he brought in the Irish kid in against my advice. I allowed it anyway because I had to give Joey a chance, so I could see once and for all if he has what it takes to run our family after I'm gone. We all know that the Irish kid is a bona fide psycho. So he killed the street bum's best friend without my okay, and it set off the bum, who turned out to be a Sicilian Rambo.

"Yadda yadda yadda," he added, making a rolling gesture with his hand. "You know the rest. All of this happened for one simple reason: because Joey wouldn't listen to me.

"Now, Joey's on trial for killing some hick, and it's all over the news." The Don leaned forward and bit down angrily on his cigar.

"Ace, I've got news for you. If Joey had done what he did in Hillsborough County, he'd be floating in the Gulf right now." He waved his frail hands. "I couldn't have stopped it. There are other families involved, and they're making billions each year. Sure, there would have been a war after he was killed. Nobody touches my son without my permission! But we would have lost a war like that. Who can win against the whole national syndicate?

"Last week, the New York families sent an emissary to give me the word. They're givin' me a chance to fix the problem, to get rid of Joey in a peaceable way. They know I've still got plenty of power, and they don't want a war. Wars are bad for business.

"So, I flew to New York City and met with the families. I talked them into a deal. Some of these guys have known me for 40 years; they know I'll keep my part. It's a matter of honor and money, and money beats honor every time. I convinced them that I could protect the old cash cow. They love that old cow, Ace," he added wistfully.

"So, to satisfy their concerns, I told them I would bring you back into the family to succeed me as Don." Hearing these words, John Dicella caught his breath. The Don looked up at him, cocking an eyebrow as if to say, 'you didn't figure it out yet, Consiglieri?'

"I said I could speak for you, Ace, and that you would agree to become the next Don. I also said that I would do my best to see that Joey leaves the country. I vouched for you, Ace, told 'em that you've still got the right stuff. They agreed to what I proposed because the alternative is war.

"If Joey will listen to me, he'll leave the country and he'll live. If he won't listen to me, he'll die. As long as nobody breaks the terms of the deal, we won't go to war against them, and they won't go to war against us.

"Ace, if they decide to take on the Provencentis, they know they have to take you out first. They can't afford to disrespect you because of your past, so you'd definitely be the first target if they made a move. You've still got quite a reputation, but that can work in your favor.

"In spite of what you've done the last few years, they remember that in the business you were a serious man: a reasonable man. There's money in it for every family if we can keep things running smooth in Tampa Bay.

"If Joey listens to me and leaves the country, he'll be safe. If not, I can't protect him. This was the best deal I could get from them."

The Don stopped talking. In the silence, they could hear him draw hotly on the cigar. The Havana crackled as the Don puffed for all he was worth, disappearing inside of a cloud of rich tobacco smoke.

"So," Ace answered thoughtfully, "what do I do next?"

"First, you've got to change your last name to Provencenti." Hearing this, Ace's scowled.

"Keep Feldmann as your middle name, if you want," the Don added diplomatically. "It's a good name. The best." Ace scratched his chin and pulled at his long hair, deep in thought.

"Look, they know you're my son. They'll accept you, since you've got an Italian father. And your mother had an Italian father, too, by the way. He was a man of respect from the old school." Ace looked at him in surprise. "You didn't know it, did you, kid? I figured she never told you. She hated our business."

"Why do I have to change my name?" Ace felt strong loyalty for his mother.

"Some of the dons are prejudiced; what can I say? Some don't like Jews, and others just don't think much of anybody who isn't Italian. Some Sicilians don't like Northern Italians, and vice versa, but we're all stuck with each other. Go figure. They're a real mixed bag. Not too many of them are culturally enlightened, but they're the guys we have to deal with. It's that simple.

"I'll refer you to a local judge, and you can get your name changed this week. As soon as Joey's trial is over, I'll announce that you're the new Don of the Provencentis. Until then, you can move in here.

"You should live with me until I buy the farm. Which, by the way, shouldn't be too long from now, since the doctor just told me that my cancer is spreading again. Fast." This news upset Ace. He turned visibly pale, and the Don reached forward to pat his hand.

"You're a good son, Ace. You've got heart. We should'a spent more time together." He took a long pull on the cigar and studied him through the smoke.

"What will happen to Joey?" Ace asked.

"We have a plan for Joey, and it's a good thing we do. We're facing a worst-case scenario here.

"It's beginning to look like the Mick won't be able to whack the witness before the trial. It looks like she's gonna testify. We were careful with the contract on the girl, by the way; the Mick has strict orders to do it alone, do it unobtrusively, and do it before the Feds get her in custody. If he can't do it on these terms, he has to call it off. After the Feds get hold of her, she's untouchable . . . it's not worth the heat.

"There should be a verdict within a week or two. If Joey walks at the end of the trial, me and him are gonna have a little heart to heart. Then, we'll put him on a plane to Colombia."

"Does Frankie know about this?" The Don smiled. *Ace always liked that guy.*

"Franco doesn't know a thing. He's not a talker, but he's not the smartest guy we have, either. I don't want Joey to guess what's up. Don't worry, we'll take care of Frankie. *With a bullet, if we have to.*

"Joey has a few men in his crew who are loyal, but none that will stand up against me. If he wants to fight, he won't have the muscle. The Mick's the only guy that Joey can count on. The Mick hates my guts, and he knows I hate him, too.

"But I can handle that psycho. We're bringin' in some talent to take care of him."

"Anyone I know?"

"Do you know Jimmy Biggs?"

"Yeah," Ace said, smiling bitterly, "I know him good. He whipped me once, back when I was a kid." *Jimmy just might be able to do the job on the Mick,* Ace reflected, *he's a major league talent.*

"He whipped you?"

"I was just a kid," Ace said, grinning sheepishly. "It was the first time I went to New York. I liked his girlfriend, and she liked me. She was 18, Jimmy was 21, and I was 15 and in love, big time. He caught us kissing in the movie theater."

The Don smiled warmly. *That's my boy.*

"Anyway," the Don continued, "back to Joey. In Colombia, there's a don who owes me a few favors. If Joey will go there, he'll put him to work. Colombia is busier than Tampa: more danger, lots of action. It's like the Wild West was in the good old days, like Chicago was back in the Twenties. Joey will love it, once he settles in. He'll fit right in. He speaks Spanish and he loves violence. It's a perfect match."

"Ace, your brother never understood about our business. He never understood that violence is not an end in itself. It's a tool, a means to an end, and we should use it with reluctance. It casts a big shadow and helps our family prosper in a crooked, nasty world. It's the big hammer. Violence should be used judiciously to drive home a point or knock an obstruction out of the way.

"We should be like wolves. We should kill to eat. Joey's like a leopard. He kills for sport."

"What if Joey's convicted?" The Don sighed heavily. The specter of the death penalty loomed large over the future of his son.

"Let's just hope Joey listens to me and doesn't do anything rash. The girl must not be touched after the trial, no matter what. It'll be too late for that. Once her testimony is part of the public record, the upside of eliminating her won't balance the downside.

"If she disappears before the trial, the heat will be bad enough. But if she disappeared after her testimony against Joey, the heat would be incredible. The other families would move hell and high water to get us out of Tampa, and we'd be in for the fight of our lives. We don't need a war with most of the major organizations in the country. I don't have to tell you the odds on that one. But who knows, we still may be able to bag her before the trial if we can find where she's staying. That's as far as I'll go.

"Anyway, you stay right beside me until I die. If Joey wants to get you, he'll have to go through me. After I die, you'll be the Don and you can take care of yourself. Joey's got the guts, but he doesn't have the brains. He's got the Mick, one of the best hitters in the country, but we've got someone just as good, and it's someone the Mick doesn't know. If Joey bucks me on this, the whole east coast will go after him, and they'll help us take care of the Mick.

"I should'a raised him better," the Don said with finality, sinking back into the huge leather chair, which dwarfed his emaciated form. "I spoiled him, and this is the result. Do you remember that book by Dr. Spock, the one about child rearing?"

"I heard about it."

"Joey's mother loved that book. 'Don't spank the boy,' she told me, 'teach him self-esteem.'

"Shoot, Ace, your brother had so much self-esteem that by age nine, he beat up the newsboy with a baseball bat. Do you remember that?" Ace shook his head and scowled.

"How could I forget? I drove the kid to the doctor in your Cadillac. Do you remember <u>that</u>?"

"Are you kidding? You were thirteen, and you took my new Caddy on I-4, speedin' right through the middle of town! When I heard about it, I had a fit. 70 miles per hour down the Ashley Street exit! Not a scratch on it, though," he admitted, smiling crookedly at Ace.

"Ace, when you think of your brother, try to remember him as a little kid, before he picked up that baseball bat. Save him, if you can." He closed his eyes.

"Okay," Ace answered unenthusiastically. He looked over at John, who was staring at him, wide-eyed. He closed his own eyes, fighting a rising wave of emotion. *So I'm finally your son, old man! Why did you wait until now, when it's almost too late?* It would have been so much easier to whack Joey just to get it over with. But he could not lie to his father about this, and the Don knew it.

A living Joe Boy posed a continual threat to Ace, but he could not ignore his father's emotional appeal. The only hope for a Provencenti succession would be if Ace took up the mantle and became the new Don. If Joe Boy defied his father, his blood would be on his own head.

"Okay," Ace said, "I'll do what you're asking. I only ask one thing."

"What's that?" the Don asked wearily, opening his swollen, rheumy eyes.

"Let me finish this gig tonight so I can tell the boys."

"Go," his father said, smiling weakly and waving his hand dismissively. "Johnny, why don't you go out to the club with Ace tonight?" The consiglieri straightened up in his chair, uncomfortable, unsure of how to act. "Go on, have some fun. All work and no play wears a man down."

John looked at the Don, then at Ace. *Okay, Ace,* he thought, *you'd better be as good as they say, or we're both dead men.*

"How old are you, Johnny?" Ace asked.

"46."

"Gee, John, you act older than Pop." He winked at his father. "The Don's right. You need to get out and shake a leg before the rigor mortis sets in." Ace stood up and pushed back the hair. Reaching into his pocket, he retrieved a hair band and gathered his long black locks into a ponytail. "Come on, let's go to the club."

"Okay," John replied half-heartedly, standing and nodding at the Don.

"And grab a couple of those extra fine Cubans for us, Johnny boy," he added winking at his father. He felt invigorated, relieved that he had been freely handed the power he had been prepared to fight for. He took two cigars from John and put them in his pocket, then put his arm around the consiglieri's shoulder.

"You da bomb, baby!" he said to John Dicella, winking at his father. "And, Johnny, just one more thing."

"What?" he asked suspiciously, looking from the Don to his longhaired son.

"Get ready to rock and roll!"

After Midnight

It was late Saturday evening. Ellen had gone to bed an hour ago. Jamie and Donny had the living room to themselves, and they were making the most of it. The stereo, turned low, was playing "Unchained Melody," and as it played, they danced.

> I need your love
> I need your love
> God speed your love
> To me.

They held each other close in the flickering light of the candles, savoring this moment at the cusp of awareness, at the beginning of shared dreams. Hope, frail and delicate, was just beginning to awaken within them. Maybe, just maybe, they could survive the coming trial and the end of Jamie's stay in the wilderness. Perhaps they could share more time together, after the trial was over. Donny hugged her tightly.

"Jamie . . . . "

"Shhh."

The music continued to play as they swayed in unison in the warm, trembling light of the candles. They were filled with wonder, drawn close in this small farmhouse beside the canal. They were hidden in the midst of a darkened wilderness that sang with life beneath the dazzling constellations.

NOT FAR AWAY, gazing at the stars, Streetcar lay in his hammock in the top of the tall cypress. The loud chorus of frogs and the whirring of the crickets serenaded him tonight, competing with the relentless roar of hungry mosquitoes. The mosquitoes had become so virulent this weekend he had put repellant on the outside of his hammock lest they bite him through the heavy canvas.

He could smell a faint whiff of burning cypress from his camp, far below. He knew that wispy trails of smoke were slowly leaking from the tiny palmetto hut he had built to preserve the meat of the wild hog that had attacked him earlier today. He had taken a chance by creating a small, smoky fire, but it was a chance worth taking. Most of the smoke was trapped inside of the palmetto smokehouse, and within days the meat would be thoroughly cured. Once cured, it would last for months.

The weather tonight was cool and breezy, and in his lap, the big cat purred loudly. *What other cat would let me haul him up to the top of this tree?* He marveled at the Maine Coon's trusting nature. *Once he bonds, he bonds for life,* Streetcar thought, ruffling his fur.

It was beautiful up here tonight, clean and pristine under the last sliver of the waning moon. Streetcar was struck with awe. High in the stratosphere, a thin cloud wafted past the front of the moon. It was a luminous thread of mist, a delicate, pure wisp of vapor that slowly crawled across the heavens. Looking to his left, he could see the cloud's shadow as it slipped across the vast marsh on the other side of the canal, across Jamie's house and into his swamp. It hid his view of the moon for a moment and continued on its way.

He sighed heavily and stroked the cat, fighting back memories of Jumbo Poindexter, of life in Ybor City and of his mad, desperate attack on the Provencentis. He could not afford to feel the pain or slip into despair. Later, when Jamie was safe, he could deal with the loss of his one and only friend.

The violence of his rampage in Ybor City still weighed heavily on his mind. He felt condemned by the choices that he had made. He knew of no way out from under the crushing load of guilt and regret, the weighty burden of blood.

His eyes turned upward. On nights like tonight, the beauty of the heavens above him, so high and lofty, so serene and undisturbed, provided the only relief from his inner turmoil.

"You do good work, God," he said softly, looking up at the stars, considering their glory. "Why do we have to mess it up?" *Because we want to,* he thought glumly, *because paradise isn't good enough for us. We've got to take our share and someone else's, too.*

He rubbed the cat, which stretched out and purred loudly, radiating warmth in the cool evening air. Wearily closing his eyes, Streetcar fell asleep.

The Sunday Scoop

At six o'clock Sunday morning, Seth Greene heard a familiar knock on the glass. It was the old school signal: *tap tap ta-tap tap*: 'shave and haircut' minus the two bits. He looked to his right at the coffee pot and grimaced sourly. *I'm glad I made plenty of coffee.* Since yesterday, he had been expecting the visitor who had now crawled to his door.

"It's open," he shouted, burying his face in the Sunday Edition of the Tampa Tribune. Preacher Durrance slouched through the door like a stray dog in a thunderstorm searching for a dry patch of ground. Entering Seth's office, he wearily tossed his hat on the sofa and slumped in one of the antique leather chairs.

Seth looked up from the paper and squinted disapprovingly. "Tommy, you look like dirt." The Sheriff's hair was rumpled, his uniform was wrinkled, and he had a frayed look that spoke of lost sleep and long hours.

"I feel like dirt," Tommy responded bitterly. "No, I feel worse than dirt. I feel like dirt feels when it gets dirty." Seth Greene put down his feet, leaned forward, and poured a cup of black coffee. It was good java, made the way they both liked it: freshly ground, scalding hot, and strong enough to float a bullet.

Without a word, he handed the cup to Tommy. Then he leaned back and picked up the paper, shaking it out, beginning to read again where he had left off. In the background, the police scanner sputtered and crackled, spitting out static and little else into the early morning air.

They sat there for more than 15 minutes without saying a word. Tommy finally broke the silence.

"Okay, okay, go ahead and ask," he said gruffly, "ask me. I know you're dyin' to know." Seth put down the paper and took his glasses off, the very picture of puzzlement.

"Well, now, I suppose that <u>you</u> know what you're talkin' about, Tommy. But I really don't have a clue."

"Right," Preacher said, rolling his eyes. "Go ahead, let me have it."

"Then again," Seth continued, "maybe I <u>do</u> have a clue. If this has something to do with the FBI agents who came to town yesterday evening, or if you're referring to the FDLE agents who showed up at your department yesterday afternoon, why, I would say that it looks like something's up in this little town of ours.

"Some folks, they say there's been a murder. But if there were any news like that around town, I'd be the first to know, right? Of course I would. Shoot, Tommy, I'm the newspaper editor! More than that, I'm your best friend!

"But I'm certain there couldn't have been a murder in this county yesterday, because if there were, my best friend, who happens to be the Sheriff, would have told me. YOU CAN COUNT ON IT!" He was worked up past the point of no return, the veins in his neck bulging, his face red. "After all, we went to the same stinkin' grammar school!" He bit the words off, then pulled up his paper and ended the conversation.

"Okay, you've got me," Tommy offered. There was no reply from behind the paper.

"I'm sorry, Seth. You're right. I should've called you with the news. But this is big, buddy, and I mean real big. I was up all night dealin' with it, and I didn't even have time to eat.

"As far as I know, no media outlet has what I'm gonna tell you. You'll be the first with this story. The paper doesn't have anything special about yesterday's murder, does it?"

"No," he admitted grudgingly, "it was buried on the last page in the local section." The Sheriff had piqued his interest; he had to admit it. He put down the paper and looked over his glasses.

"So, this is big? Really big? Bigger than the trial?"

"Maybe."

"And nobody else has the story, you say?" Tommy nodded.

"Nobody. This may be the biggest story ever to come out of this part of Florida. But, we won't know until next week, after the evidence is tested by the FBI. I just have to ask you one favor, and it's a big one."

"You want me to sit on the story, right?"

"Yeah. Sit on it. At least, until we know what we're dealin' with."

"What if other reporters start digging into it?" Tommy sighed.

"Okay, if other reporters start snooping, you can break it. The whole story, whatever we know at that time. I'll be sure to fill you in as we go. And I'll let you know if we have any inquiries from the press."

"It's a deal," Seth replied quickly.

"Deal."

They stood abruptly, the chairs scraping loudly on the floor, and shook hands formally, as they might have years ago on an elementary school playground. Then they sat back down simultaneously, reached out in unison, and picked up their cups to take a deep sip of strong, black coffee. They sipped the hot brew slowly, savoring the bitter tang that scorched their mouths and plummeted down their throats like a flaming meteor. Outside, on Main Street, a tractor-trailer rumbled by as the police scanner sputtered twice, then was silent.

"So, Tommy, tell me" Seth began, "what's been goin' on around here?"

Wake Up Call

The sun arose painfully on Tuesday morning, as bright and shiny and hard as a brand new hammer. When Joe Boy lifted the blinds in his hotel room, the unfiltered sunlight struck a sharp blow across his brow, blinding him for an instant as he squinted and turned away.

Joey groped for an ashtray, exhaling and blinking and coughing as he tried to clear the red-orange image that danced before his eyes like an amoeba of light, a bright blob that overlaid everything in sight. Finding a glass ashtray overflowing with dirty butts, he stubbed out the remains of the morning's first cigarette and called angrily to Franco.

"Get outta my bathroom, Frankie! You got your own!" The door to the bathroom was shut and the exhaust fan was on. From within the bathroom, Franco's voice called loudly in reply.

"I can't use it. My toilet's clogged."

"So, what, you want to ruin mine, too?" He pulled on his bathrobe and jerked the belt tight as a knock on the door signaled the arrival of David "Slappy" Bustamente and Leonard "Lenny Twigs" Tuigliomo, two long time members of Joe Boy's crew. Joey hurried to the door and swung it open.

"Okay, come in. Where've you guys been?"

"We ate breakfast at the little joint down the road," said Lenny, walking into the room and flopping unceremoniously on the only chair not covered with clothing or newspapers. "It ain't bad: bacon, grits, eggs, pancakes . . . . " David followed Lenny, ducking his head to clear the top of the doorway.

"It's barely seven A.M. Since when do you guys get up so early?"

"Slappy couldn't sleep, so we went out."

Joey walked over to the closet and flipped through his clothes, pulling out a flashy blue double-breasted suit and a conservative black two-piece as David sat down at the table. Lenny picked up the remote control and turned on the television while Slappy proceeded to read the newspaper.

"Hey, Slappy, what do you recommend?" Joe Boy asked hopefully, holding up the two suits.

"The pancake and egg special," he replied, thumbing through the funny pages. Seeing that he was being ignored, Joey was overcome with rage. He picked up the heavy glass ashtray – filled to overflowing with carbonized tobacco and filthy, saliva-stained butts - and fired it sidearm at Slappy, aiming squarely for his head.

The ashtray shot from Joey's hand like a crystal cannonball, leaving behind a cloud of ash and a toxic spray of airborne butts that flew in every direction. It streaked within inches of the preoccupied hoodlum's head, ripping through the newspaper in his hands before ricocheting off the wall. The heavy glass ashtray did not shatter but changed directions a high rate of speed, skipping across the living room floor and rebounding against a distant baseboard before finally coming to rest on the tile floor of the kitchenette, spinning like a top in the sudden, profound silence.

"You idiot!" Joe Boy shrieked, beside himself with rage. "I'm on trial for my life, and all you can think about is the pancake and egg special!" David looked at him in surprise, his eyes wide-open and his broad face the picture of innocence. He was a huge man with awkwardly oversized hands and feet and doublewide shoulders that made him turn sideways when passing people in hallways.

"I thought you wanted to know about breakfast," he answered, dazed by the unforeseen storm of fury.

Franco emerged from the bathroom, shutting the door tightly behind him. He glanced from Joe Boy, apoplectic with rage with a suit in his hand, to Slappy, the somewhat-gentle giant of the Provencenti family. Quickly reading the situation, he defused it with a single sentence.

"You gotta wear the dark suit every day, Joey, just like our legal eagle said," he offered soothingly. "Forget about the Italian silks."

Joey looked at Franco, blinking as he tried to refocus his energy. *At least somebody around here has some sense.*

"Sure, conservative suits aren't your style," Franco continued, "but the jury down here will buy it. A suit like that says that you're respectful, from a good family: not too flashy. That's the way they like it down here."

"Okay, good," Joey said sternly, reasserting his authority. "Now, you boys scram while I get dressed. I'll meet you downstairs in the lobby, and we'll go to the courthouse." As they rose, he smiled grimly. "We get to see a real show today. The Energizer Hick is gonna give her testimony."

"Let's just hope she chokes in the clutch," Franco replied as he walked toward the door.

"Oh, she'll choke, all right," Joey said softly, smiling wickedly. "You can take that to the bank."

Testimony

Associate State's Attorney Marcia Woodruff rose slowly to her feet and approached the witness box. Her footsteps echoed through the packed courtroom. The rich tone of hard heels on solid wood was a sound that had filled this room for more than 100 years.

Oree County had been a county seat since the days when Florida's counties could be counted on two hands. The recently restored high-ceilinged courtroom - with its white walls, dark trim, and majestic tiger oak furnishings - had seen many trials, but none so prominent or sensational as the one that was currently being tried within its weathered walls.

Today's trial was huge. Representatives of the media overflowed the press box, and camera teams from national news organizations were waiting outside, poised like vultures on a fencepost ready to devour and regurgitate every scrap of information that could be gleaned from the legal wreckage.

With her footsteps echoing through the room, the attorney strode up to the box and stopped, briefly nodding to the witness. Then she turned to the jury of five men and seven women. The tall, slim attorney was a striking figure: her olive complexion and severely swept-back onyx hair contrasting markedly with the fair complexion and auburn locks of the young witness in the box.

The eyes of the jurors shifted from Marcia to the witness, looking small and fragile behind the large dais. She was dwarfed by the heavy door and sides of the box, the high ceiling and empty walls overlooked by the great, whorled hardwood sides of the judge's regal bench.

Jamie was plainly out of place in the large, ornate witness box. She was a diminutive figure in white: nervous, but determined to tell the truth.

"What is your name?"

"Janelle James," she replied softly in a voice that was barely audible.

"Please speak up," Maria said, turning to Jamie with a brief, reassuring smile.

"Janelle James," she repeated, swallowing nervously. "My friends call me Jamie."

"Thank you, Ms. James. Did you know a young man named John Delaney?"

"Yes, I did. I was with him on the night he was murdered."

"How long had you known him at the time of his murder?"

"Almost two years."

"How well did you know him?"

"He was my best friend. We were both from out of town. I guess we both felt like outsiders. We really got to know each other well."

"We're you involved in a romantic way with Mr. Delaney?" This question was irrelevant to the case, but could be relevant to the jury. Marcia could sense that a challenge was coming on this issue, and she thought that a preemptory strike might settle the matter in jurors' minds before the defense had a chance to stir up doubts.

"Never. We were best friends, and that was all there ever was to it," the witness replied without blinking. Marcia stepped closer to Jamie.

"Can you describe what happened last year, on the morning of November 16th?"

"Yes. Johnny and I were driving around and talking. We did it all the time, just cruised around on the weekend nights, talking about all kinds of things. It was 1:30 A.M. when we saw lights up ahead."

"How do you know the time?"

"I had just commented on the time. I told Johnny that it was late, and we should head back into town."

"So, where were you when you saw these lights?"

430

"We were in Homeland Estates near the county line, out on the back roads where there is no development. There are no houses there, no street lights, nothing. We saw lights in the distance. I wanted to turn around, but Johnny wasn't concerned. He was driving, so we kept on going.

"When we got to the lights, they flagged us over. I was looking as hard as I could, and I thought I could make out a plane parked in the middle of the road ahead of us with a big truck backed up to the cargo bay. I don't think Johnny saw it, though. He couldn't see very well in the dark, especially when there were lights in his eyes."

"They flagged you over? What do you mean by that?"

"Two men signaled for us to pull over to the side of the road, waving their flashlights."

"And can you describe the two men?"

"One of them I couldn't see because he kept shining his flashlight in my eyes. The other one put down his light and asked us some questions, and I got a good look at him."

"Is that man in the courtroom now?"

"Yes."

"And could you point him out for us?" In response, Jamie rose from her chair and left the box, slowly walking across the room to the defendant's table. When she stood less than six feet away from the men seated at the table, she gave her reply.

"This is the man," Jamie said, pointing at Joe Boy, "he's the man I saw that night, standing in front of our car." Joe Boy stared at Jamie impassively in the dead silence, looking - for all to see - like a wronged man who could not understand her actions. As whispers broke out in court, Jamie returned to the witness box and took her seat, closing the door behind her.

"Let the record show that the witness has identified the defendant," Marcia said, meeting the jurors' eyes as she spoke. She turned back to Jamie.

"Do you know the name of the man you just identified?"

"Yes. He's Joseph Provencenti."

"Can you describe what happened next?"

"Yes. The man asked us some questions. Then, without any warning, he reached behind his back and pulled out a gun and began firing. He shot Johnny, and I heard him scream," Jamie said, without apparent emotion, successfully suppressing the flood of grief that arose spontaneously, threatening to overwhelm her. "Then he turned to shoot me, but I was already moving. I ducked below the dash, dove out of the door and rolled into the ditch. Then, I ran for my life. I got away."

"How did you get away?"

"I ran through the ditch beside the road until I came to a lake, and I swam out into the middle of the lake among the weeds. When they came out to find me with a searchlight, I backtracked toward the road and found one of their cars with the keys in it. I took the car, and that's how I got away."

"What kind of car was it?"

"It was a Lamborghini."

"And whose car was it?"

"It belonged to that man," Jamie replied, "the man who shot Johnny. Joseph Provencenti."

"How did you learn his name?"

"Later that morning, in Ybor City, I found a wallet in the glove box with his drivers license. That was when I learned his name."

"So, on the morning of November 16th, after you 'got away' by taking the Lamborghini, what did you do next?"

"I drove to Ybor City."

"Why did you do that? Ybor City is at least a two hour's drive from Oree County."

"My best friend lives there, Ellen Bromley. We went to school together in Tampa."

"Why didn't you go immediately to the police?"

"I didn't know who to trust. I was totally panicked, but I knew I could trust Ellen."

"What happened when you got to Ybor City?"

"I tried to call Ellen, but she wasn't home. I left the phone and drove the car to a convenience store just down the street. That was when I was attacked."

"What do you mean, you were attacked?"

"Two men grabbed me when I came out of the store and dragged me into an alley. They tried to put me in the trunk of their car." Marcia picked up two poster-sized pictures from the end of the prosecutor's table and showed them to Jamie.

"Are these the men who assaulted you?"

"Yes."

"Let the record show that the men identified by the witness as her assailants are Nicolas Matalona and James Bianamabella, two convicted felons who were identified in a recent arson investigation as employees of Joseph Provencenti Sr., the reputed head of the Provencenti crime family."

"Objection!" interjected the attorney for the defense, rising shakily to his feet, "That is prejudicial and totally unfounded. We ask that it be stricken from the record. The scurrilous rumors about Mr. Joseph Provencenti have never been proven." The attorney was a decrepit but brilliant counselor who had served the Tampa mob well for a number of years: a short, thin, balding legal powerhouse who had shed his hair and several ex-wives with equal abandon in the course of a storied career.

"So ruled," said the somber judge, a young black woman from an old Pezner family who had been recently elected to the bench. "The jury will disregard the unproven allegations regarding Mr. Joseph Provencenti, Sr., and his employees. You may continue, counselor, without any further references of that kind."

"Thank you, your honor," Marcia replied, turning to face the jury as she raised her eyebrows ambiguously and studiously cleared her throat. "I'll put it another way. The two men identified by the witness as her attackers have been identified during past legal proceedings as employees of

Joseph Provencenti Sr., the father of the defendant." She turned back to Jamie.

"What happened next?" she asked her witness.

"Before they could put me into the trunk, I was rescued by Streetcar . . . er, by Salvatore Benuto."

"Who is he?"

"I didn't know him at the time. I learned later that he was a street person who lived in Ybor City."

"How did he rescue you?"

"He just appeared out of nowhere in the alley after the men grabbed me. He told them to drop me and to leave. When they tried to draw weapons, he beat them up, and we got away."

"You say, he 'beat them up?' Both men?"

"Yes."

"How did he do that?"

"I'm not sure. It was fast. He handled them both, though."

"What happened next?"

"We ran to the Lamborghini and got away. We left the car at a mall in Tampa and took a bus to the University of South Florida campus. That evening, my friend Ellen drove us to Oree County. I talked to Sheriff Durrance and Major Rawlings, and I've been here ever since."

Caught in the Crossfire

"Ms. James," the attorney for the defense began, strolling from his table toward the witness box, "how long have you lived in Oree County?" He was a shriveled, bleached-out prune of a man: wan, white-haired, and stoop-shouldered, dressed in a conservative dark blue suit with a white shirt, maroon tie, and mirror-glossy black shoes. His eyes, large and moist, appeared to be mildewed. On his face he wore the puzzled, disgusted expression of a man who has bitten into an apple and discovered half a worm.

"I've lived here for more than two years," Jamie replied warily.

"And during that time, did you ever have occasion to return to Tampa?"

"Yes."

"How often?"

"Oh, three or four times a year, to see Ellen."

"Three or four times each year. Is that all?" Benjamin Knowles, attorney for the defense, lifted his eyebrows and gave Jamie a kindly smile. His narrow, wrinkled face seemed inviting, harmless, like the worn face of a beloved grandfather showing concern for a favorite granddaughter.

"Yes. I think so. Maybe once or twice more."

"Now, you say that you were in Tampa on November 16th, on the morning after your lover was murdered."

"Objection," Marcia interjected, rising to her feet.

"Sustained," the judge said, glancing sternly at the defense attorney.

"Johnny was my best friend, not my lover."

"Uh, yes," he said doubtfully, "your 'best friend,' I believe you called him. On the morning after his murder, you say you were in Tampa: in Ybor City, to be precise."

"Yes."

"And you were assaulted by two men, Nicholas Matalona and James Bianamabella."

"Yes."

"Where are these two men, now?"

"They're dead."

"They're not just dead, are they? They were murdered. Their bodies were found burned beyond recognition, weren't they, after a terrorist blew up a city block in Ybor City?"

"Yes, sir. That's what I heard."

"And the man who, according to your account, saved you from these two men, isn't he the chief suspect in this horrible arson fire, this brutal terrorist act?"

"I'm not sure," she replied. "I haven't been watching television." She looked around the courtroom, trying to catch the Sheriff's eye. When she saw him, he nodded respectfully.

"Do you have any idea where Mr. Benuto might be now?"

"No, sir."

"Was there any money in the glove compartment of Mr. Provencenti's Lamborghini?"

"Yes," Jamie replied, looking around the court.

"How do you know?"

"After we parked at the mall, Streetcar - Mr. Benuto – went through the glove box. He said there was some money."

"What happened to the money in Mr. Provencenti's glove compartment?"

"Mr. Benuto took it."

"Are you saying that he took all the money, just like that? Someone else's money?" He raised his eyebrows, looking at the jury as if he were surprised.

"You had to be there," she replied, glancing from the jury to the judge. "It wasn't like that. We were running for our lives. Those men tried to kill me. I guess he thought he might need it just to stay alive."

"Please answer the question, Ms. James," the judge said courteously, looking over her spectacles at the witness.

"He helped himself to all of the money?" the attorney asked again.

"Yes, he did," Jamie replied defiantly. "We were running from the man who owned the car. We were running for our lives."

"At any time, did you tell Salvatore Benuto not to take Mr. Provencenti's money?"

"No," Jamie answered glumly.

"And are you aware that sugar was poured into the gas tank of the car, after it was parked at the mall. Are you aware that this destroyed the engine?"

"No! I didn't know any of that," she responded, fighting back a smile. "Did that really happen?" She was obviously surprised.

"You knew nothing about this deliberate damage to my client's property?"

"No, nothing at all. I knew that Mr. Benuto left me at the bus stop for a few minutes, but I didn't know what he did while he was gone." She paused. "I guess I know now."

Jamie smiled at the jury demurely as the courtroom stirred with scattered laughter. The judge frowned at the spectators and reached for her gavel until, under the steely eye of her authority, the laughter died away. The attorney for the defense straightened up, eyeing her sorrowfully, as if she were a beloved child breaking his heart with her shameful behavior.

"Please describe the man who was with you in this stolen car, the man known as Salvatore Benuto."

"He is a tall man, slim, close to 50 years old. Salt and pepper hair, beard. He looks Italian."

"Do you like the looks of tall, dark men?" he asked, turning around suddenly to face her.

"Objection!" cried Marcia Woodruff.

"Sustained," stated the judge firmly. "Counselor, you will refrain from that kind of question."

"Yes, your honor. Is he a good looking man, this Salvatore Benuto?"

"I suppose that he might be to some people, in a rough sort of way, but . . . . "

"Isn't it true that you had a relationship with Salvatore Benuto that preceded the night of November 15th?"

"Absolutely not!"

"Objection, your honor," Marcia interjected hotly. "Relevance."

"Your honor," the attorney stated somberly. "I will be able to demonstrate relevance if I am allowed to question the witness."

"You may proceed," the judge stated skeptically, "but only if you can demonstrate the relevance of this line of questioning. And soon," she added sternly, gazing over the top of her glasses.

"Ms. James. Didn't you meet Salvatore Benuto on the night of November 15th, after you had driven with John Delaney to Ybor City?"

"No, I did not!"

"And didn't your 'friend,' John Delaney, get jealous, when he saw you meet with Mr. Benuto: when he saw the real reason you wanted a ride to Tampa? Wasn't there a quarrel at that time? Didn't this street person, this highly trained killer, murder Johnny Delaney and dispose of the body and the car? Didn't he hide the broken and abused body, using all of his jungle combat skills, at a remote location in the victim's home county, to mislead authorities and allay suspicion? And after these things, days later, didn't he murder Nicolas Matalona and James Bianamabella - along with several other innocent persons - in a hideous attempt to eliminate any possible witnesses who might contradict the fantastic story that you had concocted?"

"Absolutely not!" Jamie said, looking around for help.

"Your honor, we object," Marcia Woodruff interjected, rising to her feet. "Counsel for the defense is making outrageous and inflammatory statements with no supporting evidence."

"If it may please the court," Benjamin Knowles interjected, "I would like to present into evidence this copy of an affidavit, which was obtained by our private investigators late yesterday evening and hand-delivered to us just before court. I also have a logbook that is included by reference in the affidavit."

"You may approach the bench and show us what you have," replied the judge, nodding to the defense attorney and the prosecutor's table. Marcia Woodruff hastily arose and approached the bench as the attorney for the defense delicately minced up to the judge and handed her the affidavit. Both attorneys stood quietly as the judge studied the documents, then passed them to the prosecuting attorney. After allowing further time for examination, the judge addressed the court.

"This sworn statement and accompanying documentation will be entered into evidence conditionally," Judge Jackson ruled, "with the understanding that further testimony will be required from all persons who are attesting to the facts described in the affidavit. I am particularly interested in the timetables regarding the receipt of this information by your team. The prosecution should have been informed as soon as possible about this information."

"Yes, your honor."

"You may proceed." The attorneys left the judge, and Benjamin Knowles turned back to his subject: Janelle James.

"Ms James, the affidavit that has just been entered into evidence shows that at 2:00 A.M. on the morning of November 16, 30 minutes after my client is alleged to have been in the southern part of Oree County with his car, my client's car was stolen from his secure townhouse parking lot by a woman matching the description of Janelle James.

"I do not know every detail regarding the dreadful morning of Johnny Delaney's murder. The coroner has testified that, due to extensive damage to the corpse, the time of death could not be determined with exactitude but was sometime between 1:00 and 3:00 A.M. However, while I do not know exactly what happened, I know, beyond the shadow of a doubt, what did <u>not</u> happen. I know that Joseph Provencenti, Jr., did not kill Johnny Delaney.

"My client is a victim in this affair. And so are the two loyal employees who were peacefully attempting to recover my client's stolen car when they were viciously assaulted by a trained killer."

"Your honor, I object," Marcia Woodruff interrupted, rising to her feet. "The counsel's speech, while creative, is not material to the examination of the witness."

"Sustained. Get to the point, counselor."

"Yes, your honor." He sharply turned to Jamie.

"Where were you at 2:00 A.M. in the morning, immediately following the murder of John Delaney?"

"I was on the highway, driving toward Ybor City."

"Ms. James, I do not believe that your statement is true. At exactly 2:00 A.M. on that Sunday morning, as my client peacefully slept in his Ybor City townhouse, his car was stolen from a walled parking lot by a young woman meeting your description. My client had inadvertently left the car unlocked, with his keys in the ignition, and the car was easy to steal.

"The security guard on duty at the Ybor City parking lot on that fateful morning has signed an affidavit attesting that he saw the car driven from the lot at 2:00 A.M. on that morning. He will appear in court tomorrow to testify to this fact.

"The guard did not know that the car had been stolen, so no report was made to the police. He questioned the driver, and she convinced him that the car had been loaned to her by its owner, with whom she claimed to be intimate."

"The security guard is an old, respectable man," the attorney offered, taking the members of the jury into his confidence as if they were old friends. "To tell you the truth," he said with a professorial smile, "his vision isn't what it used to be. But a Lamborghini is impossible to miss. And so is a

440

head full of distinctive burgundy hair," he added with a sidelong glance at Jamie Jameson.

"We have submitted the original copy of the guard's handwritten log which notes the car's exit from the lot and the exact time. Because Ybor City is a two-hour drive from the northern border of Oree County, as the prosecuting attorney has stated, my client could not possibly have committed the crime of which he is accused.

"Thanks to the sworn statement of this brave security guard, which was made in spite of his declared fear that he might become the target of overzealous prosecutors," the attorney added, turning to the jury and appealing with his eyes and hands, "we now have proof that verifies what we knew all along.

"Our client could not have committed this terrible crime. Our client was not even here at the time. He was not in the county where, according to the prosecution, the murder took place. Our client is totally, irrefutably innocent."

In the silence following his statement, all eyes were riveted upon the attorney for the defense, who stared at the jury, his eyes wide with outrage. Then, a small voice spoke up loudly, resounding through the room. It was Jamie.

"That's not true. Joseph Provencenti's car was not in Tampa at 2:00 A.M. that night, and I can prove it."

"Objection, your honor," the attorney replied impatiently. "The witness has already testified."

"Overruled," replied the judge brusquely, glaring at him, "this witness is still sworn." Turning to Jamie, the judge gazed over her spectacles with a sternness that belied her youth. "Miss James, are you saying that this is a false affidavit?"

"Yes, your honor."

"And how can you prove that this affidavit is not true?"

"He just said that, according to the affidavit and logbook, the car was stolen from Tampa at 2:00 A.M. Well, at 2:05 AM, I got a ticket for speeding in Oree County. I was heading north towards Tampa at the time on Highway 27, and the ticket recorded that fact. I keep a copy of it in my wallet," she added, addressing the judge. "I can show you now, if you'd like."

"By all means." Jamie stepped out the box, retrieved her wallet from her purse and produced the ticket, smoothing it before she handed it to the judge.

"Here it is, your honor."

The mob attorney, who had been prepared to vigorously refute any claim she made, was stunned. He stared at her in amazement, totally nonplussed with his jaws slack and his mouth wide open, openly displaying the extent of his shock.

"You can check it out with the Sheriff's records," Jamie said directly to the defense attorney. "Since the ticket shows that I was in Oree County at 2:05 AM, there is no way that the car could have been seen in Tampa at 2:00 AM."

"The car could not have been my client's," the attorney replied, at a complete loss for what to say.

"Well, just in case you don't know," Jamie responded, "there are not a lot of Lamborghinis driving around Oree County." The crowd laughed heartily at this remark, earning a rap from the judge's gavel. At the sound, they immediately fell silent.

"The policeman asked for the registration," Jamie continued, "and he wrote the registration number on the ticket. You can look it up." Benjamin Knowles' legendary legal mind was racing, scanning the details of the case as he sought any flaw in her story.

"Why have you withheld this information?" the attorney asked. To reply, Jamie turned to the judge.

"I haven't withheld this information, your honor," she said. "I didn't know that the defense would claim that I wasn't in Oree County when Johnny was murdered."

"But," the attorney rejoined, "you said earlier that you first saw my client's wallet after you arrived in Ybor City. Yet you produced a registration for the officer who gave you the ticket. How could you do that without having his wallet?" He was going down fighting, grasping at straws.

"The registration was tucked into the visor," she replied, "right where I keep it in my own car. Your client is a cold-blooded killer, Mr. Knowles, but I have to admit one thing. His car was as neat as a pin."

"Objection," the defense attorney bleated weakly, "request to strike."

"Sustained," replied the judge, "strike 'cold-blooded' from the record. The jury will ignore this term." Angered by the defense's apparent attempt to deceive the court with a fraudulent affidavit, the judge gazed down sternly at the attorney. "Is there anything else?" she asked bluntly.

"I would like to reserve on that request, if possible, your honor," the attorney replied, totally befuddled and at a complete loss regarding how to respond to the dramatic demolition of his client's carefully constructed alibi. Then, he managed one last rally.

"Why wasn't my team provided with this information?" In response to this question, Marcia Woodruff stood.

"Your honor, if I may, we provided a copy of the ticket in our documentation to the defense. The court also received a copy."

"We would like to request that this issue be researched further to confirm the validity of this ticket," Benjamin Knowles offered weakly.

"So ruled. Bailiff, you will conduct the search of public records regarding the traffic ticket identified by the witness and present your detailed findings to the court tomorrow afternoon." The attorney for the defense reflexively pulled out his handkerchief and wiped perspiration from his pale, beaded brow.

"Thank you, your honor."

"You may step down," the judge said to Jamie. She looked down quickly at the paperwork on her raised desk, successfully hiding the smile that threatened to break out on her somber face.

The Way Home

As the hammer fell on the day's testimony, the scribes of journalism swept from the courthouse in a single motion. It was almost as if they were a unified, well-rehearsed team instead of a mixed bag of elitist working stiffs and cutthroat, ink-stained piranhas who smelled the scent of blood. As the scribes swarmed out, the picture-takers swarmed in. But behind the fleeing writers, using their momentum to add to the push, the Big Green Machine made its move.

To an aggressive and voracious press corps, the green-clad deputies and police officers presented nothing less than a flying wedge. It was an effective full-court press pass that protected the frail but resilient star witness.

She moved well in the pocket.

In the lead was Major Delia Rawlings, parting the thundering herd of reporters like an iron cowcatcher fronting a steam locomotive. One by one, the dumfounded journalists were bumped off the tracks in quick succession until the compact engine of human progress reached the squad car and deposited Jamie safely inside.

Jamie leaned back into the seat and sighed deeply as Delia slipped into the front passenger's side. The car, driven by Red Johnson, lurched away from the curb. Noisy air conditioning drowned out a flood of final questions desperately barked by the pack of abandoned news hounds as the vehicle sped down Main Street until the swarming crowd and the ancient courthouse were a distant blur in the rear view mirror.

"Thank God," Jamie said emphatically. "That was terrible."

"You performed incredible well in that courtroom," Delia replied admiringly. "You were like Popeye after he ate the spinach."

"I felt more like Olive Oil," she responded earnestly. "I was scared witless. I guess my survival instinct just kicked in.

It was a blur, Delia. I don't remember most of the stuff I said." Delia chuckled wryly.

"You said plenty," she observed. "Much more than the defense wanted to hear. He laid a trap, and you dropped a bomb and blew it up." She paused, her brows drawing together. "I wonder why the attorney didn't know about your traffic ticket?"

"I don't know," Jamie offered. "I told Clay about it early on, and he said, if a fact isn't contested, don't try to prove it."

"Well, we certainly didn't withhold any evidence. I happen to know that a copy of the ticket was included near the bottom of a thick stack of marginally-relevant documents that were submitted to opposing counsel." She smiled slyly at Jamie. "I guess the defense just got lazy and missed it," she added. "Maybe it was copied on the back of some boring document, hidden in a huge pile of single-sided copies. Who knows?"

"I get the feeling you know," Jamie replied with a wary smile. "Some things are better left unsaid."

They turned off the highway onto one of the long, meandering country roads that characterized this county. Behind them, a patrol car pulled across the road with its lights flashing, effectively blocking all traffic.

"That should give us the edge we need," Red said, slipping on his aviator-style sunglasses. His long face, cracked like golden mud baked too long in the sun, broke into a smile.

Red's sunburned mug was wreathed with a mist of fine white hair that began to blow in the wind slipping in through the open window. "In the next 22 miles, this road has more than 20 outlets, each of which feeds into a highway or another county road. With the road blocked back there behind us, the reporters can't follow us. They won't have any idea where we're headed."

He punched the gas pedal to the floor and the supercharged engine roared to life. The stoked cop car launched down the narrow asphalt road like a bullet shot from the smoking mouth of a high-velocity gun.

The sunlight slanted through the long, lanky pines that lined the roadway, illuminating the broad expanse of bright green pasture behind the trees. The pastureland on both sides of the road was fertile and moist, an ocean of turf scattered with distant spots of black and brown and white and red: the forms of various Angus, Hereford, and mixed-breed cattle.

The trees whipped past rapidly as the big car hummed along. Sunlight pressed on her skin, filling Jamie with a wonderful feeling of motion, warmth, and pleasure.

"This is nice," she murmured contentedly, slipping on her dark green shades, "real nice." She sighed and snuggled deeper in the seat.

"Turn right at the water tank," Delia said to Red, pointing to a dun colored tank a quarter-mile ahead on their right.

"Pull over into those trees," she said when they pulled off the highway a few seconds later. Red wheeled onto the narrow clay road that wound into the thick trees just past the water tank and rattled to a halt.

Beneath the trees, in the quiet shadows, Delia and Jamie climbed out of Red's car and looked at their ride. It was a battered pickup truck with oversized tires, fishing poles and a gun rack. "See you, Red," she said, slapping the side of his car.

"Y'all take care," he shouted out of the window as he slammed the car into reverse and turned it around. He accelerated abruptly, spraying gravel as he bumped back onto the road. Reaching the pavement, the car burnt rubber and barreled away at a high rate of speed.

"That Red's a real card when he gets going," Delia observed. "But when he's not in the mood for fun, he can be as serious as a heart attack. When he grinned a few minutes ago, I thought it would break his face. That's the first time I've seen him smile in a week."

"Boys like to go fast," Jamie said. "Even the old ones."

"So do girls, given the right situation." Delia added.

The dented driver's door on the old pickup groaned painfully as Delia opened it and pulled out a denim shirt, slipping it over her Sheriff's Deputy's uniform. She climbed into the truck and smiled as Jamie climbed in feet first through the open passenger window. Jamie bounced onto the seat with her hair askew, nursing a broken nail.

"The door was stuck," she offered in explanation, smiling apologetically.

"You don't have to tell me about that door. This is my brother's truck. I've been telling him to fix that thing for ages." Delia turned the key and the big engine rumbled to life, throbbing deeply beneath their feet. "This baby's a real hummer," she said, looking over at her young friend. "So, how are you doin', kid?"

"Delia, I am so glad that I don't have to go back to court," she replied, shaking her head as if she could not believe that she had the nerve to testify. As Delia let out the clutch, the truck pulled out of the trees and bumped its way toward the road.

"Well, I'm glad I don't have to leave you tonight," Major Rawlings said. "It wouldn't be good for you to be alone. Maybe tomorrow, if you'd like, we can do a little fishing with these cane poles. Maybe we can even take out that slick little canoe. How does that sound?"

"Marvelous. Absolutely marvelous."

Tomorrow, neither Jamie nor Delia would be expected in court. Closing arguments would likely occur during the late morning or early afternoon.

"I can use the company, Delia. I got spoiled with Ellen visiting last week." Ellen had left on Monday, returning to the responsibilities that awaited her at her office in Tampa, where she had recently become branch manager.

"That Ellen, she's a real corker," Delia observed as they wheeled out onto the road, accelerating abruptly.

"You're not kidding. You should have seen her in high school."

447

"You'd better put on the hat and hunker down in the seat," Delia said. She was ever the cop, always serving and protecting.

"Yes, mommy."

"Why don't you just slide down in the seat and lean back against the door? Don't worry; it's safe. As you've discovered, it's welded shut."

"Okay," Jamie replied, sighing deeply as she slumped down in the seat, following her advice. Looking up, she could see a mountainous range of clouds, as white as snow against the deep blue sky. The beauty of the sky was almost hypnotic. *I wonder what my life would have been like if I had known my mother,* Jamie thought idly, *would she have loved me? Would she have been nice, like Delia, or would she have hated me, like my father?* She considered these things without a trace of self-pity.

Jamie sighed again and shut her eyes. She relaxed in the rhythmic thud and sway, drifting amid the throaty rumble of the muscular engine as the truck hurtled down the deserted highway in the failing light of dusk.

The Sign

Streetcar was sitting on the lowest branch and preparing to climb to the top of his sentinel cypress when the beeper on his hip vibrated, signaling the arrival of a car at the main gate. *That should be Jamie,* he thought, *accompanied by the long arm of the law.*

He had begun to interpret every event as routine, half expecting that he might never be forced to defend his young friend from the mobsters who had once tried to kill her. But Streetcar knew better than to relax. The most successful assaults occurred when trouble was not expected.

The last vapors of light were fading from the western sky. The sunset dissipated like a dream of past glory as the lights of the night came out one by one: first the planets, green and red, then the dominant stars and clusters, which arrived with silent pomp like the nobility of the universe emerging from a royal antechamber.

As he began to climb to the top of his tree, ignoring the clouds of mosquitoes, Streetcar silently thanked God for mosquito repellant, a key benefit of the post-industrial age. He paused on a branch halfway up, absently stroking the cat that clung to him tightly, wrapped inside his nylon windbreaker.

From the top of the tree, the view was superb. He could see the battered pickup truck as it rumbling across the pasture. The big engine throbbed as the truck entered the grove of oak trees near the farmhouse. The headlights bobbed up and down crazily, alternately illuminating the Spanish moss and the clumps of grass as it bumped along the two-track rutted road. *Good choice of vehicles,* he thought, *that one definitely blends.*

It was then that Streetcar heard the airplane. He looked up quickly, searching the sky, straining and staring until he finally detected a dark shadow against the backdrop of starlit sky: a one-engine plane flying at over 5,000 feet of altitude, pulling a wispy shape behind it. *Is that plane trailing a banner? That must be it,* he decided, *it must be the Bass Baiters' promo plane I saw earlier today.* A plane had passed overhead during the morning, trailing a promotional message from the Bass Baiters' organization. He had assumed that it was part of a membership drive.

But what would such a plane be doing out past dark? There was no benefit in trailing a banner at this time of day, and from the maps that he had so carefully studied, he knew that there was no airport in the direction in which the plane was headed.

He was uneasy, but was not prepared to jump to conclusions. Nevertheless, he would not relax in his hammock.

"We're not stayin' here tonight," he whispered to his companion. "We're movin' closer, just make sure that everything's okay." He began to climb down from the top of the tree, carefully moving from handhold to handhold, using the rope to navigate the long stretches of trunk between the clusters of branches. He descended mechanically, without conscious effort, buried deep in a world of thought.

There was always the chance that this plane represented a true worst-case scenario. The plane could have been hired by the Provencentis to track Jamie after her court appearance. After all, given the size and nature of the county and its roads, such a plane would provide the only realistic chance to track her to her home and catch her unawares. As he considered the possibility, the hair on his arms stood up as if brushed by a passing spirit and a rush of fear coursed over him, covering him with bumps. *Oh, man, no!*

If this were truly a worst-case scenario, he considered that he would need all of his savvy and not a little luck to survive the night. *Luck is the will of God,* he mused, remembering one of his mother's sayings. *Well, if that's the case,* he reasoned, *let's hope my luck hasn't finally run out.*

Evil for Good

The pilot was exultant. He had accomplished a difficult and daunting task, and now he was prepared to reap the benefit. He could hardly believe his good fortune.

Below him, as he turned to the north in a long, leisurely bank, the vast wilderness stretched in every direction shrouded in a profound darkness broken here and there by scattered pinpoints of light. Over his shoulder, the outline of vast Lake Oklawaha rapidly receded, its glassy face a distant glimmer.

The pilot turned on the cockpit light and picked up his cellular phone, reading the number from a crumpled business card. *Just to think,* he thought, savoring the pleasure as he dialed the number, *I'm 26 years old, and I just made five thousand dollars for two hours' work.* As a newly certified crop duster, he had never dreamed of such a payday. But it was not every day that a famous trial was being held in Oree County.

"Hello," a detached voice answered on the other end of the phone.

"Jimmy Collins here," he said, turning off the overhead light, "your 007 eye in the sky."

"Okay," the dry voice responded. "Did you get the location?"

"Well, Mr. Ace Reporter," he replied, leaning back in the seat and cracking the top on an iced cold bottle of R. C. Cola, "I guess you could say so. I got the address that every reporter in America would like to have as his or her own." He paused and took a long swig, gulping it down until his throat burned and his eyes watered. "Are you interested in it?" he added slyly, wiping the corner of his eye with his knuckle.

"Where is she?" the voice interjected, "just give me the address."

"Will you mention my name in your article in the New York Times? I'd like that."

"Where is she?" the voice asked hungrily. It was an unremittingly harsh voice, so emotionless as to be tinged with rigor mortis: as grim and humorless as death itself.

"You're no fun," Jimmy drawled. "Okay, I'll tell you. She's in a ranch house out near the end of Deer Creek Road. The house is on the Oklawaha Canal, the north bank, just a stone's throw from where the canal meets the lake. The driveway is the last left turn before the end of Deer Creek Road. There's a cattle gate. It's just before the swamp begins. It's way out in the middle of nowhere, but it'll be easy to find on a map."

"Got it," the voice interrupted, all business, "great. Good work."

"Okay, you got your scoop," Jimmy replied, "now, when do I get my just reward?" He felt a thrill in his stomach, thinking of what he and Heather might be able to add to their brand new, doublewide mobile home. Would it be a washer, a dryer, or both?

"Oh, it's definitely time for your reward. How far are you now from that ranch house?"

"A good 20 miles," he replied, "I'm only five miles from the airport. I've got this baby on full throttle so I can get home to my wife and kids. I'm late for dinner!"

"Good, that's real good," the voice replied calmly. "Look under the passenger's seat. Remember the other day, when you showed me your plane?"

"Yeah, sure."

"Well, I knew you were the one to get the job done, so I went ahead and tucked the rest of your money up under the front seat for you." The cockpit light was turned on, and the pilot bent over and dug beneath the front seat, pulling out a package wrapped in brown paper.

"What, no bow?" he asked. There was no response on the other end of the line, so he hastily began to unwrap it. "I can't believe you did this. How'd you know I would find her?"

"Oh, I knew you were the right sort." The young man tore off the remaining paper and paused before lifting the lid.

"Man, you're a piece of work," the pilot said, marveling at the moxie of the man he believed to be a reporter.

"No, you're the piece of work," the voice replied. "Or should I say, pieces of work."

"What?"

"Open it up, son. Hell, open it up!"

"Hey, you can't talk that way over the airwaves. Do you know what I mean?"

"Who are you, the morality police?"

"No."

"Well then, hell, son, open it!" Suddenly annoyed and troubled, the young man turned off the phone.

"I'm not your son," he said aloud. He paused, staring at the package in his lap as a sickly feeling swept over him. *Could this be a bomb?* he wondered, and then quickly rejected the thought. *Where did that idea come from?*

Suddenly, he snatched the lid off the box. Inside, on top of the contents, was a note. He picked it up and read it in the cockpit light.

"GO TO HELL!" the note declared. It was hand written in large, neatly printed letters.

"No way!" he whispered in shock and dismay.

A clicking sound inside of the box drew his attention, and he stared transfixed at the whirling mechanism. Inside of the cardboard box was a device as complex as clockwork: smoothly polished and precise: humming and clicking as it began its abbreviated timing sequence.

It was a bomb.

"Jesus, help," he breathed, horrified by it all.

The bomb blew up in his face, shredding his body into myriad chunks of former human being, blowing his consciousness far, far away. He watched the plane as if in a dream, as if he were standing beside it, drifting on the cool April breeze. A deep peace permeated his being, and a light far brighter than the sun began to illuminate the scene.

The event seemed somehow distant and remote, a movie that he watched as he peeked though a window. It hardly looked like his own plane as the light flashed inside the cockpit and the windows shattered, flames billowing out as the side blew out in great fiery chunks and the vapors in the tank ignited, destroying it all at once in a spectacular fireball that should have been loud but was not.

That was the strangest part of all.

As the plane blew up, he could see it all clearly.

But he could hardly hear a thing.

Home Alone

Delia and Jamie talked animatedly inside of the farmhouse, preparing a dinner of chicken and dumplings and fresh tossed salad. To make their dumplings, they used biscuits right out of a refrigerated can, following one of Delia's family recipes. They scarcely heard a sound like distant thunder as the plane detonated more than 20 miles away.

At the edge of the swamp, however, Streetcar heard the sound clearly. He noticed the distant flash of light and the ensuing rumble with distinct unease. It sounded like an explosion to him, not like thunder at all. It had been 30 years since the last time he heard heavy ordnance exploding in the distance, but the sound was immediately familiar. And yet, he was not sure.

From his treetop, he had seen clouds approaching from the east, and the clouds may have brought thunder with them. That was the local pattern, and the sound must surely be thunder, he told himself. But even as he reassured himself, he felt somehow uneasy. *It sounded just like a bomb.*

After ruminating about the matter, he decided that it could have been the plane . . . and the plane could have been following Jamie. There might be trouble tonight: deadly business, to say the least. He had prepared against this day for months, and now he decided to put his plan into effect.

Streetcar sloshed through the darkened swamp until he reached its edge within sight of the farmhouse. He emerged from the trees slowly, looking cautiously across the pasture for indications that headlights might be approaching. He planned to follow the narrow band of woodland that lined the water's edge, climbing up the gentle rise until it he reached the broad oak hammock that sheltered the venerable farmhouse.

He crept slowly out of the water and onto thick grass that squished sloppily under his feet. At this place, the pasture was a sloppy grass veneer, a pale excuse for turf that lightly covered the marshy soil and surrendered to his combat boots without a fight. His every step sunk deep into the fragrant black muck.

The ground grew firmer as he drew closer to the farmhouse. He maneuvered in the dark, dense shadows of towering trees, slowly feeling his way past rotting branches, cypress knees, and armadillo holes. He stealthily continued toward his goal, ignoring a feeding armadillo that rustled through the underbrush. As he passed, the armadillo snuffed deeply, like a horse sniffing after a sugar cube. Sensing the man's presence, it hastily crashed away through the heavy mat of cast off twigs and leaves.

He moved closer to the edge of the canal as the light of the farmhouse drew nearer. In the dim light filtering through the trees from the floodlights at the corners of the house, he scanned the close-cropped banks of the canal carefully, watching out for the coal-black curves that might reveal the presence of a wary cottonmouth lying motionless on the leaves. But there were no serpents in his path. Or at least, there were none that were visible.

He came to a familiar pile of leaves at the foot of a rotten tree and carefully knelt to brush the leaves aside. Here he found a familiar form buried beneath the debris in the broad mouth of a deserted armadillo hole.

"Hello, Fred," he whispered quietly to the unmoving figure, "long time no see." Fred, a life-sized dummy stuffed with wax paper and clothed in camouflage gear, did not respond to Streetcar's courteous greeting. Streetcar slid him out of the hole, checked to make sure he was still in fighting shape, and nodded in approval. "You've held up pretty good, Fred," he whispered, poking him in the stomach, "I'd'a thought you'd be looking pretty peaked, but you look just as good as you always did."

Picking up the canvas chair that he had hidden beneath Fred, Streetcar carefully arose, hoisted everything to his shoulders, and crept toward the farmhouse. Entering the clearing, he silently ran up to the house. Ducking low, he crept past the kitchen window and paused in the shadows, quietly setting the dummy and the chair on the ground as he kneeled and looked about in every direction. He had to move quickly.

For an instant, he thought of the cat. *I hope he forgives me,* he mused, remembering the wild palpitations as the cat had struggled inside the gunnysack he had left hanging from a tree in camp. In spite of himself, he smiled at the memory.

He had chosen this spot months ago. The dummy would be partially hidden in the shadows, readily visible to a person approaching the house on foot. The driveway looped to the left when it entered the clearing, ending in a wide parking area on the left side of the house. Because this spot was on the right side of the house, a person arriving by car would be unlikely to see it. But anyone approaching from the south or the west would see a human figure that appeared to be sitting still in the shadows, keeping watch on the house and its occupants.

He heard laughter within the house and detected the distinctive sound of clanking dishes as he began to set up the chair. He put the dummy in the seat and arranged it as conversation drifted out through the cracked kitchen window.

"So, this is your grandmother's secret recipe?" Jamie asked Delia skeptically as she began to set the table.

"It is. Absolutely."

"Your grandmother used Poppin' Fresh biscuits for her homemade chicken and dumplings?"

"She got this recipe straight from the doughboy himself. That was after the Big War. Way, way after it, as a matter of fact. Granny always said that the Pillsbury Doughboy was the best thing going." Delia nodded knowingly. "She remembered the War to End all Wars. That's World War I for you younger folks. Back then, a doughboy really counted for something."

"Okay, I believe you," Jamie chuckled, placing the steaming pot on the table. "Let's see if she was right."

"Huh!" Delia responded skeptically. "Don't you go doubtin' my Granny!" They laughed as they sat at the table, preparing to enjoy their meal.

Outside, carefully arranging the decoy to resemble a man who had fallen asleep sitting in the chair, Streetcar tried to ignore the muffled sounds of conversation coming from inside of the house. But somewhere deep within him, he hurt for human companionship, especially for the companionship of people like these two decent women. To talk to them again, to laugh with them, to see their faces light up, to spend time with people who were so real, so nice . . . such an experience would be more than he could hope for.

He felt condemned to a life of thankless service swathed in blood. His was a bleak existence spent fighting fire with flame, defending the innocent against those who lacked fundamental human decency. Streetcar considered himself to be an exterminator of human vermin, destined to destroy twisted figments of reality: bad men grown worse by evil practice. He was fighting monsters created not from the fevered imaginations of children, but from wasted lifetimes filled with cruel decisions.

Streetcar's adversaries were the wretched offspring of bad ideas grown rotten with age. They were the children of hateful desires superheated in a cauldron of perverted imagination.

It was discouraging to realize the bitter truth: some people would kill any person and betray any trust to have their way in this world. And the unbridled desires of such people led them to prey on those who wished to live in peace. His life had been a series of exploits that confronted and destroyed such people.

The easy banter, the friendly conversation of friends seemed like something achingly distant to Streetcar: a simple pleasure that he would never know. He counted himself a freak - good only for murdering the kind of monstrous men who were even worse than he.

The sounds from the farmhouse served to emphasize Streetcar's isolation from the social graces so casually shared by more civilized people. Fighting the pain, he wrenched his mind to the task before him, carefully arranging the camouflage netting over the dummy's face and arranging the arms and gloved hands to mimic a man asleep in the chair.

Delia and Jamie were friends. They had friends or family, but he had nothing. He felt his hope ebb away as despair rolled in, leeching the light from his heart, sending a wash of salty tears like a bitter tide that burned the wounds in his bared and bloodied soul.

There was one thing that he knew, and he knew it well. These women were worth dying for.

These women were worth living for.

When others had treated him like a freak, these women had treated him with respect. They had treated him as a friend.

Their kindness had been wonderful, better than anything he had ever known. As a result, the two women were more precious to Streetcar than his own safety, his own life or death or his comfort or deliverance: more precious than his aching, inscrutable, tortured, incurable, battered, embattled, and compromised soul.

Personal History

"Do you mind answering a few questions about yourself?" Jamie asked Delia as she dried the dishes, happy and relaxed.

"Not at all. Fire away."

"Okay," she answered, eager to begin. "How did you wind up in Oree County?"

"Well, I guess it all started about ten years ago, when my father died of a heart attack."

"I'm sorry."

"Don't be. He had a great life, and he was ready to go. Daddy was an attorney who specialized in accidental injuries and deaths. He had a successful practice and was a terrific father, though I didn't appreciate it when I was a teenager. He was much older than all of my friend's fathers, and I was embarrassed by his age. But with time, I learned how wrong that was. He always forgave me for every wrong. He loved me come what may.

"After Daddy died about ten years ago, my mother moved to Memphis to live with her sister. I begged her to stay in Tampa, but she wouldn't hear of it. She had grown up in Memphis, and she wanted to go home.

"A couple of years before Daddy passed on, my brother moved to Quilting Bee. He loves it down here. He grew up in the big city, but he's a country boy at heart. By the way, his construction firm helped build the new bank, the one at the edge of town. Did you know that?

"No, I didn't. That's impressive."

"Yes, I suppose. He's made quite a success of himself."

"So your mother moved from Tampa back home to Memphis?"

"Yes, my aunts all live there. So, I was left in Tampa with no family. My brother wanted me to move down here, and when he heard about an opening for a Lieutenant's slot in the Oree County Sheriff's Department, he talked me into applying. I really wasn't that interested in the job. It was a cut in pay, to tell you the truth. I was a detective sergeant on the Tampa force. But I had just been through some pretty rough changes in Tampa and I was anxious to get out of town. So I applied, and Tommy hired me. Now I'm the highest-ranking member of the force. Next to the Sheriff, of course." As Delia stopped talking, Jamie put up the last of the dishes and paused thoughtfully.

"Do you mind if I ask you something more personal?"

"I guess not," Delia replied. The two women had come to know each other well, and she did not mind questions from her friend. "But I'm not guaranteeing that I'll answer."

"Have you ever been in love?" In response to Jamie's question, Delia smiled wryly.

"I was in love once. It ended badly."

"What happened?" Delia looked away from Jamie, searching for the words.

"I loved a man, but I guess he didn't love me the same way. We were married, and he wanted children. I wasn't able to have children for him. After the third miscarriage, he just packed up and walked out. He never came back."

"I am so sorry," Jamie said, regretting her questions.

"I'm not, Jamie. I was sorry at the time, but I'm not sorry anymore. And I'm definitely not sorry that you asked the question." She looked at Jamie intently, reaching out, placing her hand on arm. "I loved him, Jamie, and I thought he loved me. Given that, it was not a mistake to marry him. It was the right thing to do.

"Never be sorry about doing the right thing, Jamie. Especially when you do it for the right reasons." She sat down at the table, and Jamie sat across from her.

"Do you want to play Scrabble?" Delia asked brightly.

"Yeah, sure, why not?" Jamie smiled slyly, hoping that this time, finally, she might win a round against her friend.

"Okay, we'll play," Delia replied heartily. "Get ready to lose."

"Delia, just one more nosy question."

"Okay, shoot."

"Have you ever met anyone down here, in Oree County? Anyone special?"

"Jamie, let me put this politely," Delia replied, chuckling in spite of herself. "I don't need a man to make me happy or to make my life complete. I have a baby brother who still wants me to sew on his missing buttons, and I don't need another baby to take care of. I run the day-to-day operations of the Oree County Sheriff's Department, and my job is never boring. I have a few good friends, and I work with some of them. That's more than enough for me."

"What about the Sheriff? Does he have anyone special?"

"Tommy?" she snorted, "His work is his sweetheart. That, and his congregation. His whole life revolves around the department and the Free Will Baptist Church. He's got no home life, no hobbies, and no family to speak of. But he's the best law enforcement professional I've ever worked with."

"No family? None at all?" *Just like me,* Jamie thought, *how sad.* Delia stopped setting up the scrabble board and stared at Jamie until she blinked. "What do you know about him, Delia? Donny told us a few things about his family, but not too many details. He said the Sheriff had a falling out with his father. Do you know much about that?"

"Well," she said, deciding to answer her question, "I'll tell you all I know about it. His momma died giving birth to him. He was the only child of the meanest man in Florida."

"Really?"

"Yes, really. His father was William Lee Bannerman Kocher, a prominent racist pig. I heard that he beat little Tommy from the day he was born. He was trying to beat the devil into him, I suppose."

"That's terrible!"

"Uh huh. Well, they say that something like one out of every four kids is abused at one time or another. But Tommy got it worse than most."

"What happened next?"

"When the law here in Oree County started checking into reports of abuse, the old man moved his family up to South Georgia. In Georgia, the local Sheriff heard about what was going on and decided to draw the line. He dug around until he got proof, but he had a problem. If he'd arrested old man Kocher, none of the local judges would have kept him in jail for a Georgia minute. The old man was rich, and he was in tight with the local political machine.

"Eventually, that Georgia Sheriff was able to get some proof, and an arrest was made by the Georgia Bureau of Investigation. The X-rays of little Tommy showed more than a dozen broken bones that had healed without treatment over the years. He was five years old when they took him from the old man.

"The old man's lawyers struck a deal with the Georgia Bureau of Investigations, and he gave up custody to avoid prosecution. Tommy was brought back to Pezner. He was raised by his mother's oldest sister, a widow named Alma Durrance. He legally took her last name. She died of a heart attack while Tommy was away at his second year of college.

"After Tommy was grown, the old man moved back to the area and tried to bring him into the family business. As you can imagine, Tommy wasn't too anxious to oblige him."

"What happened to that Sheriff in Georgia? The one who saved Tommy from his father?" The account of Tommy's youth was very painful to Jamie, but she had to hear the rest.

"He was killed about six months after Tommy's father was arrested," Delia said. "He was shot from behind as he worked on a tractor on the family farm. The GBI could never could pin it on the old man, but everybody knew he was behind it."

"It's no wonder Sheriff Durrance became a lawman." Jamie said thoughtfully

"Yeah, it makes sense, doesn't it? If it weren't for that Georgia Sheriff who was willing to put everything on the line for one little kid he didn't even know, Tommy might have been killed."

"That's enough to make <u>me</u> want to be a cop." Considering Jamie's words, Delia sized her young friend up soberly.

"I'll bet you'd make a good one."

Hardscrabble

Jamie and Delia began to play Scrabble. They were quietly immersed in the play when Delia's curiosity finally got the best of her.

"What about you, Jamie? Do you mind talking about your personal history?"

"Usually, I do mind," Jamie responded. "But for you, I don't mind." She rearranged her scrabble tiles and frowned. "Is granola a word, or a proper name?"

"Granola? That's a word." Jamie brightened and placed the tiles on table.

"There you go. Granola." She placed the letters carefully on the board, one by one.

"Okay, here are my questions," Delia began. "You're only 20, but you act like you're 40. And I mean that as a compliment, by the way." Jamie smiled at her friend.

"Okay, if you say so."

"You must have had quite a life. What was your childhood like?" Jamie looked at her for a moment, rolled her eyes heavenward, and sighed.

"Hmmm, let's see. I guess it was kind of like . . . dinner and movie, followed by ten years of torture on the rack." She smiled and turned back to her tiles.

"What?"

"Well," she continued, pausing to think, "I guess it was more like a cross between Leave It to Beaver and American Psycho. It was unusual, to say the least."

"Tell me about it." Jamie looked out the window, into the impenetrable night. Then, she began to talk.

"Well, you could say that I have a lot in common with the Sheriff. In my case, I wasn't rescued until I was 16 years old.

"My mother left home when I was two. Daddy held a grudge, and I was handy, so he took it out on me. Over the years, he paid me back for mama's exit on a daily basis. He cracked my skull, broke my fingers and toes, burned me with cigarettes, shocked me with jumper cables, whipped me with clothes hangers, starved me, stuffed dead things in my mouth, locked me in a dark closet for weeks at a time – and he only used the closet during summer vacation, of course. He was too smart to do anything obvious. But if some demon could dream it up, and if it didn't leave marks that could be seen when I was wearing clothes, dear old daddy would do it."

"No," Delia gasped.

"Yes. But, please, don't tell anybody. Now that Ellen's back in Tampa, you're the only person in Oree County who knows."

"Why didn't they stop him?"

"He was a cop. He was a very popular cop. Nobody believed that it was possible. Daddy convinced them that I was vindictive and crazy, and that I was hurting myself so I could blame him." In response to this revelation, Delia shook her head ruefully. *What a life,* she thought. *You never know what a person has been through.*

"By the time they arrested and charged him, I was a junior in high school. The social workers let me move in with Ellen and her mother, and I testified at his trial. He got two years on each of ten counts, to be served consecutively. 20 years, total, with a chance of parole after seven years." She studied her Scrabble tiles and looked at the board thoughtfully. "He was murdered in prison."

"I'm so sorry," Delia said, amazed at her story.

Jamie was such a beautiful person: so stable, so nice. How could she have emerged intact from such a life? How could she have survived with such a serene appearance and such a sunny disposition?

"That's not the half of it," Jamie continued, letting the words rush out. "Almost every night, he'd stumble into my room, drunk and angry and anxious to finish what he had started earlier in the evening. From as early as I could remember, he came in stinking of cheap whiskey and raped me." Delia gasped in dismay as Jamie continued. "I thought that everybody lived like that.

"When the anger rose up inside of me, I would blame myself. Of course, that didn't help anything. It made it worse. Way worse." She gazed at Delia placidly, as if these events had been only a minor blip on the radar of her life.

"If it weren't for my friend Ellen, I think I would have gone mad. Her mother did everything she could to blow the whistle, but none of my father's friends would believe it. He had a lot of friends.

"What finally got him was when I went to the rape clinic on my 16th birthday. The DNA evidence couldn't be argued against. And these couldn't be, either." Jamie lifted the bottom of her shirt to reveal the bottom of her ribs, and Delia gasped. Across her midriff were ugly blue trenches: three large, deep, unsightly scars. They were obviously the result of untreated, potentially deadly wounds.

"These were three of the counts against him," she said offhandedly, "I won't bother showing you the other six counts. The seventh was the rape on my 16th birthday." Jamie exhaled and returned her gaze to the tiles, looking up to smile brightly at her friend, who was staring at her in shock. "I was Sweet 16. I had been raped. But at least I hadn't been kissed." She blinked myopically, deep in thought.

"Well, enough of that," she added airily, leaving the subject behind. "Let's move on to something more cheerful."

"Tell me," Jamie asked her stunned friend, gazing at the Scrabble board. "Is 'emu' a real word, or was it invented by a Scrabble player?"

News from the Front

It was 11:30 in the evening when the preacher's squad car rolled up and parked beside Delia's battered truck on the broad concrete parking slab beside the farmhouse. The Sheriff climbed out of the car and paused, blinking up at the floodlights as he pushed his remote door lock. He walked heavily toward the farmhouse, his footsteps echoing loudly as his new shoes clacked on the moldy brick path. He was not dressed in his sheriff's uniform, but in civilian attire: navy pants, gray shirt, gray and navy tie, and comfortable black shoes. He was at the steps before he saw them sitting on the porch.

"Good evening, Sheriff," said Jamie.

"Whoa! I didn't see you there. You gave me a scare."

"That's good for your heart, Tommy," replied Delia. "I told you we'd wait up for you."

"What are y'all doin'?" he asked, pausing on the sidewalk to squint into the darkened screen porch.

"Jamie said that a family of deer has been visiting the front yard lately. They come right out into the floodlights. We thought we'd sit here for a while to see if they'd show up."

"Did they?"

"Not yet." He opened the porch door and joined them, sitting in a large oak rocker. "This is nice," he whispered as the frogs began to sing again and the crickets began to whir in the trees, their vibrations quavering an ethereal chant that rose and fell in perfect synchrony. Combined into a unified wave of noise, the crickets sounded more like an otherworldly life force than a full-voiced chorus of insects.

"Why are you so dressed up, Sheriff?" Delia whispered as a breeze began to stir.

"We had a potluck supper at church," he replied quietly. "We're havin' a revival. I got called away on business just down the road. About 20 miles, to be exact. That's why I'm late. After I checked that out, I came straight here."

"Look, I told you!" Jamie hissed softly. "There they are." At the edge of the wide circle of light, where the clearing ended and the forest began, a doe stepped delicately out of the woods, her nostrils flaring. The house was downwind from the doe. Detecting no scent of imminent danger, she lightly walked a few feet from the woods, lowered her head, and began to graze on the lush native foliage that grew from the pastureland serving as Jamie's front lawn. The lawn was a rich and varied dining table to the hungry deer, a well-maintained wilderness salad bar: aerated and regularly fertilized by herds of contented cattle.

Behind the doe, a buck stepped out, his head held high as he looked to the right and left and warily tested the wind. The breeze began to increase, tossing the tops of the trees as the buck followed the doe's example. The Sheriff leaned toward the two women.

"I have to tell you something," he whispered.

"What?" Delia replied, transfixed by the sight of the two deer.

"A plane went down north of here tonight," he said, "and there may have been foul play. Two fishermen showed up at the crash site. They said they saw it blow up in midair." Delia's head whipped around, and she gaped at the Sheriff.

"Another murder?" she whispered heatedly, "I can't believe it!" Murders were not unheard of in their quiet county, but they were not common occurrences. And the local murders were invariably of a predictable, pedestrian kind: barroom stabbings, shootings after arguments, senseless domestic violence. There was no precedent for the past six months, during which the corpses of hapless murder victims had been found in trees, scattered in multiple graves, and now, perhaps, incinerated in a burning airplane.

"Jamie," the Sheriff whispered hoarsely, straining to be heard above the sound of swirling leaves as the wind shook the tops of the trees, "I don't like the way things have been going. We had a murder last weekend, and now this. I don't have a shred of evidence to connect them, but my instinct tells me they may be related . . . that is, they may related to the folks who weren't happy with your testimony, to put it plainly. I don't want to scare you, but I can't ignore the possibility. Now that your testimony is over, I think it's time for you to consider a change of scenery." Jamie looked at him like a wild animal caught in a trap and prepared to fight for its life.

"But I've started to really like it here."

"I know, and we love having you here. We really do, Jamie. You're a great kid, a wonderful person. But the people you've gotten the best of . . . I just don't like what they're capable of."

"I know," she said, "but let's talk about it tomorrow." In response, the Sheriff leaned back in the chair. They settled into silence as the wind died down. From the trees, a larger buck emerged, followed by two does and two delicate, tottering fawns.

For tonight, Jamie planned to savor this beautiful wilderness. Tomorrow, she would deal with the Sheriff's suggestion.

"Look, at the little ones following the doe," Jamie whispered to Delia. "They must be twins."

Upping the Ante

Streetcar's instincts were troubling him. He fretted as he watched his friends talking on the porch. Seeing the deer in the clearing, upwind of his perch in the tree, he relaxed somewhat, knowing that the sight or scent of an intruder would scare the deer away. He watched patiently for a few minutes, mulling the recent events over in his mind until the front door opened and his friends went inside.

Streetcar was attempting to be rational. But the more he thought about the airplane, the more upset he became.

It was good that the Sheriff had shown up, for he was growing more certain by the minute that Jamie's location had been discovered. Unsure of what to do and unwilling to give his position away, he decided to risk a call on his cellular phone, hoping that the wind in the trees would cover the sound.

When the phone rang inside of the house, Jamie looked at Delia in surprise. Both women glanced quizzically at the Sheriff.

"Don't look at me," he said with a shrug, "I don't know who it is. The only people who have this number are Delia, myself, Clay and Marcia."

"Well, then, you'd better pick it up," Delia said, nodding at the Sheriff. "Clay might have something to say to you about that plane." He frowned and walked over to the kitchen counter, abruptly taking the phone from its cradle on the wall. It was a bright yellow antique, a relic from the fifties. It had been the model of sleek plastic modernity in those halcyon days. Made to last, the telephone had survived as a reminder of the calls of yore.

Delia smiled as the Sheriff picked it up. Without intending to, she waxed sentimental for a moment, reflecting on the many years she had spent working beside this intense but lovable man. He had grown on her, not unlike a gruff older brother. His rough exterior, which he wore like a shield, could not hide the way he cared about his friends and fellow officers.

But now, as she watched, the Sheriff's tough exterior began to crack. The intense stare faded and the dark tan drained from his face, replaced by a sickly shade of white as he listened to the voice on the phone.

"You think so?" he said into the receiver. "Maybe you're right. About 8:00 o'clock this evening, a plane blew up about 20 miles north of here. Where are you?" he added brusquely, "What made you suspicious?" He listened for a moment. "How can we contact you? No, wait!" He stood still, listening intensely. Then, he hung up the phone.

The Sheriff glanced toward Delia and Jamie as if he were processing new information with all the power he could muster, his eyes glazed over and his mind a thousand miles away. His eyes focused suddenly and he blinked, his gaze flashing from Delia, to Jamie, and back to Delia. He addressed Jamie, his voice unnaturally calm.

"That was your friend, Salvatore Benuto.

"Streetcar!" she cried, smiling in spite of herself. "Are you sure?"

"Tommy recognizes voices like we recognize faces." Delia replied.

"I'm sure, all right. Delia, please lock the windows and doors and shut all the blinds. Jamie, help her, please. I don't want to frighten you. Let's just do this is just to be safe." Delia had already begun, but Jamie stared at him, hesitating. "Jamie," he asked calmly, "do you understand?"

"Yes," she nodded, and left the room to shut the blinds in the rear bedroom. The Sheriff picked up the phone and rattled the metal hook, then stopped. The line was dead. He quickly shut the kitchen blinds as Delia and Jamie returned, staring at him curiously.

"Okay, what's this about?" Delia asked.

"Do you have your cell phone?"

"It's in the truck. What's this about?"

"Streetcar said he was calling from somewhere nearby. He said that a small plane passed overhead just after you arrived here tonight. He thinks it may have been tracking your truck. He said this happened just after dark, which makes it about 15 minutes before a plane blew up 20 miles north of here."

"The same plane?" Jamie breathed.

"Maybe. The bottom line is, our enemies may know where we are. But that's not all. The phone just went dead."

"Great," Delia observed.

"I've got to go out to my car to use the radio." He stared at them intently. "I don't want to sound scary, but I don't like this. What do you think, Delia?" She nodded.

"I'm with you, Tommy. Let's play it safe." She turned to Jamie. "We're going to behave as if there are bad guys outside, just to be cautious. Do you understand?"

"Of course," she said. "I'll go get the shotgun." She swept from the room as the Sheriff and Major smiled at one another in spite of themselves.

They did not have to worry about Jamie collapsing in the clutch. As she was once again demonstrating, Jamie was not the fainting kind.

"I left my weapon in the truck, Tommy."

"I left mine in the car, so I guess I'll have to write us both a reprimand."

Jamie came back into the room with the 12 gauge semi-automatic shotgun in one hand and a large box of 00 buck shot and rifled slugs in the other. She handed it to Delia, who checked the safety, opened the chamber, checked the barrel, and rapidly unscrewed a cap at the end of the stock. Turning the gun upside down, she slid out the spacer that limited the gun's capacity, screwed the cap back on and loaded 10 shells in rapid succession.

"There," she said emphatically, "the State of Florida may not approve of what I did, but we just doubled our firing capacity."

"I think we can claim a legal exception," Tommy said, smiling weakly. "That was fast work," he added with a nod of respect, as if he were judging a competition at the Sheriff's Academy. He raised his head and riveted his gaze on them, glancing from one to another.

"Listen," he began, "this is the plan." As he paused and they awaited his word, the background noises seemed to be amplified.

They could hear a rich mix of familiar sounds that seemed strangely ominous, given the circumstances: the hum of the refrigerator and the sounds of outdoors: frogs singing in the canal, crickets whirring, and a rogue wind bitterly shaking the trees.

"We're going to turn out the floodlights," he said. "And as soon as we do I'm going to go to my car and call for backup. When they arrive, we'll secure the area and the gate to the main road and we'll go out together. Jamie will be hidden in one of the cars. We'll split up on the main highway, and her escort will take her to the station. But until our backup arrives, we're staying here in this house."

"That's the plan?" Delia asked.

"That's the plan, for now," he replied, exhaling sharply. He spun around and walked toward the front door, turning and beckoning to Delia. "I'm going to turn off the floodlights. Could you please stand here and wait for me until I come back?"

"Sure, Tommy." She jacked a round into the chamber. "Is there anything special you want me to do?"

"Yeah, sure," he replied with a grim smile. "If I don't come back in short order, turn the floodlights back on."

He paused and looked at her, at a loss to continue. He felt an ominous, oppressing presence. Into his mind came the clear impression that this was the last time he would ever talk to Delia. *Dear Jesus, keep us from evil,* he prayed.

"Look," he said, and paused. In the doorway, the dim light illuminated their faces as they shared a glance of shared respect and mutual disbelief at the strangeness of their circumstance. *My instincts have to be wrong,* he told himself. But judging from Delia's expression, it was clear that she shared the Sheriff's sense of rapidly approaching doom.

Extreme Sports

S treetcar might have seemed vulnerable, hidden as he was in the top of the tree. But the foliage was thick, and the Spanish moss around him was thicker. Long ago, this particular position had been strategically scouted and equipped against tonight's danger. As one of several tall, isolated oaks inhabiting the sparse woods on the northwest side of the clearing, the tree provided a commanding outpost with a panoramic view of the house and yard, the road, the pasture, and the canal. The tree also offered a commanding view of the dummy, Fred.

Fred sat stoically in his chair against the house, motionless in spite of the gusts of wind, showing no signs of exhaustion. Fred was a wild card of sorts. In the event of an assault, it was possible that Fred would serve as the first point of attack, revealing the positions of combatants as they tried to take out the dummy.

After his phone call to the farmhouse, Streetcar hung up, scanning the area desperately to see if he had been detected. Flipping down his night vision goggles, he could see the moss in the magnified starlight, tossing wildly in the wind. He watched as a possum ambled slowly down the middle of the driveway under the trees, oblivious to his presence. He had to avoid gazing at the floodlights, but he was able to see the deer at the edge of the woods with singular clarity.

The goggles were effective, but not omniscient. They could not see through the trees or the house. There was no position in the area that would have allowed him to guard every approach. He could not see the south and east sides of the farmhouse, and the southeast corner of the yard, where the eastern border of the woods met the bank of the canal, was totally obscured from sight. Attempting to maximize the chance of success, he had staked his gambit on an approach from the north or the west or from the canal directly behind the house, where the dock extended into the coffee-colored water.

Now, as he watched from his treetop, the deer in the clearing raised their heads and suddenly scattered. Then, as if the event were timed, the floodlights were turned off.

The Unbearable Brightness of Courage

Jamie approached the doorway carefully, walking with short, mincing steps. She was suddenly terrified: not for herself, but for her companions. Her clear blue eyes were opened wide; her nostrils flared as her gaze darted from Delia to Tommy and back, again and again, like the tail of an anxious cat.

The clock in the hallway chimed loudly, almost painfully. To Jamie the moment was surrealistic, the timing somehow obscene. She had expected good things to come their way, but instead of the good, danger was surprising them. She felt haunted by hopelessness, hunted by relentless evil.

Instinctively, Jamie understood that she and her friends were poised at the brink of tragedy. Their adversaries were armed with money, pride, and position. Arrayed against their adversaries' willingness to break any rule of common decency, her friends upheld the rule of civil authority. In this struggle, they were supported by their faith, hope, and courage.

Her universe seemed to be playing the poet, hinting of deeper dangers that swirled just beneath the surface. Jamie's mind wandered, and she picked up a disposable cigarette lighter that lay beside a candle on a narrow table in the entranceway. She flicked it on, off, and on again as the Sheriff prepared to open the door.

"Look," Delia said, "this is probably a just false alarm." Jamie did not look up.

"Most likely, that's the case," Tommy said. "We're just being safe."

"I understand," Jamie whispered, absent-mindedly putting the lighter into her pocket.

"No problem," Tommy said, winking at her and smiling, "we do this stuff all the time." She glanced at him sideways as he turned off the floodlights and quickly stepped onto the porch, slamming the door behind him.

As STREETCAR CONSIDERED the significance of the deer's sudden flight, the floodlights were extinguished and a dark figure stepped out of the house. It was Tommy Durrance. *Don't!* Streetcar whispered under his breath. *The deer just scattered; there's a predator out there!* Realizing the risk faced by the Sheriff, he committed to a risky gambit.

Leaving his rifle behind, he snatched the nylon rope tied to the branch above him and threw it to the ground, gripping it tightly as the rope unraveled below him.

This was his emergency exit.

He had no time for gloves. He stuffed the night vision goggles into his pocket and jumped, sliding down swiftly, burning his hands. On the other side of the clearing, Tommy Durrance trotted down the brick walkway to his car, pushing the button to remotely unlock the door.

Streetcar landed on his feet with a bone-jarring thump. He gained his balance, snatched the sawed-off shotgun from the sling behind his back, and ran toward the house at top speed, hugging the edge of the trees, then bearing left to race across the darkened clearing. He ran smoothly, devouring the distance with long, fluid strides: back bent over, body low to the ground, shotgun in hand. He was far behind the Sheriff, trying desperately to catch up.

As Tommy Durrance jogged past the corner of the house, he felt a hostile presence in the deepest part of the shadows. Glancing to his right, he saw a figure standing at the back corner of the farmhouse.

With no weapon in hand, his options were limited. He accelerated, hoping to dive behind his patrol car. But it was a case of too little, too late.

Before he heard the shots, the bullets ripped into his body.

The slugs blew through his torso like a jagged spray of liquid fire, ripping into him like sparks from the tip of a white-hot blowtorch. The fiery pain melted his hip in a shockingly intense caldron of pain that arced across his consciousness. The pain was a brutal revelation, a live wire spitting evil fire deep into his soul as it scorched a trail of pure, uncut agony.

He was aflame.

He was burning up.

He was consumed into cinders, melting into the earth.

In the throes of such agony, Tommy scarcely felt his own collapse. He barely sensed his fall, or the shock of the distant blow as his head slammed against concrete and he tumbled to a stop, sprawled on the slab like a marionette with cut strings.

Hot sparks cascaded across his field of vision, wilting downward as they mingled with the pain. The colors were vivid: almost as vivid as the agony itself. He watched the colors in horror as they swirled before his eyes in a sickly, sinking parade of lights.

The shooter did not hesitate. He stepped forward to finish the job, the mouth of his Uzi softly exhaling a smoky stream of burnt gunpowder. The acrid scent was somehow comforting to the mobster. It was familiar and final: the scent of a job well done. He jumped over the top of the fallen lawman and fired a burst through the window of his squad car, shooting directly into the two-way radio.

The Sheriff scarcely heard the shots.

Stunned and dismayed, in the throes of unspeakable agony, Tommy Durrance tried to crawl back toward the house, contorting his body into an impossible position, his torso facing the house and his legs jutting awkwardly out to the side at a 45-degree angle. Even in the dim starlight, it was easy to see that his back was broken.

As the Sheriff strained to get away, the shooter stepped in front of him to administer the coup de grace. Tommy was sprawled on his stomach, trying to push himself to his feet, attempting to force motion from hopeless legs. He looked up and blinked.

The shooter was a complete stranger. Tommy stared up at him in disbelief, scarcely comprehending that this unknown man had completely destroyed him.

This can't be happening, he said to himself.

But it was.

The stranger who loomed above him was a garish caricature of a gangster. He looked a bad actor impersonating a hood, but he was the real thing. He was Ignatius "Iggy" Tagliotta, a loyal member of Joe Boy's crew.

"Good night, Sheriff," he said, leveling the gun. But before he could squeeze off a round, the floodlights blazed into life above the shooter and a movement caught his eye.

Streetcar rounded the corner at something less than top speed, having slowed at the last moment to gain complete control of his body. Bent low with the short-barreled shotgun held loose in his hands, he took in the entire scene at a glance.

Before Iggy's gun could swing up, Streetcar squeezed off a deafening blast that hit him squarely in the chest. The percussive impact of the buckshot blew through the pudgy shooter like an evil wind, exploding his heart as it launched him upward and backward onto the hood of the squad car.

Streetcar hit the ground and rolled up to the Sheriff as Iggy slid off the slippery hood and landed on the hard concrete. Iggy slammed down onto his side, staring at nothing with eyes as dead white as those of a china doll.

As his life poured out into a slippery pool beneath him, the gangster's mouth worked weakly. But try as he may, no words would come. Instead, his thick, meaty tongue slipped from his mouth sideways. Like a purple eel escaping the net, it limply signaled the gunman's coming death as he slipped from this world into the next with the glint of life slowly draining from hopeless, deadened eyes.

Desperate Measures

When she heard the shots, Delia ran to the rear bedroom with her shotgun in hand. By the time she was snatching aside the curtains, Jamie had turned on the floodlights and Streetcar was rounding the corner of the house.

As Delia raised her gun to shoot through the window, she saw the gangster blown backwards onto the squad car by a blast from Streetcar's shotgun. Streetcar hit the ground and rolled close to car beside the Sheriff. And then, as the gangster rolled off the hood onto the concrete, Streetcar unleashed a second shotgun blast that blew out the floodlights, plunging the scene into darkness.

But in the final moment, before the floodlights were doused, Delia had realized the extent of Tommy's injuries. The Sheriff had looked up into her window, and their eyes had met. Through his pain, with his body twisted into an impossible position, struggling to rise in spite of his broken back, he mouthed a single word.

"RUN!"

Delia had worked with the Sheriff for years. She trusted his judgment implicitly, and her resolve crystallized as she fought back a rush of emotions. As the lights were shut out, the image of the fallen Sheriff was seared into her mind like the halo one sees after glancing at the sun.

"Jamie," she shouted into the next room, turning away from the window, "turn off all the lights and meet me at the back door. We're getting out of here."

UP AGAINST THE SQUAD CAR, lying beside the fallen Sheriff, Streetcar assessed the situation. He strained .to hear something, anything that would reveal the presence of his adversaries. He rolled onto his knees in a single, swift motion and began to scan the tree line, peeking above the hood of the car with his night vision equipment. He saw nothing.

"Are you dead, Sheriff?" he asked gruffly.

"Not quite," Tommy groaned. "But my legs can't move."

"It looks like your back is broken," he replied bluntly. Streetcar's own voice sounded strange to him, as if his vocal chords had cracked and rusted from disuse. It had been months since he had spoken to a human being.

He reached out his hand and groped beside the Sheriff, feeling for a reservoir of blood that would signal the lawman's doom. But instead of the deep pond that he dreaded, there was scarcely a puddle.

"You might live if you don't move, Sheriff."

"It burns. Oh, man, I'm burning up." The pain was beginning to peak, and Tommy gasped as tears coursed down his eyes and the agony rolled over him in heavy, sickening waves. His universe was melting, turning orange and pink as his head swirled and blood drained slowly from his body. "Jesus, Messiah, have mercy on me," he whispered softly.

"What's that?"

"I'm praying," Tommy gasped as the pain returned. His eyes rolled back into his head, and he whispered again, louder, "Jesus, Messiah, have mercy on me!"

"Oh," Streetcar said, surprised, not knowing what to say. *Praying? Well, it's a good time to pray.*

To Streetcar, this was an awkward moment, to say the least. *He's dying. What can I say?*

Streetcar had never been a religious man. He had never owned a Bible, or any book from any religion. But he believed in God, and it seemed reasonable to him that God might be persuaded by the power of prayer. *After all,* he had once reasoned, *who's to say that God wouldn't have a heart?*

"I think I know where those punks are," Streetcar rasped, returning to the matter at hand. "You stay put. I'm gonna do my best to take 'em out."

Streetcar could not afford to wait here. He had left his rifle behind, but the shotgun in his hands was effective at short range. He would attack his adversaries up close and personal. Beginning from the corner of the clearing he would roll them up, working around the tree line. If he could make it to the trees where they met the canal, he would have a fighting chance. But if he had no chance, he was determined to die trying to kill these wretched men.

This time, when Streetcar ran across the clearing, the killers would be expecting him. If they had night vision equipment and knew how to shoot, his chances for success were minimal, to say the least. But if he stayed here, at a spot that could be approached effectively from several angles, he might as well shoot himself and get it over with.

Unless he got moving, he would not stand a chance.

JAMIE AND DELIA STOOD at the back door, ready to flee for their lives. The lights had been doused, and it was completely, eerily dark inside the farmhouse.

"Help us, Jesus," Jamie whispered.

"Amen," replied Delia softly. They paused for a moment without breathing, listening for any sound that might indicate the presence of an attacker near the back door.

It was palpably dark, thick and clammy with a darkness that you could feel. They could not see their hands in front of their faces. In the night sky above the farmhouse, a huge, low-flying cloud was passing, hiding the starlit heavens from sight.

Delia raised the shotgun and pointed the barrel at the ceiling. She clicked off the safety and took a deep breath.

At this moment, a barrage of shots erupted outside. *Was that Streetcar?* Delia wondered. *Is he still alive?* Within a minute, the fusillade faded away and an explosion shook the ground.

'What's that?" Jamie gasped.

"I don't know," Delia answered. "Just follow me."

"Where to?" Jamie asked, breathless.

"The canoe at the end of the dock." As they cracked the door and looked outside, the cloud passed by above them and starlight began to shine down upon the scene.

TWO MINUTES EARLIER, as Delia and Jamie had crept toward the back door, Streetcar had mentally mapped his next move.

He was preparing to run for the trees when he heard the Sheriff speaking. The lawman's voice was firm, and Streetcar had to hand it to him: this guy was keeping his cool in the face of almost certain destruction.

"Streetcar?"

"Yeah."

"Have you called 911?"

"No. I left my phone in the top of the tree."

"I think there's a phone in the truck," Tommy gasped. Streetcar, who had been scanning the tree line over the hood of the car, ducked and crawled back to the Sheriff.

"Where?"

"Under the seat," he replied through clenched teeth.

"Okay, I'll try for it. Here," Streetcar said, on his knees again. He wrenched an Uzi from Iggy's lifeless grip. "Cover me." As he handed the gun to the Sheriff, the lawman grinned in spite of his pain. It was ridiculous to think that he could cover anyone.

Streetcar clambered toward the pickup truck. Kneeling beside it, he snatched the door open and dove inside.

A fusillade erupted from the trees: the big guns were opening up. On the floorboard inside the truck, Streetcar dug the phone out from under the seat as bullets whacked through the truck body with heavy thumps and pings, shattering windows, showering him with glass like brittle confetti. The bullets whined overhead like a swarm of angry steel hornets, relentlessly seeking a victim.

He pushed the start button and the phone lit up weakly. The battery light came on as he dialed 911, and when he pressed the transmission button, the light dimmed and went out.

"Great." For an instant, he paused. *What is that smell?*

He smelled something strong enough to taste. It was a familiar scent.

Gasoline!

Rocketing backward out of the truck, Streetcar grabbed Tommy under the shoulders. Pulling with all his might, he dragged him away from the cars and around the corner of the house as bullets sliced through the air around them.

The truck blew up in a blinding fireball, frying the spot where Tommy had lain just a moment before, blistering the paint on the house and propelling huge chunks of steel in every direction. Burning pieces of pickup truck twisted lazily in the air as they soared upward into the dazzling night.

Looking to his right, along the back of the house, Streetcar saw the back door burst open and realized immediately what it meant. *It's Jamie and Delia. They're coming out.*

Leaving Tommy in a safe spot behind dense hedges, Streetcar wheeled and made his move, running away from Jamie and Delia, heading toward the trees as chunks of burning steel, plastic, and melting rubber rained like infernal hail all around him. Streetcar was a slippery moving target leading murderous eyes away from his friends.

In the glow of the burning vehicle, the thin, bearded veteran was illuminated like a sprinter under the stadium lights. He ran with the shotgun loose his hands, looking for someone – anyone - to unload on.

But he knew better than to expect a convenient target. His cause was hopeless, and he knew it. *Here I am, almost 50, still playin' the soldier.*

But he ran.

He staked his life on his legs against the speed of the bullets, the power of the screaming steel hornets. He raced like a cheetah, covering several feet with each stride as he panted after the safety of the woods.

He was desperate to draw attention to himself, and he succeeded beyond his wildest dreams.

Moving Targets

Delia and Jamie surged out of the house through the back door. They did not see Streetcar as he began to run, leading all eyes away from them in a heroic, suicidal dash. They did not see Tommy Durrance, who had been dragged behind a dense hedge and propped up against the side of the house. They did not notice the strange beauty of the firelight playing against the venerable trees with a red-golden glow that pulsated and flickered across swaying, moss-draped oaks.

Delia and Jamie were focused on their objective.

At the end of the dock, the canoe awaited.

The canoe was as narrow and lithe and swift as any craft that had ever plied these waters. It was not a factory-made aluminum canoe. It was a cypress dugout carved in the Indian style, hand-chiseled from old-growth cypress by a Seminole firm based on the Big Cypress reservation. It was as heavy as stone, narrow and deep and superbly designed: swift and maneuverable and low to the water. Tonight, this cypress canoe was their ticket out.

They raced with abandon toward the dock, launching their bodies high with each kick, their feet touching down for another launch that carried them closer to their goal. They reached the dock, ignoring the gunshots and shouts behind them as they thundered down the heavy boards. Reaching the end, they sat down and slipped into the canoe, steadying the craft against the dock while Jamie untied the rope and the little dugout rocked crazily in the dark, warm water.

STREETCAR HAD ALMOST REACHED THE TREES, running as fast as he could, when his legs began to give out. As he drew close to relative safety, his pace seemed to slow. *Run, run, run!* he told his legs, but they were beginning to fail him.

I'm getting too old for this.

A movement in front of him caught his eye. The trees loomed near, and at their border he clearly saw the image of a man. In the light of the burning truck, the heart-shaped, unblemished, cherubic olive face was unmistakable. It was Joseph Provencenti Jr., squinting down the barrel of a rifle, staring directly at him. A light flashed at the end of the gun, but he did not hear a thing.

Something bit him.

Something bit him hard.

Something smacked into the side of his head like a ten-ton train hitting him dead on and pounding the fight clean out of him. Like air escaping from a punctured balloon, his consciousness was blown into the thoughtless world of sleep and fitful dreams. But as his legs collapsed and he crashed into the rich earth - as his world turned red, then orange, then white - Streetcar remembered his mission.

God, help me! he prayed, knowing that he had failed. And then, exhaling softly, Salvatore Benuto lost consciousness.

AS THEY PICKED UP THEIR OARS, Jamie glanced back and saw a small flash of light near the trees as Joe Boy shot Streetcar. She recognized the shape of her friend as he collapsed, backlit in the glow of the burning truck.

There was nothing that she could do to help. To turn back would be to cheapen his sacrifice, and their survival was the best way to honor his heroism. But before they could push off from the dock, they were stopped by circumstances beyond their control.

A bright spotlight swept up the length of the dock. Seeing that the light was headed their way, Jamie and Delia pulled desperately against the dock's pilings and slid the canoe underneath just in time, barely escaping the sweep of the beam. The spotlight crossed the planking above them, shining through the thick weeds that lined the water on each side of the structure. Dense weeds, rising from the water, provided cover to hide their canoe . . . for the time being.

Delia had fished and hunted during her youth in west Hillsborough County, and she knew to look away from the spotlight lest her eyes appear as glowing red coals to the person behind the beam. She urgently hissed to her friend, "Don't look at it, Jamie! Look away!" But it was too late. Before Jamie could react to Delia's command, she had stared into the bright light.

"Hey!" a deep voice shouted, "I see two eyes under the dock."

"Is it a gator?" another voice replied.

"Maybe a gator, maybe a girl. There's something down there. Let's check it out." The two gangsters, both Ybor City boys, had spent more than one weekend fishing and hunting in west Hillsborough County. They were familiar with the wilderness, but not quite comfortable with it. In their hearts, they were thoroughly urbanized. The prospect of alligators unnerved them.

David "Slappy" Bustamente clambered noisily onto the dock. As he shined his light across the small wooden pier, illuminating the weeds and the dark brown water. His companion hung back, pausing at the edge of the woods.

Lenny Tuigliomo, a.k.a. Lenny Twigs, took one last look at Streetcar's body and smiled in grim satisfaction. The street bum was sprawled on his back like a broken doll, blood covering his bearded face. Lenny pushed at the limp body with his toe and smiled at Joe Boy.

"You did the job, huh, Joey?"

"Get down there with Slappy and check out that dock," Joey replied angrily, kicking Streetcar's body. "We gotta find that girl." As Lenny trotted toward the dock, Joe Boy ejected the gun's empty magazine and slammed in a new one.

"Lock and load," he said, smiling grimly. *This is gonna be fun.* As he lifted his gun, a voice spoke, startling him.

"Congratulations, Joseph." It was a soft voice, low and hungry. "That man caused us all a lot of trouble." In spite of himself, a chill ran down Joey's spine. It was his old high school chum, Mickey O'Malley.

"He saw me just before I shot him," Joey boasted. He turned around to look at Mick. "You should'a seen his eyes. He was, like, 'Oh, no, man, I'm dead!' Then I shot him, right in the head."

The Mick acted as if he had not heard Joey. His eyes swept the clearing.

"Nice," he said with a thin smile. "Just make sure he really is dead." He stepped away toward the farmhouse. "I've got business."

"They already looked in the house," Joey called. "The girl's not there."

"We'll get the girl," Mick called back, "I want to take care of the Sheriff."

Mickey O'Malley had to admit it; he liked working with Joey's crew. They were idiots, but at least they were homicidal idiots. It was nice to share the joy of a job well done with people who could appreciate the value of a good night's evil.

Surprisingly enough, their plan had been executed smoothly. The shock troops had absorbed the punishment, and Mickey was prepared to mop up.

This was the fun part.

FOOTSTEPS ECHOED ON THE DOCK as two heavy men began to walk cautiously down the planked length, shining the powerful spotlight through cracks in the floorboards. They could see the weeds and water below the dock until they reached the last few feet of dock. This part of the structure had been built with older wood that did not shrink after it was nailed down. There were no cracks through which they could peer.

"If the girl's under the dock, she's right here," Lenny whispered in Slappy's ear. "We've checked out the rest. Why don't you get down there and take a look?" Taken aback, Slappy stared at Lenny as if he were mad.

"What if it ain't the girl? What if we saw a gator? I don't want to stick my face down there and have it bit off!"

"Listen, stupid," Lenny hissed, "just do it! Or do you want the Mick to come down here so we can explain to <u>him</u> why we didn't look?" They both shuddered at this thought. Lenny kneeled and put down his Uzi, drawing a semi-automatic pistol from his belt.

"Okay," he whispered, lying on his stomach. "Shine the light for me."

BELOW THE DOCK, gently rocking in the water, Jamie and Delia held their breaths as the bright light was shined onto the water, casting a blazing halo on the weeds to the left of their canoe. But now, as they stared, they saw something else.

They saw something that shocked and horrified them.

Darkly silhouetted against a background of illuminated cattails and reeds, the S-curved shape of a huge Cottonmouth moccasin hung from a crossbeam that supported the dock. The snake was remarkably large and very much alive.

The venomous viper probed the air cautiously with its delicate forked tongue, tasting for scent. Almost half of its body projected out into the air, while the other half was wrapped tightly around the beam. It was slow moving and hypnotic: impossibly massive and unbelievably hostile: unsettled by their presence, and ready to strike.

The big snake hissed at the two women, then looked toward the light as the dock thumped loudly above them. Above their heads, Lenny was lying at the edge, preparing to take a look beneath the dock.

The angry reptile tasted the air as its powerful length of mottled brown and black swayed majestically against the painfully bright beams of the spotlight. It was thick and muscular and as big around as a weight lifter's arm. The body flexed, and the head slowly turned their way.

The flattened head rose up and down as the body pulsated reflexively. The snake's dull eyes stared at Delia and Jamie, then turned again to look at the light. The forked tongue flashed out, silhouetted against the luminance. They heard another heavy thump above them, and a pale hand holding a gun came into view.

Delia raised her shotgun as Jamie fought back a gasp.

IN THE CLEARING beside the woods, Joe Boy stood over Streetcar and savored the moment. This was his hour of victory, and he was preparing to finish it with a bang.

The truck still burned brightly beside the farmhouse. It cast a kaleidoscopic swirl of warm red light that intermittently illuminated the inanimate human shape sprawled at Joe Boy's feet. Joe Boy nudged the limp body with his foot, but saw no signs of life: no breathing, no movement, nothing.

"You weren't so tough in the end," he said, savoring the moment. "All show and no go. What'd'ya have to say for yourself?"

Joey needed this victory badly. He had taken a huge chance.

Tonight's escapade had not been authorized. The Don knew nothing about it.

Unapproved killing, unless it could be explained by circumstances beyond the killer's control, was a death-penalty offense in La Cosa Nostra. In spite of this, Joey was sure that his father would forgive him. He was his only legitimate heir, after all. And what's more, he had just murdered the bum who had bombed their headquarters.

Joey would be a hero.

"You ain't so tough," he said, spitting on the body and raising his gun.

At first, he did not hear the sound.

It was hidden among the background noises.

Obscured by the groan and pop of the burning truck, the low-pitched yowl could scarcely be detected.

But as the sound grew louder, he slowly became aware of it.

It was a chilling, wretched sound: a wild, desperate, feline wail of anger and grief and outrage.

493

Joey's heart stopped as he recognized what it was.

It was a cat.

It was very big cat, an angry cat. It was howling madly, and it was coming his way.

A lightning bolt of terror washed over Joey from his head to his feet, weakening his knees and causing his head to spin. The wail grew louder, and he identified its direction. It was right behind him, and it was coming fast.

Joey whirled around with his Uzi in hand. Then, he saw it.

His ultimate horror was closing the distance between them with blinding speed. A massive cat streaked towards him, fast and deadly and mad with rage.

It was the big Maine Coon.

The cat ran hard and heavy and low to the earth, like a cannonball skipping across the field of battle, and as he ran, he uttered a desperate yowl from the depths of its being. The sound was chilling. It was the abandoned, hopeless shriek of a creature that has lost all that it has or could ever hope for.

To Joe Boy, with his phobic dread of all felines great and small, this was the nightmare of nightmares. He swung up his Uzi and wildly squeezed off a burst, kicking up a puff of dust as the cat hurtled headlong toward him, a gray blur sweeping across the face of the earth. In another instant, the Maine Coon was within leaping distance of his prey.

As the cat launched, Joe Boy screamed with a sound that scarcely seemed human. It was the cry of a wraith: the shriek of a terror-stricken soul lost in a chamber of horrors.

The big cat slammed into Joe Boy's face and drove him backwards, bowling him off his feet. Joey hit the ground hard, landing on his back in a fresh pile of cow manure. The cat bit into his forehead and drove his front claws into Joe Boy's face, raking his throat and chest with powerful hind legs. The sharp claws ripped through Joey's fancy silk shirt as if it were tissue paper, shredding strips of muscle and sinew with every mighty gouge.

Joey screamed, mad with pain and terror. In one swift motion, unable to think and desperate for deliverance, he whipped the Uzi up and fired a burst at the cat, emptying the magazine.

Unfortunately, in his haste, he forgot that the cat was clamped to his face. Joe Boy blew the top of his own head off, scattering brains and blood and bits of bone liberally across the grassy terrain.

This was Joe Boy's coup de grace. This was the last grisly event from his own personal hell week.

As his life drained into the soil, Joseph Provencenti sank like a stone into the abyss, feeling the nameless terror as it expanded beyond his wildest nightmares. He did not see his shattered body as it convulsed on the damp pastureland, spouting a gusher of blood into the thirsty earth.

He could not see anything at all.

He could not see, but he could feel. He felt loneliness beyond measure, torment beyond imagination. This was his brave new world: so dark that the deepest cavern on earth would have seemed bright by comparison.

There is a hell! he thought as he squirmed in the fire, writhing in agony.

This should have been the punch line to one of his jokes.

But this time, no one was laughing.

UNDERNEATH THE DOCK, silence surrounded Jamie and Delia as they watched events unfold before them. The snake writhed on his perch, backlit by the bright spotlight as one of the mobsters on top of the dock prepared to take a look at the action below.

The hand with the gun dropped lower, near the head of the big cottonmouth. Staring at the intruding hand suspiciously, the snake swayed slowly back and forth.

A man's beefy, florid face came into view. It was Slappy Bustamente, the man who had lain on the dock to take

495

a look beneath it. He blinked to accustom his eyes to the darkness.

He saw Delia and Jamie, but he did not see the snake.

"Hey," he cried.

"What do you see?" a voice answered.

"Nothin', Lenny, nothin' at all," he replied, staring into the mouth of Delia's shotgun. For the moment, there was a stalemate.

Slappy stared past the open mouth of the shotgun, looking into Delia's eyes. Her face streamed perspiration and her lip twitched once, twice. Then, something else caught his eye.

He glanced to the left of the barrel, and he saw the snake. It was weaving back and forth, mere inches from his face. Slappy paled instantly, as if an inner switch had been thrown to trigger the effect. He went visibly limp, paralyzed with terror.

"What do you see?" the voice called from the top of the dock. But he could give no answer.

Slappy was lost. He was mesmerized by the dull, cold glance of the serpent, bewitched by the flickering tongue and the slow, deliberate weave of its head. As terror took hold of him and shook him by the neck, heavy drops of urine began to seep through the dock. Jamie smelled the thick scent of fear amid the stink of rotting vegetation and the musty aroma of rich Florida muck.

Slappy's mouth moved, but no sound came out. The massive cottonmouth hissed loudly in his face, lit up by reflections from the powerful spotlight. The inside of the snake's mouth was pale and puffy. Two dark fangs curved downward like twin blood-blackened scimitars that dripped death and hot venom. The poison in the sacs formed a tiny bead at the tip of the deadly fangs.

Paper-thin stripes of light leaked between the boards, sliding across the mottled, scaly back of the snake as the big man watched, afraid to draw a breath. The snake's flat head moved slowly, and it hissed again, loudly.

"Hey, what's that sound down there?" the voice on the dock called. "Is that a snake?"

Slappy tried to answer, but was scarcely able to move. His mouth opened slackly in a vain attempt to reply.

Seeing the motion, the snake struck with all of its might.

The strike hit the bridge of Slappy Bustamente's nose, breaking it cleanly as the huge serpent drove his fangs deep into Slappy's face. The venomous scimitars plunged through the bone, sinking into the marrow of his cheekbones and hooking the back of his eye socket as Slappy jerked away and instinctively flopped backwards onto the dock.

With its fangs embedded in Slappy's bones, the snake could not disengage itself. As the man snatched his body up and away, the big Cottonmouth was whipped off the beam.

The snake sailed out of the women's sight. Above them, on the dock, pandemonium was unleashed.

Lenny Twigs watched in horror as his friend jerked back onto the dock with a long, massive, serpentine shape attached securely to his face. For a moment, Lenny could not imagine what it was. Then, he realized that it was a snake.

As Slappy fell onto his back, the heavy serpent slammed onto the floorboards above his head. Shrieking loudly, Slappy's flailing legs kicked Lenny in the shin. Lenny tripped and fell backwards onto the dock, frantically scooting away from his stricken friend.

Slappy sat up and shook his head wildly. The heavy snake whipped back and forth as he desperately tried to shake it loose. The tail hit Lenny's feet as he continued to try to scramble away. Mad with anguish, thrashing blindly on the dock, Slappy kicked his gun into the water and fell flat on his back again, convulsing spasmodically and pulling at the snake with blind motor instinct.

But the jig was up.

This was no ordinary cottonmouth.

This was a monster.

Slappy's cries of pain and terror continued, and his curses and blasphemies were unearthly in volume and intensity. The sound was beyond horror. It was the wail of the lost and the damned.

Hearing the crash and clamor above them, Delia seized a piling and pushed mightily, launching the canoe past the end of the dock, out onto the dark canal.

MINUTES EARLIER, as Slappy and Iggy had begun their fateful walk down the dock, Mickey O'Malley had been completing his search of the farmhouse. Satisfied that the Sheriff was not inside, he had slipped out through the front door to search the hedges around the perimeter of the house.

Cautiously, he glanced around the edge of the farmhouse, scanning the foliage. He slipped past the corner and began to methodically work the hedges. Mickey knew that the Sheriff was paralyzed; he had seen as much when the bum dragged him away from the burning truck. He knew that his prey would not be far away.

He was right. The Sheriff was nearby. In fact, the Sheriff was watching him.

Tommy Durrance caught a glimpse of Mickey O'Malley as the killer rounded the southwest corner of the house. The man was obviously a professional. He moved swiftly and silently, with no wasted motion: eyes open wide: head low, gun in firing position. He provided an adversary with no clear shot, darting past openings and scanning the terrain from secure positions.

Watching his approach, Tommy raised his gun and breathed a silent prayer. He would need all of the help he could get.

Mickey slipped behind a thick bush less than 15 feet away from the Sheriff. The lawman was behind and beneath a huge azalea bush, hidden in a deep depression dug many years ago by a rambunctious family dog. But he knew that his anonymity would not last for long.

Footsteps compressed the leaves. The Sheriff did not move, determined to hold his fire until the killer was close enough to touch. A stream of perspiration cascaded from his brow, streaming down his face, burning his eyes, making his nose itch.

As Mickey O'Malley prepared to empty the magazine into the dense azalea hedge, a loud scream drew his attention to the canal.

Mickey looked toward the dock and saw Slappy Bustamente writhing in the bright spotlight with something long and dark attached to his face. The serpentine object on Slappy's face lashed to the right and left as he tried to pull it off.

Lenny Twigs fell flat on his back trying to get away and dropped the powerful spotlight, which slowly rolled off the side of the dock. But as it rolled across the planking, just before it fell over the edge, the powerful beam swept across the canal and illuminated the cove beyond, where the black water flowed into a vast lake.

As the bright light swept across the top of the water, the Sheriff caught his breath. For an instant, Delia Rawlings and Janelle James could be seen in the bright light, paddling their canoe toward the open waters of the lake. Then, the light fell off the dock.

The beam dimmed immediately as it entered the water, revealing a curious tableau: clouds of mud, startled tadpoles, and backlit vegetation that swayed slowly in the ripples caused by the light's entry into the water. The sight was strangely beautiful, but no one was there to see it.

"Ssssss," the Mick hissed loudly in anger and disgust. He pulled the pin on a grenade and rolled it toward the greenery, ducking behind a concrete block wall as it exploded. Then, he dashed away from the house.

He did not run toward the fleeing canoe. He ran in the other direction, away from the lake, toward the point where the canal met the tree line at the southeast edge of the clearing.

Hunkered down safely in the hole behind the azaleas, the Sheriff was stunned and deafened by the blast of grenade. His ears seemed to be bleeding, and he could scarcely hear a sound, but that was the least of his worries. He saw the killer running away from the house and realized that he was losing his last chance to stop him.

Fighting a sudden rush of pain, the Sheriff swung his weapon out from beneath the azalea, leveling it at the fleeing man. With the killer in his sights, he squeezed the trigger.

Nothing happened.

The safety was on.

He felt the trigger catch and knew immediately what it meant. His finger expertly punched the safety off, and he sighted down the barrel again, but it was too late.

The runner had disappeared into the woods.

JAMIE AND DELIA PADDLED AWAY from the dock to the accompaniment of the shrieking, snake-bitten hoodlum. They heard the plop of his gun as it fell into the canal and the slow clack-clack of his heavy steel flashlight as it rolled across the dock. Finding their stroke, they began to pick up speed as the flashlight teetered and fell off the edge, dropping down into the water. But as it fell, the beam swept across them, revealing their position before the light sank in the canal.

Digging into the water, pulling against their paddles until their tendons popped, they heard a sudden, heavy splash as Slappy rolled off the dock and fell into the tepid water. As he went under, his ear-splitting shrieks were instantly replaced by an eerie, total silence.

As the gangster sank in the shallow water, the snake popped loose from his face. But it was too late for Slappy Bustamente.

At the first jolt of the snake's strike, his face had exploded in unimaginable pain. From that moment, he had known nothing but agony and horror: an unendurable burning that roared through the grid of his nervous system like a jigawatt jolt of unholy power. His spasmodic return to the surface of the dock and his wild thrashings in the spotlight were scarcely perceived in his own consciousness. All was a blur of instinctual horror: a mosaic of fractured awareness obscured by thunderous clouds of dark, sticky pain jammed deeply into the quick of his being. He did not even notice that he had plunged into the water until he felt the oozy warmth and tried to breathe, sucking in water instead of air.

Slappy tried to open his eyes, but they were swollen tightly shut.

He could not see the spotlight that illuminated the murky water beneath a colorful cloud of swirling muck. He breathed the water deeply as faint alarm bells went off in his mind: too little, too late, and to no avail.

He did not know it, but he had mere seconds left to live. The venom had been injected into the back of his sinus cavity. Not pausing to observe the niceties of civilized discourse, the deadly juice had been fed directly into the tiny arteries that flowed into his brain.

If you had been there, snorkeling in the warm water, you would have seen his contorted, swollen face, as big as a lopsided melon: eyes squeezed shut, his hair floating above his head as the spotlight mercilessly revealed the extent of the damage. Death, as always, was ugly beyond measure.

And Slappy was a dead man.

Dead Run

Mickey O'Malley raced past the bodies of Joey and Streetcar without a second glance, donning his night vision goggles on the fly. This was what he lived for: the thrill of the chase, the scent of blood, and the thought of a doomed woman soon to be under his total control.

With a single, catlike leap, he cleared the side of the high-octane bass boat and landed on the flat fishing platform. He pulled his knife and cut the mooring line as he turned the key, and the two hundred horsepower Yamaha engine fired up like a finely tuned Ferrari.

THE CLEARING WAS STILL. As the boat began to speed away, silence settled in for a few, brief moments.

The Maine Coon cat did not raise his head as Mickey O'Malley rushed by. Wounded by a shot from the Uzi, he lay squarely in the middle of what once had been Joe Boy's head. Around him glistened splinters of bone and flesh: blood-soaked grass and scattered chunks of the crimson oatmeal that had once been Joe Boy's brain.

As the boat departed, the big cat stood up, fell down, and stood again, his leg slowly leaking blood. When he tried to walk, the leg failed and he shook his foot, yowling angrily. Not giving up, he began to crawl toward Streetcar. At his side, the cat stopped and stared, nostrils flaring. He made angry, growling noises, as if to scold his fallen friend.

Streetcar lay as he had fallen. He was on his back with his arms cast wide, his mouth open, legs limp. His head was turned sideways. His bloody temple faced the heavens, covered with thick, sticky blood that had congealed into multiple solidified rivulets: crooked maroon trails that spread out in every direction like wiry fingers trying to grasp his wounded head. The tiny, dried streams were a crimson roadmap leading from nowhere to nowhere for the sake of nothing.

The big cat lay down with his back against Streetcar's body. He began to growl softly.

It was not a feline sound at all. It was a deep, dismaying, almost human sound of bereavement. It was an abject sound of grief beyond measure, of love beyond words: of love that was lost beyond hope, forever.

As MICKEY O'MALLEY RAN THROUGH THE TREES toward his high-octane bass boat, Tommy Durrance tried to pull himself out from under the big bush. *God help me, please, Jesus!* he prayed. And as he prayed, he believed that he would receive the help he was asking for.

As his adrenaline surged, his arms regained strength, and he pulled himself free from the shrubbery. Then, with surprising speed, he began to drag his body toward the canal.

He felt the warmth in the middle of his back and realized that he must be bleeding freely, pouring his own life out on the ground with his every ounce of effort. But for all that, he would not give up. He had taken an oath to enforce the law, and what was more, he had made a commitment to Almighty God to give his life away, if need be, to defend the innocent.

Like a wounded champion at the sound of the bell, he began to pick up his pace. Reaching forward from where he lay on his stomach, Tommy swung his arms up and slammed his hands into the ground, burying his fingers in the turf, digging in with all his might. Clutching the earth, he dragged himself slowly ahead until his nose reached his hands. Then, he repeated the process. Again and again, with his personal throttle at full bore, Tommy Durrance repeated these tortuous steps: slamming hands into the turf, burrowing fingers in, and dragging his body forward.

He heard the sound of the big outboard engine as it roared to life. He knew what that meant. Delia and Jamie's canoe could not possibly outpace such an engine, and it was likely that this professional killer had a rifle in the boat. Delia's shotgun was effective at short range, but the canoe was headed toward the open water, where there were no bushes or trees behind which they could hide. On the vast, deserted lake, a rifle could reach the two women long before Delia's shotgun could be brought into play.

As he made one last, desperate pull against the turf, Tommy Durrance reached the top of a small rise. Here he paused, listening as the outboard engine was slammed into forward gear. From his position, he had an open view of the canal.

He reached back and grabbed the Uzi from its sling. Rocking onto his left side, he jerked the gun up to his face, accidentally spraying moist dirt into his mouth. He flipped up the long-range sight and clicked the safety off.

Behind him, the heat from the burning truck reached its zenith, cooking the car that was parked beside it. At this moment, the flashpoint was reached within the squad car's gas tank.

The squad car exploded like a two-ton bomb, disintegrating with a deafening roar.

The flash of light was spectacular in its intensity. The entire clearing was illuminated: trees trailing lengthy beards of Spanish moss, dead bodies scattered like dung on the face of the fertile earth, the canal, dock, and the cypress trees on the other side of the water.

And there, before his eyes, was the killer's bass boat, picking up speed. The boat's two-thousand-dollar paint job glistened in the firelight, reflecting the light as if it were dusted with luminescent diamonds. The driver stood tall behind the wheel: lanky and relaxed with a million-dollar smile playing on his lips.

As the boat sped along the waters of the canal, lit by the light of the burning car, a tire exploded behind the Sheriff with a percussive boom that shook the earth and made his ears ring. As it detonated, Tommy Durrance sighted down the length of the short, trembling barrel, sweeping the gun slowly from left to right, synching up with the boat before it passed the dock. But as he began to squeeze off his shots, a large piece of burning rubber fell out of the sky and landed on the small of his back.

Surprised by the unexpected pain, the Sheriff's hand jerked spasmodically, and he emptied the entire magazine at the speeding boat. He screamed, reaching behind his back to sling aside the flaming piece of tire.

MICKEY'S BOAT WAS SPEEDING TOWARD THE OPEN LAKE when the squad car ignited and the tire loudly exploded, stoking the inferno beside the farmhouse. He was almost to the dock when he heard the whine of scorching hot steel hissing through the air around him. His spotlight was shattered, and steel slapped steel as the outboard motor took a bullet through the heart.

The big engine uttered a single, sickly cough and unceremoniously died.

The sudden cessation of movement rocked Mickey O'Malley forward into the steering wheel. In the sudden quiet, the backwash sloshed loudly against the fiberglass hull.

The killer dropped flat and picked up his rifle, peering down the sights. The fire continued to crack and pop, and another tire exploded as the killer's eyes hungrily scanned the clearing.

He saw motion, and he focused sharply on the area. He watched as an arm flung away a burning object.

It was more than he had hoped for.

On a swell of ground near the house, outlined against the spectral sunrise of sky-high flames, billowing smoke and melting vehicles, was the dark figure of a man sprawled out upon the ground. The man was struggling, attempting to hide himself behind a small swell of earth.

Mickey O'Malley smiled thinly and shook his head. In a single, fluid motion, he squeezed off a burst of shots.

IMMEDIATELY AFTER THE SHERIFF FIRED HIS GUN, he knew that he was dead. But he would not give up. He cast away the burning rubber and pushed himself backwards, desperately trying to hide in a shallow depression.

Help me, Jesus, he prayed. As he struggled to move out of sight, another tire exploded. And then, something curious happened.

An orange cloud moved over him. His consciousness faded. His entire universe swayed as if it were tumbling in the surf. His extensive loss of blood, which had thus far sickened but had not disabled him, now robbed him of his consciousness.

He sank into a deep and dreamless sleep.

He did not feel the bullets that hit him, shattering flesh and bone as his body spasmodically twitched upon the bloodstained ground. He did not hear the killer's distant laughter or his curses as he attempted to start the outboard engine. He could not see the man as he started his small auxiliary engine and pointed the boat toward the mouth of the canal.

Although he did not feel them, the bullets did their work. After 20 years of deprivation, hardship and regrets, Sheriff Durrance could finally rest. He was completely, and utterly, at peace.

Race for Refuge

Jamie and Delia fell into a powerful rhythm, digging their paddles into the water in unison, pulling through each stroke, pausing, then digging in again. The canoe hissed through the water as they passed the mouth of the small cove and skirted the outlying weeds, bearing right. But at this point, the sound of an outboard motor forced them to change their plans.

Along the shores of the wild, deserted lake, the nearest human habitation was a fish camp more than a mile away. Initially, this was where they were headed. But at the sound of the powerful outboard engine, they looked at each other in dismay.

"Let's go to the island!" Delia hissed. "What do you think?"

"Yes!" Jamie replied, and they dug into the water with their oars, turning toward the middle of the lake. Less than one-half of a mile from shore, the black shape of Wild Island loomed ahead of them. This was a desperate move, but they had no choice.

It would be obvious to their pursuer that they were headed for the bright lights of the fish camp. They could not outrun him, and could not fight through the weeds to reach the shoreline before the massive outboard could catch up. Before the killer realized where they had gone, they might have a chance to reach the overgrown island. There, in the thick woods or in the marsh among the tall reeds, their shotgun could be used to advantage. They would have a chance against the man who was hot on their trail.

They heard the explosion as the squad car went up in flames, heard the boom as the first tire exploded, the sound of distant shots as the outboard engine died, the second burst and the sound of the second engine. By now they were more

100 yards out, headed away from shore, and they could not afford to turn back.

Other sounds seemed to fade away, and they entered into a zone of unfettered focus. They heard their own labored breathing, the quiet slap of the oars, the hiss of the canoe as they sped out into the open lake, drawing nearer to their goal stroke by painful stroke, straining to reach the dark shape that loomed in the distance ahead of them.

Their arms and lungs burned, and their cause seemed hopeless. And yet, in spite of it, they dug in with all of their might.

IN THE BASS BOAT, the throttle was floored. The boat slowly gained speed as it began to leave the cove, swinging right toward the lights of the fish camp. Mickey O'Malley slammed the T-shaped throttle with his fist, trying to eke out extra speed as he scanned the horizon, searching for his quarry.

It was dark out here. It was smothering, stifling dark.

He could scarcely discern the shoreline and the tall beds of cattails and reeds. He would have to be close to see his victims, so he focused intently on the water ahead of him. His night vision equipment had been lost in the canal when he jumped into the boat, and he had to rely on his own perfect vision. But he was good, very good, at his profession. He would sniff out his prey like the professional he was.

He sensed that that they were near.

He reveled in their nearness, anticipating that special moment when he would confront them at last. He longed to hurt them, hungered to see the look in their eyes. *That's it; I want to see that look, the look of total terror . . . the look of fear and submission.* He reached down and fumbled through a compartment, coming up with a large flashlight. *This is better than nothing,* he reasoned, *I'll use it.* He flicked it on and shined it to his right, scanning the shoreline, looking for their canoe.

He searched in two places: ahead of his boat on the open water, and in the weeds that lined the shoreline to his right. He pounded the throttle again, searching the darkness for the prize that awaited him: the reward that he so eagerly anticipated.

AFTER TEN MINUTES, Mickey O'Malley idled up to the fish camp. The camp consisted of a drafty general store, a small marina, and a run-down cluster of windowless wooden cottages that loitered dolefully beside the lake, hunched over the water like mildewed cardboard boxes ready to tumble in at the first good puff of wind. At the center of the marina, a post light at the end of a long, sun-bleached dock revealed a cloud of insects and two weathered fishing benches.

A man was seated at the end of the dock in a well-cushioned folding chair. He was a fat man. Or perhaps it would be more polite to say that he was a rotund fisherman sporting a sleazy three-day stubble, dressed in worn overalls and a NASCAR baseball cap. Three cane poles, trailing wispy lines into the water, revealed the hopeful reason for his presence at this late hour on the end of this deserted pier.

"Good evenin'," Mickey O'Malley called with a neighborly smile. "How's the fishing?" The man sourly raised his eyebrows.

"Not too good." His eyes narrowed. "Hey, did you hear those big booms a few minutes ago? Were those M-80s, or were they firin' off dynamite? And how about those firecrackers, or gunshots, or whatever they were? What on earth were they celebratin' down there? Everybody around here knows that those people shoot off fireworks sometimes, but this is over the top."

As he spoke, the unlucky fisherman began to look more closely at the stranger with his fancy bass boat. He noticed the bullet holes in the engine, and his eyes widened. He floundered to his feet, gaping at the visitor.

"What are you using for bait?" Mickey asked genially.

"Uh, nothin', just worms."

"They're not bloody enough."

"What?" the man asked, beginning to back away. He felt bad, very bad, about this stranger with so many bullet holes in his nice, shiny bass boat. Staring transfixed at the ominous visitor, the fisherman blanched as Mickey smiled.

The big man made a split-second decision. He turned as quickly as he could, sending the chair flying as he began to run up the dock, futilely fleeing from the man in the boat.

Mickey drew his well-silenced handgun and pumped three quick shots into the broad T-shirted back of the pathetic, lumbering fisherman. The big man turned back toward the killer and opened his mouth, trying to speak.

He stood at the edge of the dock, staring in unbelief as hot blood began to pour out of his own mouth, cascading freely onto his shirt and overalls. The free-falling crimson river hit the surface of the water, and the fisherman coughed loudly, spraying blood in every direction beneath the bright streetlight. Then he doubled forward and collapsed like a marionette with cut strings, flopping straight down into the water with a tremendous splash. Bubbles came up, and a small wake rolled outward, expanding until it rocked Mickey O'Malley's boat.

"Now, that is bait," Mickey said with some satisfaction, "proper, bloody bait. Enough for the hungriest fish." He unscrewed the silencer and replaced it with a new one, thoughtfully staring into a great burst of bubbles that signaled the fisherman's final exhalation.

"Well, I guess my little girlfriends didn't come this way." He turned and looked out toward the lake, rubbing his chin. Turning the wheel, he pushed down the throttle.

"This is good," he mused as he tucked his gun into his waistband and gave it a friendly pat. "They must be headed for that island."

His reasoning was sound. The women's canoe was obviously swift, but not swift enough to have made it to this camp before him. They had not ditched the canoe on the shore, or he would have seen it, and he was certain that they had not gone south, where there were no houses for miles. Except for the tree-lined shore and a narrow strip of woods, the land south of the canal was open pasture, offering no good hiding place.

They had to be on the island. They must have gone straight out into the lake, gambling that he would not realize where they had gone.

He pounded the throttle with the ball of his fist, cursing as he smiled to himself. These were worthy opponents, indeed.

Tonight's wild adventure would be something to treasure for years to come.

This was beyond business. This was heady pleasure.

His unfair game had crossed the Rubicon. It had surpassed desirability and had entered the realm of succulence.

Wild Island

They drew closer to the island stroke by desperate stroke, but their goal was not yet attained when they heard the boat rev in the distance. The killer was leaving the fish camp, and after two minutes, they were sure that the engine noise was getting louder.

"He's coming," Delia panted. Jamie did not reply as they pulled, reached and pulled, reached and pulled: arms burning, lungs aching, fighting for breath as their muscles screamed for rest. The sound grew louder, and Jamie cast a glance over her shoulder. Behind them, a thin glimmer of light danced across the tops of the waves.

"Pull!" she whispered. "Pull!"

Behind them, they could hear the roar of the boat's little engine and the sharp slap of the hull against the waves. Their canoe cut through the tall waves like a knife, scarcely rocking as the women were dusted with fine, warm spray. The island's shoreline loomed larger now, dark and ominous before them.

As the canoe hit the island's outermost bank of waterweeds, they scarcely slowed down. They dug into the water with their paddles frantically, ignoring the risk of snakes and other unseen dangers, fearful that their speed would slow and that they would lose momentum in the thickening weeds. They heard the bass boat drawing closer. Blithe and carefree behind the wheel, the killer was singing.

"My Cherie amour," he crooned sweetly, "pretty little girl that I adore . . . . " The sound send chills up their backbones.

His voice was surprisingly lyrical, almost professional in its quality, and the music carried well across the quiet water. The words seemed to float past them, as if the man were humming in their ear. They dug in desperately, still headed toward the shoreline and gaining on their goal. Then a stream of light panned across them, swung back, and locked on their canoe.

"Bail out!" Delia cried, grabbing the shotgun and rolling to her right. Responding immediately, Jamie rolled in the same direction. They both took a deep breath as the canoe tumbled over, dumping them into the blood-warm waters of the lake.

Dead in the Water

In the rich, sealed womb of warm, mucky water, they both knew what to do.   At a depth of three feet deep, with visibility of zero, they began to run along the squishy bottom, headed toward shore.

Their feet slipped in the mud as they jammed them deep: taking long, ponderous strides, swinging their arms in wide breaststrokes with their lungs burning, eyes shut against the silt and the weeds.   A spray of bullets plopped harmlessly into the water beside them.   The steel bullets slapped the surface and dove to the bottom with a curious whining sound.

They burst out of the water simultaneously at a depth of 20 inches.   They surged toward shore at a dead run, feet rising high above the water, striving desperately for the dark shoreline just a few feet away.   Delia held the shotgun in one hand with the barrel streaming water.

As his outboard engine stalled in the dense weeds, Mickey O'Malley cast the empty Uzi aside and sighted down the barrel of his rifle.   With his left hand holding a long-barreled flashlight against the stock, he aimed expertly, drawing a bead on Delia's back.

"Goodbye," he said quietly.   A grim smile scrolled across his placid features as he began to take his shot.   But as he began to squeeze the trigger, something large and heavy slammed into the bottom of the lightweight fiberglass hull, knocking his aim awry and forcing the shot into the air.   By the time he recovered, they were gone.   His flashlight scoured the shoreline in vain.

Jamie and Delia had escaped.

IN THE LAST MOMENT before they reached the shore, the late-rising crescent moon emerged from behind the clouds.   It was gorgeous.

Showing the way for the two women, the moon lit the earth and the trees in a diaphanous wash of platinum luminance.   The women ran onto the muddy shore and continued into the blackness beneath the scattered trees. Under the trees, they slowed down to wend between through the marshy terrain.   As the trees got denser, they paused, panting loudly.   Beginning to see the beginnings of a path through the woods, Delia touched Jamie's shoulder.

"Come with me," she whispered, "and watch out for cypress knees."   She began to creep through the woods crouched low, with Jamie behind her, holding on to her shirt. Finding a cow trail, they followed it until they emerged from the stand of cypress trees into a broad marsh full of tall cattails, softly swaying in the faint moonlight.   The frogs were in full-throated glory, filling the air with a powerful, whirring blend of huffs and clacks and synchronized amphibian chants.

"This way," Delia hissed, "stay in the water."   They turned to the left and began to move more quickly, sloshing along, attempting to make time before the predator was within hearing range.   After 50 yards of progress, they squatted in the weeds and listened, panting heavily.

Suddenly, the frogs fell silent.   Delia gripped Jamie's hand.   A bullet hissed through the cattails, and Delia collapsed into the murky water with a loud splash.   There had been no loud gunshot, only the sinister cough of a well-designed silencer.

"I heard that splash," a man's voice called softly from the edge of the marsh, "either I hit a cow, or I hit a cow. Either way, it was a lucky shot, eh?"   After a pause, the voice spoke again.   "What, no tears?   No cries of pain?   You girls are tough.   I have to admit it.   You're all that I hoped for, and more."

"Jamie," Delia whispered, grimacing, "I'm hit in the leg."   She shoved the shotgun into Jamie's hands.   "Take this and run."

"But, wait . . . . "

"I'm dead if you don't lead him away from me," she whispered fiercely. "Get out of here! Save yourself! Go!" Jamie stared at her friend, then turned and began to run into the marsh, through the tall weeds. Her feet made loud splashing sounds in the knee-deep water. At the sound of another bullet hissing though the cattails she dropped and began to swim through the weeds in the warm, soupy water that was now at least two and one-half feet deep. As she swam, she saw the head of a small alligator on top of the water. She pushed it aside with the gun barrel and continued her quiet progress. Compared to the predator on her trail, the alligator scarcely rated a second glance.

Jesus, help me, she prayed fervently, *show me a way out.*

And, as she prayed, something surprising happened to Jamie. Her courage began to return.

Jamie had a plan.

Star Bright

At the edge of the marsh, the predator stood and watched, his eyes searching the tops of the reeds in the dim light. He saw the beauty of the night, but he was not moved by the magnificence of the wilderness. He was untouched by the wild mystery of creation.

He was totally focused on the matter at hand. His ears strained for sound as his eyes searched for movement, seeking the telltale clue that would reveal the whereabouts of his prey.

A profound quiet descended upon the marsh like a shroud. Beneath a muffling layer of mist, the predator watched and waited as the fog rolled across the tops of the weeds like an animate being, stretching soft tendrils above the quiet wetlands.

The remnants of the last clouds had departed, revealing planets and stars that teamed up with the crescent moon to dimly illuminate the fertile marsh. The sky's luminescence contrasted starkly with the dark horizon. Below the luminous sky, a black line of trees ringed the marsh. The trees jealously hemmed in the horizon, blotting out sight of the lake and the lowest stars.

Above them, however, the stars had free reign.

They swarmed in dense clusters. They gathered in clouds in the hearts of unnamed galaxies. In their delicacy and intensity, they beggared the crescent moon: innumerable, infinitesimal pinpricks of light swimming in the oceanic depths of the sky. They drifted in distance immeasurable, shedding brave light that spanned the universe with a pale, lustrous shimmer that rested lightly upon the cattails and the water.

The killer ignored the beauty of the night. He was torn by unholy desires, entranced by depraved pleasures that were soon to be his.

Should he slip away to his left, where he was almost certain to find the victim he had just shot: dead or, better yet, wounded? Or should he stalk the healthy one, wading out into the marsh where she had fled? *They way that she ran through the water, it must be the girl. So swift, so young,* he breathed, *so sweet, so ready for life. So ready for death!*

He reveled in the intensity of the moment, in the tension as he paused between two alternatives. *The knife, or the gun?* he asked himself, smiling inwardly. *The steak, or the lobster? The wounded cow, or the iron maiden?*

He heard a loud slosh in the middle of the marsh, and made up his mind. *This is too good to pass up. She's young, probably armed . . . and deliciously dangerous!* The very thought caused an electric cluster of butterflies to flutter in the middle of his stomach.

He paused at the edge of the marsh, not wanting this moment to end. Soon, he would make his move. He smiled, trying to imagine the moment of capture. It was always different, and this time promised to be the best. *I'll wait here for a while,* he thought happily, *I'll be on her trail soon enough.* Soon enough, he told himself, he would begin to stalk her, easing into the water as he headed for the center of the marsh.

THE MUCK IN SOUTH-CENTRAL FLORIDA has a peculiarly rotten, sour smell. The dewy scent of marsh water and black muck was thick in Jamie's nostrils as she swam through the warm water, quietly sliding between thick clumps of tall weeds or pushing them aside to burrow through.

The animals in this remote marsh, almost a mile away from the site of tonight's assault, had been little troubled by the sound of distant gunshots. Accustomed to occasional salvos of fireworks from the farmhouse, they had scarcely looked up, quickly returning to sleep or to their nocturnal activities.

As Jamie continued to swim quietly through the marsh, a massive snapping turtle, offended by her progress, paddled away without a ripple. The frogs began to croak again, their confidence returning bolstered by the eerie silence. First one started to croak, then another, until the entire marsh vibrated with the huffs and clacks of ten thousand love-crazed, vocally ambitious amphibians.

Jamie had painstakingly traversed almost three hundred yards when she rounded a thick cluster of swaying cattails and gasped. She looked up in astonishment, her eyes widening.

Looming above her, sound asleep on his feet, stood a massive Black Angus bull. He was a splendid specimen, displaying a somnolent vitality that attested to the virtues of life at the edge of civilization. His face loomed over her, and his hot breath blew on her face. The breath smelled clean, somehow, like summer hay. She could see him clearly in the moonlight. He was a great, healthy brute. His skin almost quivered with vitality.

This bull was a freight train: built for power, not for speed. Yet, in spite of his obvious strength, the bull's short horns did not appear to be deadly. To the contrary, his wide, delicate face was almost angelic: large lashes lightly overlaying wide, closed eyes: broad nostrils flaring daintily as his hot breath blew upon her.

The bull snored with a deep, subdued rumble as his breath rolled in and out of a chest as broad and hollow as a timpani. His head hung down low, leaning slightly to Jamie's left, suspended by bulging muscles that surrounded the neck like a twitching, pulsating wreath of untamed power.

Jamie caught her breath. And then, her mind made a connection.

Her eyes widened as she realized what had just been handed to her. She had not spent the last six months in this remote area without learning the ways of cattle. Cattle had browsed on her yard and communed all day in the pastures around her.

She was certain of one thing. This bull was probably not alone. Where there was one head of cattle, there were likely to be more.

Jamie backed up carefully in the water and began to swim. She moved away from the bull, heading directly toward the center of the marsh. As she softly slipped through the water, she passed more sleeping cattle. *Excellent,* she thought, regaining her courage.

She had found the edge that she had prayed for. Her plan gelled in her mind, and now she was ready to execute it.

Slipping past one last cow, Jamie circled back, approaching the herd from behind. The last cow was a small hybrid heifer, part Black Angus and part Hereford.

With a loud slosh, Jamie leaped from the water and slapped the little heifer on the rear end, shouting at the top of her lungs. The result, to say the least, was startling.

These cattle were anything but domesticated. They were as wild as weeds in the wind.

Left to fend for themselves on this deserted island, they had grown up fleet of foot and exceedingly shy, the better to avoid the occasional panther or jolly rancher with herding dogs and painful cattle prods.

When Jamie leaped from the water and slapped the little heifer on the rear end, she kicked reflexively and took off as if she had been shot out of a cannon. Behind her, running with all of her might in a frantic attempt to keep up, was Janelle James.

The faster Jamie ran, the faster the little cow ran away from her. They sloshed through two feet of water as if they were skipping through puddles.

As she gained on the little cow, she could hear the frantic lowing of other cattle and the wild cry of the angry bull. Her left arm burned from the stress of carrying the shotgun, but she ignored it. She was fully committed to her plan. She would not let go, and she would not slow down.

All the cattle were in motion now. The herd splashed through the marsh as if a sluice had opened in a bovine dam, pouring cattle through the gaps of the towering reeds. They ran wildly, intemperately, almost as fleet as a herd of deer, rocking the water and spraying thick chunks of muck and muddy water in every direction.

Jamie suspected that the cattle were right on target. As she had hoped, they appeared to be running directly toward the spot where Jamie and Delia had first entered the marsh.

ON THE BROAD RIDGE that ringed the island, Delia dragged herself painfully along the leaf-strewn ground, pushing dead limbs carefully out of her way as she crawled past cypress knees and fallen logs. She was headed back toward the boat, hoping that somehow, in some way, she could find a way to make a difference in tonight's ongoing conflict. But her path was tortuous, her progress hard-fought and slow.

Her leg was killing her. The agony was the worst that she had ever endured. She moved on her good side, dragging her damaged leg behind her, every movement accompanied by a high-powered jolt of stomach-churning pain.

She was 15 feet from the edge of the marsh when she heard the cattle. To her, it sounded as if a single, gigantic monster were sloshing out of the marsh. The sound was thunderous. When she heard the bawls of the cattle and the deep scream of the bull, she smiled in spite herself. *Jamie's stirring things up.* She was not surprised by that fact.

THE PREDATOR STUMBLED BACKWARDS out of the marshy water, startled by the wild cries. A creature of the cities, he had no idea that cattle could make such loud, haunted sounds. He could not imagine what kind of creatures he was facing, and he panicked at the tumultuous onrush of large bodies crashing through the marsh, headed in his direction.

The situation was obviously out of his control.

He raised his Uzi as the sound reached a fever pitch. The juggernaut was about to roll over the top of him, sloshing ɔawling and shrieking and stomping. Then a cow burst ɔt of the cattails to his left and ran into the trees behind him. *A cow?*

He turned as a huge bull crashed out of the cattails less than 30 feet away from him, heading in his direction. Firing from the hip, he emptied the gun into the dark shape that hurtled at him like a runaway freight train.

The big bull collapsed into the water and skidded up to the ridge, pushing a wave before him that swelled over the top of Mickey O'Malley's shoes. He bellowed and tossed his head, struggling to rise, so close that the killer could have kicked him. But Mickey was all business as he slammed in another magazine and fired a burst into the bull's skull. *Survive that!*

In the end, the bull died peacefully.

The great barrel lungs rumbled softly as the Angus bull exuded his final breath, and the angelic eyes closed as if he were falling asleep. The lord of the marsh was dead.

Transfixed by the gory magnificence of the fallen king of the island, Mickey O'Malley stared at the massive, unmoving form. Then, he remembered why he was here. *The girl!* His head snapped up and he scanned the shore to the left, then right, then back to the left again.

But the girl, like the panicked herd of cattle, had passed by him and was gone.

Rite of Survivorship

She crept through the darkened trees, following the muddy cattle path. Her athletic shoes squished with each surreptitious step as she picked her way through the dark undergrowth and emerged on the shores of the lake.

Jamie did not hesitate. She waded out from shore and dropped down into the water, holding the shotgun in the air as she slid through the weeds like a turtle crossing a pond, her head and gun barely above the water line, moving among the lily pads with her body hidden beneath the surface of the thick water. She headed for her target on a trajectory that was as straight as any arrow, swerving neither to the right nor the left.

On shore, creeping through the trees, the predator had guessed correctly. He carefully crept down the cattle path, quietly following her trail.

WHEN HE REACHED THE LAKE, he paused and looked carefully in every direction.

A faint breeze teased at his hair as he looked out across the expanse of water, scanning for movement in the weeds near the shore, letting his eyes roam over the water beyond the wide shoals of weeds. The surface of the lake gleamed with shimmering light, reflecting the moon, the stars, and the ghostly light of the planets. *It must be 3:00 A.M. Maybe later.*

For a moment, he paused as he appreciated a simple truth. *It is beautiful out here.* This, for him, was completely out of character. But even the most predictable souls can experience unimagined surprises.

He was finally affected by the beauty of the night.

Nature had finally gotten to him.

He had never felt his throat draw tight at the sight of beauty, had never marveled at the transient whimsy of

.ght upon the water. He had never wondered at the ..les on a lake in a universe of magnificent order. *The handiwork of God,* he thought uneasily, troubled by his unexpected surge of emotion. *Yeah, right!*

He shook it off.

Finding no shape on the water, no dark blot that signified the presence of his prey, Mickey O'Malley turned quickly away from the troubling beauty of the night. *She's somewhere out there, in the darkness,* he thought. The idea made him shiver with excitement. He glanced up the shore to his left, straining to see the shadowy shape of his intended.

As THE KILLER NEARED THE WATER'S EDGE, Jamie slipped underwater and began to swim slowly toward the boat. She could not afford to make any sound, so she forced herself to proceed at a slow but steady pace, her lungs burning, her mind screaming to surface. She continued until she passed beneath the fiberglass hull of the bass boat and surfaced on the other side, quietly gasping for air as the breeze rattled the cattails around her.

She peeked over the water past the end of the boat, gazing between the motor and the hull, and saw the killer at the very moment he stared out over the lake in unexpected appreciation of its beauty. She carefully reached over the gunwale, groping around for the object of her search.

He looked to his right, in her direction, and she froze, still peeking at him between the engine and the hull. Her arm was inside of the hull in the recessed engine area, and she prayed that he would not see her. Then, he turned away, and she continued to feel about, her fingers lightly running over the surface as she stood up and reached boldly into the boat, risking it all on the chance that he would not turn and look in her direction.

But now, as he continued to gaze away from Jamie, her fingers wrapped around the goal of her frantic search.

THE KILLER had always trusted his instincts. They had been infallible guides: the instincts of a feral cat. They had never betrayed him. But at this moment, to his surprise, all intuition deserted him.

He felt nothing at all: no crawling sensation on the back of his neck, no warning of danger, no sixth sense like a hidden radar that divined the presence of his prey. He waded past the first row of weeds to the clear patch of water beyond it, knee deep in the mysterious lake. He knew that she may have the shotgun, but was confident that she would be too fearful to use it effectively, even if she tried.

He heard a snort at the edge of the lake and looked in that direction. On the shore, a diminutive shape poked out of the shadows.

The small mammal emitted a snuffling noise that was outlandishly deep and powerful. It sounded like a giant whiffing snuff: inhaling, then exhaling with a prolonged nasal sigh. A hairy, armored creature crept into the moonlight, searching in the moist muck for an early morning snack. It was an armadillo.

This island is a zoo. Gazing toward shore to his left, watching the small creature, the killer heard a faint flicking noise behind him. *What was that?* It was a familiar sound, but he could not quite place it.

One hundred feet away, at the furthermost limit of the weeds at the edge of the open water, the bass boat exploded. It went up all at once with an infernal whoosh and a heavy, thunderous thud that punched him in the gut, so great was its power. He whirled and saw the boat on fire. Flaming chunks of fiberglass and streams of burning gasoline shot from the wreckage in every direction, as if the boat had become a floating Roman candle.

Standing next to the boat, Mickey O'Malley saw an image that was instantly burned into his mind. It was the girl. It was his intended.

But something was wrong. She was not fleeing in
.c.

Streaming water poured from her clothing in the light
of burning boat, and she looked at him down the barrel of a
shotgun. As his rifle whipped up, the girl squeezed off a
resounding blast that flashed fire from the end of the barrel,
propelling a weighty clump of solid steel pellets that scorched
the air between them.

The constellation of buckshot smacked him squarely in
the chest with tremendous force, sending the rifle flying from
his grasp and blowing him off his feet, straight back into the
water.

Flat on his back, Mickey O'Malley sank below the
surface. His head dangled loosely, and his body swayed
slightly in rippling water.

A small puff of smoke drifted away from Jamie's
shotgun and blended into the smoke from the inferno. She
stared at the killer, not quite believing what she was seeing.
Because he had never discarded his streamlined life vest,
Mickey bobbed on top of the water, only partly submerged.

Jamie walked carefully forward, pointing her gun at
him the entire time. Pulling the trigger, she sent another blast
into the drifting body and continued to draw closer. She
stepped right up and bent over, pushing aside the lily pads
with her right hand to take a closer look. She was filled with
morbid curiosity. She wanted to see the face of this man, this
killer who had almost taken her life.

Straining to see the details of the face rocking on top
of the muddied water, she finally made out the features. He
appeared to be well tanned, with a long, hooked nose and
white hair that drifted in the water like an infernal halo. His
mouth was open, and his eyes stared at her blankly.

Then, the man's eyes focused on her.

He exploded out of the water in a swift blur of motion.
Jamie screamed as the killer's right hand seized her shotgun,
and he smashed her temple with a roundhouse left: a heavy

blow that crunched against her bone and caused her ears to ring loudly as she fell into the water.

He leaped upon her and held her head underwater with powerful hands, skillfully throwing his full weight upon her. Jamie fought him with all that she had, swathed in pain and terror.

She could not breathe. The water deepened over her head and, kicking and twisting, she struggled to right herself, wrenching her body around until her legs were beneath her and she felt her shoes sinking into the muck.

Using her legs, Jamie pushed upward with all of her might, her lungs screaming for air. She was scarcely able to draw a breath before his weight and strength prevailed and she was shoved beneath the water again.

Her lungs ached, her mind screamed in agony as she fought for her life. But try as she may, she could not right herself again. She was outweighed by too great a margin. Stunned and dazed, she began to breathe water. The water seared her lungs, and from somewhere deep within her, Jamie found new determination to fight. Her feet found the lake bottom, and her hand came loose and popped above water as she swung with all of her might, her fist hissing through the air.

Luck is the will of God, some people say. If so, her punch was lucky. She connected perfectly with the bridge of her opponent's nose.

Mickey O'Malley's nose broke cleanly with a resounding crack. His nose had never been broken before, and the extent of the pain shocked and dismayed him. Rearing back, his hand flashed up to his face as the blood streamed freely into the shallow water.

Jamie burst from the murk at his feet, sucking air in desperation.

"Idiot!" he screamed, kicking her in the face.

She fell backward and sat down in the warm mud, up to her waist in water. She stared numbly at the red-faced man who stood over her, cursing and yelling. He slapped her face, and she scarcely felt it.   Ripping aside his life preserver, he exposed the dull glint of flattened buckshot, smashed wafer-thin against a high-tech bulletproof vest.

"Whoops!" he cried, feigning surprise, "Gee, Mrs. Cleaver, you didn't kill the bad guy, after all." He smiled at her in spite of the pain, intoxicated by the anticipation of violence, feeling an adrenaline surge as he reveled in the moment, wallowing in drunken glee. His was the twisted pleasure that springs from hatred as it savors the fruit of domination.

"You disgust me!" he screamed, mad with joy. "You make me sick!" He laughed heartily, putting his hands on his hip and shaking his head. "You are a freaking piece of dirt!"

In the flickering light of the burning boat, she saw his outline clearly: tall and thin, dressed in black clothing that poured water. And, as she gazed at him, her presence of mind returned. *He will kill me!* she realized. *This is it!*

"Jesus, help me!" she cried, "Jesus Christ, deliver me!"

"Shut up!" he shrieked, punching her in the temple and grabbing her by the hair, "He won't help you!   Oh, he <u>could</u> help you if he wanted to, but he won't, because he hates you. Who do you think sent me here after you?"

"Jesus!" she screamed, sobbing wildly, "Help me!

"I said SHUT UP!" he shrieked, backhanding her. "I am your God, little girl. SAY IT!" She stared at him numbly, her swollen face showing no fear. He smacked her again across the face. "SAY THAT I AM YOUR GOD!" he screamed, "SAY IT!" He let go, shoving her away as he stepped back. Leaping out of the water, he whirled in the air.

It was a chillingly perfect martial arts move, superbly executed. He slammed the heel of his foot squarely against the side of her head. But for all that, he did not manage to knock her out.

Jamie's head bounced backward, rebounded forward into the water, and then was slowly lifted out of the water as her muscles worked automatically to keep her breathing. She stared at the man blankly, her swollen eyes glazed over in shock and despair.

Mickey O'Malley marveled at the beauty of his handiwork. *She is stunned into submission. I am _really_ that good.* He stepped back and put his hands on his hips and began to laugh heartily, from the bottom of his belly.

As the reality of the moment became clear to her, Jamie was stricken with fear, unable to move. Shock was beginning to set in.

Lord, if you want me to be with you, I'm ready to go, Jamie prayed fervently. *But whether you take me home or leave me here, I'm not going to call this man God. You're God, and he's not.*

She looked up at the killer, who towered over her with his hands on his hips, still laughing. She watched his lips move, but could not hear a thing he said. *This is it,* she said to herself as her mind began to wander. *Your will be done,* she prayed, remembering the prayer of Jesus on the night before he was crucified. *Not my will, Father, but yours.*

"Didn't you hear me?" the man screamed madly, incensed. "I AM GOD, BABY DOLL. AND BELIEVE ME, DARLIN', GOD HATES YOUR GUTS!" He laughed with abandon, rocking on his heels, loose and happy and overflowing with glee. *This is going to be good!* he thought, savoring the moment.

"I've killed little girls all across this great nation," he chortled, "and now I'm going to kill you. I'm Dr. Sawbones, little missy." He watched closely to revel in the moment of apprehension, the moment when she realized that he was going to kill her. But she stared at him dully, as if she were not impressed.

"DIDN'T YOU HEAR ME? I'M GOING TO KILL YOU. I'M SAWBONES! PUT THAT IN YOUR PRAYER PIPE AND SMOKE IT!"

He moved closer and pulled out a large pocketknife, popping the blade into position with a loud, metallic clack. The blade swayed in front of her face in the hot, heavy air, held loosely in his hand, drifting back and forth like the head of a cobra.

He watched as her eyes focused on the moving blade. He smiled knowingly, approvingly. *This is how they all are, just before they realize they are about to die.*

As Jamie watched him, with her head beginning to clear, the picture before her came into sharp focus. The killer laughed with abandon, dimly illuminated by the waning light of the burning boat.

The dying fire lit the scene with flickering beams of red and yellow and orange tinged with purple, choking the air with a thick, heavy pall of toxic smoke that poured upward from the plastic and fiberglass hulk. In the failing light, the killer's smiling face was distorted, swollen with monstrous joy. His expression was inhumanly gleeful, engorged with hatred, anticipation, and lust.

At that moment, as Jamie wondered at the sheer depravity of the twisted creature standing before her, a strange thing happened.

She began to pity him.

In a moment, in an instant of time, she seemed to understand the motives at play behind the scenes. *No love, no hope, only anger and pride and hatred,* she thought. *What happened to him? How was he raised? Did anyone love him? Why did he give himself over to hatred so completely?*

Truly, some people seemed to be evil from the earliest days of their youths. But what kind of tidal accretion of anger had influenced this man's choice to turn upon all of humanity – to turn in rage, like a mad dog, on his fellow men and women? He had chosen to kill, and kill, and kill again: innocent women, men, and children. No torture or torment or anger that he had suffered in his youth could justify such a choice.

There was no excuse.

This man had freely chosen to live by violence. And by violence, he must die. As she thought these things, her terror fell away. In its place, she felt an intense, supernatural peace.

"Do you know where you're going to, if you die right now?" she asked him, suddenly concerned about the man. *If he dies like this, he has no hope.*

He stared at her blankly, utterly astonished. The color drained from his face, as if her fearlessness terrified him. It had never been this way.

They had always begged for their lives. His power had been absolute. The girl's fearless calm was eerie and powerful.

In the sudden silence, the blood dripped from the tip of his finger slowly, plopping into the water once, twice, a third time. The smoking boat crackled and popped and hissed as its plastic cushions bubbled up into the sky, hotly converted to gas and flame by the dying fire that cast rays of red and blue upon the misty lake.

The killer struggled to control an unfamiliar surge of fear. *Fear? Where did that come from?*

"You're hurt," she said, noticing the wound where a pellet of buckshot had torn through the edge of his forearm. His shirt was soaked with blood.

This was astonishing to him. *You're hurt? Why should she care?* Then the rage surged up within. *She's trying to control me. It's a mind game.*

"Nice try," he said, "you almost got me." He bent down and picked up a strand of her hair, admiring the lustrous, burgundy hue. "You don't mind if I keep your scalp in one piece . . . for a souvenir? It's so pretty, I hate to carve it into pieces with the rest of you."

"I'm afraid I do mind if you cut off my hair," she said bravely. "You understand, of course." In response, he backhanded her across the face.

"Let's finish this," he hissed.

And then, quite curiously, something happened.

He thought it was no longer possible, but he was wrong. After all of these years, he could still be taken unawares. He never would have believed it.

Like a business card from hell, something took Mr. Mickey O'Malley by surprise.

At first, he did not understand what was happening to him. A wave of intense fear swept over him. For no apparent reason, his eyes widened, his nostrils flared, and the hairs on the back of his neck stood up. Goose pimples covered him from head to foot.

"What?" he whispered. *Where did that come from?* he wondered. His instincts screamed danger, but his mind told him that this impulse, with no evidence to support it, was unfounded.

Then, something even stranger happened. With a heavy swoosh, the water swirled loudly behind him. His face displayed an expression of puzzlement, then a look of utter surprise.

Suddenly, with an unexpected jolt, his hands flew into the air and he was slammed, face down, into the dark water.

But before he disappeared beneath the surface, one wiry hand flicked out and seized Jamie's left arm.

His grip was painfully strong, and she could not resist. She stared in surprise as he was jerked backward, away from her. His head disappeared beneath the surface and, trapped in his vise-like grip, she was dragged along in his wake.

The water surged over the top of Mickey O'Malley as he was dragged backwards, in great pain. As he and Jamie were towed rapidly toward the open water, the lake water swelled around them like the wave in front of a submarine.

It was as if some monster, some phantom of the lake were dragging them out into the darkened deep. Astonished and horrified, Jamie fought in vain against the killer's brutal death grip.

Her head was dragged beneath the brackish water. She popped up, gasping for air. But although she could breathe, she had not found relief. She was still being dragged away from shore.

Directly in front of Jamie, in front of a swiftly moving hump of water, the killer's face popped out of the water. It was contorted by terror, not by hatred.

"HELP ME!" he screamed wildly.

His eyes focused sharply on Jamie, and the hatred returned like an evil flame. Still being dragged toward the deep, he began to pull her closer to himself as his other arm popped out of the water. In that hand was the open knife.

"I'LL KILL YOU!" he screamed, as if she were to blame for what was happening to him.

Jamie struggled frantically to get away, thrashing in the water as he drew her closer to the blade. And as she fought desperately, floundering on top of the water, her right hand struck something solid. It was a thin green oak log, rock-hard and thoroughly waterlogged. Grabbing it tightly, she pulled against the killer's grip with her left hand and reoriented her body in the water.

"Come to papa!" Mickey leered, ignoring the fiery pain in his crushed legs, focusing on the murder that he was about to commit. As his knife hand began to strike, she whipped the skinny log against his head, swinging with all of her might.

The power of the blow stupefied him.

He dropped the knife for an instant, loosening his grip.

Jamie snatched her hand away before he realized what had happened. He reached back instantly for her, but his hand slapped the water in vain.

In unspeakable agony, with his face contorted with pain and rage, Mickey O'Malley was pulled underwater.

Jamie's head swirled. Scarcely able to believe that she was free from his grip, she began to swim backwards through the thick weeds, headed toward shore. As she swam, she watched the unfolding spectacle, transfixed by the terror of it all.

The broad hump of water that had trapped Mickey O'Malley surged through the last, swaying shoal of weeds as it moved into the lake. And there, in the open water, an underwater tempest was unleashed.

A vortex began to swirl, gaining in fury, increasing in intensity, churning the dark water like a massive washing machine that spun bubbles and waves into a tempestuous whirlpool, splashing foam and spray and flecks of fresh blood into the warm spring air. It was simply awful.

Horrified by the spectacle, Jamie could not turn away. She watched, not quite believing her eyes. And then, something dreadful happened.

For one last time, for one final breath, Mickey O'Malley arose from the land of the dying.

For one fleeting, helpless moment, his face broke the water, and he shrieked.

He did not scream like a man.

His was the terrified squeal of a wounded deer brought down by wolves: the hopeless wail of a soul without hope, lost and abandoned: of a spirit torn to shreds in the claws of hungry demons as cruel and merciless as he. The sound was dreadful.

"EEEEEEE!" he squealed in a disturbingly high-pitched voice, sounding more like a lost child than a hardened killer drowning in the jaws of a nameless horror.

And then, as suddenly as it had begun, the struggle was over. With a deep whoosh, he disappeared beneath the surface. The hump of water moved deeper into the lake and gradually disappeared.

Predation's End

The water calmed, and once again the lake shimmered under the moonlight, eerily placid as it glistened with an untamed, spectral beauty. In the weeds close to the shore, the burning boat snapped and popped, giving off more smoke than light as a few small waves, the final remnants of the ghoulish vortex she had just witnessed, began to gently lap against the beach.

Jamie stumbled backwards out of the water. She was overwhelmed by the horror of it all.

"NO!" she screamed, "NO! NO! NO!" She did not know why or how she screamed, but she screamed nonetheless. Her own voice sounded distant, like the voice of someone she did not know.

Where the muddy land met the muddy lake, she tripped and fell backwards into the moist muck and weeds. The back of her head slammed into the soft ground, parting stiff grass that pricked her scalp and doused her hair in tepid, mucky water. The muck smelled rich and earthy, like eggs turned slightly rotten.

Jamie smelled nothing. She heard no sound and scarcely felt a thing.

"No," she whispered, again and again. Unable to think, almost mad with pain and anguish, she began to cry, blinking up at the crescent moon.

Then, something surprising happened. A peace beyond comprehension began to envelope her. Beginning gradually and increasing in strength, the peace filled as she lay on the ground and wept at the sky.

The moon and stars shone down upon the surreal scene: the smoking hull of the burned-out boat, the small, wet form laying flat on the beach.

Here, on this forsaken shore, peace surrounded Jamie like a halo. The shimmering clouds of God's heaven, so high and noble and untouched by the wickedness of men, filled her heart and her soul as Jamie fell asleep.

IN THE OPEN WATER, the big alligator released her lifeless prey and rose to the surface. She rested for a while with only the top of her head and tail showing above water.

She breathed deeply, savoring the complex scents of this wild, free lake. All thirteen feet of her swayed in the waves like a reptilian log that was warily adrift, loitering just below the surface.

She was gratified by tonight's success. The hunt had been one more prosperous transaction in a richly satisfying life built on a foundation of self-gratification.

Like all successful creatures of the night, she would return to her hole before dawn. There, safe at home, she looked forward to a hearty breakfast and a good day's sleep.

MICKEY O'MALLEY is dead. He opens his eyes in a land without light.

Mickey O'Malley is in hell.

How can he describe this absence of life, this place in a flame past the chambers of death? There is no one here to impress with his knife: no horror to share, no power to wield.

But the torment is real, the pain is complete, and the suffering beyond any touch, pain, or heat.

All of the murders, the blood and the screams, the pleadings for mercy that fell on deaf ears are piled like hot embers against him. His soul writhes inside a great, infinite nothing of unanswered promise and final regret.

"HELP ME!" he screams. But he cannot perceive his own thoughts, or the sounds as they leap from his mouth. He hears no reflection: no voice: no thought: no echo to show that he lives in this void. There is no way to prove he exists.

He does not live here. In this land, he withers and perishes in death's endless wind.

There is no life here in this world beyond death. Here, beyond mercy, beyond men or angels, past demons or fear or the light of the sun, past sight of the stars or the taste of the rain, here, in this darkness, no life can take hold.

Oh, for the sweet taste of rain on his tongue! He writhes in the flame and dies deep in his soul, here in the bottomless, endless abyss, here in the land of unending regrets.

They were right. There is a hell. They were right after all!

He cannot believe that this is happening. But his unbelief lacks the power to persuade, and cannot dissolve the reality in which he is immersed. This is really happening. The pain is real, whether he believes it, or not.

<u>This</u> is what is:. the land of pain and nothingness: no light and no sound, no contact, no hope.

<u>This</u> is what is. And now, at last, Mickey O'Malley knows the truth.

God didn't want me to go to hell, but I loved death, I dealt in death, and now death is my fair reward.

If he were not in the middle of hell at the moment, the moral symmetry of his judgment would appeal to his artistic sensibilities.

Now, he knows the truth. Stripped of excuses, he realizes what has happened.

During his time on earth, he stubbornly rejected life. He slammed the door in the face of God. By his own choices, he damned himself forever.

God actually cared about him. God wanted to save Mickey O'Malley from death. But that gift - the offer of life and grace - was not good enough for him.

And that is what hurts more than anything else.

His life did not have to end this way. Life was his for the asking, and he hated to hear about it. Life was his for the taking, and he laughed in His face.

That realization - that it did not have to be this way - hurts worse than the flames.

THE SUN SHONE brightly from a cloudless sky. Jamie stood on the dock, facing the farmhouse and the clearing that had become so familiar in the past few months. The air was clean and clear, the sun cool but painfully bright, beating down upon the landscape, reflecting from walls of the clean, white farmhouse. Each feature stood out with supernal clarity: the canal, the trees, the clearing and farmhouse. Noticing a movement at the edge of her eye, Jamie focused on a jumbled heap in the middle of the back yard.

It was the Sheriff.

Tommy Durrance lay face down on the ground, his body twisted, arms sprawled wide. But as she watched, he lifted his head. Seeing her, he smiled. His body straightened as he rose to his feet and reached out to her, smiling and relaxed. Remarkably, he looked younger than she had ever seen him. He was tanned, fit, and utterly content.

She found herself running toward him, overcome with joy. She ran like a little girl to a kindly grandfather, like a sister to a cherished older brother. She hugged him tightly, aching deep in her chest as the tears welled in her eyes.

The intensity of the moment overwhelmed her. *He's alive,* she thought, *and he can walk again.* She hugged him fiercely, overflowing with gratitude and with inexpressible happiness.

"Are you all right?" she asked. In reply, he pushed her back to arms length, his hands on her shoulders as if to better look at her. He smiled and nodded.

"I'm so proud of you, Jamie," he whispered. "Wake up, honey," he added, with his expression changing to one of concern, "somebody needs you."

Impulsively, she hugged him tight, as tightly as she could squeeze. She began to cry freely, unable to contain her grief. She was so glad that she had known this honorable man who cared for her so profoundly, this man who had loved her so purely and completely. He had been willing to lay down his life for her. *This must be heaven,* she thought. *This must be a dream.*

"Will I see you again?" she asked, her face covered with tears. "You're like . . . I mean . . . you're such a good friend."

"Wake up, Jamie," he answered, "somebody needs you."

Wake Up Call

"Wake up, Jamie," Delia said, shaking her friend's shoulder. "We have to get out of here." Jamie was crying as she awoke. She opened her eyes and blinked, slowly comprehending that she was awake, lying on her back in the mud. Her head lay in dirty weeds and brittle stubble that pricked her scalp when she moved.

She looked up at the sky. It was still dark, rimmed with streaks of light that were just beginning to reveal another dawn. She sat up, and pain surged in her head.

"Ohhhh," she moaned, reaching her hand up, then jerking it away when she touched her tender face. "That hurts." She was badly bruised from the beating she had received.

"Oh, honey," Delia said, "I'm so glad you can talk. When it got quiet last night, after I heard the gunshots down here, I thought you had been killed." Jamie noticed that Delia's face, like her own, was streaked with tears. "But I guess he didn't kill you."

"No such luck," Delia murmured.

Jamie rose shakily to her feet. Looking down, she saw that she was filthy and that Delia was equally smeared with dirt: filthy and badly wounded, with her swollen leg laying in the water and muck. *That leg looks bad. We have to get help right away.*

Going into action mode, Jamie sloshed straight out into the water. Pausing when it reached her waist, she took a deep breath and disappeared from sight for a full minute. She arose from the shallows directly in front of Delia, straining to drag their canoe out of the water.

"How did you find that thing?" Delia asked, astonished.

"See the tall cattails?" Jamie panted as she began to pull, "That big clump, right here? Last night, we ditched the canoe there." Jamie laboriously dragged it onto the shore.

Turning it on its side, she maneuvered it close to her friend. "This ought to make it easier," she suggested. "Are you ready?"

Carefully, she got behind Delia and lifted under her arms as her friend struggled to crawl into the canoe, fighting off the pain. When most of her body was inside, Jamie helped her lift her right leg into the canoe. Then, shoving hard, she righted the heavy cypress dugout.

"Grab the paddle, I'm okay," Delia said, grimacing on her side in the bottom of the narrow vessel.

Minutes later, they were in the open water. The sun began to rise above the eastern shore, dazzling Jamie's eyes as she dug into the water with the paddle. She was aching all over, but they were finally headed toward home.

Homecoming

As the canoe headed east, gliding smoothly across the surface of the calm lake, Jamie squinted her eyes and fixed her gaze above the horizon. The fading remnants of last night's stars were leaching away, and light began to wash the edge of the sky with the promise of the coming day.

Jamie was fascinated with the beauty of the thin strand of smoke that ascended lazily into the pale eastern sky. The smoke was backlit by the sun, which was still hidden below the curve of the earth. Like the vapor trail of a rocket, the illuminated column seemed to point a slender, gilded finger toward the heavens, towering high above cypress trees that lined the distant horizon.

The tall trees still held the darkness of the swamp close to them, as if they were afraid to let it go. In spite of their height, at this distance the trees appeared to be little more than an ominous smudge upon the water's edge.

The smoke, by contrast, was majestic. To Jamie, who was almost catatonic with exhaustion, the smoke was a symbol of liberation. It was a skinny, golden needle slicing upwards into an otherwise pristine sky: a strangely beautiful, knife-thin finger of soot, sparks and cinders that led the eye upward into the heights, then back to its point of origin.

Hidden behind the distant trees, at the source of the column of smoke, was a longed-for sight still hidden from Jamie's eyes: the little wooden farmhouse that Jamie had come to call home.

AT EDGE OF THE SWAMP, preparing to launch his canoe, a man noticed a distant speck on the waters of the lake. He raised his spotting scope, and focused in.

Even in the darkness, he could see that it was Jamie. Putting down the scope, he smiled and pushed off from shore.

---

20 MINUTES LATER, with the canoe quietly cutting across the water, Jamie rounded the point and entered the mouth of the canal. In that small bay, surrounded by lily pads, she finally caught sight of the farmhouse.

It was still standing. It had not been burned to the ground. The roof was intact, and the house was remarkably undamaged: scorched but not consumed by the fire that burned just a few feet away.

Fire trucks were parked in the driveway. Yellow-clad firemen busily directed strong streams of water onto the smoldering vehicles, which were hidden from her sight on the east side of the house. Even from this distance, she could hear the harsh roar as water hit the molten remains and boiled upon contact, sending a vaporous torrent of hot, filthy steam soaring upward to mingle with the smoke that rippled up from the wreckage.

The yard was covered with dark green Sheriff's Department cruisers, their blue lights flashing futilely in the misty morning dampness. Two green-clad deputies, bowed under the weight, carried a body bag off the dock, accompanied by the deputy coroner. Another full body bag rested on the shore beside the dock. Behind the two deputies, on a small rise near the house, Dr. Gene Thompson knelt and took measurements beside a dark shape that appeared to be yet another corpse.

A short, stocky deputy who was approaching the dock from the house suddenly noticed the canoe approaching from the west, cutting smoothly across the glassy waters of the canal. The man's mouth dropped open, and he waved his arms, frantically jumping up and down.

"She's over here!" he shouted at the top of his lungs, "Over here!" He ran toward the dock, and the two deputies almost dropped the body as they turned around to take a look. As officials came running from every direction, Jamie paddled the canoe swiftly towards shore and beached it securely in the muck. She stood up and stepped into the water.

"Get an ambulance," Jamie called to the officers, "the Major's been shot."

At the sight of their wounded fellow officer, the deputies swarmed the canoe, shouting for a stretcher and ignoring Jamie. She stepped up onto squishy grass of shore and drifted out to the fringe of a small crowd of law officers and emergency personnel.

As she watched them, she realized that a light blanket had been placed around her shoulders. *Where did that come from?* The weather was warm, but Jamie was cold, glad to have the blanket. She turned slowly, as if in a trance, looking around the clearing. The yellow police tape caught her eye. *This is the crime scene. This is the crime scene.*

"The crime scene," Delia groaned as four men lifted her out of the canoe and placed her on a stretcher. "Secure the crime scene! What are these cars doing, parked in the yard? You're ruining the crime scene!" Jamie watched from the edge of the water.

"It doesn't matter," Jamie answered, speaking mostly to herself. "They're all dead, anyway."

"Is Tommy all right?" Delia asked, lifting her head and looking around frantically. Realizing that her question was being ignored, she called to Jamie, trying to sit up as the medics secured her leg. "Jamie, check on Tommy. Let me know if he's okay."

"Okay," Jamie replied absently. She was suddenly exhausted, strangely numb, curiously unmoved by the scene that was swirling around her.

"Sergeant," Delia said sternly to a tall, red-haired man who stood by, looking at his wounded Major in obvious dismay.

"Yes, Major." His eyes were big as he watched the medics gently lean her back, securing her on the stretcher.

"Get everyone out of here who's not on the forensics team. Nobody should be walking around this crime scene except the coroner and forensics. Do you understand?"

"Right."

"And Sergeant?"

"Yes, Major?"

"Is Tommy okay?" He turned away for a moment, his eyes misting. What could he say?

She was badly wounded, and she and Tommy had been as close as twins. Whenever you saw one, the other was just around the corner. How could he tell her the truth? The pain hit Delia again, and she lay back abruptly, her eyes watering as she struggled to keep from screaming.

The crowd around the Major began to accelerate toward the ambulance that was parked beside the house. Jamie turned toward the east side of the house and looked toward a small rise in the back yard. An irregularly shaped lump lay on the ground beside Gene Thompson, the County Coroner, who was kneeling in the grass.

For the moment, Gene had paused from his work. He stared idly into space, as if lost in deep meditation. Jamie began to walk towards him, drawn by his thoughtful expression, his calm in the midst of such destruction.

"Jamie, find out what you can!" Delia called out after her as she was rolled away, "Call me at the hospital!" She was swept along by a human wave of medics and deputies who deposited her in the ambulance like a piece of human flotsam washed onto a beach.

"Okay," Jamie called, continuing to drift toward the coroner. She moved through the scene of destruction without flinching, seemingly unaffected by the destruction and carnage.

It was as if she were safely hidden somewhere else, peering at this world through a lens. She was watching everything from a distance. Jamie felt no emotion at all, only a powerful, pervasive numbness. Feeling a hand touch her arm, she did not bother to turn around and look at the tall Sheriff's deputy who stood behind her.

"Do you need a doctor?" he asked.

"No, thank you."

"You're sure?"

"Yes."

"Then - uh – well, I'm sorry, ma'am, but you'll have to leave. We can give you a ride where ever you need to go. Do you have anyone we could call?" It was the sergeant, busily executing Delia's orders to clear the crime scene. As Jamie turned her face to his, he gasped, shocked by the bruises on her face and her badly swollen eye. In the heat of the moment, as they had rushed to take care of the Major, the deputies had not noticed Jamie's obvious wounds.

Why do I have to leave? she wondered. *This is my home,* she reflected, looking up at the man's face. She was bathed in a surreal, intense calm, but no words came out of her mouth.

"I'll be responsible for the young lady, Sergeant," the coroner said, rising to his feet.

"Yes, sir," he replied. He turning abruptly on his heel, determined to clear the remaining live bodies from the yellow-taped crime scene.

"Ms. James," the coroner said gently, reaching toward her, but stopping before he touched her, "Jamie, are you all right?" Jamie did not respond to his question, but stared at the coroner as if he were a stranger. She did not look down. She was afraid to look at the body that lay at his feet, afraid of whom it might be.

"Come on, Jamie. Let's walk around to the front yard." He took her hand and led her, like a child, away from the broken body of Sheriff Tommy Durrance.

Where the coroner had knelt only moments before, the earthly remains of Tommy Durrance lay perfectly still. The body was grossly deformed: legs and feet contorted into an unnatural pose that openly declared that his back had been broken. His arms were sprawled in front of his body with the

Uzi stuck to one locked, ice cold hand. His chest and shoulders were laid open, ripped to the bone by the killer's well-aimed salvo.

The Sheriff's face was neither pretty nor peaceful. It was purple and contorted, reflecting the horror of the Sheriff's final moments: overwhelming pain, intense concentration as he fired at the speeding boat, and final, unfelt shock as five bullets struck within a single second, cutting him off from this world.

He had lived well, but he had died hard.

He had perished fulfilling his highest calling: protecting the innocent from the cruel.

The coroner was stunned. He felt raw inside, as if his heart had been physically wounded. He had not thought much about it before today, but he had really liked Tommy Durrance.

Gene Thompson hated death.

Long ago, Gene had decided that poets and philosophers were fools to rhapsodize about death. In a perfect world, death would not exist.

Gene had once been a transcendentalist. He had believed that life and death were two sides of the same coin, linked inextricably in an eternal cosmic interplay. But now, he believed something altogether different.

If an all-powerful God existed, life without death was a logical probability. Why wouldn't God want to weed out evil until only the good remained?

Gene no longer believed human beings were bodysurfing creative entities spending an eternity passing back and forth between good and evil, switching from death to life like some kind of supernatural alternating current. There had to be something better than an eternal 'dance of life' that was wedded, forever, to death.

Gene Thompson hated death.

Death stole husbands from their wives. Death savaged little children and ravaged families. For now, it might serve a purpose in the divine scheme of things, but death was never good. It was never sublime. In an ideal universe, death itself would be condemned to die.

Gene Thompson hated death.

As he saw the extent of Jamie's shock, a sympathetic resonance occurred deep within him. Fighting the emotions that threatened to arise, he wrenched his mind away from his personal grief. He had always dealt with death as a professional, and had handled it with professional detachment. For sanity's sake, he could not let himself falter now, when he was need so desperately by such a courageous woman.

They walked across the dew-soaked grass, headed for the car that he had parked beside the road where the clearing first began. He opened the passenger door, and Jamie sat down on the front seat as he walked around and slipped behind the steering wheel. After two minutes of silence, she spoke.

"Was that body - the one you were examining - was that the Sheriff?" She looked around as she spoke, staring blankly at the strange scene in the clearing: firemen rolling up their hoses, the scorched wall of the farmhouse, the two steaming lumps of smoldering steel and rubber that had once been a car and truck.

"Yes," Gene replied, taking off his glasses and blinking. "That was the Sheriff."

"He's dead?"

"Yeah. He's dead." She sat quietly, taking it all in.

"The Sheriff was a good man. I think he was best I ever met."

"Yeah, I know," he sighed. "Me, too."

"What about Streetcar. Is he dead, too?"

"Who?"

"Streetcar. Salvatore Benuto."

"What did your friend look like?"

"He was tall, about six feet two inches, kind of skinny."

"We didn't find anyone close to meeting that description, Jamie. Besides Tommy, that is."

She sat up abruptly.

"Are you sure?"

"Except for the Sheriff, all of the deceased appear to have been members of the Provencenti crime family. Their physical appearances matched up with the IDs they were carrying. Your friend, Salvatore Benuto, was not among the bodies. And I can assure you, we have diligently searched the entire area." He did not add that they had found the body of Joseph Provencenti, Jr. She had suffered a great deal, and he did not wish to provide any more information unless she requested it.

"You didn't find him?" She paused, not sure of what to think. *Could he be alive?*

"Right." They paused for another minute. Then, the coroner spoke.

"What are you going to do?" he asked her.

"I don't know."

"You look like you might need medical attention," he said, looking at her bruised face. "Are you okay?"

"Yes. I'm bruised, but I'm not broken. The doctors can't do much to treat bruises, can they?"

"I suppose not."

"Right."

"Would you like me to call a friend, someone who could come and pick you up?"

"No. I'd like to sit here for a while, if you don't mind."

"You're welcome to sit here as long as you want." There was an awkward silence.

"I have to get back to work."

"I understand."

"Are you okay?" He was concerned about her mental state, not quite happy about leaving her alone, but unable to think of a more merciful alternative.

"Yeah, sure, I'm okay." She blinked and looked away. "Please, go now." As his door slammed shut, a tear trickled down her frozen face. But somehow, in spite of the crushing pain, she could not shed more than that single, solitary tear.

Against the Flow

The narrow creek flowed from the north and ended in the lake, passing through three counties on its way. Along the way, the slow-moving waters meandered on a lazy, circuitous route, as mysterious and changeable as the land itself. He paddled north against the gentle current, leaving the lake far behind him.

A heavy mist covered the creek, and no one heard him as the canoe slipped past a quiet fish camp on the east side of the creek. He passed beneath the highway bridge as the sun was rising above the horizon.

While he was under the concrete bridge, two cars whipped by overhead, speeding toward the farmhouse. They were Federal agents headed toward the scene of last night's bloody crime.

For hours, Streetcar continued to paddle north, pushing hard to distance himself from the powerful reach of the Federal government. He pressed hard all morning, wending his way northward until the sun seared his eyes and the heat pressed heavily on his back.

He expertly propelled the tiny canoe around narrow bends and past fallen trees, accelerating when he could and slowing when he had to. Just before noon, the high bank to his left gave way to a swamp. He turned left, weaving through the trunks of towering trees. When he could no longer see the canal, he stopped the canoe in the water and closed his eyes.

He would stay here and rest awhile. After night fell, he would paddle back to the creek and continue north. He would travel by night for the remainder of his journey.

As he rested in the cypress swamp, he breathed in the familiar, musty scent of dark water on black muck. It seemed almost cozy, somehow. It seemed like home. He turned around carefully and squinted toward the canal, confirming that he was completely hidden from sight.

"Whoa, Cat," he whispered to his companion, "is this good enough for you?" The big Maine Coon, in spite of his pain, began to purr.

Streetcar was alive.

He had awakened at three in the morning with his temple throbbing. When he had touched his head, the pain had kicked him hard. But the blood had been dry and caked, and there was no massive hole, only a scabbed-up gash: clean, with no bone fragments. The bullet must have grazed his temple, knocking him out without clipping his skull.

As soon as he had lifted his head, he had seen the cat. Without a moment's hesitation, he had jump-started his body and struggled gamely to his knees. He had picked the big cat up carefully, bundling him in his shirt, ignoring the fact that the heavy fur was hard and stiff from time spent in a puddle of Joe Boy's blood. Streetcar had staggered hurriedly to his feet.

He returned quickly toward his home base, wondering whether Jamie had made it to safety. *Can I still help her?* he wondered. *Is she alive?* It had been hours since he had been shot, and dawn was coming soon.

By now, he reasoned, Jamie's crisis was likely over. By now, she was either dead, or alive.

He could not hope to track Jamie in this present darkness. Time was wasting, and unless he could see or hear some kind of clue – something to go on - he would have to try to save himself.

Back on his little island in the middle of the swamp, Streetcar had lit a bright lantern and examined the cat's wound. The bullet had entered at the top of his haunch and exited at the back of the thigh, splitting flesh but not breaking the bone. He sedated the cat, then cleaned and stitched the gash using supplies from his emergency medical kit.

His own open wound had been more difficult because sedation was out of the question. The cleaning and stitching of his gruesome gash had tested the extent of his determination. But by half-past four, he had finished his work.

Streetcar left the small island for the last time, carrying everything he needed on his back like a human hermit crab.

He found the aluminum canoe where he had left it months before. After he pulled it to the edge of the swamp, he saw a distant speck on the lake. With his spotting scope, he saw that it was Jamie, alive and well. He launched the canoe, headed for creek that - he hoped - would lead him away from trouble, once and for all.

After months without hope, Streetcar was beginning to dream again. And, quite predictably, his dreams did not include free dinner and lodging in jail - with Federal law enforcement officials grilling him about an inexcusable arson-murder that, by now, he sorely regretted.

His exit strategy had been well thought-out, and for the time being, it looked as if his strategy might work. He had helped to give Jamie and her friends a fighting chance and he had saved the cat's life. For the past several months he had gotten away with murder, and it looked as if he might finally shake his pursuers.

All in all, it had been an eventful period in his life.

Salvatore Benuto had completed his mission. He was ready to go home.

All he needed was a home to go home to.

Requiem

Of course, it had to rain. The day would not have been complete without it.

The memorial service had been emotionally wrenching, to say the least. The remembrances had been poignant; the tributes had been touching beyond measure. And now, at the graveside, the obligatory rain set in with a vengeance.

A late cold front was wringing the moisture out of the clouds, dumping the weight of the heavens upon them. The gloomy tribute reminded them miserably of their loss, adding chilly emphasis to grief that was still an open wound.

The tributes from Tommy's friends were nice, but the did not assuage the pain. Their pain could not be eased by the comfort of fading memories, no matter how sweet they might be. This was the real thing.

Delia had insisted upon attending the Sheriff's funeral, and had threatened to crawl out of the hospital if the doctors tried to stop her from attending. She had finally agreed to a compromise, traveling in an ambulance that had parked unobtrusively beneath a tree near the gravesite. She had watched the service through the open back door of the truck.

This one hurt.

This one hurt bad.

Delia felt the loss of her friend to the core of her being. And to see the huge crowd in so much pain, weeping unashamedly, only made it worse. She had never realized it, but now she knew it for a fact: Tommy had been her best friend.

Delia turned to her big little brother, who was sitting on the bench to her left. He was dressed in a dark blue suit, solemnly watching the ceremony. He looked strong and reliable, at peace with himself. This was how brothers should look, but seldom did.

"Thanks, baby," she said to him, reaching out and patting his hand. "Thanks for coming." He took her hand in his and gave it a squeeze.

"You couldn't have kept me away," he replied.

It seemed as if most of the town had come to the graveside to share their misery. The people were gathered in sad clusters under the darkened noonday sky that flashed sporadically and boomed loudly, showering giant drops of water remorselessly upon them. As the honor guard fired a salute and a team of bagpipers played Amazing Grace, the tears of the mourners mingled with the rain, flowing freely down their faces. The pastor stood to speak the final words of the service.

"Tommy Durrance was a man who was greatly loved," the pastor said with his gruff, gravelly voice. "I loved him. We all loved him.

"He was a preacher of the Gospel who lived by what he preached. He was as kind and decent as any man I ever met. I met him more than 15 years ago, and during that entire time, I don't think that Tommy ever met a man he didn't like . . . or didn't love, for that matter. That applied to the women in his life, also. He was a friend to all. A true friend." The pastor paused to fight back tears that welled unexpectedly into his eyes

"Tommy used to say that what people need is love: unconditional love. He was sure, just like I am, that Jesus Christ demonstrated the ultimate love. Jesus' death on the cross, taking the place of you and me, was the ultimate act of selflessness. Tommy believed that this was the ultimate truth, and he wasn't shy about saying so.

"Tommy used to say that God's love is the ultimate paradigm. In the suffering and resurrection of Jesus Christ, the love of an innocent God is revealed.

"God cared enough to suffer for us. God did not abandon us. God came to us. God was in Jesus, reconciling the world unto Himself. All who believe that Jesus is the one, true Messiah receive the free gift of this reconciliation. This gift costs us nothing, but it cost Him everything." The pastor lifted his eyes, red and brimming with tears, and looked around at the crowd of people. They were packed in front of him, shifting from foot to foot beneath a solid roof of black, ribbed umbrellas, hiding in vain from the falling sheets of bitter, ice-cold rain.

"In death, as in life, Tommy Durrance realized his greatest ambition. When he gave his life for those he loved, he followed in the footsteps of his Master. And when Jesus Christ returns in Glory and power, Tommy will be with him."

"Amen," the people said in unison.

"May the blessings of our Lord and Savior Jesus Christ be upon all who long for His return," the pastor added.

"Amen," they repeated.

As they spoke their final amen, the thunder clapped loudly as if the heavens themselves were shooing the crowd away from the wet cemetery. The people hurriedly departed, stepping gingerly past damp, weather-beaten headstones, trying not to step on graves as they returned to the cold comfort of their well-heated cars.

As the service was ending, Delia glanced to her right, where Jamie sat on the other bench, staring at the mourners as if she could still not quite take it all in. Jamie looked small and shaken and unhealthily pale.

"Are you okay?" Delia asked. Jamie turned and flashed a smile, then quickly turned away. Her face was soaked with tears.

She could finally cry.

Poor Jamie, Delia thought, *the Sheriff may have been the first decent man she ever knew.* Delia had once been a beautiful young woman, like Jamie, and she knew how most men behaved, married men and single men alike. The combination of womanly youth and stunning beauty seemed to turn almost every heterosexual male on earth into a hopeful, eligible bachelor.

Delia sighed and whispered a prayer for her young friend. Then she found herself talking to Tommy Durrance in her mind. *Tommy, you really should see your funeral. It's a sight.* She smiled to think of him in paradise, free from the weight of his troubled past.

The painkillers must be kicking in, she mused, feeling woozy. She was losing track of events as her mind began to wander. *I'd like to sleep,* she thought, noticing that the van was moving. Or at least, it seemed to me moving. *Dear God, thank you for Tommy. Thank you, Jesus,* she prayed with all her heart.

She looked up, and Jamie was gone. *I'm glad she was here,* Delia thought as she fell asleep.

The Month of May

Delia would undergo intensive physical therapy for months, and the doctor's orders were that she should not return to work until mid-June. Within weeks, however, she was walking with the help of crutches.

It did not surprise Delia that Jamie decided to stay in Oree County. Neither did it surprise her that Jamie wished to return to the farmhouse at the edge of the wilderness where she had lived for the past several months. She began attending Delia's church, and their friendship, founded in a time of trouble, flourished in the time of rest and recovery.

So it was that, early in the month of May, on a hot, sunny, painfully bright afternoon, Delia and Jamie were applying a third coat of paint to the farmhouse wall that had been scorched so badly less than two months before. They talked and enjoyed the steady work with the sunlight pressing on their shoulders, enjoying the clear heat of the day and the clean scent of trees and grass.

Jamie heard the car while it was still far away. They put their brushes into a bucket of water and sat down to rest in the shade, waiting for the unannounced visitor to arrive.

"This is nice," Delia observed, watching a hawk circle high in the empty sky. "I can see how you could get used to this."

"I'm used to it, all right," Jamie answered. "That's the problem. I don't want to leave, and I don't know how much longer I'll be able to stay. Red hasn't told me a thing. He just says, 'Let me worry about that, you just take some R & R.' I guess I should do what he says, but I can't stop worrying about it."

"Jamie, do you mind if I ask a personal question?"

"Go ahead, that never stopped you before." She smiled brightly at Delia. They had become good friends, and Delia smiled back. "What's the question?" Jamie asked.

"What ever happened to that nice young cowboy?" Jamie's face became serious.

"I don't know." She paused for a moment, and then the words came out in a rush. "He said he loves me, and I told him to go away for a while. I told him I need time. I think he wants to marry me, Delia." She stopped. "The truth is, I'm scared to death. You know a little bit about my life. It's not easy for me to trust any man. Even him."

"Hmmm," Delia replied, not sure of what to say. She knew that Jamie liked this boy, but she respected her need for time and safety. Jamie had lived through more than most people could imagine in their most malignant nightmares. As they sat there together, lost in thought, the car finally arrived.

A shiny indigo Mercedes rolled out from under the huge live oaks and into the sunlight of the clearing, glistening like a dark, metallic jewel as it coasted onto the freshly painted concrete parking slab. Jamie and Delia stood to greet their visitors. The passenger was Red Johnson himself, who had just retired after 30 years with the Florida Department of Law Enforcement.

The men climbed out of the car and blinked, shielding their eyes against the searing light. Red, freckled and gray haired, was dressed in a cowboy shirt and boots, while the driver, a dapper, 50ish dandy, was dressed in a gray silk suit, starched white shirt, and a glossy, midnight blue tie that matched the paint on his dazzling German sedan.

"Delia, Jamie, it's good to see you," Red said, shaking their hands. "This fella I'm with has some business with both of you, I believe." Mr. Gentleman's Quarterly shifted his weight and looked around tentatively, slipping on a pair of dark sunglasses. Stripped of his luxurious cocoon of leather and steel, plunged into a caldron of roasting heat beneath the relentless rays of the central Florida sun, he appeared unsure of himself, like a turtle without its shell.

"I'm Lewis Starke of Starke, Hoffman, Venable and Crabtree," he offered, as if that might mean something to either of them. But Delia and Jamie were from Oree County by way of Tampa, and they knew nothing about his firm, the most prestigious partnership in Orlando.

"Please, come in," Jamie offered courteously. Her curiosity was aroused. She glanced at Delia with raised eyebrows and led them into the house. Ten minutes later, seated with them at their kitchen table, the suited visitor had begun to recover from the heat.

"I'll get right to the point," he stated brusquely after polishing off a glass of lemonade. "I'm here as executor of the will of Mr. Thomas Wimberly Durrance."

"Wimberly?" Jamie asked, looking at Delia quizzically. I spite of their best efforts, Jamie and Delia burst into laughter, unable to control themselves. It was a true belly laugh, the first they had enjoyed in two months. At the end of the outburst, they wiped away their tears and asked the man to continue.

"You have to understand," Delia added, realizing how their laughter must look to the stranger. "Wimberly just doesn't fit the Tommy we remember. No wonder he never used his middle name." The man smiled thinly.

"My grandmother was a Wimberly," he offered starchily. Their laughter was instantly squelched.

"I knew Mr. Durrance," he continued with a mechanical smile, "and I think I can understand your loss." He opened his lambskin folio and placed a single clean sheet of legal-sized paper on the checkered tablecloth.

"This is the last will and testament of Thomas Durrance. He wrote it himself three months ago, and signed it at our office. He insisted on doing it himself. Mr. Durrance could be rather unyielding about such things." The man smiled thinly.

"I would have approached you earlier, but my client's instructions were that, if he died by violent means, I should wait at least eight weeks before the reading of the will. I think that he hoped to spare his loved ones from the shock that the will might provide. The probate judge has been more than willing to comply with my client's request.

"I would like to read the will. Shall I proceed?" Delia looked at Jamie for assent, then nodded.

"Please, go ahead."

"Certainly." The man picked up the paper and slipped on a pair of reading glasses.

"I, Thomas Wimberly Durrance, being of good health and sound mind, do hereby render my final will and testament. This will negates any and all prior wills and testaments, and represents my express intent for the distribution of all of my resources after my death.

"To my beloved friends, I hereby bequeath the following:

"To my secretary and her husband, to be shared jointly, my house at 1412 Fairview Court, all vehicles that I own, and any of my possessions that are on or about that property.

"To the pastor of my church, James Watson, all of my stocks and bonds with the exception of shares in financial institutions. The worth of said stocks and bonds is currently estimated to be in excess of 50 million dollars.

"To Janelle James, I bequeath the farmhouse on the Oklawaha Canal and the surrounding land, totaling 1,263 acres, which I purchased in January of this year. I also bequeath my holdings in treasury bonds and other notes issued by the government of the United States of America, currently worth in excess of seven million dollars. These bonds should provide for her financial security.

"The remainder I give to my two best friends in the world in appreciation of their friendship, which is dearer to me than I could ever say.

"To Seth Greene, I give all of my land and holdings within the Pezner city limits, including my controlling shares in the First National Bank of Oree County.

"To Delia Rawlings, I give all oil lands and the income from all oil leases that I own. I also leave her all properties - real, tangible, and intangible - that are not explicitly mentioned in this will and testament. This includes stocks, bonds, ranches, orange groves, and holdings in Oree, Glades, Collier, and Palm Beach Counties. These holdings have a current market value in excess of 200 million dollars.

"I direct that this will be read first to Delia Rawlings and Janelle Jameson, then to the other beneficiaries. If my death is by violent means, I hereby direct that the executor should request of the probate court a delay of eight full weeks from the date of death before the will is read. This will allow them a measure of recovery before the reading of the will.

"All assets explicitly referenced in this will are described in detail in the signed and witnessed attachment to this will and testament. Due to the changeable nature and exhaustive extent of my holdings, a full accounting would rapidly become dated. For this reason, on the event of my decease, an accounting of the entirety of my assets will be provided by the firm of Biggs and Jensen, working in conjunction with firms chosen by the beneficiaries.

"In the presence of my attorney, I hereby declare this to be my final will and testament."

The attorney glanced up over his glasses. "That's about it. Would you like me to read the attachment now, or would you prefer to read your own copies?"

The two women stared at him blankly. Delia was the first to speak.

"We'll read it later," she whispered, her throat suddenly tight. She glanced at Jamie, who was staring at the floor, and turned back to the two visitors. Regaining her composure, Delia smiled politely.

"Would you like some more lemonade?"

Capo di Capos

In the month following the Don's death, James Feldmann Provencenti, the musician formerly known as Ace, moved quickly to assert himself as the new Don of the Provencentis. He rapidly dealt with the few loose ends that he had inherited from his father.

There was the problem of Joey's former right-hand man. Franco had been the only soldier who had escaped the disastrous assault on the farmhouse. But he had not escaped for long.

For engaging in an unsanctioned action that involved murder, Frankie was turned into an example to the rest of the family. He was shot in the back of the head on a warm, muggy night as he sat on the sandy bank of his favorite fishing hole, watching the cork bobbing in the water. An instant before his murder, the unsuspecting soldier had been reflecting that his luck was surely about to turn.

After Frankie's bitter end, the lesson was clear to all Provencenti soldiers. Family employees should trust, but verify.

Capital operations could be approved only at the highest level, and those who violated this rule would not go unpunished. Franco's body, dumped into the gulf, would never be found.

As Don, Ace fortified his ties to the major families by increasing the flow of contraband through the secure Tampa gateway. At the same time, Ace reached out to make peace with Atlanta. Hiring the best image consultant in the country, he began to restore the respectability of the Provencenti name in the greater Tampa Bay area.

Through a variety of venues, the image consultant planted subtle seeds of spin that reminded local citizens of the Provencenti Family's decades of public service. Thus began the process of reestablishing the respectability that had been demolished in a single night by the unpleasantly public actions of Joe Boy and his muttly crew.

The surviving members of Joe Boy's crew – those who had not traveled to Oree County - were merged into other crews in order to dissolve any lingering traces of camaraderie. They retained all rank, and were not punished for events outside of their control. This move demonstrated the new Don's wisdom and generosity, important traits for any mob leader who wished to earn the respect of his men.

Ace quickly showed himself to be a genius in his role as the new Don. The Northeastern dons who had supported his ascension in hopes of preserving the cash cow provided by the Provencenti dynasty were thrilled. Other dons, who had supported Ace in hopes of watching him crash and burn, were bitterly disappointed.

With surprising speed, James Feldmann Provencenti had become a Don to be reckoned with, a man of respect who blew as warm or cold as the situation demanded. For his family's sake and for his own survival, he was determined to succeed in his new role. He would be a don in the old model, a delight to his friends and a terror to his enemies. And after only two months, Ace was well on his way to his goal.

On this particular day in June, Ace was sitting in his office with his feet up, discussing the potential acquisition of an options trading firm with his consiglieri, John Dicella. A buzzer sounded, and his secretary's voice came over spoke over the speaker.

"Mr. Provencenti, you have a call from a man who knew you when you were a musician. He convinced me that you would want to take this call."

"Okay, put him on," Ace said, reaching for the phone. "Let me know what you think about that idea, Johnny," he said to his consiglieri as he picked up the receiver.

" Provencenti here."

"Ace," a husky voice rasped, "this is Streetcar." Ace sat up in his chair, looking sharply at John. "Is this line secure?" Streetcar asked.

"Yes."

"Are you the only person who can hear me right now?"

"Yes," Ace replied tersely.

"Did you tell your family that you saw me at their headquarters, on the night I took my revenge?"

"No."

"You're the Don now, ain't you, Ace?"

"That's what they say."

"Bad choice."

"Probably. Why did call?"

"To make peace, if you'll have it. I want you to know something. I'm never gonna tell anyone that you were there in the headquarters on the night I blew it up."

"Okay."

"We're Sicilians, Ace. I ain't talkin'. Do you know what I mean?"

"Yeah. I believe you."

"Good. Now, look, I've got an idea. I don't want us to be at war anymore."

"I'm listening."

"I have an offer to make."

"Okay, but wait just a minute. My advisor is here with me," Ace signaled to John. "Do you mind if I put you on speaker? I need to bring him in on this."

"I don't mind," Streetcar said, as if he were an executive negotiating a deal. "Put him on." Ace punched the button and leaned back in his chair.

"Okay, so you were telling me, you are the guy who destroyed our headquarters and killed our men." John Dicella sat bolt upright, his eyes widening.

"Yeah, that's me. This is Sally Benuto, the guy they called Streetcar. I did it, and I shouldn't have done it. It was wrong. But I did it, all right."

"Okay, we've got the picture," Ace continued. "So now, you're saying that you want to make peace?"

"That's right. You leave the girl and her friends alone, you leave me and my people alone, and I leave you and your people alone. That's the deal."

"Why should we consider this offer? You killed eight of our men and destroyed an entire city block. Three of the men you murdered were made members of our family. One of the men was our consiglieri."

"Okay, let's hash it out," Streetcar replied. "I killed eight men. But you've got hundreds of soldiers. All together, what did you lose, maybe two, three percent of your family? Well, your guy wiped out 100 percent of my family in one day. One hundred percent. When he killed Jumbo, he took out everyone I had."

"Okay. So, even if I thought that was a valid point, what about the property damage you did to our headquarters?"

"You've got insurance. Come on."

"Give us a better reason to make a deal," said John Dicella, his voice sharp, edgy. "Why should we consider your offer?" Leaning forward in his chair, he marveled at the man on the other end. The sheer brass of this street bum – this unknown who had so completely cleaned their collective clock - was amazing.

"Who is this talking?" Streetcar asked.

"This is John. John Dicella."

"Haven't I heard your voice before?" John smiled.

"Yeah. You met me at a greasy spoon in Pezner, Florida. I almost served you up with the grits." John was irritated by the entire conversation, and did not try to hide it.

"I almost got you, too."

"So, like I said," John continued, "why should we consider your offer? What if we reject it? What are you gonna do about it?" There was a pause at the other end of the line.

"I think you've already seen what I'm capable of." In the ensuing silence, Ace looked at John and raised an eyebrow. John Dicella leaned forward tensely.

"Don't play with us."

"Look, I want to bury the hatchet," Streetcar offered, "and not in your head, believe it or not. I want to apologize for what I did to your men. I'm telling you, it was wrong. I was wrong. I'm sorry I did it." Ace raised his hand, cutting off John's planned reply. He cleared his throat.

"Streetcar, this is Ace. Will you keep this conversation confidential?"

"Omerta," Streetcar replied. There was a pause as they considered his comment.

"Okay, Streetcar. John and I are going to discuss this in private. I'm putting you on hold."

"All right." Ace punched the button and turned to his counselor.

"John, what do you think?"

"Well, you know, it's crazy. My heart says string him along, tell him everything's okay, make nice, then whack him. But my brain tells me something else.

"We've got to deal with reality here. And as weird as it sounds, this guy is holding the cards. He knows where we are, but we don't have any idea where he is. This guy isn't the usual street punk; he won't come back to the old neighborhood, sneaking around like a goat with a bulls-eye on his back.

"The news reports say that he lived in a swamp for months. He helped save the girl from Joe Boy and the Mick. Joe Boy was a solid fighter, and the Mick was one of the best. What's more, this guy took down our headquarters like a kid torching a tool shed.

"I say, take the deal and stick to it. He doesn't sound like he wants to come after us. But if we try to hit him and botch the job, he'll come after us again. And I hate to say it, but from what I've seen, I don't like our odds." Ace nodded, hiding his pleasure behind a poker face.

"I was thinking along the same lines."

"He's Sicilian, right?" John asked.

"Right."

"Then he'll probably keep his mouth shut. Take the deal." For several seconds, Ace was silent.

"Okay," he said suddenly, pushing the button on his phone.

"Streetcar, are you there," he asked hopefully.

"Yeah Ace, I'm here."

"Okay, listen up. As Don of the Provencenti Family, I accept your offer of peace, but only if you accept two conditions."

"What are they?"

"Number one, the terms of this deal must remain secret forever. Number two, you can't come back to Florida. Ever. If you're in Florida right now, you've got 24 hours to clear out. Violation of these conditions will cancel everything. Do we have a deal?"

"Deal."

"One more thing I want you know," Ace added. "I was not involved in your friend's murder, and it wasn't sanctioned by the family." He stopped for a moment, waiting to see if Streetcar would respond. When there was no response, he continued. "You shouldn't have killed Marky. He was one of my best friends."

"I'm sorry, Ace. I really am." Streetcar sounded truly remorseful.

"Okay," Ace said, rubbing his forehead wearily. "As Don, for the good of our family, I commit to the terms we've agreed to. Do we have an deal?"

"Deal."

STREETCAR TURNED OFF his cellular phone and stared out across the tops of the snow-capped mountains, savoring the cold air on his cheeks as he rubbed the fur of the purring cat. The sun was going down, casting a heavy wall of shadow that slowly crawled up the steep wall of the valley directly across from him. Below, in the middle of a rich, grassy slope leading up toward the high pass to his right, three Basque sheepherders lit an evening fire as their dogs rounded up strays.

Exhausted from a hard day's work, Streetcar considered the beauty of this place with a heart filled with awe and gratitude. *You do good work, God,* he thought, and his conscience struck hard as he remembered his sins.

God had been merciful to him. But he, Salvatore Benuto, had shown no mercy to his own adversaries. He had slaughtered them like animals, allowing no space for apology or repentance. Thinking these things, Streetcar began to pray.

God, he prayed, lowering his eyes, *I don't deserve your mercy. I don't deserve another chance. But I'm asking for one, anyway. I'm sorry for what I did . . . for every wrong thing.*

Memories of his life flooded him: the beatings he had suffered from street punks as a little child and how he had learned to fight, becoming a victor instead of a victim. He remembered his mother in their tiny apartment in Hell's Kitchen, cutting onions over a steaming pot.

He recalled the people he had known, the good and the evil. For the most part, they had been evil.

Please, God, he prayed, *show me the way.* He lifted his head, feeling a tremendous sense of relief. The sensation was remarkable, as if a crushing weight had been lifted from his spirit. He knew that somehow, in spite of everything, he had been given a fresh start.

He looked around the valley, marveling at the beauty of this place. This was the family ranch of Wally Thompson, his best friend from Vietnam. Like Salvatore Benuto, Wally had survived the ambush long ago in the rice field.

Only one week ago, Streetcar had met Wally and told him that he needed a place to stay, begging him not to ask the reason why. Wally, a man who read the newspapers even less than he watched television, did not suspect that Streetcar was wanted by the authorities, but could not have cared less if he had known it. Out of loyalty and gratitude for the man who had once saved his life, Wally offered to let him live on his ranch free of charge, with room, board and clothing provided for as long as he wanted to stay. Here Streetcar had chosen to work, learning to herd sheep with the Basque herders.

Sally Benuto looked forward to the life of a shepherd in these wild mountains with only the lightning and the snow and the grizzly bears to beware of. In time, he would learn the ways of the Basque. He would learn how to blend into their close-mouthed society, so similar to the culture in which he had grown up. With them, he would disappear for months into the vast mountains, traversing the 100 square miles of this incredibly vast ranch.

The pay was nonexistent, but the view was spectacular.

Streetcar had to admit it; life was good. Jamie was alive, his Cat was beside him, and the beauty of Montana lay at his feet with the mercy of God shining around him.

His heart had been changed within him. At the beginning of a new life, reality was exceeding his wildest dreams. He would get his hands on a New Testament, and he would learn how to live life as it should be lived.

After all of these years, Streetcar had finally quit running.

When his strength had failed him and his luck had ran out, Sally Benuto had struck it rich.

The Water's Edge

On a Saturday morning in early July, Jamie rested for a moment in her dugout canoe beside the bank of the canal. As she began to push the paddle against the shore to launch into the water, she heard the unmistakable drone of a small outboard engine. *Who could that be?* She hastily clambered onto the bank and walked to the end of the dock, holding her hand above her eyes to shade out the bright sunlight.

It was Donny Hawkins.

She brushed back her long hair and caught the line he tossed her, securing the boat as he climbed onto the weathered structure. He clambered to his feet and stood awkwardly before her, surprised as always by her beauty. His gaze shifted from her hair to her eyes, then dropped to his own muddy boots. Jamie wanted to say something, but she was unable to speak.

"Hi, Jamie," he began.

"Hi." She turned away and walked toward the house, leading him to the cedar picnic table beneath the big live oak. There, in the dense shade, he sat next to her, savoring the breeze that stirred from the direction of the lake.

"I missed you," he began, and then he stopped, at a loss for how to continue.

"Me, too," she replied hesitantly. For several seconds, they sat quietly, unsure of what to say. A crow cawed raucously from the direction of the canal, and another answered from deep within the cypress swamp.

"Look, Jamie, I hope you'll forgive me for showing up like this. You said you wanted time to think, but I hadn't heard from you. I've been waiting for so long. I just had to see you."

She looked away from him, not knowing what to think. *Why does it have to be like this?*

"If you don't want me to come around anymore, just say so, and I won't ever bother you again." Jamie looked at him sharply with fear showing on her face. He was shocked by her expression. She was usually so strong!

"Don't go," she said tremulously, sounding like a little girl, lost and alone.

"Oh, baby, I don't want to go away," he said reaching out and touching her shoulder. "I wouldn't go unless you insist. Even then, it would be the hardest thing I've ever done.

"I love you, Jamie. I've never felt this way before. I think about you when I wake up; I think about you before I go to sleep, when I'm working, all the time. I can't stand the thought of spending my life without you."

"I can't, either," she said, beginning to cry. Her lip did not tremble, her shoulder did not shake, but the tears cascaded down her cheeks freely, as if a switch had been thrown. Seeing her in such agony, Donny spontaneously reached out and wrapped his arms around her, holding her close. She resisted, and then slumped against him, sobbing: her arms hanging limply at her sides as he squeezed her tightly, crying along with her.

"I don't want to lose you, Jamie. Ever."

"I don't want to lose you, either," she said, beginning to regain control, stemming the tide of her tears. She laid her head on his shoulder.

Slowly, like the petals of a flower unfolding in the sunlight, her arms reached around his back. Her hands pressed against his shoulders, and she turned her face to one side as she hugged him.

"I love you, Jamie," he repeated uncertainly.

At this moment, beset by doubt, Jamie made a leap of faith. In a brave decision filled with hope and limitless promise, she set aside her fear. *I will not fear what man may do to me,* she thought, *for my help is from the Lord.*

In spite of all that had happened, Jamie would not be defeated. She would not let her past destroy her dreams for the future.

She squeezed Donny tightly, holding him close.

"I love you, too," she whispered, savoring the words. In spite of her tears, she smiled. She looked over his shoulder, across the bay to the lake beyond. She marveled at the beauty of the water as it rippled in the wind, dancing with light beneath a bright, cloudless sky.

"I love you, too, Donny Hawkins," she repeated softly. "What do you think about that?"

To purchase this novel —

Retail Customers —

The Ultimate Paradigm can be purchased in your local bookstore or bought online at the Internet address, **www.UltimateParadigm.com**

Booksellers —

Booksellers can purchases this book wholesale via the publisher's web site, which is listed in Bowker's <u>Books in Print</u> database.

Other novels by M. C. Rudasill -

➢ **Jewel of the Mind**

➢ **The Brilliantly Rainbowed, Semi-Transparent, Red or Aqua-Tinted Adventure**

Literary Lights, the publisher of this novel, is a small publishing house with a simple mission: to further mercy by sharing the Gospel in a fresh and innovative way.

At the Literary Lights website, **www.LiteraryLights.com**, unique new inspirational fiction, essays, and poetry can be read online and downloaded free of charge.